FRONTIER TEMPTRESS
Patricia Pellicane

ZEBRA BOOKS
KENSINGTON PUBLISHING CORP.

To Joi Nobisso,
more like a sister
than a friend and
oh so greatly missed.

ZEBRA BOOKS

are published by

Kensington Publishing Corp.
475 Park Avenue South
New York, NY 10016

Copyright © 1989 by Patricia Pellicane

First printing: February, 1989

Printed in the United States of America

Prologue

Mattie's head gave a hard bounce against the dirty
window. She moaned sleepily, her hand reaching automatically for the small injury, her eyes blinking open.
Even then, her heart raced on. The dream refused to
end. It had been two years and still she heard the
screams.

The train took a curve. Even at this crawling pace,
she imagined it to totter on the edge of the railing,
apparently undecided if it should continue to follow
the commands of its driver, or proceed at its own will
across the endless stretch of flat, green countryside.

She strove for control and yet her body seemed unable to let the dream go. She had been through this
often enough to know it would take time for the effects
of the dream to dissipate. Her hands shook, and had
she a mirror, she knew her skin would be pale, almost
gray in hue, her eyes wide with fear.

At first she stared with some surprise at her sur-
roundings. A small part of her mind still expected her
to awaken in the warm sunny room that had been hers
since she was born. Mattie gave a wry smile, for the
comfort of her room and the big house she had grown
up in were gone forever.

She looked around the car, unwilling to remember
the pain of leaving all she had once known. Closely
packed, a wide assortment of humanity accompanied

5

by their meager possessions dozed in the early-morning hours. Cool, damp air rushed in an open window two rows up and caused her sweaty body a great shiver. She sighed wearily, as she pulled her cloak more firmly around her. When would they stop? She needed to stretch her legs. How much longer?

After days of listening to the steady, rhythmic click click of the train's wheels, the passengers had slid into a sort of stupor. If it wasn't for the constant jarring and occasional stops, and, of course, the nightmares, she, like them, probably could have slept all the way to Independence.

Mattie slid her hand into the pocket of her cloak and felt for the paper again. She had copied the names onto two slips. One she put in her purse and another into her carpetbag. But there was no real need. She had already memorized the list. One of these men would take her to California. And then she would kill John Ellis.

Chapter One

Mattie forced away the grimace of distaste as she shouldered the grimy swinging door to the noisy, smoke-filled tavern. Taking a small lace-edged handkerchief from her sleeve, she held it to her nose for a second, fearing she would choke on the stench of unwashed bodies and cheap perfume. Good God, she had walked this dirty, overcrowded town from one end to the other, but this was the worst yet. Idly, she wondered how the occupants managed to breathe in a place like this?

Mattie's cheeks grew pink and she averted her eyes from a tasteless, nude painting hanging over the bar. Gaudy red paper, shot liberally with gold, peeled in curling torn shreds down the walls, exposing dirty smudges of gray, bare clapboard. Heavy red curtains covered every doorway and window, allowing not a breath of air to enter the room. The floor was filthy. She could only imagine what had made it so slimy. The idea didn't bear consideration. Mattie shivered as her fingers reached automatically to her skirts to avoid a possible brush against it. The best she could say about the room was the haze that floated from about eye level to the ceiling, partially obscuring any clear view.

The moment she entered, a particularly filthy young man moved toward her. His hair was blond, she thought, although she couldn't be sure of the exact color, since it hung in greasy unwashed strands to his shoulders. He smiled revealing grotesquely blackened teeth, the reward, she imagined, of chewing tobacco.

Mattie forced herself to return his smile, and if hers was slightly stiff and more than a little cool, he seemed not to notice.

"Name's Bill, ma'am," the young man said as he boldly stepped closer. Suddenly his eyes widened and he gallantly took his hat from his head and held it respectfully against his chest. It was obvious, he realized upon closer inspection, she wasn't the sort of woman who regularly visited this type of establishment. "Would you be lookin' for someone?"

Mattie almost swooned as she caught the scent of him. The man reeked of dead animal. How could anyone stand to smell like that? Perhaps, she reasoned, he was a trapper, just returned from the wilds and he hadn't a chance as yet to see to his personal hygiene. Whatever the reason, Mattie imagined he couldn't smell worse were he long dead himself.

"I am, sir," Mattie returned, her low voice and soft southern drawl an obvious plus in her favor, for she thought the man's eyes were sure to pop from his sockets as he leaned even closer. Forcing her features into an amicable expression, despite the disgust she felt, she continued, "I was told a Mr. Callahan might be found here."

"Hot damn," the man's eyes glowed with appreciation as he boldly took in her diminutive size and shapely form, "Callahan always gets the good ones."

Mattie couldn't be absolutely sure, what with the cloud of smoke hanging above her head, somewhat marring her vision, but she thought she saw him wink. Her blue eyes rounded with surprise. "I beg your pardon," she gasped. Could this man actually believe she was the type of woman who would arrange a clandestine rendezvous in a place like this?

"Oh there ain't no need to do that," the young man returned in all innocence. "You ain't done nothin' 's far as I can tell."

For the first time in too long, a genuine smile curved Mattie's lips. She flashed white teeth, all but for one straight and even. Her one crooked tooth often brought Mattie some measure of embarrassment, particularly when obviously noticed, since she considered it yet another flaw in a body already far from perfect. But not so the men upon whom she bestowed that smile. It wasn't unusual to see their eyes alight with instant hunger, for many imagined, without the least effort, running their tongue over that deliciously inviting, slightly crooked tooth.

Mattie shook her head, totally baffled. Did he believe her to be apologizing for something? Her confusion lasted but for a moment when she suddenly turned red with embarrassment as the young man pursed his lips and issued a high-pitched whistle. The crowd quieted immediately. Gone were the blaring sounds of loud male voices, screeching female laughter, and tinny music, and yet the man apparently felt the necessity to yell, "Hey, Callahan! Someone wants to see you."

Needless to say, Mattie would have preferred a more discreet form of introduction. Instead of the unobtrusive entrance she had imagined, all eyes suddenly turned on her and the place grew so quiet one could hear the harsh breathing of every man she passed. She felt her cheeks growing redder with each step she took toward the man pointed out and fumed that he felt no need to stand and greet her, nor dislodge the clinging woman sitting in his lap.

Cursed luck! Why did this man have to live here? Why was she forced to search him out in the loudest, dirtiest tavern in the loudest, dirtiest of towns? But Mattie knew the answer to that question. He was the only one left. The last on her list. The one she prayed would help her.

Mr. Cassidy's train was pulling out on May 7, just four days from now, and Mattie planned to be on it. It didn't matter how. She didn't care who she had to bed, what she had to promise, from whom she had to steal. She would be on that train.

Mattie sighed unhappily as she took in the sight of

the man she approached. He didn't look any better than the rest in this place; in some ways he appeared even worse. His hair was dark, close to black, and if he had let it grow to his shoulders, at least it appeared clean. But the full beard that covered half his face and succeeded in disguising what she could only guess to be fairly average features caused her a moment's pause. The problem was he had let it grow until it reached almost mid-chest. The effect was unsettling to say the least, for he appeared half man, half grizzly.

Mattie shivered. He looked so uncivilized. Like a mountain man, like a bear. The whites of his eyes were red. It was obvious, even from across the room, he was either deep in his cups or had gone some time without sleep, and yet his dark-blue eyes narrowed, growing cold with suspicion, she thought, alert and filled with some unnamed emotion as he watched her approach.

Mattie gave a mental shrug. It didn't matter. Mr. Kyle pronounced him to be a reliable and decent sort, to use his own words, and she trusted Mr. Kyle's judgment. If the man chose to overindulge in spirits and preferred the company of certain ladies in between jobs, who was she to judge? Nothing mattered but that she accomplish her objective. She was going west and she didn't care who it was that got her there.

"A moment of your time, Mr. Callahan?" Mattie asked as she reached his table at last.

The redheaded painted whore sitting comfortably on his lap giggled. Callahan shot the woman a look of annoyance and sighed with disgust as he listened to Mattie's accent. It was just his luck to run into a woman who looked like her and have her turn out to be southern. Damn, but he'd had enough of those bitches, their looks of scorn, their uppity attitudes. As a captain in the Union Army, he had been forced to take their hatred in stride, but not anymore. He didn't care what she looked like, she and the rest of her kind could go to hell. He never bothered to disguise his feelings as he remarked, "The name's Callahan, lady. You can forget the mister."

Mattie controlled the soft gasp that threatened. A Union officer! Was he one of the wretched beasts who had sacked her town and burned her home? He wore still the faded blue jacket, his captain insignia proudly shining. She felt a wave of dizziness as her plans seemed to shrivel and die before her eyes and clutched the table, lest she fall to the floor. Mr. Kyle had never mention . . . He knew how she felt about the Yankees, especially their officers! Why hadn't he told her?

Beyond the fact that this man was the most hated of all earthly creatures, Mattie realized his obvious scorn. Her eyes widened with surprise. Why, she didn't even know the man. Why should he dislike her so? It was she who had every right to hate. It wasn't he who had lost his home and family. Mattie pushed aside her horror, gritted her teeth, and forced herself to ask, "May I speak with you a moment?"

"Talk."

Mattie almost groaned. God, how she hated that clipped northern accent. Would it forever bring chills of terror down her spine?

"You all right, honey?" the woman asked, noticing the way Mattie had whitened and swayed.

"She's all right," Callahan answered for her, his voice dripping sarcasm as he fought the ridiculous urge to take her in his arms and make sure he spoke the truth. The need to do so caused his voice to harden all the more. "Her kind might look all soft and weak, but you're as tough as nails, aren't you, honey?" The last slapped his hate in her face.

Mattie's back stiffened. She didn't know why he felt this instant hatred, but it couldn't be stronger than her own. After all, she alone had the right. It was she who had suffered at the hands of these animals. Suddenly an idea dawned, the irony of it almost making her laugh. Wasn't it justice that one Yankee officer should have a hand in the downfall of another?

Mattie looked at the woman, hoping she would excuse herself, but the woman either didn't care or cared

11

too much to leave them alone. "Would you give me a moment?

Callahan's arm tightened around the woman. "I ain't got no secrets from Lucy, here. Say what you've come to say."

Mattie sighed. It really didn't matter. She could ask what she must, not matter who was present. "I intend to join Mr. Cassidy's train. I've need of a driver, Mr. . . ." she hesitated, belatedly remembering his request, "Callahan. Mr. Kyle suggested you might be interested in the job."

Callahan became instantly alert, but schooled his features to show not a glimmer of his surprise. His heart thundered in his chest. Jesus, he wouldn't have believed it to look at her! Mitchell had told him just today to watch out for anyone looking to join the train at the last minute. God, he almost sighed aloud with disgust. He had assumed the culprit would be a man. Obviously they were smarter than anyone had given them credit, because no one would suspect this little piece of baggage. Why, it was getting so you couldn't tell the good guys from the bad anymore.

Of course he was already signed up, but she wouldn't know that. He gave an almost imperceptible shrug. It wouldn't do to appear too eager. "Might be. You payin' the usual rate?"

Mattie thought of the small sack of gold tied to her waist beneath her petticoat. It was the last of everything she owned in the world. She had sold her gold pendant, given to her by her father on her sixteenth birthday to finance this trip, but it didn't matter. She'd use all she had and steal the rest, if need be. "Name your price, Mr. Callahan. I must get on that train."

His brow rose with feigned surprise. I can imagine you must, he mused in silent sarcasm. Over the years Callahan had become a master at hiding his true feelings. So it was with little effort that he managed in seeming innocence, "Why's it so all fired important? And why ain't your husband doin' the hirin'?"

12

Mattie's hands fidgeted nervously. Unbeknownst to her, her lie was obvious to any within hearing. "My husband is in California, Mr. Callahan," she murmured, almost choking on the falsehood. Basically honest, lying didn't come easy to her and Mattie nearly groaned as she finished with, "I need a driver to bring me to him."

Callahan almost laughed out loud at that one. A sick mother, he might have believed. The need to get away from a war-torn south, from which she'd obviously come. A lecherous uncle, any one of a dozen excuses, but a husband expecting his wife to travel west? Alone? Ridiculous. No man in his right mind would leave a woman who looked like her to find her own way. He knew he sure as hell wouldn't. They, whoever they were, should have concocted a better story than that. Still, he gave a mental shrug. It was none of his concern what story they had come up with. What was important was the fact that he had recognized the lie for what it was.

"I reckon I'm available."

Lucy laughed a shrill sound. "But not too available, honey."

Mattie gave the woman a tight smile. For a brief moment, her relief at finding a driver was so great, she forgot her manners. Mattie was a lady in the truest sense of the word and would have been mortified to know the distaste she felt showed clearly in her eyes. "I've no wish to further interrupt your evening, Mr. Callahan. If we could meet in the coffee shop across the street tomorrow, say around noon, I could give you the money you'll need to purchase supplies."

Through narrowed eyes, Callahan watched the woman standing opposite him. Idly he wondered what it would be like to travel in her company for months on end. He couldn't remember ever seeing anyone quite so beautiful. He felt his gut twist with the tantalizing thoughts that suddenly flooded his brain. How many nights would they share a lone campfire? What would their sleeping arrangements be like? How often were

13

they bound to come in contact, before . . . before. Callahan almost laughed. It would be interesting to see just how far a lady in her line of work would go to achieve her ends.

She was a delicious piece, to be sure, but there was something about her that rankled. Finally he realized what it was. She was looking at him and his companion as if they were bugs. He knew Lucy was no prize package, but at least she was honest about plying her trade. Could this woman say the same? Suddenly annoyed, he found himself squirming under her obvious appraisal, knowing by her expression she clearly found him lacking. Damn! How the hell did she do that? How did she manage to make him, a grown man, feel self-conscious about his appearance with one superior look. For a moment, he might have been a child, while she his schoolmistress, sneering with disgust at his dirty fingernails.

All right, he conceded in belligerent silence, so it was more than obvious he could use a hot bath and a haircut. The stench of his clothes was disgusting, even to him. But he'd be damned if he was going to make excuses to *her*.

It wasn't unusual to find him in this condition, after spending a few weeks at his mountain cabin, which he tried, time permitting, to visit between assignments. He needed the solitude to rid himself of the tension his work nearly always brought about, and the skins he usually took back to town only lent credence to his cover. All hereabouts believed him to be exactly what he appeared, a trapper. For his own well-being, he had no intention of correcting what he had deliberately allowed them to assume.

The problem was, this time he looked and smelled worse than ever. This morning he had tangled with a mountain lion. Luckily he had been wearing his gun and finished the cougar, barely clearing leather before he got off his shot. But the animal had been in the midst of a lunge and had landed on his chest. The impact had

14

knocked him from his horse and left him covered with blood.

Damn it, he swore silently, while growing angrier by the minute. He stank of dead animal. He should have cleaned himself up the minute he got back, but Lucy had insisted they have a drink while his supper and a tub of steaming water were being prepared. The thought of a glass of whiskey after two long months of abstinence had been just too much to resist.

Yes, her distaste couldn't have been more in evidence and yet there was excitement there too. Callahan had been with too many women not to recognize that look. It was obvious she thought him beneath her and yet she was strangely attracted. Yes, he knew her kind well enough. Hadn't he married a bitch just like her?

Still, his pride smarted. Who the hell was she to pass judgment on him? All he needed was a bit of soap and water, while she needed . . . . Shit. If she was who he thought she was, and he hadn't a doubt she was, for no woman of any moral fiber would travel without the company of family or at the very least a hired companion, heaven only knew what she needed.

He was thoroughly annoyed and promised himself her high-and-mighty attitude would be the first thing to go. This one needed to come down a peg or two. His eyes glowed with daring as Callahan reached his hand to Lucy's breast and deliberately caressed the soft flesh before Mattie's astonished eyes. Silently he waited for her to comment on his actions.

Mattie's cheeks reddened with embarrassment, while Callahan's grin was obvious even through his shaggy beard. Clearly he was enjoying her discomfort. His eyes were bright as he silently and foolhardily dared her to take back her offer. Callahan cursed. Christ, that was a stupid thing to do. How the hell was he going to catch her and her cohorts in the act, if he so disgusted her that she found another to do her driving? The damn train was so big they might never come face to face until their final moment of truth. And then he'd likely have no

15

warning. He couldn't imagine what had caused him to do such a damn fool thing.

"Tomorrow then, Mr. Callahan?" Mattie asked as she automatically and unthinkingly extended her hand.

Callahan nodded. "It's Callahan. I told you forget the mister."

Mattie shuddered with revulsion that he should take her hand immediately upon releasing the woman's breast. But her disgust was instantly forgotten as the warmth of his big hand enveloped hers and brought searing heat racing up her arm. A puzzled frown creased her forehead. For a long moment she simply stared at their joined hands, wondering if she could be imagining the sensation.

Callahan, more worldly wise, instantly recognized the attraction between them for what it was, but even so, found himself amazed at the longing that suddenly filled his being and overrode every sensible thought. If he had wanted her on first sight, and he most definitely had, it was nothing compared to the desire that bloomed full upon touching her. But the fire that gleamed briefly in his eyes was instantly doused. He was first and foremost a professional. There was no way he was going to jeopardize this mission by letting her know what effect she had on him.

Gaining control, he breathed a sigh of relief to find his actions hadn't brought about irreversible damage, and asked in a voice that sounded low and strained to his own ears, "Since I'm working for you, do you think I might know your name?"

Mattie slowly grew conscious of the fact that their hands were still joined. Suddenly she pulled hers sharply away. The oddest shiver ran up her spine as her eyes met his. She was trembling and she hadn't a clue as to why. All she could do was pray the man didn't notice her confusion.

He did.

With eyes downcast, she whispered, "Mattie Trumont." Mattie, in her innocence, answered honestly,

16

never realizing she had just sealed her fate. "Till tomorrow, Mr. Callahan."

Even Lucy, who most considered, and rightly so, none too bright, was aware of the heated exchange between the two. She could almost hear the sizzle when their hands touched. Lucy, a good-natured sort, didn't have a jealous bone in her body. And when she offered her advice it was done so with caring for her longtime friend. Her eyes were on Callahan as he watched the woman walk away. "Be careful of that one, honey."

Callahan's gaze was drawn beyond his will to the dark woman's slender back, as one wild fantasy after another flooded his mind. Try as he would, he couldn't pull his gaze away. God, he had felt attraction before, but never anything to equal this. Jesus, he felt as if he had taken a blow to his midsection.

"She get to you, that one?"

"What?" Callahan asked, oblivious to the fact that the woman on his lap could feel his stirring desire.

Lucy ran her hand down his wide chest and flat belly until she found what interested her most. She didn't care that Callahan was obviously excited by another. He was great in bed and she'd be a fool to pass up this opportunity. "Let's go upstairs," she whispered near his ear as her tongue flicked out and sampled the taste of his neck.

Callahan brought his dazed eyes back into focus and smiled. He sighed with pure enjoyment as she stroked his growing hardness. This was what he needed. Lucy didn't care if he bathed or cut his hair. Lucy wanted him just like he was. He'd be a fool not to take what she offered. No telling how long it would be before he found Mattie Trumont half so willing.

Chapter Two

Mattie sat at the table nearest the window trying to control the temptation to fidget as she waited. The street was crowded and noisy as was everything in Independence, with those preparing for the coming journey. Children played on and off the wooden sidewalks, sometimes venturing dangerously close to the hooves of a passing horse. Stores almost burst their walls with merchandise as emigrants sought that one, oh so important last-minute object.

Suddenly, her eyes widened with shock and her heart began to thump wildly. Out of the crowd stepped one particularly striking man. He had come from the tavern and was now walking across the street, heading for the coffee shop.

Mattie immediately dismissed the thought. It couldn't be him! Of course it couldn't. But deep inside, she knew with some sort of fatalistic horror, it was. "Dear God, no!" Mattie gasped as she watched him approach. She never realized she had spoken aloud, nor did she see the peculiar looks of her fellow patrons being cast her way.

Although in daylight, he possessed not the slightest resemblance to the Mr. Callahan of last night, Mattie hadn't a doubt as to who he was. How many men were that broad in their shoulders? How many had hair so black? How many of them lived above the tavern?

18

Mattie groaned, almost as if in pain. How could she have been such a fool not to have recognized the man beneath the dirt? Godalmighty, what had she done? Mattie gave a silent groan at the jolting almost painful sensation that crashed over her, and twisted her stomach into a hard knot of foreboding.

She could see now what she should have sensed last night. He had cut his black glistening hair to collar length. His beard was short and neatly trimmed. Gone was the dusty, stained Union jacket, to be replaced by a clean white shirt and black leather vest that did nothing to hide the massive size of his shoulders and chest. Nor, for that matter, did the tight black trousers disguise as they clung to muscled thighs.

She had left the tavern last night feeling totally confused. She couldn't understand why her heartbeat had suddenly accelerated upon touching his hand. She couldn't imagine a man more unattractive. And yet she felt . . . What? What had she felt? By dawn she had convinced herself the strange happening she suffered at their meeting was merely a reaction to the length of time since she had last eaten. She had thought the matter over long and hard and came at last to the only conclusion her mind would allow. It was simply impossible to have thought the man tempting. He was dirty, unkempt, stunk of animal, and worst of all, although he possessed only the slightest of accents, a Yankee! There was no way she could have felt attraction to such an unsavory character. As far as she was concerned he possessed but one redeemable trait. And that was his ability to take her to California.

Mattie was gasping for breath. Her cheeks flushed and her heart was thumping wildly in her chest by the time Callahan walked into the small shop. Mattie watched as he made his way toward her, positive she couldn't have uttered a sound if it meant her life. But when Callahan stood over her at last, she surprised herself by raising her hand to him in a gracious if cool greeting. "Mr. Callahan."

Callahan breathed a silent curse, as her softly spoken words caused a hard ache in the pit of his stomach. If he was half as smart as he prided himself on being, he'd tell Mitchell right now he wanted no part of this assignment. A small part of him longed for the coward's way out. But of course he wouldn't take it. He almost groaned aloud as he thought of the months that lay ahead. Did he have it in him to go up against another southern belle? His wife had shown him the evil deceit that lay behind their softly spoken words and teasing smiles.

Callahan gave Mattie a hard look of determination. He was trained to put aside any emotions in performance of duty. It didn't matter the chaos this woman brought to his senses. There were those who swore he'd turn in his own mother if necessary. And he'd do it to her as well. If it killed him, he would.

Callahan's mouth tightened with self-disgust. He had meant to spend the night in Lucy's arms. Besides the comfort and relief his body always found there, he had hoped to rid himself of any and all desire for this woman. It was hours later that he gave up the effort at last.

Their mutual disappointment was obvious, if unmentioned, but there was nothing he could do about it. His body wouldn't cooperate. He couldn't find pleasure in taking his old-time friend. Even for the sport of it, for pictures of chocolate eyes and black silky hair had cursed the fun he should have known.

Callahan masked the longing he felt. There was no way he was going to let her know the feelings she stirred in him, thereby giving her a weapon to use against him. No, she couldn't ever be allowed that advantage. That he would have her, he hadn't a doubt. What she didn't need to know was how much he wanted it.

Callahan nodded a silent answer to her greeting and

took her hand, but released it almost instantly as he sat across from her. During the night he had convinced himself that his eyes had deceived him. He had sworn the whiskey had gone straight to his head. No one was as beautiful as he had imagined her to be. But his hopes had been in vain, for she wasn't as beautiful as he had remembered. She was more so.

Over steaming mugs of tea, Mattie related her story. She and her husband had come from Richmond, Virginia. After the war, there was nothing left. John had left for California last year. She had only recently received word to join him.

Callahan sighed at the nonsense she spouted. Was he supposed to believe this? Apparently she was ignorant of the fact that it took eight months to travel west. How had her John made the trip, found his fortune, and sent her a letter all within space of a year?

He had known last night her story to be false. Now he wondered at the absurdity of it. Why had they given her such a weak cover? What was their reasoning behind it?

Mattie went on to tell him what he already knew, the time and date of the train's departure. Her voice was cool, her manner clipped. Callahan had the uncomfortable feeling that she was looking right through him. She gave no evidence of even remembering what had passed between them last night. By the time she had pushed her small sack of gold coins in his direction for the purpose of purchasing a wagon, oxen, and supplies, Callahan was beginning to believe last night must have been the result of too many days spent away from civilization. Surely she couldn't act so calm and cool if the emotion he felt shiver through her had actually existed.

"I think that's everything, Mr. Callahan," she said at last. "You have the list and the money. I'll meet you Saturday morning outside of town."

Callahan nodded his agreement.

"Oh, one more thing," she added as they both stood. "Mr. Cassidy, the wagon master, will not allow unchaperoned ladies to ride his train." Mattie hesitated, for what she was about to ask of him was outrageous indeed, especially when she considered the shivering response she had felt at his touch. She worried her bottom lip with her teeth as she sought the right words, never noticing Callahan's stiffening as his gaze lingered on her all-too-appealing mouth. "Since you could hardly qualify as my chaperon, I suggest we prevent some nasty gossip and possible expulsion from the train by pretending we are married."

Callahan's carefully guarded expression faltered at her suggestion. But his shock quickly turned to pleasure, and finally a definite leering quality entered his formerly expressionless eyes as he allowed his imagination to run riot. There was no way they were going to remain strangers thrown into such intimate contact during the months ahead. No matter the danger she posed, he'd have to be half a man to resist what she was offering. His voice was silky smooth with promise when he asked, "Lady, do you realize what you're suggesting?"

Mattie's cheeks grew pink with embarrassment. Her eyes lowered shyly as she moved at his side toward the door.

God, she was good. She really was good! If he didn't know better, he could almost believe her innocent act. Callahan balled his fists as he forcibly restrained his hands from reaching out to touch her. His breathing grew steadily labored, for he'd never seen anything quite so lovely.

"I'm not suggesting anything improper, Mr. Callahan. I hope you realize that." Her dark eyes grew fiery with some unnamed purpose. "I wish only to go west. If, because of Mr. Cassidy's Bible-thumping ways, I'm forced to twist the truth a bit," she shrugged, "so be it."

Callahan almost laughed out loud. "Is that what you

call it? Twisting the truth?"

Mattie didn't answer, but turned redder than ever.

They had reached the sidewalk and Callahan, just before he turned away, muttered with an elaborately nonchalant shrug, "I hope you know what the hell you're doing."

He hoped they both did.

Callahan laughed as his bulky form filled the doorway to the mayor's office. "I thought it was you I saw racing down the sidewalk. Jesus, woman, have you forgotten how to walk?"

Nora Pace squealed with delight, spun about, and flung herself into his outstretched arms. Without hesitation, she planted a kiss on his smiling lips.

"What would your dear old mother say if she saw your most unladylike trot?"

Nora tipped her head back and lifted silver-gray eyes to his. "Likely as not, she'd blacken your eye for calling her old."

"A figure of speech, pumpkin," Callahan grinned, using his old nickname for her, as he squeezed the lady tightly to his chest. "I've missed you."

"Sure you have," she answered in clear disbelief as she took a step back. "That's why you hide yourself out in the mountains between jobs. It's obvious you only go there to search out my bubbly personality behind every rock."

Callahan grinned at Nora's exaggerated flirting as she furiously blinked her dark lashes in his direction.

"Would you have me joining the rest of your beaux? Shall I patiently wait in line for you to notice I'm alive?"

Nora poked his chest, her eyes narrowing with warning. "You leave my beaux alone, Callahan. They don't need what could only be the most god-awful example of how a man should treat a woman."

23

"Are you saying I don't know how to treat a lady?"

Nora raised a brow and gave him a pointed look. "Callahan, you wouldn't know a lady from your a— Jake!" Nora turned as she spied the man entering the room. "You got here just in time. This beast . . ." she pointed over her shoulder at a grinning Callahan.

"Are you two at it again?" Jake asked, giving her no further chance to continue. "Why don't you just get married and be done with this fighting?"

Nora laughed at the absurdity of the notion. "One of us would surely be murdered before the honeymoon was over." She gave a wicked chuckle. "Now would you want to see this poor man cut down, even if he is past his prime?"

Callahan gasped in pretended outrage. "Past my prime, eh?" Slowly he began to stalk her, having every intention of tickling her unmercifully once he got his hands on her. "And who says I'll be the one to be murdered?"

Nora squealed as she ran behind the desk with Callahan in hot pursuit.

"It's beyond me how two of my best agents can act like such complete idiots. How am I supposed to rest easy knowing you're on the job?"

It was with some effort that Nora and Callahan finally smothered their laughter as Mitchell walked into his borrowed office and shooed them away from the desk. "If I could interrupt this nonsense for a moment," he asked as his stern gaze moved over all three of his agents, leaving each with no doubt of his disapproval.

Whatever he was about to say was lost as his assistant burst through the door, almost knocking it from its hinges. "Sir! A telegram from Washington!"

Mitchell turned an annoyed look toward Manning and nodded. "Read it."

Manning cleared his throat. "Received information placing two agents on train. Sabotage possible."

The silence was almost palpable when the young man finished.

Mitchell's lips whitened. He shrugged a slender shoulder and waved an almost feminine hand, while giving his agents a hard look. "You know what to do."

The two men muttered sharp curses at this bit of information.

"If you know the shipment is in danger, why don't you send it under the guard of the Army?" Nora asked logically.

Mitchell shrugged again. "There are those who believe it safer to be less ostentatious. Besides, it mustn't get out that the United States is backing Juarez or chance an open confrontation with France."

Callahan asked, "Are they positive there are two?"

Mitchell's eyes narrowed. "Why?"

"A Mrs. Trumont hired me on to drive her west. Do you think . . ."

"Is she alone?" Mitchell interrupted.

Callahan nodded.

"I'll check into it," Mitchell replied as he scribbled notes.

He glanced up at the other two. "Nora, are you and Jake ready?"

Nora nodded.

"Robinson and Perry will be joining the rest of you. I've already met with them. Everything is set."

Callahan shook his head. Before they were finished all those traveling this train would likely be agents of one kind or another.

"Do we know each other?" Callahan asked as he nodded to his fellow agents.

Mitchell shrugged yet again. "Can't see how it would matter none."

25

Chapter Three

A sharp cry and the sound of male laughter outside the swinging doors of the tavern brought Callahan's mind from the three queens he held in his hand. His heart thudded with sudden fear. It was her! Somehow he knew it was her. What the hell was she still doing in town? And what had she gotten herself into?

Lucy was almost dumped on the floor, so quickly did he come to his feet, and left with her mouth hanging open as Callahan cursed and ran, elbowing his way through the crowd already gathering at the door.

Callahan took in the situation with one sweeping glance. She wasn't in any serious trouble, but she was terrified, that was no act. Some of the boys were having a little fun. Apparently they had snatched her hat. Her hair had lost its pins and tumbled in a riot of black curls and waves to her waist. Callahan felt his belly tighten and he watched the beautiful lush hair swing free as she attempted to retrieve her belongings. By all rights, he should have minded his own business, but he recognized the look of dawning hunger in the men's eyes, shown clearly by the light of the two lanterns hanging on each side of the tavern's front door. He knew more would likely come of this if he didn't put a stop to it now.

"Roscoe," he ordered in a friendly tone, "give the lady back her hat."

"Aw, come on, Callahan. We're just havin' a bit a' fun."

"I know, but you're scaring my boss. Now what kind

26

of a hand would I be if I let you do that?"

"Shit," Roscoe grumbled good-naturedly as he released Mattie's shoulders and handed her back a somewhat bedraggled bonnet. "Can't have no fun around here." He glanced at his still-grinning friends and asked, "Wanna go over to Beverly's?"

The men left in a chorus of agreement, while the expectant crowd, now clearly disappointed, lost interest and moved back inside.

"Th . . . Thank you, Mr. Callahan."

"What the hell are you doing here?" He looked around, "Alone and at night?" Callahan's eyes widened. He was sure she hadn't heard a word he said. From the looks of her it was a miracle she could stand. He'd never seen a body shake like that before. Godalmighty. How did she do it? He could have sworn her innocence no act, but his pocket held the telegram confirming his suspicions. Mrs. Trumont, formerly of Richmond, Virginia, had died in childbirth twenty-three years ago. Lord how he wished he was mistaken. Why couldn't she simply be a woman who needed him to bring her West? Without a doubt, she was a liar and God only knew what else. Still he found his voice softening appreciably. "No need for you to tremble like that, lady. They meant no harm."

Mattie tried to laugh, but the sound came out a strangled sob. "I see that now."

"You want me to walk you back to your place?"

Mattie couldn't seem to stop shivering. She shook her head. "I'm staying over there." She nodded toward the tent city that stood about a mile outside of town. "I was shopping for a few last-minute things." She reached for a package so far gone unnoticed at her feet, but twice it slid from shaking fingers.

Callahan saw two more lying nearby. "You shouldn't come here at night and especially not alone."

Mattie smiled wistfully. "There are some things that can't be helped."

Callahan picked up her packages and eyed the

27

horses tied to the post out front. "Which one is yours?"

Mattie shook her head. "I have no horse. I walked."

Callahan took her arm, desperately trying to ignore the sensation of heat that smashed into his stomach like a hot poker when he touched her. "You'd better let me go with you. It's dark out there and there's no tellin' if the boys had their fill of fun tonight."

To her mortification, Mattie found herself leaning into him. She couldn't stop the trembling that had taken control of her body. What in the world was the matter with her? "Perhaps I should sit down for a minute."

"Are you goin' to faint on me?"

Mattie laughed at that, feeling somewhat steadier at the sound. "I probably should have told you at our first meeting. I never faint, Mr. Callahan."

Callahan bit the inside of his lip. She was referring of course to his unnecessarily nasty comment when they met. It annoyed him that he should feel this pang of guilt and yet he felt no recourse but to take her gentle setting down. Callahan pushed aside the need to apologize and gruffly remarked, "Well, there ain't no place to sit, unless you're thinking of the ground. Suppose I carry you. You're such a little thing, it wouldn't take no effort at all."

"Oh no!" she almost shouted as he turned and lifted her into his arms.

"Don't make no fuss, lady." Callahan grunted with a silent curse. Jesus, if she kept moving against him like this, he was going to explode. Was he out of his mind? Why had he touched her? And how the hell was he going to stop touching her when he suddenly couldn't think of wanting anything else?

No matter his effort at control, the clean scent of her filled his senses and he felt his knees weaken with almost overwhelming instant desire. Suddenly he didn't care who she was. He needed to hold her close. To taste her lips, to linger over her lush curves. Callahan turned his face, breathed deeply, and forced his

28

wild emotions aside. Take it easy, man. There'll be plenty of time. Don't rush her. A moment later he stepped off the wooden sidewalk and moved across the dark street toward the hundred tents that blanketed the countryside. His voice sounded oddly strained as he commented, "I'll have you home directly."

"Mr. Callahan, please. I'm perfectly capable of walking."

"Probably right about that, but it won't hurt none to be sure."

Mattie began to tremble again. Only this time it wasn't fear that sent her nerve endings into an uproar. Or maybe it was. No, she vehemently denied. She wasn't afraid of this man. Then why, she silently questioned. Why are you shaking? Mattie had no answer.

They passed beneath the low-hanging branches of a heavy oak. It was dark, the moon offering not a glimmer of light as it hid behind a sky of low clouds. Suddenly Callahan stumbled in a deep rut left by a carriage wheel and went down. Before he hit the ground he swung his body so Mattie fell on him.

She was stunned, and for a second only blinked in confusion to find herself stretched out upon this stranger. Suddenly a gleam of laughter entered her eyes and she chuckled. "Do you still contend I'm better off being carried?"

Callahan answered the laughter in her voice with his own. "Well, it's better than falling without a cushion."

"Perhaps," she reasoned almost gaily, "but you leave much to be desired in the way of softness."

"You don't."

Mattie gasped as his words. She was suddenly conscious of their all too intimate position. Conscious also of the way her body curved all too well into his and the suddenly wanton desire of keeping it that way. She pulled away and came quickly to her feet.

"I can walk the rest of the way."

"You all right now?" he asked as he again picked the spilled packages from the ground and walked at her side. He didn't dare touch her. He knew he couldn't control the need she caused if he did.

Mattie smiled weakly. "I'm fine, Mr. Callahan. Thank you." She gave a sudden gasp as her ankle turned in still another rut.

Mattie started with surprise to find his steadying hands at her waist. She didn't notice at first that he was lifting her. For just an instant she couldn't imagine what he was about, not until she felt herself turn and press lightly against his body. "I don't think . . ."

Callahan knew the moment he touched her it was a mistake. He was afraid he hadn't the power or the will to let her go this time. Suddenly he had to taste that mouth. Had to touch her creamy skin. It didn't matter if it was too soon. He had to!

His body trembled as he hesitated, trying desperately to fight against this raging desire to know her, but he finally gave a helpless groan as the will to fight fled and pulled her tiny form into his arms.

His mouth touched against her lips. Tenderly, hesitantly, almost as if he realized the terror of discovering what lay beyond. And yet the ache to do so was more than he could bear. His lips grazed her flesh and went on to sample the texture of her cheeks, the smoothness of her forehead, the whispering scent of flowers at her neck.

Mattie gasped and shivers of delight ran up her spine as his soft, clean beard and mustache tickled her skin. She never thought to push him away, but groaned instead as his mouth left a moist path of fire along her nerve endings.

Callahan lifted his head, straining against the dark to see the beauty held in his arms. His brow puckered with bewilderment. When was the last time a chaste kiss had brought him to tremble? When had a woman last so affected him? He felt a terrifying unwanted warmth invade his soul. He wanted to curse her. To lash out. She didn't have the right to so affect him. He took a deep, steadying breath. He had to gain control.

30

He almost smiled as he felt himself winning against the battle that raged. He nearly put her from him then, his whispered apology already forming on his lips.

But Mattie, having no knowledge of what this man believed her to be, never realized the suffering she brought about. She only knew she had never before felt such wonder. Without thought, she reached a hesitant hand to stroke his bearded face and his resolve disappeared as though it had never been. He gave up his struggles with a strangled moan and took her mouth with all the fiery need he had known since first touching her.

His mouth slashed across hers, forcing her lips apart. He felt her stiffen against him as his tongue sought entrance. From far away came a thought that this experience was new to her, but Callahan shrugged aside the absurdity. No one could work in the profession she had chosen and remain pure and untouched. She knew what it was to kiss a man. Her hesitancy was simply part of her act. Damn, but he'd have to be careful. She was the best he'd ever known.

His knees almost buckled as he felt her soften against him. He swung them both so his back rested against a tree, his legs parted, his hands guiding her hips closer to his heat. Her mouth opened wider, her teeth no longer an obstacle against his tongue, he groaned as he gained entrance to this forbidden haven and groaned again at the delight he discovered within.

"I don't think this is going to work, Mr. Callahan." Mattie sighed breathlessly as he released her mouth and nuzzled the sweet flesh of her throat. The taste of her was beyond his ability to resist. Her skin was so soft, so sweet, he couldn't stop his mouth from sampling its texture and scent.

Whisper soft, his beard grazed her cheeks, her eyes, her lips, and jaw. He was losing control, but it never mattered less. He couldn't ease the hunger and the more he touched her, the stronger it grew.

Callahan raised his head and wordlessly took her

31

mouth again, his longing for yet another tasting pushing him past the point of rational thought. He was wild for her. Her every touch and taste drove him farther along the path of disaster. He was like a man possessed. Never in his life had he known a need such as this.

With superhuman effort he managed to drag his mouth from hers. "I know," he breathed miserably into her hair. He gave a silent curse. Why the hell couldn't she have been whom she professed? He didn't need this complication. He wasn't going to be able to keep his hands off her. Did he have the strength to use her body and remain emotionally detached? He had no choice, he must. In his gut he knew she was dangerous. In his line of work, he'd encountered the most villainous of criminals, but he suspected none to be more dangerous than this woman.

Both were gasping for breath as he placed her gently but purposely away from him. As Mattie took a step back her legs wobbled slightly. Slowly her mind began to clear of the passion he so easily instilled. She trembled as she realized how close they had come to giving into this wild impulse.

Mattie lifted wary eyes to his. Even in the dark, she could see the glitter and recognized the hunger that still lurked within. She, in her innocence, didn't know the effort it had taken for him to stop. What she wondered was what in God's name was she to do about this newfound complication? She stared at him for a long moment before sighing with defeat. The train was leaving in three days. No matter the temptation wrought, she knew she had no choice. There was no one else to turn to. He had to do it.

Mattie took another step. She dared not search for her packages. There was no telling what might happen if they should again touch in the dark. Just before she turned and left him alone with his agony, she murmured, "Saturday at dawn, Mr. Callahan."

32

Chapter Four

Dawn was only now breaking over the horizon and already a few anxious souls were milling about, apparently more than ready to begin their journey. Mattie wondered if Callahan was up and about. She saw not a sign of him, nor, for that matter, knew which of the almost endless line of wagons was hers. She sighed with disgust and sat upon the trunk she had been dragging around. No sense moving it farther until she knew where to put it.

Mattie looked around. Still no sign of the man. She didn't feel up to another venture at the tavern. Being forced to search him out was not exactly the way she had planned on beginning this trip. Actually, the day had barely begun and she was already tired, for the night had proven to be most unrestful.

It was far into the night before the excited occupants of the camp had finally settled enough to allow sleep. And then left alone with her thoughts in the dark, Mattie found herself suddenly unable to take her mind from their last, near disastrous meeting.

How in the world was she to travel with this man when there existed between them such emotion? Mattie tossed and turned half the night away. She wanted only to reach California as soon as possible. She didn't need the trouble this man was sure to bring.

Mattie was in the midst of a huge yawn when a deep male voice came suddenly and startling close to her ear. "Mornin', lady." At that exact moment, Callahan settled himself cheerfully at her side.

Mattie gave a short squeal of surprise and jumped a good foot off the trunk. The problem was she had crossed her one leg over the other upon sitting and now found herself seriously off balance.

Callahan's hands went instantly around her waist and pulled her back, just as she was about to tumble headfirst upon the dusty road.

Once she was able to breathe again with any degree of normalcy, Mattie shot him a look of aggravation. Her eyes narrowed dangerously as she snapped, "Was it necessary to sneak up on me like that?"

Callahan chuckled. "I didn't sneak up on you." And when she continued to snarl in his direction, he asked, "Are you always so grumpy in the morning?"

Mattie ignored his question, but asked with some apprehension, "Don't tell me you're one of those people who smile the moment you open your eyes?"

Callahan laughed at her look of disgust as he came to his feet and reached for her trunk. Mattie had no option but to move aside as he lifted it to his shoulder with a low grunt. "I'd say being able to open your eyes each morning is reason enough to smile."

Mattie only moaned at his cheery remark.

"I hope you haven't eaten yet. I've got a stack of flapjacks about yea high," he gestured with his free hand, "back at our wagon."

"I never eat breakfast, Mr. Callahan."

Callahan nodded as he looked her over. "I expect that's why you're so puny. How do you hope to keep your strength up if you don't eat?"

Mattie bristled under his close and clearly clinical examination. Puny! How dare he call her puny?! She was a woman, grown. She didn't need some giant telling her how or when to eat. Mattie took a deep, calming breath. This day was not starting at all as she imagined. "Fat is not necessarily healthy, Mr. Callahan. Contrary to your opinion, I do eat. I'm simply not hungry in the morning."

"Ya ever think a good breakfast would be the thing to cheer you up?"

Mattie ignored his question along with the accompanying low chuckle as he stopped beside one of the wagons. "I'll join you for tea after you put my trunk into the wagon. I'm afraid that's the best I can do." Mattie

34

couldn't control the sneer in her voice. She just wasn't up to this much cheer in the morning. "I shiver to imagine it but you'll probably get even happier after you've finished your meal."

Callahan laughed out loud as he went about the chore. "I already ate. I was savin' the rest for you."

Callahan grunted again as he managed to push her trunk inside. "What have you got in here? Bricks?"

Mattie couldn't hide her smile. "I guess I'm not as puny as I look."

"You didn't cart this from Virginia by yourself?"

"I did," she returned proudly.

Callahan could only shake his head in amazement.

"Good morning, Mrs. Callahan" came a voice from behind Mattie. "I'll bet you're excited about starting out this morning."

Mattie had completely forgotten that since she was supposed to be Callahan's wife, she'd be addressed as such. Therefore, it never registered that someone was speaking to her.

Callahan grinned as he moved to Mattie's side and casually wrapped his arm around her slender waist. "My wife's a bit hard of hearin', Miz Stables." He directed his next words at Mattie, with a low laugh. "This is Miz Stables, honey."

Mattie jumped at his all too familiar touch, thereby lending credence to his words.

Mrs. Stables nodded knowledgeably and then proceeded to yell, "How are you this morning, Mrs. Callahan?"

Mattie's eyes widened with alarm as Callahan ran his hand down her back and up again. His unwanted and definitely uncalled-for action, coupled with the lack of sleep and shrill sound of the woman's voice, brought about the beginnings of a headache. Mattie would have jumped away from his touch, but realized just in time how odd that would have looked. Still, she managed a somewhat stiff smile. "Just fine, thank you."

"You were sleeping last night when my Jim and I made

35

our visit."

Mattie looked up with some puzzlement at her supposed husband, obviously waiting for clarification.

Callahan grinned as Mrs. Stables left them with an extraordinary loud farewell to answer her husband's call.

"I couldn't tell them my wife preferred to sleep alone rather than share our cozy wagon, now could I?"

"Am I supposed to be deaf?"

"Well, you didn't answer her. I had to think of something."

"And you thought hugging me would clear up this imaginary ailment?"

Callahan shrugged as he returned to the job of clearing space for her trunk. It was obvious he was finding it difficult to control his merriment. "I was only acting like a husband, lady. You want everyone to believe we're married, don't you?"

"All husbands do not rub their hands up and down their wives' back when they talk."

"The ones I know do."

"Well, the ones I know don't!"

Callahan shoved the trunk farther inside the wagon and casually leaned against the back. He crossed his legs and hooked his thumbs into the waistband of pants that already rode dangerously low on his hips. The action brought Mattie's gaze to linger where it had no business being. His lips curved into a knowing smile. "Which example shall we follow, lady?"

As she stomped off toward the small cooking fire Mattie, her cheeks growing pink as she realized what had caught her attention, muttered some advice about whose example she'd be happy to see him follow and where she hoped that example would take him. The sound of his low laughter caused her to viciously kick dirt over the small blaze. Mattie gave a muffled and most unladylike curse as her toe hit against one of the large stones that edged the fire. Even though the pain raced up her leg in mindboggling agony, she gave not a sign of her discomfort. Only when she heard him move away in answer to one of his neighbor's calls, did she give in to the need to pull off her boot and rub her painful injury.

Mattie sighed with disgust as she sat before the now dead fire, holding the cold pot. Belatedly she wished she had controlled her temper. There was no time to start another fire, even had she the knowledge, and she needed a cup of tea. Altogether, this was not one of the better beginnings to a day.

Less than an hour later, Callahan and Mattie sat upon the high wagon. Coffee was not her favorite beverage, but the hot liquid offered by Mrs. Stables did much to restore her humor. The train began its slow winding path west.

"Mr. Callahan . . ."

"Lady," he interrupted, "why can't you just call me Callahan? This mister business is driving me crazy."

She pursed her lips. "It's very rude to call someone by his last name without . . ."

"I'm giving you permission. As a matter of fact, I insist. It's my name, after all."

"Well, you call me 'lady.' That's not my name."

Callahan grinned as his warm gaze moved leisurely over her small form. "Lady suits you."

"Very well," Mattie began hurriedly, not at all sure she liked the way he was looking at her, or perhaps liking it a bit too much, "have you ever been west, Callahan?"

Callahan shrugged. "Guess that depends on how far we're talking. I've been to Texas. Worked as a hand on a spread for a time."

"Texas?"

He nodded.

"Did you like it?"

"Parts. Mostly where I was it was dry as kindling and about as warm as where you were wishing me this morning."

Mattie lowered her head and bit at her lip, suddenly contrite. At times, she could really be a monster in the morning. She'd have to try to control her temper. After all, Callahan had done nothing to deserve such a show of

37

ill humor. "I'm sorry about that, Callahan. As you can tell I'm a bit out of sorts in the morning. I'll do my best not to snarl at you in the future."

Callahan grinned, his eyes forward. "Can't hope for more than that, I guess."

Mattie was exhausted by the time the wagons pulled to a stop for the night. Stopping only for a hurried midday meal, they had covered an amazing seventeen miles. And Mattie's backside felt personally acquainted with every pebble and stone the wagon had bumped and thumped over.

Belatedly, she realized riding a wagon was probably the most uncomfortable mode of transportation in existence. From now on she'd walk. A smile curved her lips. Perhaps she could convince Callahan to occasionally lend her the use of one of his two horses. Even saddle sores were preferable to this unyielding wagon seat. Anything, absolutely anything, was better than the endless jarring and the clouds of dust she was forced to swallow all day.

The day had grown unseasonably warm. Her white, button-down shirt was covered with a thick layer of brown dust and stuck like second skin to her back. She felt in desperate need of a bath. Thank God they had stopped near a farm. In the not too far distance, a line already formed around a well. For tonight, at least, there would be plenty of water. Mattie wondered how she could bear it when there wasn't.

Callahan swung her down from the high seat. Mattie gasped when she felt her knees crumble beneath her as he settled her on the ground and released her waist. Instantly his hands were holding her again. He smiled into her astonished eyes. "You're not used to this yet. Your legs won't grow so weak if you do a bit of walking tomorrow."

Mattie nodded and rubbed at her sore bottom, forgetting for the moment the man at her side. "I think I'll do

38

more than a bit."

Callahan's expression tightened as he watched her hands move over the roundness of her backside. Quickly he turned away, not trusting himself lest his hands suddenly join her own. His voice sounded oddly strangled as he bent to examine one of the wagon's wheels. "You need help starting the fire?"

Mattie's eyes rounded with surprise. Fire? Oh dear, she hadn't thought about that. She'd be expected to do the cooking, of course, and she didn't have the slightest notion of how to go about it. She sighed tiredly, unable at the moment to even think about the chores that yet lay ahead. "I'm sure I'll manage."

Suddenly a garter snake slithered across her path. Mattie, born and raised on a farm, was quite used to such happenings, and if she were at home wouldn't have given it a moment's thought. But out here in the open, her mind instantly imagined a far more dangerous form of reptile. Her low squeal and quick movement as she jumped back brought her crashing upon Callahan who was still wondering why the wheel should squeak with so much grease applied.

With no little surprise, Callahan suddenly found himself sprawled upon the ground with Mattie's back lying against his belly. An instant later she heard the laughter in his voice. "I told you I'd help with the fire. You didn't have to wrestle me to the ground."

Mattie sat up and shot him a look of annoyance. "I saw a snake."

"Umm," he nodded, the teasing light in his eyes lost in the ever-deepening shadows of approaching darkness. "A likely excuse."

Mattie came to her feet. To cover the sudden fluttering in her chest, she glared at the man before her as he dusted off his seat. "I suppose you're suggesting some ulterior motive?"

"Not at all," Callahan grinned as he recognized the testiness in her voice. "If you say you saw a snake, then you saw a snake."

"Well, I did," she snapped as she turned to walk away. "And I'll thank you to keep your evil thoughts to yourself."

Callahan chuckled as he took her arm and turned her back to face him. "How do you know I've evil thoughts?"

"Because . . . because I just do, that's all," she whispered, suddenly breathless and excited at the turn their conversation was taking.

Callahan stifled a groan. Their playful words had turned into something quite different and unexpected. From the sound of her voice, he could tell she was as greatly affected as he. His hands slid around her back. He pulled her close against him. Callahan groaned against the pleasure that crashed through his body. She was just too much to resist. He couldn't stop.

All day they had sat side by side, speaking of the most commonplace everyday matters. Not once had they allowed their conversation to wander toward forbidden paths. But he knew what had been sizzling just below the surface of their all too civil words. He remembered their every meeting as clearly as she and knew the seething embers that had instantly burst into flames when last they met.

"Because you have them too," he suggested. His back was against the wagon. Gently he brought her to stand between his legs.

"I don't," she choked as he pressed her hips against his.

Callahan chuckled at the obvious lie. "You shouldn't lie, lady. You don't know how."

"Stop," she whispered feebly as his mouth lowered toward her own.

"I'm just going to kiss you, lady, nothing else."

Mattie was melting into him, her whole body growing liquid. She could barely stand. Once his lips touched hers, she would surely crumble helplessly to the ground.

"The fire," she moaned weakly as his mustache and beard grazed her face.

"Can wait."

"I don't know how to start it."

40

Chapter Five

"What do you mean, you don't know how to start a fire?" Callahan stiffened noticeably and held her slightly away from him.

Mattie sighed with relief, knowing she had managed to get his mind off kissing her. There was no telling where that little indiscretion might lead, especially since they were already posing as man and wife. Considering the flutterings that were almost always present whenever he was near, she couldn't chance this kind of temptation. Mattie gave a small, helpless shrug. "I've never done it before."

"And you waited till now to tell me?"

"How was I supposed to know it was expected of me? I've never been on a wagon train."

"Jesus, lady, have you forgotten? The war freed all slaves. Maybe you thought I hid a few in the back of the wagon, so you could lounge in the shade?"

Mattie stood stiffly before him, her mouth twisting with disgust, her chocolate eyes bright with anger. What more could she expect from an ignorant Yankee. It took her a moment, but she finally got control of her temper and answered as calmly as possible. "Do you believe it necessary to insult my intelligence?"

Callahan pushed aside the truth of those words. He was being unnecessarily harsh, only he couldn't seem to help it. "Look, there ain't nobody on this train that don't work."

"I never said I wouldn't work," she bristled under the

unfair accusation. "I just don't know how to build a fire."

"What about cooking?"

"What about it?"

Callahan groaned with disgust, barely holding on to his temper and between clenched teeth he asked, "Can you cook?"

"I know how to make plum pudding," she stated proudly.

"Wonderful," he grunted sarcastically. "I'm sure I'll appreciate the fact if we're still on the trail come Christmas."

Callahan muttered to himself as he went about the chore of starting the fire before tending to the oxen. If the coffee was ready by the time he was done with his own chores, at least that would be something.

Mattie listened for a long moment to his low words generously laced with savage curses before she dared to speak. "For God's sake, you needn't carry on so. It's not the end of the world, you know."

"Right," he nodded and added deliberately, "It's the end of supper."

Mattie stood helplessly by as she watched Callahan gather large rocks to form a small circle. A few minutes later dry leaves and broken sticks became a small blaze, shining brightly at the circle's center. Once the fire took hold, larger pieces of wood were then carefully added.

That didn't seem difficult at all, Mattie reasoned as Callahan stomped off to the wagon to get the coffeepot. God, the man certainly was unreasonable.

A moment later, the pot was left to simmer upon one of the rocks. "Would it be too much to ask for you to haul some water? I ain't goin' to drive all day and then do the cooking, see to the animals and repairs to the wagon, and haul water to."

"You needn't be so nasty about it. You only have to ask me," Mattie snapped.

42

Callahan bit back the sharp retort that threatened and sighed. "I'm askin'."

Mattie's arms felt like they had stretched at least a foot by the time she walked back to her wagon with two large buckets of water. But for all her efforts, did she get so much as a thank you? She did not. Callahan only looked at her and remarked, "Is that the best you can do? They're only half full."

Mattie looked with some surprise at the buckets and then at her soaked skirt. "I guess some spilled on the way back."

Callahan bit his lip so as not to smile. God, she was lovely, deliciously flushed and breathing heavily from exertion. Callahan didn't even try to disguise his interest as he watched her breasts rise and fall with every deep breath taken. Her hair had started to come loose from its pins and damp, midnight-black tendrils clung to beautiful pink cheeks.

With no effort at all he poured both buckets into a large pan. "This will probably be enough for supper. But I'm going to need a lot more for the oxen," he nodded toward the two horses and cow that were tied to the back of the wagon, "and them."

"How much more?" Mattie asked while eyeing the nine huge, thirsty beasts with grave apprehension.

"As much as they want," he shrugged indifferently.

Now it was Mattie's turn to mutter expletives, centering in particular on the question of brilliance regarding the wagon master's order to set up camp so far from water. The well had to be at least five hundred yards away. Had the man no sense? Anyone could see the logic in moving the camp closer. Anyone, unless you weren't the one doing the hauling. Again, with two empty buckets in hand, she trudged to the well, tripping as she moved, in the dark, over small mounds of earth and hidden ruts.

On a trip to London, Mattie had once as a child visited a zoo. She remembered how she had stared in wide-eyed amazement at the apes, their long arms scraping the ground as they meandered almost gently about their cages. Mattie groaned with pain, her back aching, her arms aflame as muscles stretched to their limit. She dumped yet another bucket of water before the animals and swore if she was forced to carry even one more drop, her arms would surely match the length of those apes.

"You took your time doin' it, but I guess that'll be enough till morning."

"Thanks," Mattie sneered with what felt like the last of her energy before she collapsed to her knees and then sat, gasping for her next breath. Cursed luck! Why had she been so ill-fated as to have chosen this lout to bring her west?

"You can wait till after dinner before you get the rest."

He almost laughed at her look of stunned disbelief. "I'm sure you'll want to wash up before bed. I know I do."

Mattie's spine straightened despite the screaming ache. "Mr. Callahan, I'm finished hauling water for the night. If you want to wash up, get your own water." She came again to her feet, grunting and groaning as she moved. "I'm going to bed."

"Eat first."

"I'm too tired."

"You're bound to get more tired and probably sick to boot if you continue to miss meals. You had nothing but a piece of bread today, remember?"

Mattie, too exhausted to put up much of an argument, was pushed back to the ground. A tin plate filled with hot, sweet beans and thick slices of bacon was thrust not too gently before her.

For a second, Mattie thought to throw the food in his face. Arrogant, know-it-all oaf. She didn't have to take this. If she didn't want to eat that was her business. But on second thought, the food did smell awfully good. What purpose would she prove with a show of temper. All that would accomplish would be to send her to bed hungry.

Despite her exhaustion, Mattie did the meal justice. She was scraping her plate with a wonderfully flaky biscuit, cheerfully delivered by Mrs. Stables, when she heard his deep chuckle. "Hungrier than you thought, eh?"

Mattie, not in the best of moods, shot him a nasty look beneath one raised brow, not bothering to answer his comment. Her actions showed clear enough the truth of his words.

"When you're done, you can do the dishes in this pan."

Mattie glanced up from her plate to see him pointing at a tin basin with the toe of his boot. She was about to object, but bit her lip forcing back the words that longed to tumble forth. After all, it was only fair, she reasoned. He had done the cooking, fed, unharnessed, and corraled the animals, seen to the greasing of the wagon's wheels. The least she could do was clean up.

What rankled wasn't the fact that she should share the chores. It was his insufferable attitude. Who did he think he was to order her around? Not even a please, or a would you mind? It was she who was paying for this trip, after all. She was the one who paid his salary. Didn't that make her the boss? Mattie, in a huff, barely waited for him to take his last bite of beans before she unceremoniously snatched his plate and spoon away. Taking a bar of yellow soap that sat beside the basin, she scrubbed a rag into suds. Her sharp indrawn breath brought Callahan quickly to her side.

Squatting, he took her wet hands in his and examined them carefully.

"Go away," Mattie snapped as she pulled her hands free.

"Goddamned stupid female," Callahan muttered as

45

he left her side, heading for the wagon.

"Right, just what I need, Mr. Callahan," she called after him. "Yell at me some more." Tears of pain and exhaustion blurred Mattie's vision and she wiped her eyes with her arms just before she determinedly reached for the soap again.

She didn't realized until her hands touched the harsh soapy water and pain sliced through her palms that she had developed blisters, most of which had broken. Her back and arms had ached so bad, she hadn't noticed her hands at all. It took only a moment to finish up her chore, but every minute her hands stayed beneath the water was pure agony.

Mattie gave a pitiful sigh. She was gently wiping her hands on her skirt when Callahan left the wagon and came toward her with a jar of salve and clean cloth. All she wanted to do was go to bed. Why couldn't he go about his business and just leave her alone? Was this a sample of what it was going to be like, traveling with this wretched man? Mattie wondered if it wasn't too late to change her mind. She hated to travel by ship, since it never failed to cause her to become deathly ill from the moment she stepped on board till she finally and most gratefully left the constantly swaying deck. But right now, even the thought of being sick was preferable to what she considered this man's most careless treatment. Perhaps she should tell him she'd changed her mind. By midafternoon tomorrow, she could be back at Independence. The thought most definitely brought a lifting to her spirits. But reality finally interceded. There was no money left. She had given Callahan the last of it. She had no choice but to go on.

Mattie sighed. She'd known this trip wasn't going to be any picnic, but she hadn't imagined anything near this hard. And this was only the first day! She shuddered to think what lay ahead. How much more was she to suffer? Not more than Melanie, surely, an-

46

swered a nagging voice from the back of her mind. Mattie sighed. No, she wouldn't give up at the first sign of inconvenience. It was up to her to find Ellis. She wasn't going to let a little hardship and discomfort stop her.

"You should have used your skirt to cushion your hands."

Mattie knew he was right and had she not been wallowing in self-pity at being forced to do her share, she might have thought of it herself. "You should have told me before, not after the blisters."

Callahan smiled at the stubborn set of Mattie's mouth. He had only to lean forward to bring that mouth within contact of his. To say he was greatly tempted was a drastic understatement. Never was he within sight of her that the idea of taking her to bed didn't assail. He only wondered how long he'd be forced to wait. Perhaps a little cajoling and sympathy might go far toward achieving his ends. It certainly couldn't hurt, if she came to like him. "Tomorrow, I'll fetch the water," he offered. "You won't have to do anything but watch."

Mattie gasped again as he liberally spread the soothing salve over her burning palms and shot him a suspicious glance. Suddenly too tired to care what his ulterior motive might be, she sighed, "More than likely, I'll be dead tomorrow."

Mattie vehemently denied the quiver that assailed her stomach at Callahan's low, silky chuckle. "You'll be alive. After a few days, even these won't bother you." He smiled. "By the time we reach California, you'll have muscles where you never thought muscles existed."

"Good."

Callahan's eyes widened with humor as satisfaction gleamed in her eyes. "Good?"

"I'll need them to knock your block off, for laughing at me."

Callahan's expression softened as his warm chuckle closed deliciously over her. "When have I laughed at you?"

"Since the first night we met, I suspect. After you finished your sneering, that is." She prayed he didn't hear the suddenly breathless quality in her voice. What in the world was the matter with her? Just because the man chose to occasionally display some humane emotion, she went all aflutter inside. It was nothing more than he'd do for one of the beasts pulling the wagon. It means nothing. Good God, Mattie, she silently insisted, get some control over yourself.

He was wrapping her hands with the cloth. Despite the discomfort, his touch was so gentle, it sent chills up her spine. His voice was low and filled with suggestive meaning when he finally spoke. "I didn't laugh at you. As far as I can remember, laughing was the furthest thing from my mind."

After a long pregnant moment of silence, he asked, "Aren't you going to ask what was on my mind?"

"If your actions since are any proof, I know well enough what was on your mind."

"And, of course, such thoughts never occurred to you?"

"Absolutely not!"

Callahan gave a gentle, low laugh.

"See, you're doing it again."

He shrugged as he tied the last of the bandage in place. "Perhaps it's only because I find you so appealing."

Mattie felt a wave of dizziness. How could he so easily do this to her? How could she allow it? Only a short time ago he had treated her as if she were no more than a beast of burden and now, after a few softly spoken words, she felt herself softening, aching to lean into him. Mattie strove for control. She mustn't let this happen. And then she suddenly remembered her story. Gratefully she clung to the lie. "I'm a married woman,

48

Mr. Callahan. I wish you'd remember that."

"How long has it been since you've seen your husband?" he challenged, his eyes narrowing as he awaited her answer.

"T-two years," Mattie replied, forgetting she had already told him one.

Callahan nodded with satisfaction. "And you've been alone all this time?"

"I was living with my father."

"Why didn't he come with you?" he instantly countered.

"He's old and sickly. His health would never permit such a trip." Mattie sighed with disgust, angry that she was forced to make up one lie to cover yet another. All she could do was hope she remembered the lot. "What difference does it make? I hired you to drive me west, not write my biography."

Callahan grinned. "Why so defensive?"

"Why do I have the distinct feeling you don't believe a word I've said?"

Mattie had no way of knowing, of course, the intrigue she had mistakenly fallen into. She had no idea her obvious lies about being married only led Callahan to believe the worst of her and therefore to suspect everything she said.

Due to his line of work, Callahan had many years of practice in the art of lying. Therefore, it took only a second to put Mattie's doubts to rest as he raised his brows with feigned surprise. "I'm sure I don't know, Mrs. Trumont."

Mattie's brow creased with a frown as she tried to reason out the oddest sensation. Something wasn't right. By his own words this afternoon he had told her he spent most of his time trapping for animal furs. How then did he suddenly lose his backwoodsman drawl and often speak as if he had received the finest of

49

educations? No, something very definitely wasn't right here.

Mattie stood in the back of the wagon. A small lantern held in her hand, she inspected the confines of the small compartment. Her eyes widened with begrudging respect. There wasn't an available inch of space that hadn't been put to use. Six curved bows of hickory held the canvas secure over the wagon. Into the sides of the canvas were sewn pockets, containing bars of soap, liniment, herbs, candles, wicks, scissors, needles, thread, and twine along with a dozen other needed supplies.

How had he ever thought of it all? Mattie shrugged. No doubt living in the mountains gave him an idea of what would be needed for such a journey. She imagined his trapping excursions to be only slightly less supplied.

Her gaze continued to search out the mattress. But no matter where she looked or what she looked behind, she couldn't find it. Mattie finally poked her head out the back of the wagon. She sighed with disgust. Callahan had already taken his tent and was probably fast asleep. What was she going to do? Where was she going to sleep?

Mattie crawled over the tailgate and jumped out of the wagon. She moved soundlessly toward the tent, only barely outlined in the light of a distant campfire. She crouched down just outside of the low portable structure. "Mr. Callahan," she ventured softly. "I can't seem to find the mattress."

No sound came from within.

Mattie shivered. It was so dark, she could hardly see her hand before her eyes. Why hadn't he added wood to the fire as had others? Why were there no more than red embers burning in the night? She didn't want to stay out here any longer than was necessary. There was no telling what might be crawling about. Why didn't he wake up? Louder, she tried again. "Mr. Cal-

50

lahan."

"I'm not in there" came a deep, humorous voice from directly behind and above her.

Mattie gasped, never expecting to hear his voice come from what she believed to be the wrong direction. Instantly she jumped to her feet. Her sudden movement caught Callahan by surprise, more so, since upon hastily rising, her head butted with bone-shattering strength into his jaw.

Stunned, Callahan stumbled back a step and watched with amazement as Mattie, equally stunned, did the same. He might have laughed, as he watched her arms flail wildly around her, searching for balance. He might have laughed but for the fact that she apparently stepped on the hem of her skirt, which brought her even further off balance. He might have laughed as she went crashing down, except that she landed almost midcenter on his tent. The sound of ripping canvas left not a doubt as to the tent's future usability.

Callahan rubbed his aching jaw, not at all pleased with the prospect of sleeping exposed to the elements, since he could no longer count the tent as protection. "Lady, that was a damn fool thing to do."

"Me!" she gasped in righteous fury as she in turn rubbed her head. "You sneak up on me in the dark and tell me *I* was foolish?"

"If you wanted to share my tent, why the hell didn't you just crawl inside? I was only gone a few minutes."

Mattie fumed. The very idea. Was his mind so demented and his personality so shallow that only one thought persisted? "You, Mr. Callahan, have to be the stupidest clod I've ever come across. I had no intentions of sharing your tent. I was looking for my mattress."

"What mattress?" he asked as he wriggled his jaw as if testing its agility. "And why would you believe you'd find it in my tent?"

She came to her feet, not at all comfortable with the

51

fact that the man loomed over her and therefore appeared to be even larger than he already was. "What do you mean, what mattress? The mattress I'm to sleep on, of course."

Callahan shot her a look of disgust. "Unless you brought one, there is no mattress."

"No mattress?" She laughed softly. "Don't be absurd. Of course there is a mattress. I put it on the list."

Callahan only shook his head.

"You didn't buy it?" she asked, clearly astounded. "Why on earth not?"

Callahan wasn't about to tell her the boxes of guns and ammunition left little space for such luxuries as mattresses. He only shrugged. "A mattress would take up too much room, and as you can see every inch of space is already taken."

"That's the stupidest thing I've ever heard. Why, it would have taken almost no room at all. Now what am I supposed to sleep on?"

"Lady, that's the second time you've referred to a lack of intelligence on my part. If I was you, I'd watch my nasty tongue," he warned silkily. "As far as sleeping goes, you can manage quite comfortably if you unfold the quilts piled in the corner of the wagon and spread them out where you can."

"And sleep on what? The floor?"

"Lady, it took you a while, but you finally got somethin' right."

Chapter Six

After going almost twenty-four hours without sleep, Mattie slept like the dead, that is, after she managed to lose her blinding rage and ease up on the useless, if silent, curse words that filled her brain. Having no alternative, she had finally done as Callahan suggested and found herself most delightfully comfortable. Of course she'd never let the beast know. If she had her way, she wouldn't speak to him until they reached California and probably not even then.

It was sometime during the night when she became vaguely aware of rain hitting the canvas. But the sound had only caused her to turn over beneath the warmth of the quilts and snuggle deeper into their cozy softness. It wasn't until hours later that she awakened to a dreary gray day of rain. She almost smiled. Callahan had spent the night outside. No doubt, he was soaking wet. She gave a heartless shrug, for she couldn't imagine a man more deserving to suffer such discomfort.

Her thoughts lingered on his nasty parting words. He had his nerve. Who did he think he was to speak to her in that insulting tone?

Mattie stretched and sighed, feeling fully refreshed. A moment later she stripped off her sleeping gown and pulled a clean dress over her head. She fumbled awkwardly with the buttons at the bodice. The bandages made her fingers stiff and it was some time before she managed to accomplish the simple chore.

Without a word of warning, Callahan took just that moment to leap up to the wagon and step inside. A stream of rainwater was running freely from his hat and he cursed as cold water ran down his back when he flung it from his head. Not in the best of moods, since he had stupidly spent most of the night dozing under the wagon in a puddle of mud. He was colder and wetter than he could ever remember being. He glared wordlessly at the cause of his discomfort as Mattie gasped with surprise.

"Mr. Callahan! How dare you come in here? Why, you could have caught me totally unprepared!"

Callahan shot her a look of disgust. "Lady, as much as the idea of seeing you in the altogether entices, I'm afraid I'm just too cold and wet to give a sh—" He caught her widening eyes and amended quickly, "to care."

Mattie watched him for a long moment before she realized he was taking off his clothes. "What do you think you're doing?"

"I'm changing into dry clothes. Surely, even you can see that."

"Here?" There was a definite note of panic in her voice.

"Do you expect me to change outside?" he asked, his tone one of ridicule as he smirked. "I expect I'll accomplish little doing that."

That made sense, of course. Still, it rankled that he should presume to use her wagon without asking. It had never occurred to her that he would change inside the wagon, but of course he would, she reasoned silently. Even in the best of weather he would occasionally need a private moment.

Mattie, deep in thought, never realized he had stripped down to only a pair of pants that were so wet they left absolutely nothing to the imagination. His fingers were slowly unbuttoning the pants as he remarked, "Of course you're perfectly welcome to stay, this being your wagon and all, but I would have thought . . ." He finished with a laugh as Mattie came instantly to her senses, her face suddenly beet red. She gave a soft cry and nearly flung herself from the wagon.

Barely had she reached the ground when an oilcloth poncho was flung after her. Mattie struggled into the covering and gratefully pulled its hood over her head as she sought out a place of privacy for her morning ablutions. She then headed toward Mrs. Stables's wagon, to remain in the lady's company for most of the day.

The traveling on that their second day out was the worst Mattie could have imagined. Mr. Cassidy was adamant. He'd lose not a day to the elements. For nothing but Sunday, a day given over to God, would this train stop.

The mud had bogged down the wagon wheels. Even six harnessed oxen had a time of pulling the wagon through the muck. Mattie barely listened to the sharp curses, muffled some by the storm, as the oxen were prodded forward. Their mournful bellows against the snap of a whip as they strained at the yokes left her with an eerie feeling that even these stupid animals knew better than to willingly set forth on this journey.

Mattie, like all the others, hadn't a choice. She knew she dared not ride one of the horses, lest he slide and fall, thereby causing permanent injury to the animal. But for those doing the actual driving, all walked, sometimes knee-deep in the oozing mud.

It was ridiculous to chance the ruin of a perfectly good pair of boots. Almost from the moment she returned from the woods, she had taken them off and thrown them back inside the wagon, aiming for, but without much hope of hitting the chuckling male still inside.

More than once she found herself almost flung to her back as rain and gusts of wind pelted her slight form. It was only the heavy mud oozing through her toes and swirling thickly around her ankles and shins that kept her upright. The hem of her skirt, heavy with mud, began to weigh her down. At Mrs. Stables's suggestion, she gathered the skirt and pulled it between her legs to tie at her waist, thereby gaining some freedom of movement. It was easier going after that, but even this newfound freedom did little toward easing the exhaustion that closed steadily over her as the day wore on.

The rain had eased to a fine misty drizzle by the time they stopped that day. Mattie thought the four miles gained hardly worth the effort. In her opinion, Cassidy was a fool. She listened to his relentless raging. "They must not give into the desire to stop at every opportunity. To do so would see them floundering only halfway to their destination by the start of winter."

In the meantime, the animals were worked to exhaustion and the emigrants fared no better. Did that make sense?

Because of the storm, it was growing dark hours earlier than usual and the men had to hurry their care of the animals. Everything was wet. No fires could be started. Dinner consisted of cold, unpalatable leftovers from the night before.

From Callahan's morose mood, it was clear he missed his evening cup of hot coffee. Mattie silently considered his disappointed grumblings to be of the most childish nature.

But if Callahan missed his coffee, more so did he miss the easy camaraderie that should be growing between himself and this woman across from him. They were seated in the wagon, the ground too wet for any to be about. Clearly she was nervous, waiting for him to leave, so she might go to bed. Only tonight he wasn't going anywhere. And the sooner that was settled between them, the better.

Callahan reached inside his vest pocket and pulled out a small bottle of whiskey. Mattie's eyes widened with alarm. She knew what the effects of drink could do to a man. Good God, why hadn't she thought of that before? Where were her brains? What in the world had she been thinking to involve herself with a man found half in his cups at the local tavern. Hadn't she seen, firsthand, the evil drink could do?

Melanie was dead because a man couldn't control his lustful nature while in the throes of an alcoholic haze. And here she had put herself at this man's mercy. All to seek out her revenge.

"I'd prefer it if you wouldn't drink spirits in my company, Mr. Callahan. I abhor the smell of them."

Callahan eyed her for a moment and then deliberately took another long swallow from the bottle. Sighing with pleasure at the warmth that slid down and wrapped itself around his belly, he then wiped his mouth on the sleeve of his shirt. He leaned back against a wooden barrel and smiled. "I think it's time we got something straight between us, lady."

Mattie shivered at the intimate sound of his words. "There is no us, Mr. Callahan. You are a driver I've hired, nothing more. And as an employee, I'd appreciate it if you would simply do the job you were hired for."

Callahan ignored her little speech and started again. "Like I was sayin', lady. There are a few things we need to straighten out. First of all, I ain't sleepin' out in this weather." He saw she was about to interrupt and he held up his hand as if to stop the flow of words. "You can save your breath. Far as folks know, we're already husband and wife. It would look a bit odd if you called for help, don't you think?

"Now, I can see you're a-frettin', so I'll settle your mind right now. I ain't goin' to bother you none. All I want is a dry place to sleep. That ain't askin' too much, is it?"

Mattie watched him for a long moment before she ventured. "How do I know I can trust you?"

Callahan took another swallow and sighed, his lips twisting with disgust. "Do you think you're so goddamned appealing that I can't bring my rutting nature under control when in your company? Do you think you're on my mind every minute of the day?" He laughed harshly and gave her the most insulting look he could manage. "Listen, lady, I ain't sayin' you're ugly or

57

somethin', but I've seen better. I've seen much better."

"How nice for you," she managed swiftly. Mattie would have died before admitting she wanted to appeal to this man and yet she couldn't rid herself of the ridiculous sense of disappointment she felt at finding herself not at all attractive in his eyes.

Through some effort, Callahan managed to control the urge to laugh. It was obvious he had hurt her feelings, but he had the distinct feeling if he let her know just how much she did affect him, how much she was constantly in his thoughts, he'd have to tie her down to keep her inside this wagon.

He knew by the stubborn lift of her chin, she wouldn't hesitate to sleep outside if she possessed the slightest hint of his true feelings.

"Now," he continued, while studying the amber liquid in the bottle, purposely keeping his eyes from her beautiful face, "I ain't askin' for no special favors from the boss. All I want is a warm place to sleep at night and I'll do my job well enough."

Mattie remained silent. What choice did she have, after all? She couldn't very well insist that he remain outside, especially with the ground covered with mud. Not without his tent. Perhaps it was just as well that he didn't find her attractive. She might be able to eventually relax in his company. Maybe they could someday become friends. Mattie had never had a man such as he as a friend.

"Is it a deal?" he asked after waiting endless silent moments for her to respond.

"It's a deal, Mr. Callahan." Mattie reached her hand toward the man as if to shake on it, but a sudden ear-splitting crash of thunder brought a scream to her lips and her body instantly lunged as if catapulted in his direction.

Callahan gasped as she fell unexpectedly upon him. Her hands circled his neck and she clung as if her life depended on touching another human being. Again came a rolling roar of thunder and she whimpered as

58

she pressed her face into his neck. Her body shook, vibrated in fact, with a terror he'd never seen in another. What in God's name had happened to her to bring about such fear? His arms closed gently around her as he felt her push herself even closer.

"It's all right, sweetheart," he murmured softly, his lips moving close to her ear, his mouth automatically leaving gentle comforting kisses as he spoke. But he knew she heard not a word of what he said. "Mattie, honey," he whispered, "it's only thunder. It can't hurt you. Can you hear me?"

But Mattie felt none of his gentle caresses, nor heard his soothing words. Every new crash of thunder brought yet another stiffening of her body and mindless whimpers to escape her throat as her arms tightened in a desperate, almost choking hold. She shuddered in her fear, returned once again to the night of her sister's death. She heard only the screams, the blood-curdling screams, the pounding of her heart, the horrible, horrible laughter as she was transported two years back in time to the drunken cries of encouragement as those animals, one by one, eased their lust.

She was lost in the midst of a nightmare that would find no end until the monster was made to stop laughing forever.

Chapter Seven

Mattie gave a low moan of discomfort. Half asleep, she wondered why her back felt so stiff, and then remembered yesterday's walk in the mud. Slightly confused, she thought, why then wasn't it her legs that ached? Finding the effort of thinking through this monumentally complex problem simply too much upon first awakening, she sighed and tried to roll to her side. Oddly enough something prevented all movement. Something was pressing against her chest. No, not pressing exactly, more like nuzzling. Something warm and, her heart began to beat a little faster, suspiciously alive lay against her naked breast.

It couldn't be, of course. Obviously she was dreaming or something. Please, please don't let it be or something!

Mattie didn't come slowly from her sleep. She came sharply and instantly awake. Her whole body stiffened with shock and her heart picked up its pace to a thunderous beat.

Callahan! Good God, she was sleeping in the arms of a Yankee! Had she tried, she couldn't imagine anything more horrid. And to make matters worse, from what she could sense, the man was naked! What had happened? How had she ended up like this?

Tentatively, almost afraid of what she might encounter, she opened her eye a crack and looked down, only to gasp at the sight before her. Her worst fears proved true. As she feared, Callahan was sleeping, his dark, curling hair in sharp contrast against her creamy skin, his head reclining with obvious comfort upon her exposed breast.

Mattie thought she might choke, so hard did her heart

throb in her throat. What had they done? Wildly she called to mind what she could of last night. She had been about to shake his hand when a crash of thunder had rendered her almost paralyzed with fear. What had she, in a dazed moment of panic, allowed him to do?

Callahan's arms were locked securely around her and she was held snugly against his hard, warm body. On closer inspection, she realized only his chest was bare. He must have taken off his shirt. The terrifying question was why? Had he grown too hot? Mattie felt a wave of cold fear and shivered. Good Lord, the probable reason for excessive heat was more chilling than she dared contemplate.

Desperately, she tore her mind from last night's possible happenings and tried to think of a way to free herself from his hold without bringing him awake. But it was already too late. Her soft gasp and the accompanying erratic beating of her heart against his ear caused him to stir.

Mattie cringed, fighting against the odd weakness that threatened to overcome her as a warm expulsion of his breath teased her exposed nipple. Oh God, how was she to get out of this? He murmured sleepily, his lips moving just enough against her skin to send bolts of unwanted erotic sensation through her.

She tried to pull away. It no longer mattered if he awakened. She didn't trust either him or herself in this position. But his arms might have been made of steel for all the give in them. She couldn't move an inch.

Mattie groaned and gave a silent curse, knowing the embarrassment she was sure to face once he awakened. Still, she reasoned, nothing was to be gained by staying in his arms. Or more rightly stated, too much might be gained. Perhaps that wasn't the best way to phrase it either. Damn! What on earth is the matter with you? Here you are tottering on the brink of disaster and what do you do? Babble on mindlessly, thinking of the most inconsequential, nonsensical ways of phrasing impending calamity.

Mattie stiffened again. She had been so intent upon removing his head from her breast that she never noticed his hand was beneath her skirt, his palm cupping her bottom. She never noticed, that is, until he started moving it.

He was awake, that was it! And she, like a fool, was allowing this almost casual and most assuredly possessive caress.

Only there wasn't a casual thought in Callahan's mind as sleep slowly evaporated and he became conscious of the fact that his arms held a soft womanly form. For just a second he couldn't remember who it was that lay beside him. Then he sighed quite happily as he remembered last night and how she had come to him in her fear. The notion that anyone would have suited at the moment was unthinkable. He didn't understand why, but he needed to believe she'd never have reached for another as she had him.

Somehow during the night the bodice of her gown had come undone. Perhaps in his sleep he had instinctively sought out her softness and warmth. In any event Callahan found himself faced, quite literally, with the most appealing sight imaginable. Her nipple was no more than a hairsbreadth from his lips. He needed only to move a fraction to take it into his mouth, and to Callahan's delight he found not the need or inclination to refuse so enticing an offer. He didn't know how he had managed to gain this wondeous position, but there was no way he was going to turn from temptation this sweet.

Mattie gasped as he flicked his tongue over her, almost as if testing the rosy flesh, watching it harden into a round bud. Her chest was rising and falling rapidly as she strained to breathe against the nearly suffocating emotion that beckoned. She didn't want this. She moved her arms, trying to push her way free, but he only rolled her over and gathered her more securely beneath him.

"Callahan." Her voice was breathless and shaken, her heart thundering, the tiny, private compartment spinning, as she watched the direction his gaze had taken.

"What?" he asked, and with obvious effort took his eyes from her breast.

"I don't want this."

Callahan smiled as he took in the telltale heated flush of her skin, the darkening of her eyes, her erratic breathing. If she didn't, she was doing a damn good job of pretending she did. Still, some women felt it necessary to protest right up to the last moment. Somehow they imagined their denials freed them of guilt, he supposed. He gave the slightest of shrugs. It mattered little to him. He'd take on her guilt and then some if he could keep her thus positioned. "Don't you?" His dark gaze grew darker still as he silently taunted her to deny what he believed them to both desire.

Mattie felt her heart flip-flop in her chest, but instantly forced her emotions into some semblance of control. It wasn't possible. She hadn't read any great tenderness in his eyes. He looked at her as he would any woman, and if she imagined anything but lust on his part, she was more the fool.

While she, of course, felt not even that. Lust was something foreign and unknown to her nature. Something, in her innocence, she could only imagine, a sinful urge seen to in the dark by depraved creatures. It wasn't something she'd ever feel or want to feel. And he, most of all, wasn't someone she'd ever want. It was true! Only why then was her heart pounding as if it sought to escape her chest? Why did she find it so hard to breathe? Why did the weight of him against her bring about the most oddly delicious sensations?

"What exactly is it that you don't want?" he asked silkily as his dark gaze returned to her tempting nakedness. "Could it be this?" he asked with a low, taunting laugh as he teased her senses and caused her a desperate aching groan by licking his tongue smoothly across her breast. "Maybe not," he murmured as he felt her back arch. "This then?" he whispered as his tongue deliberately circled her nipple. He smiled as he watched her breast rise instinctively, almost reflexively toward his mouth.

"Could it be this?" he asked as he suddenly took her soft flesh deep into the startling fire of his mouth.

Mattie would have tried to stop it if she could, but the soft groan of pleasure escaped her throat before she knew it was coming.

Callahan growled when he heard her and the pure male sound, coupled with the sensual suckling, brought exquisite pleasure racing down her body to her feet and back up again, to grow into a delicious ache somewhere in the pit of her belly. Somehow, instinctively, she knew she pleased him and the knowledge brought a flood of pleasure anew.

Mattie probably could have forced his face from her. After all, her hands had been left free. She thought for a moment she might, for even in the midst of this delight, she knew to allow this was absolute madness. But when she touched his face, her thumbs slid into the hollows of his cheeks, made more so by his suckling. Something happened then. Instead of pushing him away, she found herself incapable of doing anything but holding him closer, suddenly greedy for more of this newly discovered exquisite sampling.

She didn't bother to think why. She couldn't have understood it in any case. This was Mattie's first tasting of passion and she found herself unable to believe such ecstasy existed.

God, why had she waited so long to know this? Most women her age were long married with a brood of kids. And here she was twenty-four and till now had never been with a man, but for Callahan had never really kissed a man. Why, she wondered, did this feel so right? Why with him? Would it feel the same with anyone?

He was gasping for breath, his arms shaking as he held the upper portion of his body above her. A buzzing sound was growing ever louder in his ears and he found himself straining to simply keep his thoughts upon this teasing conversation. "Tell me what you want, my lady fair. Tell me and I'll give it to you," he whispered just before he took her lips. Gently, his mouth moved over hers, tenderly teasing, tormenting her senses, on and on until she thought she'd go mad with wanting. But his mouth would only touch upon hers, to dart instantly away. Again he ventured to brush lightly, sweetly against her mouth and then again, the crash of disappointment as he left her lips aching for more, much more.

"Callahan," she cried almost incoherently as wave after wave of dizziness assailed. She'd never known this aching, almost painful need. Her lips parted breathlessly, waiting, pleading for him to take what he would.

"Callahan, please," she moaned, nearly mindless in her need, and then groaned deeply with pleasure as he took her mouth at last. He had kissed her before, but Mattie gasped at the sensation that now assaulted her senses. How she didn't burst into a raging flame, she had no idea. His mouth held firmly to hers while his tongue slowly traced the inside of her lips, his teeth alternately nibbling at what he could. She couldn't stand it. He was driving her insane. Her mouth opened wider, silently pleading that he forgo this exquisite torture, and they both groaned as he found his way deep into the sweetness of her at last.

"Tell me," he insisted, as he tore his mouth free, his voice no more than a low, gasping growl. "Tell me what you want."

She could have told him then. She could have said, I want you to get off me and leave me alone. She could have said any number of things, but she didn't. "I don't know," she murmured, and for an instant, he almost believed she didn't.

Callahan smiled. Even in the throes of passion, and he had enough experience to know she couldn't be faking this, she managed still to remember her innocent act. For just a second he wondered if he wasn't unequal to this delicious adversary. Would she prove to be the master here? Would she win? Callahan gave a mental shrug. It mattered not her strength. He wasn't alone in this mission and no matter the danger, he wasn't about to refuse this sweet offering. "Do you want me to kiss you again?"

"Yes," she moaned as he nuzzled her throat, his beard sending chills of delight down her back.

"Do you want me to touch you?"

"Oh yes, please," she sighed in breathless anticipation as his hand slid under her rumpled skirt, up her leg, reaching the top of her stockings at last, lingering for exquisite moments upon the soft exposed flesh he found there, coming closer, closer.

"Mrs. Callahan, dear" came a voice from outside. "I've managed to warm a bit of coffee. Would you and Mr. Callahan want a cup?"

Callahan let loose with a stream of muffled curses against the side of her throat and then sighed with disgust as he slumped heavily against her. He never heard the sounds of morning as campfires were started and oxen were once again harnessed to wagons. Children were crying. Men were swearing. Dogs barked. Pots banged, and yet he might as well have been on the moon for all the notice he'd taken. He smiled into her dazed eyes. He hadn't noticed anything but her. The wagons would soon be ready to pull out and here he was. He smiled again as he allowed his gaze to dip below her throat. He rubbed his chest against her and watched her nipple respond. Yes, here he was. His finger caressed the softness of her lips, his eyes shining with pleasure as he called out. "I'll be out directly, ma'am. We're running a bit late this morning."

Mattie, coming to her senses, made to cover herself, suddenly embarrassed lying so brazenly exposed. But he took her hand, and after removing her bandages, kissed her palm with lingering tastings. Gently, expertly, too expertly Mattie would later realize, he closed the bodice of her dress and redid the buttons.

"As delicious as you are," he sighed, a smile playing at the corners of his eyes as his mouth toyed with her lips, "I'm afraid you can't compare to a cup of coffee." He grinned and kissed her hard and hungry, one last time. An instant later he was pulling on his boots and sliding his arms into his shirt as he headed for the rear of the wagon.

Mattie lay still for a long moment after he left. A gentle smile touched her lips. Of course he was teasing. The smile disappeared. He was teasing, wasn't he?

She sighed softly as she sat up. It didn't matter. What mattered was why she should feel so . . . so strange? It wasn't disappointment exactly. It was more like empty. Mattie groaned with disgust. Now why in the world would she feel like that? Her lips twisted into a sarcastic smile. When had she felt full? Oh God, she was so confused. What was happening to her? Why should his silly words mean so much? They didn't, of course, she silently insisted. Why should she care if he teased or not? Why was she letting him affect her like this?

Mattie straightened her dress and searched out her boots. She refused to think about this morning, or last night for that matter. She didn't care a fig for the man or his preferences. So what if he knew, really knew, how to kiss. So what if his kisses were so entrancing as to make her forget everything but the need to be in his arms. How had he done that? She shook her head as if to clear her thoughts, her lips suddenly snarling with disgust. Have you already forgotten he's a Yankee, the most hated creature on God's earth? Mattie gave a low, wry laugh. You couldn't have forgotten where you met and the lady on his lap at the time. No doubt visiting whores, and this a pastime she believed only a disreputable Yankee capable of, had proven most informative. Surely that's not what you want in a man. At last Mattie could honestly agree with her thoughts. She definitely did not!

Mattie smiled with delight at what she considered her greatest accomplishment. They had stopped early again, it being two o'clock and too late to attempt to ford the river that crossed their path. Tomorrow morning would be soon enough, said Mr. Cassidy, to move the train across.

All the women, Mattie being no exception, took this

chance to wash their clothes. Most, also including herself, took the opportunity to walk farther down the riverbank to a secluded section. There, under the watchful eye of a few who had established themselves as guards, she enjoyed the luxury of a bath and a vigorous scrubbing of her hair.

While Callahan, Jim Stables, and a few others had gone hunting for meat, Mattie had worked for hours preparing a fire, which, as it turned out, wasn't as easy as it appeared and then followed Mrs. Stables's recipe most carefully.

Mattie puffed a stray wisp of hair from her sticky forehead and smiled again. She felt like dancing, so proud was she. Wait, just wait till he tasted these biscuits. He wasn't going to believe she'd done it all by herself. She'd show him she wasn't completely helpless.

In a large tin bowl, she had mixed flour, warmed water, soda, and salt. Carefully she kneaded the dough. Finally she spread it flat into a heavily greased pan. She covered it, set it upon the now-sizzling coals, and heaped hot rocks upon the lid.

Mattie brushed her skirt free of flour as she moved along the side of the wagon. The clothes she had hung out were very nearly dry. She glanced up at the setting sun, knowing to wait much longer would only invite them to remain damp. They would dry the rest of the way inside the wagon.

She was gathering the clothes into a pile across her arm when the men returned to camp. Mattie turned, her eyes widening with mild curiosity to see Callahan dismount, tie his horse to the wagon, and approach her with a purposeful stride. In an instant, and to her utter shock and mortification, he took her in his arms and bestowed a hungry kiss right on her lips!

Embarrassed beyond words, Mattie turned crimson. Had she had the nerve to look around her, she would have realized no one seemed to notice his outrageous behavior, but for Mrs. Stables, who bestowed upon the young couple a gentle smile of tolerance. After all they were newly married.

Mattie said nothing as he released her lips at last. Flustered and slightly dizzy, she stared at the fallen articles of clothing at her feet, missing completely his satisfied, happy grin. "Have you any coffee ready?"

She couldn't find her voice as she swallowed convulsively, and she most certainly couldn't look at him. Finally she simply shook her head.

"Well then, it seems I'm stuck with only you to taste."

Mattie's gaze shot suddenly up to lock with his. He leaned forward, his lips curved into an innocent smile, but Mattie had no doubt he would repeat his most disgraceful behavior. She ducked quickly beneath his arm and almost yelled, to his happy laughter, "I'll make some."

While she was about the chore, Callahan settled himself upon the ground, his back against the wagon wheel. Before him lay the small deer he had brought back from the hunt. He whistled a jaunty tune as he cut the deer into thin sections for drying, while saving a choice piece for their next meal.

Callahan smiled as he quickly finished, his eyes settling on the lovely lady crouched low over the fire. If he didn't know better, he could easily believe her to be an innocent. How, he wondered, did she manage to blush like that? He felt an unaccustomed ache tighten his chest as some unnamed emotion threatened to take hold. What was it he felt? Passion, lust, desire? Yes, but more was involved here. He thought for a long moment, but could find no reasonable answer. Finally he gave an almost imperceptible shrug. Why was he trying to figure it out? He wanted her. It was simple enough. It didn't matter who she was. And he knew as sure as he breathed, he wasn't going to have to tie her down to get what he wanted.

So why this misplaced sensation of guilt? Because some part of him wanted to believe her act. Why? Callahan shook his head, again having no answer. It didn't matter. Nothing mattered in the end, but that he accomplish his mission and if he took Mrs. Mattie Trumont to bed along the way, so much the better.

"What's for dinner?"

Mattie smiled. "I made biscuits."

Callahan's eyes widened with honest appreciation. "Did you now?"

Mattie nodded happily. "Mrs. Stables gave me the recipe."

"And what are we having with them?"

Mattie blinked and repeated stupidly, "With them?"

Callahan smiled at her obvious confusion. "Weren't you planning on eating anything else?"

Mattie you idiot! she berated silently. How could you be so dumb? She was so proud of her first attempt at making biscuits that she had completely forgotten about the rest of the meal. "Of course I was planning something else," she lied.

"What?" he asked as a smile of disbelief threatened. God, but she lied so badly. He could read her every thought in her eyes. How in the world had she or her government imagined she might succeed in this venture? Or was that part of her disguise? Was this an act? Could it be she was so well trained as to make him believe she couldn't lie? Callahan gave a mental shrug. It didn't matter. He was enjoying her too much for it to matter.

Mattie shrugged. "I was busy with the wash. I didn't realize it was time for dinner already."

"So what are we having?" he pressed on mercilessly.

Gaining some control over her confusion at last, Mattie smiled brilliantly as the thought occurred, "I thought perhaps whatever you brought back."

Chapter Eight

Mattie gave a silent sigh of disgust, almost choking on the mouthful of biscuit. Wasted. All her hard work for naught. Her biscuits had turned out looking beautiful, and flaky enough, to be sure. The only trouble was they tasted like salty, dry mud. Mattie stared at the offending object held in the palm of her hand. A puzzled frown marred her smooth brow. What had happened? She had followed the directions exactly. How could they possibly taste this bad?

Apprehensively Mattie glanced beneath lowered lids at Callahan. But at his expression, her disappointment completely evaporated. She almost laughed aloud as she watched his throat convulse against the salty concoction. Hungrily he reached for his coffee, no doubt to wash the taste away.

Mattie turned her head, hiding her grin. He looked so comical. His mouth had puckered from the salty taste, his eyes widened with surprise. She wondered how he managed to swallow without strangling.

Mistakenly believing her devious intentions well hidden behind an all-so-innocent smile, Mattie asked, "Are the biscuits to your liking, Callahan?"

Callahan glanced up guiltily. What the hell was he supposed to say? If he told her the truth, he'd hurt her feelings. If he lied, he'd be forced to eat another. Suddenly, in the light of the campfire, he caught a glimmer of the smile she'd hoped to hide, and grinned. "I've never tasted anything like it," he answered in all honesty.

Mattie smiled openly, finding it close to impossible to keep her laughter from bursting free. Unable to resist, she brought the pan closer. "Please. Don't be shy. Have another."

Laughter rumbled from deep within his chest and Mattie's heart felt suddenly light and gay. "I haven't been told I was shy since I was boy."

Mattie made to think on his words. Chocolate-brown eyes glittered with mischief as she pretended to study his face. "That long ago, eh?"

Callahan looked down at her with some surprise. His dark brow lifted as he questioned. "Just how old do you think I am?"

Mattie gave a tiny shrug, her eyes lowered to hide their laughter, her lips twitching with humor. "I wouldn't want to hurt . . ."

"You already have," he interrupted.

Mattie giggled helplessly.

Callahan flung his plate to the ground at the soft sound, and with his hands on her arms pulled her easily upon his lap. "You little wretch."

Mattie was laughing now, her position never dawning on her as her arms circled his neck for balance.

"How old do you think I am?"

"Oh, ancient," she answered with dramatic emphasis. "I'd say close to," she shrugged, "thirty-five?"

"Thirty-three. And you?"

Mattie laughed again, the sound soft and silky. Callahan felt his belly tighten as it covered him like a warm, sweetly scented blanket. She pursed her lips in a prim and proper fashion. "A gentleman never asks a lady her age, Mr. Callahan."

He squinted his eyes as if studying her. "Were I to guess, I'd say twenty," he grinned, "nine or ten?"

Mattie laughed as she smacked his shoulder. "Beast! How could I be twenty-ten?" She listened to his deep chuckle. "For your information I'm twenty-four."

"All of twenty-four?!" feigning shock. "You *are* getting on."

Mattie shot him a warning look, and then giggled. "They really were awful, weren't they?" she asked as she

72

eyed the nearly full pan of cold biscuits. "I wonder what I did wrong?"

Callahan brushed aside Mattie's question, more interested at the moment in the lady herself and the position in which she sat than her abilities or lack thereof in the kitchen. "It may be there are other things in which you excel."

Mattie gave a wicked chuckle and Callahan felt a definite tightening in his loins. "Indeed. I've been to school in France. I've learned to do flower arrangements. Dance. Hold inane conversations at social gatherings." She laughed at herself. "Too bad I can't show you how good I am."

"Oh, I don't know. I imagine you could, if you tried."

Mattie, in her innocence, never caught the underlying meaning behind his words. "How did you know I was teasing?"

Callahan shrugged, his voice growing suddenly lower. "The same way I know your husband doesn't know how to kiss."

Mattie gave a horrified gasp, realizing too late her position and his obvious reaction to it. Her cheeks darkened. She could feel his excitement pressed hard against the side of her leg. Her hands instantly released her hold on his neck and slid to his shoulders as she tried to push herself free. But Callahan was too quick for her. His arm was already around her waist, his free hand gently pressing against the back of her head, bringing her mouth toward his. "Don't say . . ."

"But it's true, isn't it?"

"No!" she insisted, almost desperate to get away from him.

"Does he do this?" Callahan asked as the tip of his tongue brushed silkily against her quivering lips. She stiffened. He persisted.

"Callahan, don't," she breathed.

"Yes."

"No," she almost whimpered as his tongue slid just inside her lips in a sensual caress, so erotic she could

73

swear her toes curled.

Her sharp intake of breath was all the answer he needed. And her soft "please" was lost in the hungry coming together of their mouths. She was trembling. Mattie could feel her resolve weakening. She had to stop this. She had to tell him this couldn't happen again. But suddenly she wondered what was the harm? She'd tell him later. Nothing could come of it, after all. There was no privacy here by the fire, while anyone could happen by. Tell him now. Don't wait. Tell him, insisted a small voice from the far recesses of her mind.

"Shut up," she murmured weakly just as he released her mouth.

Callahan grinned, his dark-blue eyes sparkling with pleasure. "Did I say something?"

Mattie never realized she had spoken aloud, but his question did manage to bring her back to her senses. Her hand reached automatically for her hair and she unconsciously patted the loose, flowing mass, as if it were neatly bound in place. "It's not what you said. It's what you've done."

"You told me to shut up."

"Did I?" She had to move away from him. It was more than obvious she forgot everything once in his arms. And there was no telling what he might do next, or what she'd allow him to do.

"I suppose I could have been mistaken."

"I suppose," she murmured absentmindedly. "Mr. Callahan, I think . . ."

"So, it's back to Mr. Callahan, is it?" he interrupted. "Shall I kiss you again?" He smiled down at her. Mattie shivered as his head dipped ever so slightly and his rough beard brushed against her cheek and jaw. "You become much more agreeable when I kiss you."

"No!" she almost shouted, her body leaning as far away as his arms permitted.

Ignoring her outburst, he continued. "You have very kissable lips, do you know that?"

"Mr. Callahan, we have to talk."

"I am talking." He grinned.

"I mean, we have to move apart and talk."

"Why?"

"Because . . . because." What could she say? I can't think when you touch me? I don't trust myself this close? She said only, "We just have to, that's all."

"You can't think straight when we're this close. Am I right?"

Her face flushed beet red, for he had voiced aloud almost exactly her silent words. "That's ridiculous," she protested lamely. And then with more determination, her eyes rolling toward the heavens, she added, "God, the arrogance of some people."

"I know what you mean."

"I was talking about you!"

Callahan laughed. "I know. I was simply agreeing with you." Suddenly he changed the subject. "You're not married, are you?"

Mattie stiffened. She felt a moment's panic that he should suspect the truth. She hadn't expected this. Was there something about married women that set them apart from their unmarried sisters? Could he somehow tell by just looking at her? Of course he couldn't, she reassured herself. He was guessing. He would have said something sooner, if he'd known. "Of course I'm married." Her heart thundered, her cheeks flushed, for the lie still came hard. "Why do you ask?"

"You wear no ring."

Mattie almost groaned aloud. God, but she was a fool. How could she have forgotten something so easily noticed? "Oh, that." She looked at her hand and then back into his eyes, stalling for time, her mind searching for a logical answer. "It grew too small. I had to take it off. Besides, if I weren't married, why would I be asking you to take me west?"

Callahan grinned, his heart suddenly as light as air. He wanted to laugh. He wanted to smother her with kisses. He wanted to hold her so tight, neither one of them could breathe. She had unconsciously looked at the wrong hand. Mattie hadn't a clue to the flood of emotions that assailed, for he kept them admirably in check. "I don't know. Why would a young lady want to go west?"

"To meet with her husband, of course."

"And yet you let me touch you and kiss you. Is this the way a wife would act?"

Mattie bristled under the unfair accusation, while tearing herself from his arms at last. "If you remember correctly, it was you who held me in your arms. Not the other way around. I didn't ask you to kiss me. As a matter of fact, I asked you not to."

Callahan chose to ignore her outburst. What she said was true, and there was little he could offer as an excuse. The plain and simple fact was, he couldn't keep his hands off her. And he wouldn't deny the need she brought to surface. With calm deliberation, he reached for his coffee and brought them back to their original subject. "Perhaps you mistakenly added a cup, rather than a pinch, of salt to the batter."

Mattie stormed off in a huff to the relative safety of the wagon, while her inelegantly mumbled expletives brought a smile to his lips. He watched her slender back and the gentle sway of rounded hips move out of the light of the campfire. It wouldn't be long, he promised himself. And he almost licked his lips imagining the pleasure that awaited.

"I don't know," Callahan shrugged.

"What do you mean, you don't know? Is she or isn't she one of them?"

Nora gave a low knowing laugh. "She getting to you, Callahan?"

Callahan shot her a quick scowl. "Shut up, brat."

"God, this is good," Nora giggled heartlessly. "I've waited a long time to see a woman get under your skin."

"Look, Callahan, if you feel you can't trust your judgment here," Jake interjected.

"Who the hell said that? I'm watching her, ain't I? If she's one of them, it's not going to matter what I do or don't feel." He gave his two partners a long, level look. "I'll do my job."

"If you want, I could get friendly. One woman can usually read another pretty accurately."

Callahan shrugged. "Suit yourself."

"Have Robinson or Perry anything to report?"

"Only that they wished they had your job." Jake smiled. "It seems Mrs. Trumont is a lot easier on the eyes than the hind view of oxen."

"Tell those two bastards to . . . Never mind, I'll tell them myself." Callahan stormed off in search of the two agents.

"He's got it bad," Nora whispered.

"Yeah, I hope," Jake shook his head, apparently deciding to keep to himself what he hoped. "He'll be all right."

Nora took his arm as they walked back to their campfire. "Want some coffee?"

Jake shook his head. "I'm going to bed."

"You want to talk about it?"

Jake froze, his eyes staring coldly into hers. "Talk about what?" he asked very slowly.

Nora sighed with disgust. "Jake, we've known each other, for how long? Two years? I've seen you bury both your wife and one of your daughters. I can see you're aching. It would help if you talked about it."

Pain sliced into his heart as he thought of his child, but Jake determinedly pushed aside the emotion. He couldn't tell her. Not even Nora could know that still another was at stake. He couldn't trust anyone. Not Mitchell, not Callahan, not anyone. His voice was flat, devoid of emotion when he answered. "It's not going to do any good. She's dead," he said, praying she'd believe the recent death of his daughter the reason for his actions of late. "No amount of talking can bring her back."

"No, but it can ease the hurt if you turned to another."

"What do you know?" he asked, his voice a broken whisper of raw agony. "What the hell do you know!" he asked again as pain slashed anew into his every pore. "Have you ever had a child die in your arms?" He gasped, almost unable to bear the pain his words brought to surface. *Have you ever had the one remaining stolen from you?* "Have you ever known the horror of watching her slip away and not being able to do a damn thing to stop it?"

Nora brushed aside his anger. He wasn't going to hide behind his usual cold reserve. Not tonight. Not ever again. "There are some things we are all helpless to stop. But . . ."

Jake snarled with disgust as he turned from her and jumped into the wagon. "Leave me alone."

Nora followed. "Jake, listen to me."

"I said leave me alone."

"No!"

Jake blinked with surprise. A moment later he shrugged, his voice flat again. "I told you . . ."

"And I told you no."

"What the hell do you want from me?" he asked, self-preservation causing his pain and terror to grow to anger.

Nora didn't answer. It had been two years since he buried his wife and almost three months ago, his daughter. She had waited for him to come to her. Ached for him, cried for the suffering she'd seen in his eyes, eyes that haunted her nights with pain. But she had waited in vain, for Jake had built up a shell of ice around his heart. She stood for a long moment trying to think of the right words. But finally realized this was one of those times when words could only sound shallow and meaningless.

Her fingers reached for the buttons of her bodice. A moment later the dress slid to the floor of the wagon.

He seemed not to notice.

Nora fumbled nervously with the ties to her petticoat. She had wanted him for so long, had loved him for so long. She trembled, suddenly unsure. But in her heart she knew this wasn't the time for timidity. If she didn't act, he might be lost to her forever.

Her petticoat joined her dress around her ankles. Her drawers and stockings next. She flung her chemise over her head and let it fall behind her. "Jake," she whispered.

"Don't do this" came his gut-wrenching warning. Blood pounded in his brain, for he had not been so lost in misery not to have noticed her actions. He felt himself harden, and his lips twisted with self-loathing. It appeared his body could still respond to a woman, no matter the state of his mind, no matter his fear for his one living child. But he wouldn't love her, he calmly and silently insisted. He didn't have the capacity to love again, no matter the temptation. He'd never survive pain greater than this. And if he lost her too . . . He left the thought unfinished, as still more pain ripped into his gut. He lowered his eyes to the floor and slumped tiredly against the wall of the wagon. "I can't love you, Nora. Don't ask it of me."

She knelt before him. "I'm not asking anything."

His eyes lifted from the floor of the wagon. He forced back the groan at the sight that greeted him. But he knew his restraint was misplaced. There would be no turning away from this. Never had he seen a woman like her. God, she was lovely. More lovely than ever he could have imagined, ever let himself imagine.

"Touch me, Jake," she whispered softly, her clear gray eyes reading correctly and reflecting his aching need. "I can't wait much longer for you."

"Nora," he groaned as he pulled her willing form into his arms. His senses reeled at the scent of her. His face nuzzled her clean, thick hair. "Nora," he sighed, feeling as if he had come home at long last when her mouth opened beneath his.

Callahan stormed back to his wagon, his thoughts

unusually black. His encounter with Robinson and Perry had come to nothing. Neither man had said a word about the lady, even though he had given them more than one opening. What had gotten him so riled? Callahan couldn't think what had put him in so foul a mood. He felt like punching someone, something, and if he didn't do it soon, he was going to go crazy.

It was that damn brat Nora and her smart mouth that had set him off, he realized at last. It wasn't true, of course. The lady wasn't getting to him. He gave a low laugh at the absurd suggestion. Hadn't he seen what could happen to a man? Hadn't he been through enough? He sure as hell had. Never! Never would he be fool enough to again allow a sweet-talking bitch to get to him.

Suddenly he came to an abrupt stop, pain slicing into his stomach. Callahan never heard the soft moan or the muttered "Sweet Jesus" that slipped from his lips. His eyes were on the wagon and the silhouetted form of the lady most constantly in his thoughts. Did she know he could see her? Did she know she was tearing him to pieces? Had she planned for him to see this? Was she doing it on purpose?

A moment later he came to his senses. "Sonofabitch!" If he could see, so could anyone who happened to glance at the wagon. Yards away, he managed to close the distance in less than two seconds. With a vicious curse, he flung the canvas closing aside and jumped into the wagon.

Mattie gave a short, startled scream, pulled her nightdress to her naked form, and, off balance, fell with a hard bounce to the floor.

"Are you out of your mind?" Neither noticed they spoke in unison.

Mattie was gasping from the shock of having him enter while she was undressed, while Callahan's gasping was for completely different reasons.

"Do you know the whole camp can see you with the lantern lit behind you?"

Mattie ignored his question, in fact never heard it. "Get out of here, Callahan. How dare you barge in like that? I was getting dressed."

"I know well enough what you were doing. I could see every movement you made."

"Well, you could have said something instead of running in here like a madman!"

He took a step toward her, his anger threatening complete loss of control. "Why the hell aren't you asleep?"

"I took a walk."

"In the dark?" he asked incredulously.

Mattie's spine stiffened. "Since when do I have to answer to you?"

"Since you hired me to get you to California," he sneered. "You're my responsibility, lady. It's my job to see that nothing happens to you."

Callahan was beginning to calm down. The only problem was his body was also beginning to notice just how much she had on, which was nothing. His eyes moved to the long length of naked leg and hip. Her gown was crushed in her fists, lying over the length of her, covering only the bare essentials.

Mattie reached for a nearby quilt and pulled it over her. She hadn't mistaken the look in his eyes. She could almost name the second when his anger had turned to desire. She shivered. With fright? With answering need? Did she want him to kiss her? To touch her? Oh God, she did. But she couldn't let that happen. Not with him. She had to get to California. There was a score that had to be settled. Somehow she knew, if he found out, he'd never let her finish. And she had to finish, or she'd never be able to start anything else. No, she couldn't allow herself to get involved with him. Not now!

"Get out of here, Callahan," she breathed softly, only her words sounded like a plea for him to stay, even to her own ears.

Callahan smiled as his fingers moved to the buttons

of his shirt. "You say the right words, lady, but . . ."

"I mean it," she said more firmly.

"Do you?" he dared, his brow lifting with mocking humor. "I wonder what you'd do if I joined you on the floor."

"Callahan, I'm warning you."

His low laugh was awful in what it did to her. He shouldn't be allowed to laugh like that. Mattie felt her will slipping away. She felt cornered, paralyzed, unable to move, barely able to breathe. She couldn't take her gaze from him. His shirt opened and he pulled it from his pants. Mattie swallowed, her eyes widened, a pulse throbbed in her throat. He was more beautiful than he had any right to be. How was it, she only now noticed how dark he was? Her cheeks flushed as the wanton thought came upon her. Was he dark everywhere? She shivered as her fingers suddenly itched to thread themselves through the beckoning black hair that covered most of his chest.

His eyes darkened, growing almost black as his gaze moved over the length of her. He couldn't see more than a hint of her outline beneath the quilt, but he could remember the creamy white glow of her skin and the silky softness so far sampled.

His shirt dropped to the floor. His boots were thrown carelessly behind him. And still Mattie sat there, unable to do more than gasp each desperately needed breath into her lungs. He was moving toward her. He reached down and pulled at the edge of the quilt. It moved easily from her grasp.

He swallowed hard. Blood pounded in his ears. The movement of the quilt had caused her gown to slide between her legs, leaving everything but a thin line down the center of her body uncovered. "Mattie," he groaned, unable to resist the beauty before him.

He never remembered moving or pressing her to lie back, and was somewhat surprised to find himself kneeling over her. When had a woman last brought about such a need as to forget everything but her?

Never, came an answer from some far corner of his mind. Never had he wanted as he did this woman.

He had to have her. Perhaps then she wouldn't haunt his every waking moment, his dreams, his constant thoughts. He had to get her out of his mind, his life. He almost groaned with dread, for he knew he'd never be anything but hers if he didn't. And he had to do it now.

Neither spoke as his gaze moved slowly over the length of her, reaching at last her eyes. She was gasping for breath, her chest rising and falling in rapid succession.

Callahan wordlessly took her balled hands and placed them at her side. Gently he began to pull her gown from her. His voice was low, husky, holding her easily under his spell. "Don't close your eyes, Mattie. I want you to watch me look at you. Look in my eyes and see what I see."

Mattie had no will but to obey. She couldn't fight this pull between them. She should have known from the first it would come to this. Maybe she had. Could she have found another way? Had she wanted this all along? She didn't know anymore, and right now, she didn't care.

The gown slid from her breasts and Mattie listened to his sharp intake of breath as his eyes took in the sight of her.

"Mattie," he murmured. "Oh God, Mattie," he choked as the gown slid lower. Slowly, achingly slow, he pulled the material from her stomach, her hips, at last uncovering her completely. Callahan groaned, and his eyes closed at the sight before him as if savoring this exquisite moment. Yes, he had imagined, but God, never this much. He leaned over her, his eyes level to hers. "If I were suddenly struck blind, it would not matter, for I've seen all that is beautiful." Somewhere in the back of his mind, Callahan was mildly surprised. He had never known himself to be particularly romantic or poetic, but he found himself aching to whisper love sonnets, for only the most beautiful words were worthy of this sight.

"I want you, Mattie. I've wanted you since the first moment I saw you."

He kissed her then, and Mattie thought she might die, or faint, or simply float away with the pure ecstasy of his lips against he mouth.

"Tell me what you want," he murmured as he traced lazy, imaginary lines over her jaw and down her throat with his tongue and then brushed the moisture away with his beard.

Mattie closed her eyes on a groan. Her neck arched, giving him easier access. "You know."

"Say it. I want to hear you say it."

Mattie opened her mouth, but the low words never came as a scream split the silent night.

Chapter Nine

Callahan shoved his feet into his boots, his eyes blazing with fury. "This is the second time. I swear I'm going to kill that woman."

Mattie hurried into her dress, her fingers shaking at the horrified sounds. What in the world was happening out there? It wasn't logical, but Mrs. Stables's scream appeared to be almost instantly answered by another. Oddly enough it began to sound as if two people were taking turns, each one trying for a louder and higher note until Mattie was sure no one on this train of more than a hundred wagons could possibly not have heard. Mattie couldn't imagine the cause. Surely, no one could maintain that intensity of fright, and she imagined it *was* fright, for that long.

The noise suddenly and drastically lowered in volume. Mattie and Callahan stopped all movement and looked at each other. It was obvious someone had put something over her mouth, for low, muffled sounds could still be heard. "Stay right here," Callahan ordered as he grabbed his gun and nearly flew from the wagon.

Mattie had no intentions of obeying, of course. She was going to see for herself what was happening. A moment later she stepped outside, intent on following Callahan, only to find herself face to face with an Indian.

Mattie gasped with surprise. What was he doing sneaking around her wagon like that? Good God, he'd nearly finished her off with the fright he'd given her. Still, she hadn't uttered a sound, knowing this Indian to be no hostile. Apparently, if the satchels lying across his horse were any evidence, he had come to trade. It was his companion who was continuing the dueling screams with Mrs. Stables.

Mattie faced the tall man before her. He was remarkably good-looking for an Indian. And then with some disgust, she silently berated her thoughts. Why would she suppose him to be good-looking for an Indian? She had no firsthand knowledge they weren't all as pleasing to the eye. His chest was bare, and he stood a good head taller than she. A long earring perhaps eight inches in length glittered in the silvery moonlight as it dangled from one ear, while gleaming black hair hung straight and thick to his naked brown shoulders.

Mattie refused to back up as he took a step toward her. She wouldn't lower her eyes as if in fear, but returned his bold look. If he thought to scare her, he was bound to be disappointed. Did he think her some kind of fool to run and hide?

"What do you want here?" she asked, her arms planted firmly on her hips. It wasn't as if she wanted to portray aggression, but her arms wouldn't stop shaking, no matter how she might fiercely deny her fear, and this was the only position that would hide the fact.

The Indian smiled, white teeth flashing in the dark, his eyes narrowing with appreciation at her brave display. Clearly he was looking her over with some appreciation. She forced back a shiver of fear. His eyes locked with hers and she had the most unlikely feeling he was going to say, "You."

Warm hands slid comfortably around her waist and a kiss brushed lightly at her temple. She breathed a sigh of relief as Callahan pressed her possessively against his chest. "I thought I told you to stay inside."

"What does he want?"

"By all appearances, I'd say you."

"Be serious!"

"Mrs. Stables is going to need someone. I'm afraid she's quite hysterical. Would you . . ."

"Right away," Mattie answered, moving quickly from his embrace, grateful to put some space between her and the dark eyes that gave her the shivery sensation that he was sizing her up for his next meal.

Mattie cursed her moment of cowardice. She knew Indians were not cannibals. True, she had heard many a horror story concerning the atrocities committed against white settlers. Still, even knowing the truth of these rumors, she couldn't imagine a human so heartless as to kill women and children, no matter his color. Why, even the Yankees hadn't murdered children, and in her experience, Yankees were to be hated and feared above all.

What Mattie didn't realize was that men were men, no matter their color or creed, and given the opportunity, especially in times of war, there would always be a few who would bring shame to the human race.

As Mattie made her way toward the Stables's wagon, she tried to rationalize away her lingering fears. This man was no hostile. She had simply been startled at finding him outside her wagon. Anyone seen lurking in the dark would have brought about the sudden lurching of her heart. She had no cause to feel this odd sense of foreboding. By the time she reached the wagon, she almost believed it.

Mattie sat by a whimpering Mrs. Stables. Gently she tried to soothe the woman. "It's all right, Mrs. Stables. The Indians are friendly. I think they want to trade with us."

Mrs. Stables was crying. "I . . . I came back from . . . you know."

Mattie could only imagine she meant a trip to the woods and nodded solemnly.

"All of a sudden, there he was, standing right in front of me. I screamed. He seemed to think that a good idea, so he did the same."

Mattie could have told her she already knew that. She and just about everyone else on the train.

*　*　*

Why had he taken so long? He sighed as he cuddled her softness close against him and breathed in her sweet woman's scent. Why had he continued to deny his feelings for this woman? Jake knew the answer all too well. To admit to loving her, yes loving her even while Cecilia lived only brought about a guilt he couldn't face. He knew it wasn't logical, but logic didn't always have a place in emotions. Somehow he felt he had betrayed his wife when she needed him most. Never would he have allowed his true feelings full rein, and yet the guilt continued to plague. And so, even after he was free and had every right to pick up the pieces and start again, almost as if he punished himself, he had purposely kept his distance.

Even now the guilt threatened to take control, but Jake firmly pushed the emotion out of his mind. He wouldn't think of it now. It felt so good to hold her in his arms, at last. Just for once he wanted to forget his nagging conscience. Just for a short time he wanted to hide from the fear of what Sarah must be suffering. Just for once he wanted to feel love.

Nora pulled her face from the warmth of his neck and sighed a most contented sound as she caressed his face with gentle fingertips.

"You should have told me," he admonished gently, his finger running down her short nose and over her soft full lips.

"What?" She smiled. "That I'd never been with a man? Would it have made any difference?"

"I would have been more gentle."

"I don't believe it."

Jake chuckled. "You don't believe what?"

"You couldn't have been more gentle."

"And you know so much about it?" he teased.

"I do now," she returned on a sigh. There was a moment of contented silence before she continued. "Can I tell you something?"

Jake felt his heart thud suddenly in his chest. He knew what was coming. That she loved him, he had no doubt.

She wasn't the kind of woman who could give less than all and only to the man she loved. But this wasn't the time. Maybe after he was done with this mission and Sarah was safe. No. Not then. They would all know then. He sighed unhappily. They could never be together, for what he was about to do would mean the end of anything she felt for him. "Nora . . ."

"I have to say it, Jake," she interrupted his low impending warning. "It doesn't matter that you don't feel the same. I love you. I have for a long time."

I know, he wanted to cry. I've felt it from the first, but there was nothing I could do. I was married. I loved her. But the worst of it was I loved you too. And now, now it's too late.

He was silent for so long, Nora felt a moment's apprehension. Perhaps she shouldn't have told him. Perhaps, even after all this time, he still wasn't ready. "Is it all right?" she smiled weakly.

"Are you asking my permission?" A hint of a smile touched the corners of his mouth. His hand was running the length of her back as he coaxed her hips close to his again.

"No," she sighed with delight, loving the feel of him against her. Suddenly and quite daringly she pushed him to his back and straddled his waist. Her eyes shimmered in the soft light that filtered through the canvas from the campfire. "I love you and it's too bad if you don't like it."

"Too bad, is it?" Jake chuckled, his eyes widening with pleasure at the lovely sight of her breasts, so unashamedly exposed to him. There was a beautifully stubborn set to her lips. "Is this too bad too?" he asked as his hands reached for her face, and with a low groan took her mouth again.

"I should have expected as much. You'd think at his advanced age, he'd have learned some manners." Nora shrugged. "I think it's all that time he spends in the mountains. What he needs is a big dose of civilization."

Callahan shot the woman a disgusted glare, his cup of coffee halfway to his mouth. "Would you mind not discussing me as if I were not present?"

Nora laughed. "Was I doing that?" She gave a tiny shrug. "It serves you right. If I hadn't taken it upon myself, I still wouldn't know this lady."

Mattie's eyes moved from one to the other, her mouth open slightly with amazement. How long had they known each other to permit such casual lightly veiled insults?

"Will you give my ears a rest, for God's sake?" Callahan grunted and then lied with perfect nonchalance. "I didn't know you were on the damn train till yesterday."

Mattie looked at the three. Something was wrong. Certainly Nora and Jake seemed happy enough, but Callahan didn't seem at all pleased to see his longtime friends. Why?

Mattie shrugged. It was no concern of hers. For herself, she couldn't have been more happy to have made a friend at last. She hadn't realized until just this afternoon how starved she was for female companionship. For so long, Melanie had been her closest friend, but when her sister died, Mattie had no time left to seek out friends. All her energies focused on the need to stay alive. There was no one in whom to confide. No one to turn to for help.

Melanie. Sweet brave Melanie. Mattie gave a small shudder as her sister's haunted eyes came again to mind. Purposely she forced aside the horror of that night. She wouldn't think about it. She couldn't afford to think about it, lest she return again to the whimpering, cowardly fool she had once been.

But the memories would not desist, and Mattie slipped back in time, her thoughts returning once again to that fateful night. The night that had changed her life forever.

She and Melanie were alone in the great white house. Her mother had died while giving birth to the twin sisters, her father a casualty at Atlanta. Her brother no doubt had met his demise in some Yankee prison camp, for he had been missing since Gettysburg.

Even the slaves had run off, leaving the two young women with a sick baby and almost no means to care for it.

The baby had been born to Millie, the young house slave. Millie, poor little thing, had died soon after giving birth. Mattie and Melanie both wondered if the baby wouldn't soon join his young mother.

He was a sickly child and cried almost not at all, but lay listless and still, his tiny chest struggling with every shuddering breath taken. There was no milk, the cows long ago slaughtered by passing troops in need. No food, but wild onions and an occasional raw potato. What little they had was scavenged in the woods during the day and hidden in the mansion's cellar at night, where the two young women now made their home.

Their carriage and horses long gone, they had not the means to go for help. And so they watched as each day brought the baby closer to his final reward.

That the baby was dying was an undeniable fact. That he had managed to live four days was in itself a miracle. He wouldn't make it another day, if they didn't find help.

Melanie insisted she was going to the McClearys' plantation some six miles down the dirt road toward Richmond. Mattie begged and pleaded, terrified of being left alone. But no amount of arguing could dissuade her sister. The baby needed milk and if she couldn't find it at the McClearys' place, she'd find it at another.

And so, in the midst of a raging storm, Melanie had left on her samaritan mission, while Mattie remained with the baby.

Melanie was gone no more than twenty minutes, perhaps only five, for time passes incredibly slowly when one is made to wait, when the house, usually as quiet as a tomb, suddenly came sharply alive with the sounds of horses' hooves and the laughter of men. Footsteps stomped overhead. Furniture was dragged about as the trespassers made themselves at home.

Mattie, her heart beating furiously with fear, stood at the stairs to the cellar, waiting with a helpless, almost debilitating sense of doom for the door to lift and her hiding place to be discovered. But that was not to be. The men who had taken up temporary residence had more enjoyable things on their minds than searching the obviously already ransacked house.

Mattie, her hand over her mouth, forced back her cry of horror as she heard Melanie's voice rise sharp above the roar of the storm.

She was pleading with those animals. But she might not have bothered. The night soon filled with her sister's screams. Would she never forget the screams? The seemingly endless screams. Would they never tire? she had wondered as she waited, consumed by alternate waves of impotent rage, paralyzing horror, fear, and pity. Would they never finish? The torture continued on for hours. Until Mattie found herself praying for her sister's death. At last, collapsed in a heap upon the cellar floor, she watched the dawn creep its dim, gray light over the horizon. The aftermath of a storm had left the earth sodden, the air thick with moisture and eerie sounds of silence from above.

The baby died that morning. He took his last breath at almost the exact moment she heard the horses trot off.

The house was silent once again. Too silent. Had they taken Melanie with them? Mattie shivered at the alternative as she slowly, silently crept up the cellar stairs.

She found her sister alone in the empty house. What was left of her, that is. Melanie lived for three days. Mattie, unable to stop the hemorrhage, had watched her sister, the last of her family, slip quietly into death.

Mattie shivered as she fought down the memory of her sister's haunted eyes. Soon Melanie's torturer would find justice. It would then be finished at long last.

For two years she waited, first for the war to end, which it must and soon, for the South could not live through much more, and then to find Ellis. For two years she planned his death, at first living, if one could call it living, like a wild animal in the woods, eating what others threw away, sleeping in the open, for her home had been torched by the Yankees not long after Melanie's death. And then later in town, working only for food and a place to sleep, in Mr. Glosser's general store, biding her time, befriending her enemy until Ellis's whereabouts could be found.

Mattie blinked with surprise as Callahan shook her shoulder. His voice was low as he leaned close. "Are you all right?"

"Of course. Why would you ask?"

"You looked as if you were in pain and you didn't answer me."

"Just thinking of something I have to do."

Mattie gave him a stiff smile as she shook off the last of her memory. She hadn't realized her mind had drifted and her newfound friend was gossiping about someone on the train. "She's the talk of the whole train, you know," Nora whispered conspiratorially and gave a sad shake of her head. "It's a shame her being so young and pretty. Why, I'll bet she could have taken her pick of just about every eligible male on this train. And then she had to go and ruin everything with her loose actions. Someone should set the girl on the right course."

"You have a big enough mouth, why don't you do it?"

Nora ignored Callahan's ungentlemanly remark. "I know most men will take their pleasure where they can find it," she gave a long sigh, "but a woman is a fool to give into such advances without the blessings of marriage."

Mattie's cheeks blazed that such talk was even hinted at in mixed company, while Jake choked on the coffee he had just swallowed, not missing the mischievous gleam in Nora's eye. Callahan grumbled a low, almost animal growl, his eyes shooting daggers of . . . what? Warning? Was that it? Was Nora trying to tell her that Callahan would use her if she was foolish enough to allow it? And he, was he warning her to keep her peace?

Mattie shivered with self-loathing. It didn't matter. Mattie knew well enough what would happen if they should finally come together. She gave a soft, sad sigh. She held no hope that the man would ever feel anything but lust for her, not with the cold, hard look most often cast in her direction. While she, Mattie gave a slight shake of her head, she didn't even want to think what she felt.

Mattie was bent over the fire as she coaxed the blaze higher. Why did it always look so easy when someone else did it? Not once in the three weeks on this trail did the flames take hold as they should. Mattie sighed with disgust. It took her longer to start the fire than it took most to cook the whole meal.

Mattie blew softly into the tiny flames and gave a grunt of satisfaction as they took hold of the kindling at last. Her hand massaged her lower back as she came to her feet.

"Coffee ready?" Callahan asked from over her shoulder.

"Coffee! Is that all you ever think about?" Mattie turned to glare at him, suddenly more than a little annoyed as sweat dampened her skin and caused her hair to cling uncomfortably to her neck. A fly refused to stop trying to dive into her eye. Her back was killing her, her legs and feet ached miserably. She was dirty, sweaty. All she wanted to do was sit down and have a good cry, and all the man could think about was his damn coffee! Didn't he realize how hard this was for her? Hadn't he a shred of compassion in him? Didn't he know how tired she was?

Callahan grinned at her burst of temper. "No, I think you know that's not all I ever think about."

Mattie couldn't imagine what had gotten into her. She couldn't remember ever being so out of sorts. All day she had snapped at his every word.

"Are you having your monthly time?" Callahan asked

easily, his eyes warm with concern, his hand brushing at the insistent fly.

Mattie gasped. The nerve! The audacity to mention such an unmentionable thing! Her cheeks colored to crimson. She couldn't look at him as tears of embarrassment filled her eyes.

Mattie made to move past him, but Callahan took her shoulders and held her firmly in place. "Is it so disgraceful a happening that it cannot be spoken of?"

Clearly mortified, she murmured, "You shouldn't . . ."

Callahan grinned as he pulled her against him. His large hand ran down her back and began to massage the throbbing ache. Mattie couldn't stop the soft moan of relief that escaped her throat. "How do you know?" she asked softly, never thinking of her words, simply enjoying his soothing touch.

"My wife used to suffer terribly. I often did this for her."

Mattie stiffened and pulled away. "Your wife? You're married?"

"I was," he gave a casual shrug. "She died some time ago."

Mattie took in the cold, hard blue eyes, that tight mouth, and almost careless stance that somehow didn't seem to fit his expression. She felt a sudden wave of gratitude that she wasn't, or ever would be, his wife. Never could she accept a man as unfeeling as he. Mattie couldn't keep the sneer of contempt from her voice. "Just about tore you up, didn't it?"

Callahan shot her a quick, hard smile. "As a matter of fact, no, it didn't. If she hadn't died, I probably would have killed her."

Mattie gasped. She knew he meant it. He said it not in anger, but with a cold, deliberate detachment that chilled her soul.

"Why?" she asked, her voice no more than a squeak.

Mattie shivered as his cold eyes looked her over from head to foot. "You know, you remind me of her a bit.

95

Although you look nothing alike. She was tall and blonde, but every inch a southern belle.

"She wouldn't have been able to start a fire either. And it would have just about killed her to dirty her soft white hands with cooking."

Mattie bristled at what she believed to be an outrageous insult, considering the backbreaking work she had been made to endure these last weeks. "I fail to see the resemblance then." She held up her hand for his inspection. "As you can see, my soft white hands are a thing of the past." She glanced over her shoulder. "And I did start a fire."

Callahan grinned almost apologetically. "Perhaps it's the accent that distorts the view. No doubt I'm a bit prejudiced."

Mattie gave a silent curse that his smile should cause her heart to skip a beat and an aching tenderness to grow in the pit of her belly. She didn't want to feel tenderness for this man. How was it she was so weak-willed to nearly dissolve with pleasure simply because he chose to now and then treat her with some kindness?

But when it came to this man, Mattie was at a loss to understand her emotions, and on this day even more so, for Callahan had not missed the mark. Indeed, she *was* having her monthly time, and that combined with the usual hard day put her considerably out of sorts.

"I'll get your coffee," she said, knowing he wasn't about to give any further details. All she could do was wonder why a man could hate his wife so much as to not care if she died. Had she been unfaithful? What else could have caused such hatred?

Mattie shrugged aside her useless imaginings. Tomorrow she'd ask Nora. Perhaps she would know.

Deep in thought, Mattie never noticed how close she stood to the now generously burning flames. She bent over to get her skillet and heard a woman's sharp scream of warning. Mattie turned to see what had caused the cry, only to find pain licking at the backs of her legs. Mattie turned again, trying to find the cause of the discomfort.

Fire!

At first she felt totally dumbfounded. This couldn't be happening to her. Mattie stood almost calmly detached, watching her gray skirt turn to black, curling ash. She had once read an article in her hometown newspaper, reporting fire to be the major cause of death among women. Some professed, although never in mixed company, that it claimed even more lives a year than childbirth. And now here she was helplessly watching her own approaching demise. Her eyes widened with surprise. She'd never thought she would die this way.

Clearly she couldn't believe this was happening. But the beautiful orange-and-red licking flames that spread quickly up her long skirt brought a searing heat that couldn't be denied. She knew she should have tried to hit at the flames. Had another been on fire, she wouldn't have hesitated to do just that. But on this, the most dangerous happening in her life, she could only scream a sound of pure terror. She knew only one thought. She had to get away from the flames.

Mindlessly Mattie began to run. She took no more than five steps, for Callahan had heard the screams and was well on his way long before Mattie had panicked. The breath was knocked from her chest as he threw his heavy body upon hers and tackled her to the ground. Quickly he rolled her over amid the choking dust, his hands slapping at any remaining flames.

Mattie was shaking uncontrollably and moaned as she came to her senses. Callahan had thrown her so hard to the ground that she had almost blacked out from the blow her head had taken.

She tried to lift her head, but found her strength had deserted her along with every ounce of her good sense. She felt suddenly so heavy. From the side of her eye she could see a variety of boots and shoes and knew a small crowd of people completely surrounded her. "I think you got it out in time" came a voice from above.

"Looks like she'll be all right" came another.

"Best take her into the wagon and see to her burns. I'll bring dinner over later." That came from Mrs. Stables.

Mattie moaned again as she was turned to her back and lifted into Callahan's arms. Why was she so dizzy? And why was something wet and warm sliding down her cheek?

Callahan muttered an unconscious stream of curses as he looked at her face. Instantly a path opened and he hurried her into the wagon.

"Must you continue to curse like that?" Mattie asked, once settled inside. He was bent over her, wiping the blood from her face.

Callahan smiled as he quickly eased her out of her ruined clothes. She was lying upon a soft quilt, her chemise her only protection from his concerned gaze. And even that was pushed aside as he cleaned away pieces of her stockings and burned drawers with clean water. Soon he was soothing an ointment over her legs.

"It doesn't look too bad. Your skirt took most of the damage. Is it giving you much pain?"

"My head hurts more than anything else. I must have hit a rock when you threw me down."

Callahan cursed his roughness, covered her burns with a clean cloth, and turned her to lie on her back. Gently he bathed her face free of any sign of blood. He could have taken care of the cut himself, and would have, had she been another, but Callahan wasn't about to take a chance with that face. Dr. Webster was called and Mattie's cut was closed.

There was still much to be done. The animals were not settled as yet for the night, and still Callahan remained long after the doctor had gone, silently watching her. "There's no need for you to sit here staring at me. I'm not about to run off, you know."

Callahan smiled, wondering at the terror that had filled him when seeing her skirts afire. Surely he would have been upset if it had been anyone, but he thought his heart would stop with fear when he realized it was Mattie.

She shouldn't mean that much to him. For all he knew she was the most dastardly of villains, and yet he couldn't seem to help himself. If anything had happened to her . . . Callahan couldn't finish the thought.

He slid a summer quilt over her. A tender smile touched his lips. "You're not going to be able to walk tomorrow or perhaps for the next few days. I'll speak with Cassidy about staying over a spell."

Mattie took Callahan's arm as he made to move from her side. "I'm not your typical southern belle, Mr. Callahan. I'll walk. If not tomorrow, then the next day." Mattie gave a small shrug and then grimaced at the pain the movement caused. "Your talk would do no good in any case. Mr. Cassidy won't be waiting this train for me. He wouldn't even stop when Mrs. Jermain's time came. Why, most thought the poor woman sure to die what with the wagon lurching and rocking and all."

Callahan smiled, his eyes alight with pleasure. "You sure you ain't a typical southern belle? You sho enough sound like one."

Mattie gave a shy smile to his teasing remark, her cheeks growing warm at his tender regard. "There is no doubt about it. The man is a beast," she said, speaking to an imaginary audience upon the canvas ceiling.

"And the woman, the most beautiful I've ever known," he whispered in return, for her ears alone.

Chapter Ten

"Look, lady," Callahan sighed wearily, the lines around his mouth deep from exhaustion. "I'd appreciate a little cooperation. I've been driving this wagon all day and I still have to take care of the animals and get us something to eat. I haven't got the time or strength to argue with you."

Mattie glanced up into his dark-bearded face. His eyes held not the slightest trace of the tenderness he had shown at the time of her injury. As a matter of fact, he hadn't spoken a kind word to her in two days. "Leave the water. I'll take care of it myself."

"And how do you expect to see behind you?"

"Mr. Callahan, please. Allow me some dignity. I'll simply do the best I can."

"Dignity, my as—"

"Mr. Callahan!"

Callahan gave an almost boyish grin at his slip. But she had heard worse, much worse, as the men of the train tried to force the stubborn beasts that pulled these wagons forward. He shrugged aside her shock. "It ain't goin' to take a minute."

"Mr. Callahan. You would do well to remember you're merely a hired hand. If I need help I'll ask one of the women for it."

"Lady, you would do well to remember I'm supposed to be your husband. Wouldn't the ladies think a sudden show of shyness a bit odd?"

Callahan almost grinned as he watched her eyes widen. She knew he was right. And when she didn't respond, he shrugged. "Now shut up and roll over."

"I won't. Get out!"

"What the hell do you want? Does festering hold some kind of appeal to you?"

"They are my wounds, Mr. Callahan. Should they fester, I will bear the burden."

"The hell you will. I have to sleep in here, remember? It's bad enough that the bacon has gone rancid and the grease stinks to high heaven. I don't need . . ."

"All right! All right," she interrupted as she rolled to her stomach. "Just hurry up and be done with it."

Callahan flung aside the summer quilt, hiked up her chemise, and gently uncovered her burns. "Do you have another pair of stockings?"

Mattie nodded. "In my trunk. Why?"

Mattie gave a sigh of disgust as she watched Callahan rummage through her things. His back to her, he was blissfully unaware of her growing annoyance. "If I use them in the place of bandages, you'll be able to get up and move about without the ointment rubbing off."

"Must you tear into everything? God, you're about as gentle as one of those oxen outside."

Callahan ignored her remarks as he continued his search. Propped up on her elbows, Mattie snapped, "Watch out, you're going to tear my . . ." she groaned with disgust, not bothering to finish as she heard the fabric of her thinnest nightdress rip.

"There wasn't much to it anyway," Callahan offered with a shrug in lieu of an apology.

Mattie's lip lifted in a sneer, furious that he should show her meager possessions such little respect. Did he think her able to replace clothing so easily? "If you rip one more thing, I'm going to take it out of your wages."

Callahan laughed at her threat. "Oh, in that case, I'll be very careful."

Mattie almost snarled at his condescension, but

101

breathed a grateful sigh of relief as he came up with the needed article at last. He cleaned her wounds and again spread the ointment over her injury. Gently he finished by pulling her cotton stockings into place.

Mattie rolled to her back and reached for her light covering. Her eyes widened with surprise to see Callahan hold the quilt out of her reach. "What?"

"I'm not finished."

Mattie's heart lurched in her chest. Gone was the cool, clinical assessment in his eyes. In its place shone aching desire, a desire all too familiar and terrifying, for it matched her own.

Mattie couldn't seem to get to the bottom of her breath. "I can finish," she replied, so whispery soft she wondered if he'd heard her.

"I know," he returned, as his gaze slid over her. Her chemise was so thin from endless washings that it offered almost nothing in the way of cover. His heart thundered. He wanted her. God, how he wanted her. He was driving himself mad knowing nothing could come of this but a painful teasing of the senses. And yet he couldn't help himself. He had to see her. His words almost stuck in a suddenly dry throat. "If I touch you, I'll never stop."

"I can't," Mattie whispered, her cheeks burning with shame. "I . . ."

"I know," Callahan returned, knowing she was still in the midst of her monthly flow. "And I don't care."

"I do."

Callahan took a deep calming breath as he fought for control. Were he to kiss her, he was positive she would soon forget her embarrassment. But no, there was more to consider than shame. She had been seriously injured. There was no doubt she would suffer even more injury were he to allow his control to slip.

Callahan cleared his throat twice before he managed to speak. "Can you dress?"

Mattie nodded.

"You're going to have to do some walking later.

After dinner, I'll help you."

Mattie breathed a long sigh, suddenly torn between relief and longing. Her lips parted and the words, inviting him to stay, nearly tumbled from her throat. But having no doubt where those words would lead them, Mattie instantly gained control of her errant emotions and watched in silence as he left the small confines of the wagon.

Mattie scowled as she forced down a bite of chicken and dumplings. Mrs. Stables had again made herself indispensable. It had been a week since her accident, but knowing Mattie was still shaky on her legs, she had come to their campfire shortly after the train had stopped for the night bearing a pot half filled with the delicious meal. Only it might have been warmed water for all the enjoyment it brought the silent couple.

Callahan sat before the fire, in almost sullen silence, his gaze holding to the remains on his plate. He spoke only in monosyllables, when he spoke at all and Mattie, her temper rising, had had just about enough of his impossible moodiness.

"What's the matter?"

Callahan glanced up from his plate, but immediately swung his gaze toward the fire. "Nothing. Why?"

"Mr. Callahan," Mattie breathed a long, weary sigh. "Under normal circumstances, I couldn't care less if you sulked to your heart's content. But since I find myself forced to bear your company, I'd appreciate it if we could establish a bit of harmony."

"Meaning?"

Mattie sighed again. The man was a dolt. Of that she had no doubt. "Meaning," she repeated, her teeth clenched, her temper barely held in check, "I hate it when you sulk."

Callahan grinned. "Is that what you think I'm doing?"

"Aren't you?"

103

"Why would I sulk?"

"I'm afraid I haven't the slightest idea. All I know is that you've barely spoken for days. Except, that is, to bite my head off."

"What the hell are you talking about?" he snapped, his voice rising as was his temper. "When have I bitten your head off?"

Mattie gave him a long level look, one brow raised, her expression silently telling him he had just proven her point. "I'm sure I wouldn't know."

Callahan sighed. "Jesus, women are enough to drive you crazy."

"Are they? I haven't noticed."

"You haven't noticed the bastard following us for more than a week either, I take it."

"Mr. Callahan, I'll thank you to keep a civil tongue in your head. Who has been following us? And why should that cause you such a snit?"

He almost told her exactly where he'd like to put his civil or not too civil tongue right now, but impatiently forced the words aside. What the hell was the matter with him that every word the woman spoke sounded a veiled entreaty to take her to bed? God, each day he grew more obsessed with the idea. And if he didn't take her soon, he held no hope for his sanity. Callahan sneered with self-disgust, "The Indian, lady."

"What Indi—" But Mattie didn't finish, for she knew what Indian. Only one had so far crossed their path. Her eyes widened, her voice trembled ever so slightly. "Why?"

Callahan shrugged. "I reckon he wants you."

"You reckon what?"

"You heard me."

Mattie laughed, the sound forced and brittle, holding not a trace of humor. "That's ridiculous. He believes me to be a married lady." Mattie grew flustered at her slip. "I mean, he thinks you're my husband."

Callahan's eyes narrowed. He'd be damned if this woman was married. Why the hell was she continuing this farce? "Apparently that don't mean much to him. He already offered me six horses for you."

"I don't believe it. Why, I've barely spoken more than a few words to the man."

"It appears you spoke enough. He says your heart is strong and brave, like the buffalo."

Being compared to one of those ugly brutes was not Mattie's idea of the best of compliments. Still, he hadn't said she looked like one and that, she supposed, was something. Mattie gave a nervous giggle. "What utter nonsense."

Callahan sighed, his shoulders slumped with a combination of worry and exhaustion. "I'm happy to see you can find some humor in this. Let's hope you keep laughing when he carries you off."

"And I have nothing to say in the matter?"

"Nothing he wants to hear."

"You . . . you wouldn't let him take me, would you?"

"I wouldn't if I was really your husband."

"But they think you are." Her gaze darted toward the long line of wagons. "What would they think of you if you allowed him to take me?"

"First of all, I don't give a shit what they think of me. Second, once these fine folks find out that you was only posin' as my wife, they ain't goin' to care what the Indian does with you."

"Is that the most I can expect in the way of protection? What did I hire you for?"

"Lady, you hired me to get you to California. Not get myself killed."

Mattie sneered her contempt. "You're afraid of him."

Callahan glared his anger. "What do you care, right? It ain't you who might wake up one morning with your throat slit."

Mattie looked down her nose at the man across from her. "Mr. Callahan, I seriously doubt you'd be waking up, if that were the case."

There was no way in hell that Callahan was going to let the Indian, or for that matter anyone else, take this little runt away from him. But it wouldn't hurt to throw a good scare into her. He almost smiled as he imagined her clutching at him begging him to take care of her. He reasoned away a stab of guilt. She needed to come off her high horse. He'd had just about enough of her smart, snotty mouth. Besides, why shouldn't he get something for risking his life? Judging by the Indian's persistence, he hadn't a doubt that the day was fast approaching when he would have to fight for her. If he didn't push her into it, he'd probably get no more than a polite handshake and a thank-you for all his troubles.

Callahan came suddenly to his feet. His huge hands reached down and brought Mattie to stand before him. "Since you're so brave and strong, how about goin' out there and talking some sense into the man?" He gave her a tiny shove. "Tell him you don't want him. Tell him you've already got yourself a man."

Mattie ground her teeth in anger. She'd die before she turned to him for help. She'd been taking care of herself for two years. She didn't need anybody, especially not this coward. "Since I don't see a man in the immediate vicinity, I'm afraid I'll just have to make one up."

"You've had enough practice to be good at that." Only she wasn't, he corrected. Every time the subject of her husband came up, Mattie seemed to almost choke on the words. Why did she seem unable to tell a decent lie?

In her rage Mattie never heard his mumbled words as she stomped toward the darkness hovering just outside the huge circle of wagons. She stopped and turned to face her sneering antagonist. "Just so I don't wander aimlessly about, perhaps you could tell me where I could find him."

Of course Callahan had never expected her to take him up on his words. He couldn't believe his eyes as he stupidly watched her walk away from him. He growled a stream of curses as he overtook her in three strides. "Just where the hell do you think you're going?"

"Since I've no one to help me, I'm going to take care of the matter myself."

"Get in the wagon," he warned, his voice low, holding a clear threat.

At that moment, Mattie knew his words had simply been meant to torment her. This man feared no one and nothing. Her spine stiffened. Her hands rested on her hips as she returned his glare. How dare he try to frighten her like this. What did he hope to gain? Did he expect her to grovel and beg for his assistance? Of course he did, she realized. Mattie almost laughed. He'd never see the day.

A blood vessel throbbed in his temple. "I'm not going to tell you again."

Mattie wasn't a fool. She knew there were times when it was necessary to stand up for a point of issue and times it was expedient to tactfully retreat. The man definitely had murder in his eyes. It didn't take much thought for her to choose the latter.

Mattie turned and looked over her shoulder for perhaps the hundredth time. She gave a long, weary sigh at the sight that greeted her. Even from this distance she could see the tiny swirls of dust as a lone horse and rider stalked the train. Wouldn't he ever give up? What was he waiting for? Did he expect Callahan to simply hand her over if he followed long enough? The thought gave her the shivers.

Two weeks had passed since their quarrel. Another wretched two weeks of silence. She wished to God she knew what was going on inside Callahan's head. There was no way of knowing, of course, since he almost never spoke to her anymore.

Lately it had begun to occur to her that he believed her to blame for the Indian's interest. Why else his

107

sudden change in attitude? Mattie felt seething anger at the mere thought. She had done nothing to make him believe that absurdity. And she wasn't going to take the blame for the man's twisted ways of thinking.

Damn, but she wasn't going to take any more. Stalked by one. Ignored by another. When they stopped this evening, she was going to take Callahan's rifle and ride out and talk to him. Maybe she could persuade him to leave her alone. Certainly nothing could be worse than this eerie feeling of constantly being watched.

Nora walked beside Mattie this morning, for the most part talking to herself, since the girl obviously had her mind on something else and rarely if ever heard a thing she said. She would have had to be blind not to notice Mattie constantly looking over her shoulder. She watched as the girl shivered and then looked and shivered again. Something was going on. Nora became instantly alert. Perhaps she should tell Callahan and Jake. Maybe Mattie was in league with the French, after all. Damn, Nora hated to think she could have been so wrong. She could have sworn the girl wasn't capable of this. Were they were about to seize the shipment meant for the Mexicans? Was Mattie waiting for the first sign of them before she put her side of the plan into action?

Nora's unconscious curse brought Mattie's attention back to her. "What?"

Nora forced a smile. "What are you looking for?"

"Me?" Mattie shrugged. "Oh, nothing important."

Nora tensed, ready for action. The girl was lying. Something definitely was about to happen. Nora reached into the deep pocket of her skirt, her fingers tightening around the small gun that was always within reach. Her voice took on a harshness never before noticed. "What is it? Tell me!"

"It's him." Mattie nodded toward the rear of the train.

"Who's him?"

Mattie sighed. "The Indian. The one whose friend scared Mrs. Stables half to death."

Nora searched the flat horizon, but could only make out the slightest swirling of dust. "I don't see anyone."

"He's out there."

"What does he want?"

"Me."

"What!"

Mattie shrugged. "That's what Callahan said. Supposedly he offered six horses for me."

Nora laughed, feeling suddenly weak with relief. "That's ridiculous."

"That's what I told Callahan, only he doesn't agree."

"The man's a fool."

"If you mean Callahan, I quite agree," Mattie said. "And, that one is always out there. He's been following us for almost a month."

"What's Callahan going to do?"

"Nothing. He says he didn't hire on to get killed."

Mattie smiled as Nora told her exactly what she thought of the man.

"Callahan, you've got to be the dumbest . . ."

Callahan had been seeing to the greasing of the wagon wheel and turned instantly on his heel. "You know, I'm getting mighty tired of the women on this train calling me stupid."

"I didn't call you stupid. I called you dumb."

He raised his brow as he glared down at her from his impressive height, but if he thought to intimidate his longtime friend, he might as well have saved his strength. "Would it be too much to ask why?"

"Why the hell did you tell her the Indian is out there, waiting for her. You have her scared to death."

Callahan had no need to ask what the hell she was talking about. What he wanted to do was tell her it wasn't any of her damn business. But knowing Nora, that would have been a waste of breath. Instead he gave a long-suffering sigh. "I told her so she'd be careful. If she knows the bastard is waiting for her, she won't venture too far from camp."

"And you told her you wouldn't help her?"

Callahan shrugged. "Not in so many words."

"Well, you must have used just the right amount of them for her to get the picture, because she's tired of waiting."

"What do you mean she's tired of waiting?"

"She's gone to confront him herself."

"What! And you let her go?"

"How was I suppose to stop her? Shoot her?"

"Sonofabitch!" he grunted as scooped up the rifle leaning against the wagon and ran to his horse.

Nora smiled with a satisfied gleam in her eye as she watched Callahan race after Mattie. She watched until he too was no more than a dot in the far-off distance. Suddenly she decided to search out the camp for Jake. Callahan might need his help. In any case, it couldn't hurt to send in a backup.

The sun was low upon the horizon by the time Mattie pulled her horse to a stop. Slowly, almost hesitantly she dismounted. Her knees were trembling and she found herself holding to the saddle for support. Oddly enough, the camp appeared to be empty. Only the low-burning, smokeless fire gave evidence that that was not the case. For a moment Mattie wondered if indeed she had come upon the right camp.

The thought that perhaps she had stumbled upon another caused her a shiver. Suddenly, as frightened as she was to face this man, she much preferred the Indian above anyone else. For the worst of villains were reported to sometimes straggle behind a wagon train, ready, at a moment's notice, to pounce upon a poor unsuspecting traveler and relieve that emigrant of his possessions and perhaps his very life.

Mattie never heard his approach, but she knew the

exact moment he was standing behind her. The hairs on the back of her neck stood up. She half expected to feel his hand on her shoulder. "I want you to stop following the train. I don't like it."

When she heard nothing but silence as an answer, she turned to face him. Mattie's eyes widened. God, the man was beautiful! The first time she'd seen him, it was dark but for the light of the moon. She had thought then he was good-looking. But she never imagined him to be quite this striking. Mattie looked closer. Her eyes narrowed. How could it be? He had blue eyes!

"I do not frighten you?"

Mattie watched the man's blue eyes darken with respect. Instinctively she knew to show fear would be the worst thing she could do. "Would it please you if you did?"

"No. White Cloud would find no pleasure in bringing fear to your heart."

"How did you learn to speak English?"

"My mother was white."

"Was?"

"She's dead."

Mattie nodded, half afraid to question him further. She didn't want to know about this man. Something told her to get away. He was dangerous. Far more dangerous in his gentle actions than she had ever imagined. Had he taken her captive, she could have hated him. Had he forced himself upon her she would have one day killed him, but this gentle persuasion was most unnerving.

"I have to go."

"No!"

Mattie backed up a step. "I'm not staying. I came only to tell you to stop following me."

"Why didn't your man come? Why did he send a woman in his place?"

Mattie cursed beneath her breath. Why hadn't she thought of this? She couldn't tell him Callahan didn't know she was here. What more of an invitation would he need to keep her with him? And if she told him Callahan knew, she'd only succeed in making him look the coward.

"He didn't send me. I came to tell you I belong to another. You must go away."

"You belong to no man. I can see it. You will be mine."

"That's not true. I belong to Callahan. I can never be yours."

The Indian smiled then. A long lazy smile that sent tingles of fear down Mattie's spine. "We shall see."

Mattie took a step closer to her horse, but the reins were suddenly, if gently, taken from her fingers. Mattie sighed. Indeed, she had been wrong to come here. This man didn't want to talk. He didn't even hear the things she said. "You cannot take what you please."

"If your man comes for you, we will finish this. If he doesn't . . . " The Indian shrugged, and Mattie knew he'd then consider her his property.

Mattie groaned. How could she have been so stupid? Callahan wouldn't come for her. He didn't care what happened to her, and if by some miracle he did, he didn't even know she was here.

"He comes now," the Indian remarked, almost unconcerned as he looked over Mattie's head into the growing darkness.

Mattie's eyes followed the direction of his gaze. Even though she strained, she could see nothing. For a moment she thought the Indian was imagining things, when a moment later the sounds of a racing horse came clearly over the silent, flat countryside. Mattie stared in stunned disbelief as Callahan suddenly pulled his horse to a stop.

The distance from the wagon train to the Indian's camp was no more than five or six miles; still, Callahan had obviously covered that distance in record time, for the animal's sides heaved with the effort forced upon him. A huge cloud of dust from prancing,

112

nervous hooves swirled and enveloped the three, bringing tears to Mattie's smarting eyes.

Callahan leveled a rifle at the proud man standing at Mattie's side. He glanced at her, silently calling her every kind of fool. "Get on your horse and ride."

Completely dark now but for the soft glow of the campfire, Mattie still recognized murder lurking within the depths of his eyes. She couldn't simply walk away and say nothing. She had to let him know there was no need for violence. "White Cloud didn't hurt me, Callahan." And when that statement brought about nothing but a look of disgust, she asked, "You're not going to kill him?"

Callahan sighed, remembering the panic that had assailed, the fury that had soon taken its place, and the relief that now filled his being. He felt completely drained of energy. How had she managed to do this to him? How had he come to care so desperately? "Do you want to go with him?" he asked, his head nodding toward the Indian, knowing all the while her answer didn't matter. She wasn't going anywhere. Not while he lived.

"No."

"Then get back to camp." And when Mattie hesitated, his voice hardened. "Now!"

From the side of his eye Callahan watched Mattie mount her horse. His look was grim with determination as he once again addressed the Indian, never lowering his rifle. "I don't feature killing you, but I will if you touch her."

White Cloud smiled and calmly stated, "I want the woman."

"She's not up for grabs."

"You have not made her yours."

Callahan gave a silent groan of disgust, knowing the truth of that statement. He knew also if he didn't settle this right now, the Indian would likely follow them clear to California. "She's mine all right."

Callahan knew the words were coming and was out

113

of his saddle charging the man almost before they were spoken. "Will you fight me for her?"

Mattie gasped as she watched Callahan throw aside his weapon and fling himself from the animal's back directly and, to her mind, without warning upon the Indian. She heard a low grunt as the two went down. Suddenly they were rolling upon the ground, creating a cloud of dust so thick she could hardly tell one from the other.

Mattie never noticed Jake as he came to a stop beside her. Her eyes strained to see the twisting, grunting men at her feet. Her heart thundered in her breast. The blade of a knife glittered in the light of the fire as they rolled yet again. Mattie cringed at the sickening sound of fists smashing into flesh. She wanted to scream for them to stop, but she knew neither would listen.

Under any other circumstances, the fight would have been a fair match, in that the two men were of about equal height and strength. But White Cloud hadn't taken into account the depth of Callahan's feelings for the woman he believed to be his. True, she was wanted by both, but the Indian had, as yet, felt only need, while Callahan, even though he didn't recognize the fact, was already in deeply—hopelessly, painfully in love.

Mattie glanced to her right. The movement of Jake's horse had brought her attention from the fight. Her eyes widened with amazement. Jake was sitting back totally relaxed, his one leg pulled up across the saddle, his hat pushed back, while a smile of pure enjoyment curved his mouth and lit his eyes.

"Do something!" she insisted.

Jake took his eyes from the twisting bodies beneath them. Mattie thought her eyes must be playing tricks. Surely the man wasn't ready to laugh. "I reckon he's doin' all right."

Again came the sounds of fists meeting flesh. And then a low gasp. Instantly they lay suddenly still. Mattie was almost afraid to look. What if Callahan lost? Her heart thundered with fear. How was she to go on without him? How was she to stand the pain?

No. She shook her head as if to clear it from dark, dangerous thoughts. That wasn't what she meant at all. How would she get to California? That was what she meant.

And then she saw the blood. Mattie moaned. A wave of blackness threatened to overtake her, but by sheer force of will she remained in the saddle.

Jake touched her arm. "Are you all right?"

Mattie nodded. She couldn't take her eyes from the two combatants. Callahan straddled the man's chest. The blade of a knife pressed against White Cloud's throat. Callahan bared his teeth and Mattie gave in to the blackness that hovered, for she knew the Indian had breathed his last.

Chapter Eleven

Mattie moaned as she cuddled her head into the comfortable hollow of his neck and chest. She fought against the coming consciousness. Somehow, even in oblivion, she knew she couldn't face the awful thing she had witnessed.

Warm firm lips touched briefly upon hers and a gentle, slightly breathless voice coaxed her to awaken. "Mattie, darling. I can't carry you. Wake up."

Mattie came instantly awake. She blinked with surprise to find herself not only back at the wagon train, but still on her horse, leaning against Callahan.

"You all right now?" he asked. At her nod and with Jake's assistance, he lowered them both to the ground.

Mattie never noticed Jake as he tied the horses to their wagon. Her attention was on the man who laboriously managed to climb into the wagon and fell with a weak groan upon a soft mat of quilts. The fact that his body was shaking and covered with a fine sheen of sweat went unnoticed. All she could think was the horror of what he'd done. In an instant she too entered the wagon.

"What do you think you're doing?"

"I don't know. What?"

"Did you believe I could bear your company after what happened?"

Callahan was in more than a little discomfort. His arm was bleeding profusely and the loss of blood left his brain a bit fuzzy. He knew Jake was right. He never should have insisted on bringing Mattie back. The effort of holding her had left him completely exhausted. Therefore, he never noticed the anger in her voice, nor fully understood her words. "Lady, don't bother to thank me now. What I need is for you to see to this cut."

"Thank you! Thank you for killing a human being?"

Callahan blinked in confusion. Her image was fading in and out of focus while a high-pitched hum in his ears obliterated most of her words. Amazingly she appeared angry. Callahan couldn't imagine the cause and finally assumed it must be his imagination. God but his arm was killing him. "Get me a drink, will you?"

Mattie moved toward the back of the wagon, heading for the huge barrels that were strapped to the wagon's sides. "I don't mean water, lady. My bottle's over there," he nodded with his head.

Mattie reluctantly did as he asked. "Do you believe this some sort of cure-all? The fact remains that a man is dead at your hand. Getting drunk won't relieve you of the guilt."

Callahan downed almost half the bottle before pulling it from his mouth. "No, but getting drunk will relieve my ears from your constant nagging. What is it you keep harping on? Who is it I'm supposed to have killed?"

"Don't try to play me for a fool, Mr. Callahan. I saw the knife pressed to his throat."

Callahan shot her a look and shook his head in weary disgust. "Did you see me push it in?"

Mattie blinked, completely taken aback. She hadn't imagined that the Indian still lived. She cursed her weakness. Why did she have to go and faint? "Well," she hesitated, "no, I didn't."

"Then shut the hell up and fix my arm. Jesus, what have I ever done to deserve this?"

"Are you telling me you didn't kill him?" Mattie bit her lip, her eyes holding to his as a slow stain of embarrassment marred her golden skin.

"One day I'll probably curse the fact, but no, I

didn't."

Mattie felt an unreasonable rage suddenly suffuse her body. She wanted to lash out. Her hands itched to strike his face. Why had he done it? Why had he put himself in such danger? And why did that fact cause her such fear?

Mattie pushed aside the unsettling thought that she worried for this man's safety. No, it couldn't be that, she vehemently denied. Suddenly a thought dawned, and she finally understood the cause. He had endangered himself, thereby endangering her. If he had lost, the Indian would have taken her as his. Mattie shivered and silently fumed at the unfairness of it all. How was it a man could dare take a woman without her consent? Damn but she hated him and the Indian both. For that matter, she hated all men.

Mattie suddenly glanced at her skirt and gasped. "Good God! There's blood all over the place."

"Very observant," he remarked snidely.

"You've ruined my dress!" she accused unthinkingly, for her mind wouldn't allow the terror that hovered close by.

"I'll buy you another. Now fix my arm."

"What?"

"Has something suddenly happened to your sense of hearing. I said fix my arm."

"Oh my God," Mattie groaned as she finally saw the blood gushing from a cut that ran the length of his arm from elbow to shoulder.

Mattie turned completely white. She couldn't take her eyes from the blood as panic filled her being. From somewhere came the thought of sending for the doctor, but she seemed frozen into immobility. Suddenly the doctor was there, obviously summoned by Jake, his dark head blocking her view as he leaned over his patient.

Mattie moaned as the shirt was cut away. The cut was deep, and what seemed like gallons of blood was pumping out, forming a puddle on the quilt. God, had

118

she ever seen so much blood? Yes, when Melanie died came a low voice of remembered horror. Did that mean he too would die? Could anyone live after such a loss?

The blood began to mingle with a brighter haze of red, and she suddenly found herself seated outside upon a crate, choking as she breathed in the scent of ammonia. Jake was standing on one side, Nora on the other.

"What happened?"

"You fainted."

Mattie shook her head. "That's impossible. I never faint."

"Under normal circumstances, perhaps not. But you did earlier and then again a few minutes ago. Are you all right now?"

Mattie ignored his question. "What happened? There was so much blood."

Jake nodded. "If that fool Callahan would have let me take you back to camp, it might not have gotten so bad.

"Are you all right now?" he asked again.

"I'm fine, Jake. You needn't worry." Mattie made to stand and found her legs quite unable to support her weight.

Jake muttered a curse just before saving her from falling flat on her face. He shook his head as he eyed Nora's smile. "I think these two deserve each other. I've never met a more stubborn twosome.

"I have to get back inside. Make her stay put, will you?"

"Go ahead, Jake, she'll be all right."

"What did he mean? Callahan carried me. Is that why I'm covered with blood?"

Nora nodded. "I'm afraid Callahan doesn't take kindly to men touching you. Not even his friend." Nora shrugged aside the absurdity of men. Who in the world could understand them? "Do you want to come back to my wagon? I could find you something to wear."

Mattie shook her head. She couldn't leave. It was bad enough that she fainted at the sight of his wound. She wouldn't just walk away as if nothing were amiss. "I should go back inside. They might need my help."

Nora smiled and held her firmly in place. "You'll do no such thing. The doctor will take care of him and Jake is there if he needs help."

Mattie and Nora plus Mrs. Stables and a few other well-meaning ladies were sitting around the campfire for almost an hour before Jake and Dr. Webster left the wagon. During that time, Mattie hadn't spoken a word, but sipped at the scalding tea thrust upon her. Mattie felt a wave of dizziness at the sight of their grim faces, but steeled herself to take the news.

Calmly, her hand hardly shaking at all, she placed her cup on the ground and rose to her feet. That he was dead, she hadn't a doubt. But she wouldn't think of that now. For the pain that was already slicing her insides to ribbons threatened to grow so severe, so terrifying she dared not allow it or go screaming stark raving mad throughout the camp.

All she would allow her mind to think on was the trip west. She would have to drive the wagon now. But at least she'd be allowed her privacy again. No more sharing her sleeping quarters. No more listening to his soft, somehow comforting snores from the other end of the wagon. No more making dinner for two. Her eyes misted with unshed tears. It was ridiculous, of course, but she was just beginning to like the taste of coffee, and she would never have to make it again.

She could hear the doctor talking, but there was a louder ringing in her ears and she couldn't make out a single word. "The artery in his arm was punctured, but thankfully not severed or I would have had to amputate. Barring infection, and I'm afraid that is a real possibility under these conditions, he should be all right."

Mattie couldn't at first fathom the doctor's meaning.

Only the last part seemed to penetrate her mind and she repeated dumbly, "He should be all right? Are you telling me he isn't dead?"

"He's not dead, Mrs. Callahan. As a matter of fact he's asking for you."

Mattie was kneeling at his side. Her face was pale, her eyes huge. Her hands shook as she lifted the light cover at his waist, prepared to pull it over his exposed chest. She hesitated for a moment. Tears of relief misted her eyes as she listened to his slow, deep breathing and watched his chest rise and fall in sleep.

Suddenly he opened his eyes. His dark-blue gaze locked with hers. "I thought you were asleep."

"And so you thought this your chance to have your way with me?"

Mattie looked confused for a moment and then realized she was still holding the quilt above him. More than likely the man had not a stitch on beneath it. Mattie blushed red. "Mr. Callahan, one wonders at the workings of a mind so deeply decadent. Sure I'd have to search far to find another to compare."

A wave of pleasure filled her as she listened to his deep chuckle. Mattie smiled in return. "Shall we put your evil thoughts to rest? I was simply about to cover you." Mattie pulled the covering to his chin. "Like this." She leaned back on her heels and asked, "Can I get you something?"

But at his grin she knew he was twisting the meaning of her words to his own liking. "Perhaps some coffee?" she went on hurriedly.

"Later. Right now, I just want you to sit with me. Perhaps hold my hand or touch my brow."

Mattie laughed. "I've often heard it said that men become the biggest babies when sick. Will you prove that gossip true?"

Callahan had drunk nearly a full bottle of whiskey while the doctor had sewn his arm. Although he was

121

apt to tease her unmercifully, it wasn't usual for him to speak so suggestively, but the alcohol seemed to have loosened his tongue in the extreme and allowed his thoughts a means of escape. And if his voice was slurred, his grin was downright evil. "I'd wager a man is no better or worse than anyone else when ill. But if you think I've grown childish since my injury, there are parts other than my forehead I'd be more than eager for you to touch to prove you wrong."

"No doubt, Mr. Callahan," Mattie replied in her most prim fashion, her eyes lowered shyly, her cheeks coloring with embarrassment.

"I wonder if you know how beautiful you are?"

Mattie's gaze returned to his. Was he teasing her still?

"I've surprised you." He smiled ever so gently. "You are beautiful, you know."

Mattie shrugged, knowing the truth of her appearance. Due to the unrelenting rays of the sun, her skin had darkened, no matter the constant use of a floppy felt hat, to an unbecoming, unladylike brown. Most always dirty, since water was first and foremost set aside for the animals and cooking, her scent was at times particularly obnoxious. Her hands had grown calloused, her nails broken. "Perhaps a person grows to believe so when there is no other to compare."

Callahan laughed. "Do you suppose we are alone on this trip? Are there not a hundred or more women traveling with us?"

Their eyes held for a long moment, Callahan wishing he had the strength to do more than talk, while Mattie sighed a thankful prayer he did not.

Finally she asked, "Why did you do it? You said you wouldn't fight him and yet you did."

"I think what I said was, you hired me to get you to California, not get myself killed. I never said I wouldn't fight him."

"That's skirting the issue, don't you think? Why did you do it?"

Forgetting his arm, Callahan shrugged and then groaned as pain sliced into his brain. His voice was harsher than he had planned and the words came tumbling out before he could stop them. "Lady, if anyone is going to have you it's me, not some god-damned Indian who's suddenly found the sway of your skirt intriguing." A white line of pain had grown around his lips. "Hand me that bottle, will you?"

Mattie stiffened at what she considered a most out-rageous comment. This? This was the beast she had worried about? Mattie couldn't understand why she should care if he lived or died. Just who did he think he was? How dare he talk about her as if she were nothing but a possession, a commodity? No matter the attraction, there was nothing between them. Nothing at all. How could he suppose her to be his for the taking? Damn, she silently swore. Damn him and all men to hell!

Mattie, lost in her own anger, never thought to offer an objection, but reached behind her and did as he asked. After a few deep swallows, Callahan sighed with relief and gave her a sheepish, almost apologetic smile.

"Does it help all that much?" she asked, her expression showing her clear disbelief.

Callahan nodded. "Try it."

Mattie glanced at the offered bottle but shook her head. "I don't approve of spirits, Mr. Callahan."

"I know you don't take to the stuff. But your hands are still shaking and you're as white as a sheet. It will calm you a bit."

Mattie shook her head again.

"Go ahead. Surely a small sip can bring no harm."

Mattie sighed with annoyance as she yanked the offered bottle from his hand. Obviously he was going to nag at her until she capitulated. If it would satisfy the man . . .

Never having taken more than a few sips of sherry in her life and those only at special occasions, Mattie never suspected the strength of whiskey. Still aggra-

123

vated at his comment, she swung the bottle to her lips and carelessly gulped down a huge swallow.

Mattie's eyes widened with alarm. The first thing that registered in her brain was . . . Fire! The liquid burned in what appeared to be a straight line to her stomach and then spread out, squeezing her midsection into a tight knot of heat. Helpless tears smarted and overflowed her eyes as her breath seemed suddenly frozen in place. Her chest continued to move, but no air was taken in or out.

But her lungs weren't about to allow indecision here. They insisted she draw air. Mattie gasped, only the gasp turned into a choke and the choke into a cough.

"You were right about one thing," she managed after some few minutes of coughing, "I can't shake when I'm choking to death. My God," she took a deep, calming breath, her anger totally forgotten as she wiped at her tears with the back of her hand, "how can you stand that stuff?"

Callahan grinned. "It's an acquired taste."

"Why would you want to acquire it?" she asked with some amazement.

Callahan chuckled. "Beats me. Seemed like a good idea at the time. Part of becoming a man, I suppose. Like smoking and having your first woman."

He watched her eyes widen. "Do you believe drinking, smoking, and taking women to your bed the mark of a man?"

"No, but you can't tell that to a boy."

"Well, someone should! Do all men think like you?"

Callahan smiled. If she only knew how innocent she sounded in the ways of men. How could she ever have hoped to pull off this farce? "Some, I suppose. How does your husband think?"

"I don't . . ." She almost said I don't have a husband, but remembered in time her lie. She finished with, "Know. I don't know."

"He doesn't drink, I take it?"

Mattie shook her head, unable to meet his eyes.

"Or smoke?"

Another shake. She wished he would stop talking about her husband or rather her supposed husband. She wanted to tell him the truth, but if she did, she'd only have to lie again when he asked her why she was going west. And worst of all, she'd have no reason, to his way of thinking, at least, to resist his advances.

"Pretty damn near perfect, wouldn't you say?"

Since he was well on his way to finishing his second bottle, it wasn't hard to imagine that she began to sway, almost as if weightless, before his eyes. " 'Cept he don't how to kiss, does he?"

Mattie gasped.

He gave her a decidedly evil grin. "Want me to show you how? We could get it perfect. This way you could teach him."

"Mr. Callahan!"

"Yeah, yeah, I know. I can't talk to a lady like that." Callahan tried to blink the haze away from his eyes, but soon gave up and swallowed again from the bottle. "Why'd you have to be a lady, Mattie?" His voice was terribly slurred now. "Know what I'd do if you weren't?"

Mattie couldn't help herself. She leaned a little closer. It was horrible of her, she knew, but she couldn't stop wondering what he was going to say.

And when she heard nothing but low, gentle snores, Mattie couldn't prevent the sigh of disappointment from leaving her lips.

"Jesus Christ! What the hell are you wearing?"

"I borrowed them from Mrs. Edwards," Mattie answered as she struggled into the wagon while balancing a pan of water.

"Are you telling me Mrs. Edwards can fit into those pants?"

Mattie shot him a look of annoyance. "Of course not. They belong to her son."

"Take them off!"

"I will not!"

"Mattie, I will not have others looking at you."

"Mr. Callahan, first of all it is none of your business who looks at me. Second, these travelers have other things to worry of besides the evil thoughts that most always plague your mind."

"Mattie, if you think a man wouldn't look . . ."

"I believe all of us are so tired, no one even notices."

"Bullshit!"

Mattie tightened her lips, her eyes narrowing in warning at his expletive.

"A man would have to be dead not to notice."

"Do me a favor, Mr. Callahan. Shut up and let me get on with this chore."

Jesus, this was just what he needed. He felt sweat break out over his lip, his body tightening against the coming pain. Not only was she prancing around, showing every goddamned curve with those skintight pants, now she was going to give him a bath. And he was supposed to remain unaffected? God, what did she expect from a man?

"I don't want a bath," he remarked sullenly.

"You'll have one in any case. Perhaps that might restore some of your humor."

Mattie pulled the light blanket to his waist and briskly soaped a rag to suds. A moment later she spread the cleansing liquid over his chest and arms, careful, as always, of his injury.

Callahan could feel himself growing hard. He lifted one leg to disguise the fact. Good God, she was driving him out of his mind. His mind screamed to take her, but his body couldn't. Not yet. He was so goddamned weak.

He was panting for breath by the time she dried his skin with a large sheet. "Are you all right?"

"I'll be a lot better when you wear skirts again."

"Why does it so affect your sensibilities? Surely you know well enough a woman's shape."

"I do, but does everyone have to know yours?"

Mattie breathed a long weary sigh. "Once you are well enough to drive again, I will return to wearing a skirt. Does that satisfy?"

"It does not."

"Too bad. It will have to suffice."

Mattie didn't care what anyone said. Mr. Cassidy could give her all the thunderous looks there were, while Callahan could rant to his heart's content. She wasn't going to wear her skirt while driving this wagon. It was bad enough her arms were almost pulled from their sockets, her once soft hands were hard and calloused, her nails broken and split, her skin burned almost as dark as any Indian, but she wasn't going to waste her time worrying about ladylike modesty while doing it. There was no time to be a lady now. Not with the care of the animals, wagon, meals, and Callahan all left to her care.

Yes, Jake and Nora often helped out, especially with the oxen and wagon repairs, but Mattie still took the burden of driving on her shoulders. What alternative had she? The train wouldn't wait for Callahan's recovery and there was no one else.

It was true Mr. Robinson had offered to drive for her, but she hated to burden him with her responsibility. Everyone had their own work and enough of that to do.

Mattie considered herself blessed to be able to stop on the Sabbath. A day of rest, Mr. Cassidy had proclaimed as if he thought of the idea himself. Some rest, she grimaced as she stretched her achingly stiff body. Why, all she had to do today was a week's worth of laundry. Thank God they had stopped close to a river. Hauling water would have been beyond her at this point. After she finished the laundry, she only had to cook for the week. The idea of cooking after a day spent yanking the oxen into line was enough to make her shudder. And then there was the baking. Enough bread to last them until they stopped next Sunday. If it was still light when she was done with that chore, she could mend all their clothes. Mattie's lips turned down at the corners as she thought of her meager wardrobe. Before long she would be wearing rags, for nearly everything she owned had been torn. Mattie shrugged. There was no help for it. This trip was at least as hard on clothing as people.

Mattie muffled the sound of a yawn and stretched again, reveling in her stolen moment of comfort while trying to gather the willpower to leave her soft bed. The wagon was unusually quiet. She glanced over at Callahan, expecting to see him awake, but realized he was sleeping on his side again. Therefore the silence.

His gentle snores had grown most comforting of late, the sound somewhat akin to the steady ticking of a clock perhaps. Mattie shrugged at the comparison knowing only that the rhythmic sound usually lulled her into sleep. She smiled as she watched his face, softened in sleep. How much younger he appeared. The harsh lines around his mouth and eyes were almost invisible in the dim light of early morning.

Mattie dismissed the tender emotion that suddenly assailed. It wouldn't do to allow a softening in attitude toward him. The man was a beast. No matter he had saved her from the Indian. He had done it with one purpose in mind. And that was to have her for himself. The man posed a danger to herself and her mission. Should she succumb to his charm, and she had to admit he possessed that quality in abundance—when he chose to use it, that is—she might very well see the end of her plans.

Her mind wandered back to last night. Callahan had sat for a time by the fire, covered in a blanket and enjoying the company of his friends. It was late by the time Jake helped her get him inside the wagon. And later still before she brought him a pan of soapy, warm water so he might cleanse away the day's accumulated

128

dust and sweat. But after two attempts at washing, he gave up, falling back to his mat with a loud sigh.

"What's the matter?" Mattie asked, returning to his side. Her eyes were wide with alarm, for she had spent most of the past week worrying over the slight fever that she feared would bring him to an ever-weakening state.

"I haven't the strength. Take it away."

Mattie watched him for a long moment. His eyes didn't appear glassy. His skin wasn't flushed with fever. So far the dreaded ailment had not come in any strength. She could only pray it would not, for more died due to fever than any other cause. Mattie shivered at the fearful thought. "Nonsense," she stated briskly. "If you are unable, I will do it for you."

Mattie should have become suspicious here, since he was well on the road to recovery and especially since he had never before professed such self-sacrificing tendencies. "No. You work hard enough. I'll probably be able to do it tomorrow."

"Are you in pain?" she asked, leaning close.

Callahan nodded his head, finding it almost impossible to hide his grin.

"Is it your injury?"

He shook his head.

"Where then?"

"Here," he said as he took her hand in his and placed it upon his belly.

Mattie's eyes widened with surprise. "Here? You have a stomachache?"

"I guess you could call it that."

Mattie blinked. What an odd thing to say. Either the man had a stomachache or he didn't. What else could you call it? "I'd better get the doctor."

He held her hand against him. "No, you could take care of it."

"I'm afraid I don't know . . ."

"I could teach you," he interrupted, his blue eyes growing dark with a need that was instantly clear.

129

It didn't take a moment for Mattie to realize the silent question he asked. Her heart pounded and she shivered. It would be so easy. You want to. You know you do. Stop fighting this pull. Take what he has to offer. But Mattie knew she would not. Even if she were free to begin a relationship. Even if Ellis did not have to be punished, this giving had to be two-sided. She had to know he wanted more than just a willing body. Suddenly she nodded as if in agreement and almost smiled as she watched Callahan's eyes widen with surprise. "I have just the thing you need."

"I know you do," he commented silkily.

Mattie nodded, and just before she left his side reached into a pocket of the canvas and handed him a bottle of mineral oil. "I'm sure this will see to the end of your problems, Mr. Callahan."

Mattie sat up with a reluctant sigh and eyed the trousers she had discarded last night with some longing. Thank goodness Mrs. Edwards's son was her size. It had been so much easier to move about and do the necessary chores without the encumbrance of a skirt and petticoats. Still, there was only one pair and those needed to be washed if she wanted to use them this coming week.

Mattie glanced at Callahan again and breathed a sigh of relief. He was still sleeping. If she hurried, she'd be dressed and gone before he stirred. God, but she was tired of dressing under the blankets. To say the least it wasn't easy to hold the blanket between her teeth while pulling a shirt over her head.

She wished he would hurry up and get well. Before his injury, Mattie would awaken to him already gone, thereby allowing her a moment of privacy.

Mattie shot Callahan a final look. Satisfied that he was asleep, she came to her feet and pulled her gown over her head. Her hands froze in mid-air while reaching for her shift. "One day I'm going to stand in front of a mirror with you dressed like that."

Mattie gave a short yelp and lunged beneath her

blanket again. Her cheeks burned. Her temper soared. He had seen her before. Indeed he had nearly made love to her. But Mattie had since tried to forget that foolish lapse of good sense on her part. "You could have told me you were awake!" she ranted to his laughter. "You could have turned away!"

"That would have been foolish, don't you think?"

"That would have been the gentlemanly thing to do."

Callahan laughed. "If I had the strength, I'd show you right now what a gentleman would do."

"Beast! Rutting beast!" she mumbled as she pulled her clothing on while hiding under the covers. Her fingers shook as his words formed erotic images in her mind.

Callahan chuckled at the growlings and rolled stiffly to his back. He gave a low groan at the ache that still plagued.

Even with his eyes upon the canvas above them, he knew she stopped all movement. "What is it?" came the muffled question, from beneath the blanket.

Callahan bit back a grin at the sound of worry in her voice. "Nothing," he replied with supposed weakness. "I'm all right. Don't worry."

Mattie pulled away her covering, tugging her chemise from around her waist. Her blouse was buttoned crooked. Her skirt had yet to be found. Her hair in wild disarray, Callahan thought he'd never seen a sight more beautiful.

He almost gasped as her cool hand touched his forehead. "Are you hot?" He could feel himself shudder. No, but with only a little effort, I could be, he answered silently. He shook his head.

"Don't you feel well?" she asked solicitously, never expecting his actions to be still another trap.

"Actually. . ." he started and then purposely stopped.

"What? What is it?" she asked, coming closer as she spoke. "Do you need something? Is there something I can get you?"

Mattie never noticed his good arm snake out behind her. Not, that is, until she was suddenly crushed against him. His hand was under her shift and moving over her rounded bottom before she thought to object.

"Callahan," she grunted as she pushed herself away. "You are the most obnoxious brute."

Callahan's fingers slid between her legs and Mattie gasped as she bolted away. But she got only a few feet when she realized he was holding to the skirt of her chemise. Damn, but he was going to tear it to shreds if he didn't stop tugging. "Callahan, stop. It's going to rip."

"Not if you come closer," he answered quite reasonably.

"I only have two others." She grunted as she yanked at the cloth, but to no avail. "Will you please let go?!"

"Come here and I will."

Mattie's laughter held not a shred of humor. Her voice was strained. "Do you take me for a fool? I said let go."

"Come over here, Mattie. I want to touch you."

"And your wants are all that are important, I take it." Her cheeks grew pink with the mere thought of where his hands had been. Mattie wouldn't even think about the ache, the need, her wants for him to do it again.

Callahan grinned. "Shall we strike a bargain?"

"What kind of bargain?" Mattie eyed him suspiciously, while never giving up her struggle to free herself.

"If you give me a good morning kiss, I'll let you go."

Mattie's grunt of disbelief was all he received as an answer.

"I promise. Only a kiss. If you want anything else, you'll have to ask for it."

Mattie laughed at that. "And of course you think I would want more than that."

Callahan shrugged his good shoulder. "It's a possibility."

132

"I'm certain it is, Mr. Callahan. But you see, there is one flaw in your plan."

"Being?"

"I'd have to want to kiss you in the first place. And I can promise you, I don't." She grunted again as she pulled.

"Don't you?" he tugged harder, bringing her unwillingly back to his side.

Chocolate-brown eyes clung to blue. "I don't," she managed, but her voice had grown measurably softer.

"Humor me then. After all, I'm a sick man."

"In mind perhaps," Mattie's brow raised as if to emphasize her words. "Still you've seemed to regain immeasurable strength."

"Have I?" he asked. His gaze had fastened to her mouth and he didn't seem capable of making too much sense. He barely knew what he was saying. All he could think about was the feel of her body a few moments ago. She was so warm. If she gave him only half a chance he could make her burn for his touch.

His hand lifted, still clutching her skirt, his finger hooked inside her blouse. Mattie gave a soft gasp as his finger brushed against the curve of her breasts. She shivered ever so slightly. It wasn't fair. He shouldn't be able to do this to her. He wanted only to satisfy his needs, while she . . . No, she wouldn't think of that. Not now. Not ever.

Gently he pulled her body lower. "Unfair, Mr. Callahan. Now my blouse will rip if I resist."

"But that's the point, isn't it? I don't want you to resist."

"One kiss," she reminded him.

"One kiss," he agreed. At that moment he would have agreed to anything, anything! The need to touch her was so strong it bordered on pain.

Mattie meant to drop a chaste kiss on his lips, fulfilling her part of this ridiculous bargain. But when her mouth brushed against his, he released her clothing and slid his hand around her neck, holding her

133

mouth for his fiery assault.

And assault it was, for there was no other word that could even come near.

Callahan drew her closer, his gentle kiss giving her no warning of what was to come. He waited until he felt her relax, his arm molding her to his side before he deepened the kiss. His tongue slid enticingly over her closed mouth, taunting her to resist the pleasure he offered. They moaned in unison as she parted her lips and allowed his tongue entry.

Callahan rolled her to her back, his mouth never parting from hers as he discovered again the sweetness of her. He nibbled at her lips, stroked her teeth, the top of her mouth, her tongue. He breathed in her scent and tasted of her until he thought he'd go mad if he couldn't have more.

His body moved against hers, his hips pinning her beneath him, his tongue imitating the movement of his hips, the needs of his body, his long-withheld hunger.

Dazzled, Mattie couldn't stop her answering moan. Waves of heat mingled with exquisite pleasure until she couldn't name a part of her that didn't ache for his touch. Chills of delight spread all the way to her toes. His movement caused thrill after thrill of excitement to race up her spine. Wild emotion filled her to overflowing, for he acted unable to stop, unable to get enough, and the knowledge flowed with the pleasure he gave, leaving her only wanting more.

They were panting, starved for their next breath when he released her mouth at last. Mattie pulled her head back, her voice shaking and breathless as she murmured, "Is that what you call a kiss?"

Callahan grinned all male confidence. "Wasn't it?"

Mattie lowered her eyes, for she didn't trust her own reaction to the desire that burned in his gaze. It took her a moment, and if her voice was none too steady, she did manage, "If you let me finish dressing, I'll make breakfast."

"I'm not hungry," he murmured, his mouth leaving

tiny kisses along the edge of her jaw. "Except for you."

Mattie forced aside the weakness his words caused. "After you eat, you might ask Jake to help you to the river so you can clean up."

"Actually, I was thinking of something a bit less strenuous."

"For instance?"

"For instance we could stay here."

"All day?" And at his nod she shook her head. "Oh, I don't think so." Her eyes widened, filled with amusement as she joined his teasing. "Whatever could we find to do?"

"Well, that does pose a problem." He pretended to think on it. Mattie laughed as his expression suddenly brightened considerably. "Wait a minute. I think I've got an answer. I could hold you in my arms. I could kiss you again. We could make love all day."

Mattie shook her head again. "Most unseemly, Callahan. Whatever would Mrs. Stables say?"

Callahan groaned at the mere mention of the woman. After only a slight hesitation, he answered with what he supposed a brilliant solution. "You could tell her I'm dying and can't be disturbed."

"And, of course, I'd have to stay at your side like a dutiful wife?"

"Exactly."

"And then tomorrow you'll have a miraculous recovery. Somehow being snatched from the jaws of death." Mattie's expression grew suddenly serious, almost sad. *And tomorrow you'll have gained nothing but a lover. A man who'll use your body and after the pleasure, and she knew there would be pleasure . . . What? He promises you nothing. He offers you nothing. Mattie, you fool, it doesn't matter the temptation. You have to finish this. You have to find Ellis.*

Callahan chuckled, never noticing the light gone from her eyes or the stiffening of her body. "I think we're finally beginning to understand each other."

"I understand you well enough."

Callahan's eyes were bright with deviltry. "Do you

think so?"

"I know so, Mr. Callahan."

Callahan groaned, suddenly realizing her change of mood. So it was Mister again. She only called him that when she was annoyed. What the hell had he done this time? He could see it in her eyes. She was going to deny she wanted him? Jesus, he couldn't remember when a woman had responded so completely. He had enough experience to know the truth. Why the hell was she fighting it?

"I suppose you're going to tell me you're not interested."

"You suppose right."

Callahan gave her an impatient shake. "Why the hell are you lying?"

"I'm not lying."

Callahan shoved her away with a groan of disgust. He turned on his back, his good arm covering his eyes. He felt her hesitate. His mind filled with hope only to be dashed as she finally moved away.

Callahan was suffused with impotent rage. He sure as hell wasn't going to beg for it. There were plenty of women on this train. Many he wouldn't have to tease and taunt and plead with until they fell into bed. Christ, but he'd had enough of waiting. And what the hell was he waiting for? What did she have that a hundred others didn't? Surely he could find one with skin as soft. He wouldn't have to look far to feel hair as thick and silky. Plenty could kiss, and if they couldn't he'd teach them just like he taught . . . Enough! He was almost well again. The moment he was able, he was going to find himself a woman. A real woman. Someone who took what she wanted and asked only for pleasure in return.

Chapter Twelve

Mattie smiled, her eyes so sad he wanted to strangle that stupid bastard. Gently she declined John Perry's offer of a stroll. "I don't think that would be wise."

"Why not?" He shrugged a thick shoulder and nodded toward the next campfire. "He's been over there for three nights straight. Do you want him to think you're pining away?"

Mattie glanced with surprise at John's knowing expression. Did everyone in camp know of their estrangement? Of course they did. Nothing happened on this train that wasn't immediate common knowledge.

"Are you afraid? Do you imagine he'll become abusive if he sees you walk away with me?"

Mattie shook her head. "It's not that, John. I'm supposed to be married to him. What would the others think?"

John grinned. "I wouldn't worry about what people think, Mattie. Do you or don't you want him?"

Mattie shrugged. John knew the situation between them. It seemed he and Mr. Robinson had been Jake and Nora's friends for years. And since they were well acquainted with the couple, they knew too of Callahan's true marital status.

Callahan hadn't lied to his friends. They knew he and Mattie perpetrated the guise so she might reach California unassaulted. What they apparently didn't know was her pretense of being married to another. It was just as well, for Mattie felt uncomfortable enough lying to one. She didn't know if she'd be able to lie to yet another four.

"It can never be, John."

"Never say never, girl." He reached out and took her hand as he came to his feet. "Now look at me as if you can't pull your eyes away." John smiled at her feeble attempt. "Is that the best you can do?"

Mattie opened her mouth, but John interrupted her words. "Never mind. He can't see from this distance anyway. The only thing he has to see is you leaving with me."

With only the slightest hesitation, Mattie allowed John to pull her away from the light of the fire. She trembled as she imagined what Callahan might do. Would he come roaring at this man? Would he make a terrible scene? Would he blurt out the truth of their relationship? Or would he simply shrug away her supposed indiscretion, content enough now that he'd found another?

Mattie shrugged away her fears. It was John's idea after all, and if violence came of it, he seemed able to take care of himself. Two nights ago the man had shown up unexpectedly at her campfire and she couldn't have been more grateful. Embarrassed, she was already dreading another night alone and wondering how many more looks of pity was she to stand from well-meaning, sympathetic neighbors, before she screamed. That brute Callahan had now left her three nights running, immediately after a silent dinner, to spend a boisterous evening with Susie O'Conner.

She had tried not to watch them, their heads together, their bodies so close they almost touched. She had sworn she didn't care, sworn she wouldn't look, no matter how loud they became. But despite her insistence, their laughter never failed to draw her gaze.

Vehemently she denied it meant anything to her. She and Callahan were nothing to each other. She had no claims on the man, nor he on her. Why then did it hurt so bad? Why did she suffer this constant ache in her chest?

During the day, Callahan had been a bear. He hadn't spoken to her since that morning in the wagon, except to yell at her for some small infraction or another. Mattie sighed. Certainly his newfound interest brought about no calming influence, for he seemed to grow more irritable as each day passed. He might laugh when in Susie's company, but his happiness lasted only until he left her for the night.

"Laugh, Mattie." And when she hesitated, John insisted. "Laugh, loud, and do it now!" Mattie did as she was told, but wondered why she had bothered, for the sound seemed more a pitiful cry than a laugh to her own ears.

"Don't be surprised if we suddenly come across the two of them. Say nothing. Absolutely nothing," he warned.

Mattie couldn't believe it, but sure enough Callahan and Susie were suddenly standing right in front of them. Mattie blinked with surprise. How had they left the fire and gained this distance that fast? Mattie gave a low moan as pain filled her chest to overflowing. She watched in silent agony as Callahan slowly took his mouth from Susie's and grinned sheepishly at being caught in the act.

John returned his grin, his hand tightening on Mattie's as if in warning. But he might not have bothered, for Mattie couldn't have uttered a sound if her life depended on it. "Even', folks," he remarked as they moved on by.

Callahan mumbled something unintelligible.

Mattie couldn't be sure but she thought she heard him curse.

"Good girl." John said, a note of pride in his voice. And then a deeply wicked, rumbling chuckle. "I almost feel sorry for the poor fool."

"Do you? Why?" Mattie asked, her voice soft, filled with pain, her eyes blinking rapidly while forcing aside the urge to cry.

"Why, it's as obvious as the nose on your face, honey. The man is in love with you."

Mattie laughed at that. For the first time in days she laughed hard and long, but her laughter turned suddenly into sobs. Mortified, she felt helpless tears flow freely over smooth cheeks. John leaned his back against a tree and pulled her into a comforting embrace. "Don't start getting hysterical on me, girl."

Mattie squashed the impulse to give in to the wild emotion. She gave him a watery smile as she wiped her eyes with the backs of her hands. "I must be tired. I never cry and I certainly never get hysterical.

"It's just that in my experience, if a man loves a woman, he doesn't show it by showering his attentions on another."

"But it's true. I see the way he looks at you. I know what he's doing."

Mattie laughed again. "Oh yes, we both know what he's doing. He's trying to get Susie to . . ."

"But there'd be no trying." John interrupted. "Don't you see? If he wanted her, he could have had her quicker than he could drink a cup of coffee. Everybody on the train knows her kind. What he's doing is trying to make you jealous."

Mattie gave him an incredulous look.

John shrugged. "It don't take no great mind to figure if you're jealous you won't be fightin' him off." He laughed. "But here's the rub. If *he's* the one that's jealous and you can bet your sweet a—, well you can bet anything you want," he corrected in time. "He's jealous all right. Don't be surprised to see the two of them strollin' by in a minute or two."

Mattie made to pull away from his embrace. "If what you say is true, he's going to . . ."

John pressed her tighter to his chest and felt an unwanted response at her nearness. If it wasn't for Maggie waiting back home, he might have given Callahan some real competition. Still, he wouldn't be a man if he didn't enjoy her softness, no matter if it was only a favor he was doing. "Don't make no never mind, girl. You just make yourself comfortable. I can take care of myself."

"Easy girl, he's coming now," he whispered, his mouth close to her ear.

Mattie heard the footsteps behind her. Her lips curved into a smile as she heard Callahan growl, "Shut up." And then Susie's whining voice, "Damn it, Callahan, what do you think you're doing? It takes me days to drag you away from the campfire and for what? To walk miles just to find a comfortable spot? What was the matter with back there?"

Callahan, almost at a run, desperate to find her, was oblivious to Susie's chatter. He knew she was talking, but he never heard the words. He came to a sudden stop. He couldn't believe his eyes. There she was standing all cozy like, under a tree, with that son of a bitch Perry's arms around her.

Susie, never expecting him to stop so suddenly, banged into him. "Ouch!" she grunted as her head hit his shoulder. "Have you finally found a place?" she asked, unsuspecting of his true intent.

But Callahan never felt her slam into him, nor heard her words. A growling sound came from his lips and a roaring grew in his ears. He never realized he moved. He never knew his hands had balled into fists until he heard the sharp snap of his knuckles against Perry's jaw.

Mattie was roughly pushed aside and John took the full weight of him as Callahan lunged at the man. But it was no contest. The fight that ensued was over in seconds. John might have been older by ten years or more, but his size and power were diminished little by age, while Callahan was so caught up in blinding rage he showed not a hint of his usual intelligence.

"What am I going to do with him?" Mattie asked as John dumped Callahan from his shoulder into the back of the wagon like a sack of flour.

John grinned as his gaze moved from Callahan's limp form to Mattie's worried expression. "I'd say it won't matter none." His brows raised and lowered as he teased, "He ain't goin' to feel nothin' for a while."

"John!" Mattie returned, her cheeks growing pink at the implication.

John laughed. "Just funnin' you, girl. Leave him be. He'll come around soon enough." His expression grew concerned as he put a heavy arm around her shoulders. "Maybe you'd best come over to Jake's fire for a spell."

It wasn't ten minutes later that Callahan came and sat himself at Jake's fire. His face was bruised. Mattie shuddered to think what it would look like tomorrow. Jake and Nora, having no knowledge of the happenings earlier this evening, gaped at the swelling under his eye. "What the hell happened?!"

Callahan shrugged. "Walked into a tree."

"By the looks of you, I'd say you ran into one."

"You haven't seen Perry around, have you?" Callahan asked, his gaze resting accusingly on Mattie.

"He was here a while ago. Don't know where he went," Nora said.

Callahan shrugged again. "No matter. I'll find him in the morning."

And Mattie, her heart sinking to the pit of her stomach, knew he would.

It wasn't so much the beating he'd taken, it was more than that. Much more. Callahan was going to make it clear, no one was going to touch what was his. And Callahan didn't care how much she objected, Mattie was his.

"You about ready for bed?" he asked, about a half hour later, addressing her for the first time in days.

Mattie nodded and soon accompanied a silent Callahan back to their wagon.

"You ain't goin' inside?" Callahan asked as he watched Mattie sit at their own fire and reach for the ever-present coffeepot.

"No, I thought I'd have a cup of coffee first."

Callahan sat across from her.

"Want some?"

He nodded. Mattie's heart raced. She'd give anything to know what was going on in his head. That he was upset was a foregone conclusion. What she didn't know was what he might do next. Damn, but the man was so unsettling. She never knew what to expect from him.

Callahan finished his coffee in silence. Suddenly he flung his empty cup aside with a muttered oath. "Okay, I give up. What do you want?"

Mattie almost jumped at the sound of his voice as it cut through the silence of their camp. "Excuse me?"

"Just name it and it's yours."

Suddenly all her apprehension disappeared to be replaced by boiling rage as she realized the meaning behind his words. Her lips curled into a sneer, her dark eyes grew black and narrowed with menace. "You really are a miserable character, Callahan. I could almost feel sorry for you if you weren't so despicable."

Her chin lifted a notch and her brow rose with obvious disdain. "I assume you're talking a trade-off, am I correct? Anything I want, for the temporary use of my body."

Callahan ran his fingers through his hair in frustration. Jesus, he'd done it again. Would he never learn how to treat this woman? Would he always speak before thinking? "I don't want just your body, damn it! If that was the case, I could have taken Susie. She was willing enough."

Mattie felt an anger unlike anything she'd ever known. She could hardly speak with the fury that filled her. She longed to lash out and strike his handsome

143

face. For a moment she wished John had done a better job of it. "Go back to her then," she flung at him.

"I don't want her!" Suddenly he came to his feet and picked up his rifle.

For one wild moment Mattie imagined him aiming the gun at her and forcing her to do his will. The moment passed as quickly as it came to be replaced with an even more terrifying thought.

Callahan's face was grim as he checked the weapon, and Mattie felt a wave of cold fear wash over her. Suddenly she knew he was going to take his anger out on John. Was he going to kill the man? Good God, she had to do something. She had to stop him before it was too late.

"What are you doing?" She came quickly to her feet.

"Checking my rifle, why?"

"We need to talk."

Callahan shrugged. "So talk."

"About tonight."

Callahan stiffened. "I'd prefer not to discuss it."

Mattie ignored his preferences. Anticipating his moving away, she stood before him. She had to tell him, lest disaster ensue. "Callahan, please don't hurt him. He planned for you to find us. Nothing happened."

Callahan's gaze snapped up from his rifle. "What are you talking about?"

Mattie twisted her hands in a nervous gesture. "He said you were only trying to make me jealous. He said I should go with him. I know it was foolish, but he said you would be jealous."

Callahan gave her a long look before understanding filled his blue eyes and a smile suddenly curved his lips. "Did he?"

"Did he what?"

"Say all that?"

Mattie nodded.

"And did you believe him?"

Mattie shrugged. She didn't know what to believe anymore. She only knew that this man wanted her in his bed and she was so confused she could no longer call her mind her own.

"Did he say why I was trying to make you jealous?"

Mattie lowered her gaze. "He said I wouldn't fight you off, if I was jealous."

Callahan laughed. His hand reached out and brought her chin up so she was forced to look in his eyes. "So, were you?"

Mattie opened her mouth, but couldn't find the words. What could she say? Yes, I was dying inside? It was killing me? I should hate you for the torture you caused?

Callahan grinned, his teeth flashed white against his black beard. His eyes crinkled at the corners. She *had* been jealous. The truth of it was easy enough to read in her eyes. Callahan felt his chest swell with joy. She was beginning to care.

He had known from the first the attraction between them, but for a long time now, attraction hadn't been enough. He wanted more. Much more from this woman. He wanted everything.

Mattie watched as he leaned closer. He was going to kiss her. Her heart fluttered with excitement. God, she suddenly couldn't imagine wanting anything more than the feel of his lips on hers. His mouth came closer still, blotting out all but his face from her view. Her lips parted as she anxiously awaited the touch of his mouth. She never heard the soft sigh of pleasure she gave when he kissed her at last.

Callahan smiled as he pulled his lips from hers. His dark-blue eyes were filled with laughter as he watched her shyly lower her gaze. His lips brushed gently against her forehead as he whispered, "I've got to go."

Mattie stiffened. Go! Go where? Did he still intend to kill John? Mattie grabbed his shoulders. "Callahan, I told you nothing happened. You can't kill him? He didn't do anything!"

Callahan pulled his face away, his mouth curving with laughter. "Who is it I'm supposed to be killing tonight?"

"Where are you going?" she asked, suddenly beginning to doubt the truth of her thoughts.

"It's my turn to take the first watch," he answered easily.

"Oh," Mattie said softly, her cheeks growing dark with embarrassment.

"Why do you believe I solve every problem by killing someone?"

"You picked up the rifle. I thought . . ."

"You thought I was going to kill John." Callahan laughed. "I might have done just that if I had a gun with me when I saw him holding you." Callahan nuzzled her cheek and ear. "He was right, you know. I was jealous."

Dumbfounded, Mattie's mouth hung open with surprise. Long moments passed before she realized she was standing by her wagon alone. Only the soft echoing sounds of his laughter remained. He had gone to take his watch.

"Anything?"

"Not a damn thing." Callahan shook his head with disgust. "Do you think Mitchell's informer screwed up?"

Jake shrugged. "Could be, but I doubt it." He hesitated for a minute. "Nora doesn't think it's Mattie."

Callahan felt a wave of relief, but pushed aside the emotion. Nora wasn't infallible. "She could be wrong."

"Why? Have you found anything?"

"Not yet, but as far as I'm concerned everyone is a suspect."

Jake nodded his agreement. "Mitchell's probably right about when they'll try to take it. Why not wait till

146

we get it to California. This way we do all the work."

"Yeah, but keep your eyes open anyway. They might not be as lazy as we think."

It was late before Callahan finally returned to his wagon. Unable to face the prospect of entering the wagon just yet, knowing Mattie slept just inside, all warm and soft, he sat at a fire that was no more than warm dying embers. The coffee was thick and only slightly warm. Callahan sipped at the black liquid, his thoughts centering on the problem at hand.

If the French had agents on this train, and from the information so far attained, he had no reason to doubt it, their cohorts would be waiting somewhere between here and Sacramento. It stood to reason there could be real trouble once they passed the Rocky Mountains.

Callahan shook his head. This shipment had to reach the rebels. Mexico had to get the French off their soil before the United States was forced to interfere.

Callahan felt a shiver of fear for the woman who most always occupied his thoughts. If anything happened to her . . . No. He wouldn't think of that. For all he knew, for all any of them knew she was one of them.

His heart might deny the prospect, but his reason couldn't. What was she doing here if she was the innocent she appeared to be? Why the hell was she, a young woman alone, traveling west?

Callahan shook his head. He had no answers. He grunted as he came to his feet and hoped his body was tired enough to ignore the temptation inside the wagon and sleep.

Chapter Thirteen

Mattie pulled her gray felt hat lower over her brow and the scarf that covered the bottom of her face higher as the wind whipped sandy dirt into tiny swirling clouds of stinging brown dust. The sun baked unceasingly down upon the weary travelers. They had been on the trail for four seemingly endless months and Mattie began to wonder if indeed they were making any progress. But for the sun setting each night directly ahead, Mattie felt, they might have been walking in circles. Nothing changed. Nothing but mile upon mile of endless flat prairie.

How much longer, she wondered wearily? The guide books said three months, but Callahan insisted it was closer to eight. Eight months! Would Ellis still be there by the time she arrived? And how would they manage another four months on this trail? Especially since they were promised the worst of it still lay ahead. They had mountains and rivers to cross. Idly she wondered how did one take a wagon up the side of a mountain?

Mattie shook her head. She wouldn't think of it now. She was bone-tired and found it necessary to concentrate to merely put one foot in front of another.

Thank God, tomorrow was Sunday. As each week passed they needed this day of rest more desperately than the last. Mattie sighed. What she wouldn't give for a bath. A real bath. God, she'd almost forgotten the sweet luxury of a tub.

Mr. Cassidy had promised tonight they'd be stopping near a lake. Mattie's mouth watered at the thought. The first thing she was going to do was jump in, clothes and all. And after she'd drunk her fill, perhaps she and Nora could find a secluded spot and bathe away this grime.

Mattie raised her head. The wind was dying down. The sting of sand eased. She pulled her scarf from her face and blotted the moisture away. Mattie smiled. No matter how thirsty she was, she always managed to sweat.

They were getting low on water, it being nearly five days since it last rained. The clouds were no more than light puffs, high in the sky. The barrels were only half filled. It had been days since she was able to even wash her face. Every drop of water was needed for the animals.

Mattie glanced to her right. Callahan was seated high on the wagon. His arm swung the whip as he prodded the oxen forward. His blue cambric shirt was rolled up at the sleeves, exposing brown arms. Mattie watched as the muscles of his shoulders and back strained to pull the animals into line. His shirt was soaked with perspiration and stuck to him like a second skin. Mattie knew he had to be as thirsty as she; still, the lack of water seemed of little consequence to him. He never complained. A smile was almost always ready. How could the man remain so cheery? Didn't he suffer as did she and the others?

Mattie stumbled over a rock and gave a low, most unladylike curse. Her lips twisted into a wry smile. If this trip did nothing else, at least it had increased her vocabulary. She could now curse fluently in two languages, thanks to Mr. Genovese's generous input.

Callahan shot her a look and realized she was unsteady on her feet. "Come up here, Mattie."

Mattie managed a smile. "It's all right. I'm not tired."

"Don't make me come and get you. Get over here."

Mattie sighed, hesitant to go near him. She knew she wasn't at her aromatic best. The shortage of water had severely limited everyone's ability to maintain ideal cleanliness. Of course she didn't suffer this temporary indelicacy alone. Most everybody stank to high heaven, some whether water was in plentiful supply or not. In truth, although she imagined her condition far worse, she needn't have worried overmuch, for her habit of changing her clothing daily went a long way toward eliminating the worst of the problem.

Mattie watched Callahan's mouth harden and knew there was no sense fighting him. If she didn't listen, he would only stop the wagon and come and get her.

Callahan did stop the wagon, but only for the moment it took to pull her up beside him. Suddenly he swallowed a curse, for the instant he touched her he knew it a mistake. She had stood on the wagon wheel, her one hand holding her skirts, the other the wheel. His hands reached for her waist. Somehow her legs became separated as he swung her over him and she landed, if for only an instant, legs apart, facing him, on his lap. For what felt like an endless, breathless moment they simply stared at each other, neither quite believing the sizzling current that ran between them.

Mattie had believed her unsavory state offensive to the senses, but Callahan found nothing to repulse him in this woman. If anything, the slightly musky scent of woman only sent a bolt of blinding, pure lust crashing through him. Stunned, Callahan couldn't remember ever feeling the emotion in such astounding strength, never realizing it wasn't lust alone that caused his body this reaction.

One look in his eyes told her the flaming need she imagined to be true. Mattie scurried off his lap and moved as far away as the seat would allow, all the while wracking her brain for something to say.

They had rarely touched these last few weeks. Not since the night he had admitted his jealousy. Mattie had gone to bed that night in a state of utter amazement and budding hope. Did his admitting to jealousy mean he cared for her? Mattie wondered why then he had made no move since to push home his point. He had been kind, gentlemanly, considerate, almost courting in his manner.

Mattie blinked with surprise. Why hadn't she thought of it before? He was courting her. A smile curved her lips and a thrill of delight touched her heart.

Finally gaining some control over his raging emotions, Callahan cracked the whip over the oxen. His voice was almost angry when he spoke. "You're so damn small it wouldn't take more than a gust of wind to knock you over."

"I'm not that small, Callahan. I managed to stand upright during the last storm."

Callahan shot her a warning look she imagined to mean she should know better than to argue with him. But the look, like every look, like every word spoken, like every accidental touch only seemed to bring alive the throbbing lust that lay constantly simmering beneath the surface. It was always there. Neither could say or do anything that didn't bring the subject to mind. This couldn't go on. Mattie trembled with apprehension and searched her mind for something to break the thick silence that had grown between them.

"There's talk about a dance tonight, if we reach water, that is. Most everyone thinks this a good excuse to celebrate."

Callahan grunted a response but kept his gaze forward. This woman was driving him out of his mind. He couldn't even look at her without wanting to touch her. He could barely maintain control. If something didn't happen soon, it wouldn't be long before he'd be howling at the moon.

Mattie felt a thrill of excitement as she smoothed her white shirtwaist over her hips and looked into the small mirror. Had she left too many buttons opened? Was she displaying too much flesh? Mattie shook her head. It would be ridiculous on this warm night to button the neckline to her throat. Mattie grunted with satisfaction as she gave her long black hair a final stroke of her brush. A white ribbon held it back from her face to cascade in thick waves down her back.

A smile tugged at the corners of her mouth. She wondered if Callahan could dance. He had never mentioned it. She shrugged. Tonight she would find out for herself.

Mattie jumped from the back of the wagon and almost skipped toward Nora and Jake's camp. Nora had just finished dressing and appeared equally excited about the festivities tonight. But for an occasional game of cards and some general conversation, there was little socializing at night. Most of the travelers were too weary to do more than sleep.

"You look beautiful tonight. With your dark hair and tan, white suits you."

Mattie smiled at the compliment. "You don't look like a wilting flower yourself."

"Yeah," Nora agreed as she eyed the pink silk dress she wore. "I'm going to knock him dead tonight." Nora winked as she purposely lowered the bodice of her dress a fraction. "He hasn't got a chance."

Mattie gave her friend a wistful smile. She wished she could be a little more like Nora. Sometimes she hated being so quiet, so shy. Why couldn't she flirt like Nora did with Callahan? Nora was obviously a woman of the world, and Callahan seemed to enjoy the teasing remarks that passed between them.

Mattie bit at her lip, dying to ask. Wondering if she had the nerve to ask what had been on her mind since they had first met.

"What's the matter?"

Mattie shrugged.

"Come on. I can see something is bothering you. Spell it out."

"I was wondering about something."

Nora nodded. "Go ahead."

"It's about Callahan."

Nora smiled. "I figured as much. What do you want to know?"

Mattie shrugged. "Well it's probably none of my business . . ."

"Ask me, Mattie, and don't worry about it. If I know the answers I'll tell you."

"Well I was wondering about Callahan and . . . Callahan and you."

Nora's eyes widened with surprise. "Me?"

"You seem very friendly."

Nora laughed. "And you thought we might have once been lovers?"

Mattie bit at her lips again, suddenly sorry she had asked. Suddenly not wanting to know. She shook her head as if to dismiss the subject. "Like I said, it's really none of my business."

"Probably not," Nora agreed. "But no, we've never been lovers."

Mattie shot her a look of surprise.

"Surely you believe a man and a woman can be friends."

"Oh, of course. It's just that you seem so close, so friendly. And he's so confusing. I don't know what to think sometimes."

"What do you mean?"

"Well, for instance, he sometimes speaks with a backwoodsman drawl, so thick I can hardly understand him. Then he'll suddenly say something so refined, as if he's attended the best of schools. He was a captain during the war, wasn't he? And officers are usually educated, aren't they?

"And another thing, sometimes I'll find him watching me with this horrible sneer as if he expects me to murder someone. If I notice, he'll suddenly smile as if nothing is amiss. I wish I knew what he was thinking. He has me quite baffled."

153

"I'm sure he must. The man is a bit complicated."

"Do you think it has something to do with his late wife?"

Nora shook her head. "I don't know. Callahan never speaks about her."

"Do you think I should ask him?"

Nora shrugged. "All he can do is tell you to mind your own business."

Nora heard Mattie's indrawn breath and followed the direction of her gaze. Callahan had apparently just come from the lake. His black hair glistened with water, his shirt as yet unbuttoned.

Nora smiled. "He's something to look at, isn't he?"

"Who?" Mattie asked breathlessly.

Nora gave a low, knowing laugh. "I love my Jake, Mattie, but I'm not blind. I know a good-looking man when I see one."

Good-looking? Is that what she thought? Perhaps she was blind, after all. How could anyone think he was anything but magnificent?

Suddenly Mattie's lips thinned as Susie O'Conner ran up to him, took Callahan's arm, and leaned suggestively against him, her abundantly lush breasts pressed enticingly to his chest. Mattie frowned. Apparently the woman said something, something provocative, no doubt, because Callahan suddenly threw his head back and laughed with pure male enjoyment.

Damn the man, he certainly seemed to find no need to dislodge himself. Obviously he quite enjoyed her attentions. Well, she wasn't going to stand here and wait like some lovesick fool for him to notice her. If he wanted to spend the evening with Susie, that was just fine as far as she was concerned. She wasn't going to stop him. She couldn't, in any case. He could do any damn thing he wanted to do and so could she. Mattie turned her back to the laughing couple. "I think I'll take a walk over to the dancing." She nodded her head toward the couple behind her. "No sense in waiting. I expect he'll be some time yet."

"Can I talk to you a minute?"

Callahan stopped on his way to join Mattie, his eyes searching the crowd some distance down the line of wagons. "Since when did you need my permission? I'm sure you'll talk no matter what I say."

"She suspects something."

Callahan swung his gaze back to Nora. "Who?"

"Mattie."

"What the hell are you talking about?"

"Mattie think something is wrong. She told me she sometimes finds you staring at her like you suspect her of something awful."

Callahan cursed. "If she suspects something, it's because of you. You talk too damn much."

"Sure. I suppose I'm the one who forgets he's not a real backwoodsman and speaks in his Harvard accent."

"Shit! What else did she say?"

Nora laughed. "She asked me if we were ever lovers."

Callahan's eyes widened, his lips curved into an interested smile. "Did she? Straight out?"

"No, not straight out, you oaf. But she hinted at it."

"What did you tell her?" he asked, a suspicious gleam in his eyes.

"Why the truth, of course." She blinked, her expression all innocence. "You might be easy on the eyes, Callahan, but I'm more attracted to men who have a bit of brains to go with their looks.

"By the way, I think you're in for a smattering of trouble."

Callahan's brows lifted, obviously waiting for her usual dramatic finish.

"Mattie saw you with Susie on your arm."

He closed his eyes, his lips thinning with annoyance. "Damn it!"

"I assume it didn't mean anything to you, but the last

155

I saw, she was pretty upset."

Callahan, his mouth set in a grim line, never answered her, but hurried toward the sounds of merry music.

Even amid the party of revelers, Callahan spotted her immediately. She was dancing, her black waist-length hair and full white skirts flying in rhythm to the guitars and violins. A wide smile curved her lips, her dark eyes gleamed with enjoyment. Callahan felt his belly tighten to a throbbing ache of longing. When would she smile like that for him?

Impatiently he waited for the dance to end. She never saw his approach. "I believe the next dance is mine" came a deep voice from behind her.

Mattie felt her knees weaken, so great was the rush of relief that assailed. He hadn't stayed with Susie after all. She almost smiled, but suddenly remembered how he allowed the woman to cuddle up to him. Mattie turned and glared at him. "I'm afraid not," she replied stiffly. "I've already promised it to someone else."

"What a shame."

"What do you think you're doing?" she snapped. A ridiculous question really, since he was, at that very moment, nearly dragging her away from the festivities. She tried to pull away. "Let me go!"

"We have to talk." Her feet were suspended above the ground now, her body effortlessly held at his side as he walked along the outside of the wagons, stopping only when he was sure of a bit of privacy.

Mattie took a startled step back the moment he released her. "I've got nothing to say to you."

"I think you do."

"Do you? And what might that be?"

"You could say you're sorry."

God, he was the most insufferable man. "For what?"

"For getting angry over nothing."

Enchanted, he watched her suddenly rush forward. She took hold of his arm and leaned heavily against him, while batting her long dark lashes. But instead of smiling as he would have expected, her teeth clenched and her lip curled into a sneer. "Does the pose ring a bell?"

Callahan, delighted in her anger, merely grinned.

"Can't remember, eh? Oh, I believe that. No doubt there've been so many the poor man can no longer decipher one female body from another."

Callahan laughed out loud. She was jealous. God, he couldn't believe his luck. A wave of happiness filled his being.

"So you think this is funny, do you? Well *this*," she kicked him as hard as she could, "should send you into near hysterics."

Because of her anger, it took a full five seconds for the pain to register. But when it did, her eyes widened with the shock of it and she fought a valiant battle against the need to groan. She had stupidly forgotten she wasn't wearing boots. But he was, and her thin slippers offered no protection at all to her toes.

"You'd better calm down before you hurt yourself."

Mattie took a deep breath in an effort to regain a smattering of composure. "Go aggravate someone else, Mr. Callahan. I'm going to dance."

Mattie turned, but Callahan's arm slid around her waist and drew her back up against him. His mouth lowered to the side of her face, her jaw, her throat, his warm breath tickling her nerve endings, sending unwanted chills down her spine. "Won't you let me dance with you?"

Mattie leaned her head back upon his hard chest. She took a deep breath, trying to control the sudden erratic beating of her heart. Thankful for the moment that he held her, she wondered if she could stand it if he let her go. God, how could he affect her like this? How could a simply spoken question send her into such a tailspin?

157

Mattie's voice broke and she had to clear her throat twice before her world gained balance and the words would come. "Callahan, don't do this to me" came a husky broken whisper.

"What am I doing?"

"I don't want a man whose eyes wander after every skirt." Good God, what was she saying? She was asking for commitment. She had no right. This could never be.

"Mattie, I'm a man, not a saint. My eyes are not blind to a pretty woman. But there's only one woman who entices."

Mattie grunted in disbelief.

"The one I want stands about this tall," he placed his hand at the top of her head as if measuring her. "She has long black hair and chocolate, spellbinding, heart-wrenching eyes. And a mouth," he sighed, "a mouth so damn kissable it's about to drive me out of my mind."

Mattie felt herself shudder as his lips brushed against her neck. She couldn't help it, her head just seemed to tip of its own accord, thereby allowing him easier access to her flesh. Just tonight. Just for tonight, she promised herself. What did it matter, after all? No man would want her after she finished with Ellis. In any case, she'd likely spend the rest of her life in prison. Why shouldn't she take just this one night of tenderness? It might be the only one she'd ever know.

Small sounds of pleasure slipped from her lips. Mattie trembled, her whole being aching to turn into his embrace. She wanted to feel the warmth of his mouth against hers. She couldn't deny the wicked thoughts. She wanted to feel his mouth against every part of her.

With the last of her sanity, she whispered, "Do you always dance like this?" and sighed with relief at his low laughter. The spell was broken and Mattie couldn't decide if the knowledge left her happy or sad.

"No," his words carried on a sigh, "but when I hold you in my arms, I can't always remember my original intentions." It took some effort, but he finally managed to create some space between them. Gentle humor filled his eyes as she turned to face him. He offered her his arm. "Shall we?"

"The stars are bright tonight," Mattie remarked conversationally as Callahan swung her in smooth graceful circles amid the other dancers.

"Are they?" he grinned. "I'm afraid I'll have to take your word for it."

Mattie's brows rose with humor. "Why not look for yourself?"

"And miss the loveliest sight of all?"

"My, we are glib tonight, aren't we?"

"Are we? I haven't noticed any compliments on your part."

"I think Susie gives you more than you deserve. You don't need any more."

Callahan laughed. "Don't I? Are you so sure then of my confidence?"

Mattie nodded. "Sure enough." And after a few moments of companionable silence, a silence filled with long, searching looks and answering, tender smiles, she asked, "Why does everyone call you Callahan?"

"No doubt because it's my name."

Mattie laughed and the pure happy sound caused Callahan's heart to pound heavily against the wall of his chest.

"What is your Christian name?"

Callahan's brow rose and fell in rapid succession, but he ruined his attempt at a villainous leer with a grin. "Oh ho, not until I have you firmly in my clutches."

Mattie smiled. "Is it so terrible?"

"You might say that."

"And you won't tell me?"

"Someday perhaps."

"I will ask Nora," she threatened.

"She doesn't know."

"Shall I guess then?"

Callahan gave a secret, confident smile. "You can try."

"Sigmond."

Callahan laughed. "Not even close."

"Merlin?"

Callahan smiled and shook his head.

"Marion? Gabriel? Travis?" And at his continued negative reaction she rattled off a string of planetary names."

He chuckled.

Mattie's eyes narrowed as she studied him. "Perhaps I'm on the wrong track here. Could it be something from the theater? Was your mother possibly a patron of the arts?"

"Shall I give you a hint?"

Mattie's eyes widened and she smiled expectantly. "What?"

"Come back to the wagon."

Mattie gave him a long puzzled look. "What kind of a hint is that?"

Callahan laughed and pulled her more closely into his arms, his heart swelling with an emotion he dared not name, yet couldn't resist. "That wasn't a hint at all. I'll give you the hint back at the wagon."

Mattie grinned as she leaned into him and muttered happily, "Beast!"

"Mmm," Callahan smiled into her hair, "you're getting close."

Mattie snuggled against him, her head resting against his chest. "I think we're already too close."

"Not nearly close enough, to my way of thinking," Callahan growled. "We've been dancing for hours. Aren't you tired yet?"

"Oh, exhausted," Mattie whispered on a dramatic sigh.

Callahan pulled sharply away, his eyes searching her

160

face. "In truth?"

Mattie giggled. "Your sudden show of concern couldn't have ulterior motives, could it?"

"Who, me?" he asked in supposed innocence.

Mattie nodded, her brow lifting in wry humor. "I didn't think so."

Suddenly a fat drop of water smacked upon Callahan's head. And then another, and another. The music came to an abrupt end. People began to scramble for the shelter of their wagons. Without a word, Callahan took her hand in his and hurried away from the fast-disappearing crowd.

Mattie was gasping for breath by the time they reached their wagon. The small fires, once lighting the entire train, were dying one by one with soft sizzling sounds. The night had grown dark. The stars were gone now, hidden behind thick, heavy clouds. Mattie made to enter the wagon and felt Callahan's hand at her shoulder. "Wait. Don't go in yet," he whispered close to her ear.

Mattie turned to face him. Rain streamed down her face and matted her dress to her form. He could barely see her, but sensed her unspoken question. "I want to kiss you."

Mattie made to step back, but came up against arms that had already circled her waist. "Here? Now?"

Callahan smiled at her surprise. He whispered conspiratorially, "No one can see us. Everyone is hiding from the rain."

Mattie giggled. "Anyone with any sense, that is." After a slight hesitation, she shrugged a slender shoulder and grinned. "Well, I suppose if no one can see us . . ."

Her words were interrupted by the sudden pressure of his mouth. Callahan groaned, lost in an instant, blinding surge of lust. God, he'd thought of nothing but her mouth all night. He deepened the kiss, his lips forcing hers apart, his tongue delving deep into the sweet

161

darkness.

With every breath he slipped closer toward the limit of his control as her scent filled his senses. Her taste drove him wild. He shifted his mouth, slashing his lips across her, desperate to take all he could at this one tasting and realized at last he'd never get enough.

He was gasping for breath, his face buried in the sweetness of her neck as he finally tore his lips from hers. Callahan shuddered. "God, I want to make love to you out here." He groaned as his mind conjured up a picture of her naked in the rain, pressed against him, warm and giving. "I want to feel your skin, slippery soft, hot and wet."

Fool! screamed a silent voice from the far recesses of his mind. You once thought to take her and rid yourself of this need. Now you know it won't work. If you take her you'll only want more. And the wanting will leave you, as before, half a man. Haven't you suffered enough? Haven't you learned firsthand what this kind of desire can do?

Callahan hesitated a long moment, striving for control. His hands shook and then dropped from around her. He took a deep calming breath. He chanced too much. He couldn't allow her that kind of control. "I can't. Go inside, before it's too late."

I can't?! Mattie silently repeated. What was he saying? What was he doing? Wasn't he coming with her? Had he been teasing her, only to slake his desires with another? No, Mattie knew that thought to be false. This man wanted her, of that she had no doubt. She had felt his body tremble with need. Why then did he suddenly pull away?

"Aren't you coming?"

"In a moment."

Suddenly Mattie remembered the last time they had been together. He had asked her then to tell her what she wanted from him. They had been interrupted before she could reply. Did he need to hear her say it?

Mistakenly she imagined he did.

Mattie's heart thundered at her boldness. After this, the man would have no doubt. Slowly her fingers reached for the buttons of her shirtwaist. One by one they came undone, exposing creamy flesh to the onslaught of a stormy night. Mattie shivered, but not from the elements, for the rain was as warm as bathwater. It was excitement that caused her trembling. Excitement and fear and, yes, longing for this man's touch.

Her bodice was open, her breasts exposed, but the night was blacker than pitch by now and Callahan knew nothing of her enticement.

"Callahan?"

Callahan cursed the need that threatened to tear him apart. Never in his life had he wanted a woman like this. Not even what he had known for Beverly could compare. He felt about to die from the pain of it. Had she been another, he wouldn't have hesitated to take her, but this woman posed a danger only a fool could ignore.

"Mattie," he cleared his voice, desperate now for control. "I'm afraid I've taken unfair advantage tonight. This is something you should think on long and hard. We'll talk in the morning."

Her heart thundered in her throat. Her fingers shook as she reached for his hands. Slowly she brought them to her breasts. Her voice was low and husky. "I've thought of near nothing else for months."

Callahan stiffened in shock. "Oh God!" came his ragged, choked response as he realized what she had done. Too late! Too late! his mind screamed. There was no going back. He shuddered, his hands filling to overflowing with her lush softness. "Oh God," he growled again, his voice mingling with longing and misery, his face burying itself in her sweet beauty.

Callahan cursed his stupidity as a sudden flash of lightning lit up the area. Jesus, anyone in the camp could see them should they venture outside. The guards! What could he have been thinking? Callahan

163

smiled. That was just it. Once he had touched her he hadn't been thinking at all.

Callahan broke away from her and jumped into the wagon. With dizzying speed he pulled Mattie in after him. Her body fell against his and they both went down.

Callahan never noticed the fall. Her body lay over the length of his, his mind took in nothing but the scent and feel of her. His mouth searched out her own, his arms almost crushing in their attempt to keep her close.

Suddenly he rolled her over and leaned gasping above her. "This isn't enough. I have to see you," he whispered against her parted lips.

Mattie tried to keep him at her side, her dazed mind never registering his words. Her arms held to his neck when she felt him pull away. "No. Don't go."

Callahan chuckled. "Just a minute."

His fingers shook as he found and lit the lantern. Determinedly, refusing to give in to temptation, to look at her, he spread quilts upon the wagon floor and kicked off his boots.

Callahan knelt upon the quilts, his fingers moving to the buttons of his shirt. Only then did he allow his gaze to return to her. He breathed a sigh of relief, for if she had not rebuttoned her bodice, at least she had pulled the fabric together and was no longer exposed to his view. He wasn't sure if he could hold on to his control if he saw what his hands had held.

"Come here, Mattie," he said, his voice so low she wondered if she might have only read his thoughts.

Mattie joined him, facing him, kneeling as he. "Let me," she offered softly as her hands covered his.

Callahan took a deep, calming breath, his eyes half closed as her hands worked to divest him of his shirt. "Nora thinks you're good-looking," she said, her voice a ragged effort at sound.

"Does she?" Callahan grinned. "What is it you think?"

Mattie pulled the shirt away, dropping it the instant it

164

came free of his body. For a long moment her eyes devoured his exposed flesh. She swallowed. Her gaze came to meet his. Her voice shook. "I think you are magnificent."

"Mattie." Callahan moaned her name as her hands reached hungrily for his bare flesh, savoring the texture of his skin, her lips parted as each shallow, gasping breath was drawn in and shakily expelled. God, he was so hard, so warm, so different from anything she'd ever known. Suddenly she seemed to realize what she was doing. She looked up, her eyes wide with surprise, her cheeks growing pink at her daring. "It is all right to touch you, isn't it?"

Callahan groaned, knowing no pain to exceed this. He was aching to pull her into his arms and yet unwilling to forgo this exquisite torture. At the moment, his feelings were growing too intense, too dangerous. Vaguely he wondered of his sanity if he allowed this to go on. Still, he knew he hadn't the power to stop it. Callahan strove for a lightness he did not feel, lest he crush her to him and take her without further preamble. "You have twenty minutes."

Mattie blinked with surprise, never expecting his answer. Her mouth curved into a soft smile. "Do I?" Her hands slid boldly down his sides and around his back, kneading the muscles she found there. Mattie licked her lips, her fingers spreading, greedy for more. They slid over his hips and buttocks, never hesitating when they encountered his trousers, silently wishing they had joined his shirt, on the floor. "What happens after that?"

"Any damn thing you want," he barely choked out.

Mattie's hands stilled, her gaze rose to meet his. She whispered, "Do you realize the power?"

"Oh God, Mattie," he groaned almost in despair, "don't you know? The power was yours from the first."

It was hot, the air thick and moist. Rain beat unceasingly upon the canvas, creating a steady droning sound inside the wagon. But the couple inside was oblivious to powers of nature. Each intent on the other they heard nothing but the sounds of their own erratic breathing and the throbbing of blood that pounded ever louder in their ears.

"Would it stop you if I returned the favor?" Callahan asked, unable to resist a moment longer the need to touch her.

"I don't know, it might."

He smiled. "I'll have to take that chance."

His hands reached for the buttons of her dress. "Stand up."

Mattie rose unsteadily to her feet and Callahan slowly slid the dress from her shoulders. Next her chemise and then her petticoat, until she stood before him wearing only ruffled drawers and white cotton stockings.

He heard her soft gasp as he pulled the last of her clothing away. She'd be embarrassed, he knew, standing naked before him, but he couldn't allow her the covering she craved. The sight before him too lovely, too tempting to resist, his mouth leaned forward and rested against her, his senses caught in a whirl of delight as her scent filled his mind.

Mattie gasped and stumbled back, her shock apparent. "No!"

His hands on her hips prevented her escape, but he felt the stiffening and knew he would wait. "Next time," he promised, as he guided her to kneel before him again.

His mouth was there waiting for her lips, hungry for her taste, for her scent, for the warm texture of her.

Callahan cursed. Helplessly he felt her stiffen as a crash of thunder shook the ground.

"Callahan," she cried as she reached blindly for him. Her arms closed around his neck and clung desperately, her face pressed hard against him. She was trembling and moaning soft sounds of terror.

But Callahan wasn't about to allow this moment to be

lost. Gently he eased himself back to lean on a barrel and gathered her into his lap. Softly crooning tender words, he ran his hands over her body, praying she'd lose these demons and come back to him. "It's all right, Mattie love," he soothed. "It's the storm, nothing more."

Mattie whimpered, her body stiff. She never heard him.

"Can you hear me, love? I'm here. I'll take care of you."

Helpless against the flood of memories, she only whimpered again.

"Don't listen to the storm, Mattie. Feel my hands, love. Feel them touch you. Think, Mattie. Think of what I'm doing."

But Mattie only clung tighter, the strength of her hold threatening to close off his supply of air. Still, Callahan continued his loving caresses, confident he could eventually sway her thoughts back to him.

Again and again he ran his hands over the length of her, but he might as well have caressed a stick of wood for all the reaction she gave. Callahan swore. He had waited too long for this night. Nothing! He didn't give a damn what, nothing was going to stop him now.

Callahan's fingertips slid gently into her body. She was barely moist, responding not at all. "Mattie," he whispered into her hair, "do you know what I'm doing?"

No verbal response, but he soon breathed a sigh of relief. She was definitely growing moist and more pliant in his arms. Patiently he waited, expertly his finger caressed the tiny nub into stiffness.

She knew nothing of what he was doing. In an instant her passion dissolved into nothingness, horror taking its place. Mattie found herself huddled once again in the damp black cellar, listening to the sounds from up above. The thunder crashed on and on almost obliterating the screams. Men laughed and she cowed closer into herself, squeezing farther into the small corner. When would it stop! Please God, let them stop.

And amazingly it began to happen. For the first time she consciously felt the terror recede. Unlike before, she hadn't fallen asleep. No, she definitely wasn't asleep. Callahan was murmuring softly spoken words above her while a delicious tightening was growing somewhere within her belly.

"Callahan," she murmured into his neck, her hold loosening somewhat.

"Yes, darling."

"What are you doing?"

Callahan chuckled, thankful she had come back at last. "I'm making love to you."

"Oh," she breathed softly, her astonishment evident.

"Do you like this?"

"Very much," she returned, her face still buried in his neck.

"Watch me, Mattie. Watch me and you'll gain even more pleasure."

Mattie, feeling suddenly shy to find herself in his arms, his hands so intimately exploring her most private parts, took a long moment before she complied. And when she did, it was his face she watched.

His blue eyes were dark, almost black as they smiled down into her amazed expression. "Watch my hands, Mattie. See how they touch you."

Mattie followed the direction of his gaze, her heart suddenly throbbing, her breath growing shallow and ragged at the sight of his dark hand against her white flesh. He lifted her slightly and she moaned as the heat of his mouth claimed the tip of her breast.

Mattie gasped. The duel sensations caused a pulling from deep within. She felt as if she might burst, but from what? Again she moaned. Her fingers threading through his dark hair, her hands holding him closer, she arched her back, wanting more.

The tightness grew. How much more? It was twisting her insides. Tighter again. Tighter! He had to stop. She had to get away from this impending pain.

She gasped. She stiffened. She panted for breath. Her hips arched from his lap, straining toward the movement of his hand, desperate now that he not stop. "Please," she groaned, not knowing for what she asked. "Please," she tugged on his shoulders, her nails biting into his flesh, "you've got to do something." She struggled to breathe, to think. "You're killing me."

She never heard the crash of thunder, her mind oblivious to all but the thunderous storm he was creating inside her body. Her head fell back. She whimpered helplessly in his arms, unable to do more than accept this torment.

Fascinated, he watched her move, her body straining, stiffening, silently crying out for release. Callahan sucked in his breath, enthralled with her response, his heart beating furiously as he listened to her broken cries and senseless words and watched her eyes glaze over. With a grunt of deep satisfaction, his mouth took her long keening wail of pleasure.

Chapter Fourteen

Callahan swung her dazed form upon the quilt and joined her there a moment later. He looked into eyes still glazed by the trauma her body had experienced and grinned. "Miss me?"

"What?" she asked.

Callahan laughed. "Just as I thought. You never knew I was gone."

"Where did you go?" she asked dreamily, her arms reaching around his neck.

"I had to take my clothes off."

"Oh?"

"You don't imagine we're finished, do you?"

Mattie was untried in the art of love, but not totally ignorant. She knew to make love was to couple. Being raised on a large plantation, she had often seen animals mate and had once, to her mortification, come across a slave and his woman. What she had never imagined was the pleasure that could be achieved during the preliminaries. Was making love equally as satisfying? Is that why so many held the idea uppermost in their minds?

A wicked smile curved her lips. "I'm afraid I am."

Callahan grinned at her teasingly. "Perhaps I'll be more stingy the next time. It will never do, you being so satisfied."

Mattie smiled. "And you know, for a fact, I'm satisfied?"

"Lady, if you're not, you give a excellent imitation of it."

Mattie never thought to be coy. Especially at this

most intimate moment she was delightfully honest. She sighed. "It was wonderful."

Callahan felt his chest swell with pride. Jesus, her simple statement coupled with the shining happiness in her eyes made him feel like a cock swaggering about a henhouse. Never had he felt more a man, that he could bring her this pleasure. His gaze, warm and tender, moved over her softened features. "It was wonderful watching you, but I'll wager not half so as being inside you."

Lightning flashed and another clap of thunder shook the small wagon. Worriedly he looked down at her startled expression. His arms tightened around her. "What happened to make you so terrified of thunder?"

Mattie stiffened only for an instant at the sound, for the feel of him, warm and naked, tantalizingly male, against the length of her left little room for haunting nightmares. A shadow passed over her eyes. Mattie longed to tell him, but knew the impossibility of it, lest he realize her reason for going west. She forced a cheery note to her voice and teased. "What thunder?"

"You won't leave me again, will you?"

Mattie smiled. "I won't leave you."

God, the feel of him against her was wonderful. His chest hair tickled and yet excited as it brushed against her breasts. His leg slid between hers and Mattie felt her thighs close of their own accord around it, moving and rubbing, delighting in his scratchy, smooth texture.

Callahan looked down at the woman beneath him and marveled at her beauty. Her hair lay damp and curling upon the quilt, her creamy skin flushed pink, her chest heaving still as her breathing had yet to return to normal. A smile of pure enjoyment touched her parted lips.

No supposed maidenly shyness marred the obvious delight she found in his arms. That she wanted more was evident in the subtle movement of her hips. His body shuddered as he remembered moments just shared. Never would he have believed such abandonment, so wild, so naked, so pure was her response. It had been almost enough just to watch her, just to witness her pleasure.

Callahan had felt no little amazement. Granted, he had enjoyed some experience with ladies, true ladies, that is. But the little he'd indulged did not make for delightful memories. Sex always seemed to be a means to an end, a bargaining tool. Be it marriage, as in Beverly's case, or jewelry, an apartment, or simply entering a party on the arm of a man. Something. They had always wanted something. Cynically he had listened to their moans of enjoyment, but never quite believed them.

Callahan's blue eyes darkened with pleasure, knowing Mattie couldn't lie worth a damn. In any case, no one could have pretended her enjoyment to this extent. She had been half crazed with the wanting and he could have sworn she couldn't have told him what it was she had craved.

Callahan answered her smile with his own. How long had he waited for this woman? How long had he searched? When had he not wanted her? When had he not longed for this moment? Or imagined the deliciousness of holding her beneath him? God, she was in his thoughts day and night and those thoughts had fed a desire that had grown into torment. Callahan closed his eyes and pushed aside the need to bury himself inside her warm body. No, this would be a slow, leisurely tasting of the senses. He had waited too long to rush through this.

Callahan lowered his mouth and ran his tongue over her parted lips. He listened for and smiled at her sudden intake of breath. Her hands came to stroke his cheeks, to hold his mouth still, but he would have none of it.

"No, darling, not yet. If I kiss you like I want to, I won't be able to stop."

"Is that so bad? Suppose I want you to never stop?" she asked dreamily.

Callahan forced aside the sudden thundering of his heart. Did she mean it? Did she truly never want him to stop? He gave a sad smile. When had he last been so foolish as to listen to and believe love talk? Determinedly he steeled his emotions and ignored the last of her remark. "Not a bad idea at all, but there are other places that must be visited first, lest they grow sad at being forgotten."

Mattie smiled, a definite gleam of interest in her eyes. "What kind of places?"

"Well, here, for one," he said as he ran his finger down her throat and over the soft mound of her breast.

Mattie gasped. "Mmmm," she murmured, and strove in vain to steady her voice. "I see your reasoning. I know firsthand the sadness if you forgot that."

"And here," he teased as his fingers slid farther down the length of her body to linger at her stomach and waist.

Mattie closed her eyes, helplessly nodding her agreement.

"There's more," he announced triumphantly.

"Is there?" Her words were slurred. "Show me where."

Callahan groaned at the explicit invitation. "Shall we start at the beginning?"

"Oh, yes, please."

Callahan moved to her feet, his mouth leaving hot, wet paths as his kisses moved up the inside of her legs. Mattie stiffened, not at all sure it didn't tickle more than anything else.

"What is it?"

"That tickles."

Callahan smiled. "In that case, I'd better leave it till later."

"Won't it tickle then?"

"I can guarantee it will not."

With a strangled moan, Callahan tore his mouth from her lips and listened to her sigh of delight. "That was very good indeed. Have you more?"

"Much more," he assured as his mouth lowered to her

173

neck, her shoulders, and at last her breast.

Callahan felt the urge to laugh. She was so delightful. Step by step she urged him on, telling him with soft sighs or low-spoken murmurs how well he excelled in each of his many endeavors. So obviously thrilled as each portion of her body was given over to his mouth and hands.

Callahan slid to her feet again. His eyes smiled with tender humor as he listened to her sighs. "I think you should give some thought to the field of teaching. Your students would benefit greatly from your constant praise."

Mattie smiled. "Do you think so?"

And at his nod, she gave a wicked grin. "Perhaps not dressed like this though."

Callahan gave a slow smile, his gaze taking delicious pleasure as it moved over the naked length of her. "No, definitely not dressed like this."

Again his mouth scorched burning kisses up her leg. "Does this tickle still?"

Immersed in the mindboggling sensation she absent-mindedly murmured, "When did it tickle?"

Mattie stiffened as Callahan's mouth came to the juncture of her thighs. "Oh dear! Callahan. Do you think you should be doing that?"

"You don't like it?"

"I don't know."

"Give yourself a minute."

She moaned as he nuzzled against her, kissing her flesh, delighting in her taste, her scent. His hands slid under her hips, holding her closer, his body trembling as he fought aside the need to end it now. Desperately he tried to think of something, anything but this delight, lest he lose his seed here and now upon the quilt.

Mattie groaned. She felt in a daze, dazzled with a pleasure never even imagined, floating upon a cloud of delight. Her hands reached for his head, holding him to her.

"Have you decided?"

"Decided what?" she gasped as the aching returned. It was happening again. Unconsciously she arched toward him. Oh God, could she live through it again?

Callahan gave a low laugh at her obvious loss of memory. But his laughter was soon forgotten. He was drowning in her scent, dying with the need to take her. If he waited much longer it would be too late.

Mattie cried out her disappointment when he left her. But she needn't have worried, for Callahan was all too conscious of her need. With skillful fingers he continued her pleasure. He listened to her sigh, while his body, thick, hard, hurting, pulsing with blood, eased gently into her.

At first Callahan gasped, and then his breath came in short, shallow pants. He wasn't going to make it. Nothing this wonderful could be borne and lived through. His eyes squeezed shut, his head flung back. His mind grew nearly delirious with the pleasure of it. She was so damned tight, he wondered if he might not die from the pure ecstasy that filled his body and soul.

Suddenly he almost shouted out his joy as his body broke through the thin obstruction blocking his path. He felt her stiffen and heard her soft moan of discomfort. He knew he should wait for her body to accept him, and he would have, no matter the cost to his sanity, but she was urging him on as his fingers brought her again to madness.

God almighty, it was too much! She pulsed against him, her muscles hard, throbbing, squeezing, daring him to hold to his control. The sensation was mindboggling, his reaction impossible to stop. He couldn't hold back. He couldn't wait.

His hands cupped her hips and lifted her toward him. He moved with a vicious thrust, and only seconds later stiffened as he arched wildly, helplessly into her. He cried out her name, his arms crushing her to him.

Callahan groaned, gasping for breath. "Not enough, not enough. Put your legs around me."

Mattie, dazed by the last few minutes, didn't think to

refuse.

Callahan sat back on his heels, pulling her from their bed, holding her against him, her legs around his hips. Again he began to move, his need not lessened with one taking. He'd waited too long. He had to have more.

Sweat glistened their skin and allowed them to slide deliciously against each other. Callahan's arms trembled, but he forced aside the weakness, his heart filled with a joy so perfect he wondered if he could bear it. He laid her back upon the quilt and leaned on his elbows, holding himself above her. He smiled. "I suppose we can safely discount the notion of a husband waiting in California."

Mattie stiffened. Her eyes were suddenly wide, her expression apprehensive. She knew he had suspected her of lying. He accused her more than once of inventing a husband. Now he seemed certain of the fact. "Why?"

Callahan, so completely satisfied, so obviously happy, chuckled, rolled to his back, and pulled her possessively over the length of him. "Did your mother never tell you the way of things?"

"My mother died birthing my sister and myself." Mattie scowled as she raised her eyes to his smug expression. "What things?"

Jesus, he had suspected her to be an innocent, but never had he imagined the whole of it. Callahan searched his mind, wondering how to best proceed. "Did you feel a bit of pain at the beginning?"

Mattie shrugged. "A little, I suppose."

"Well you won't feel it again."

"No?" Mattie laughed and stretched comfortably, completely at ease, upon him. "Taking for granted, of course, there will be an again."

"Of course," Callahan murmured, losing his train of thought for a moment, as her lips ran a line of kisses down his neck. "Stop that a minute. I want to tell you

176

something."

Mattie's face burned by the time he was finished. "Therefore, the proof. You are not married." Callahan waited only a beat and asked, "Why did you lie to me? Why do you want to go to California?"

Mattie was astonished. She had heard stories of men knowing if their wives were pure or not, but put it down to nonsense. She had never expected such a thing, nor a man's knowledge of it. Certainly the subject had never been hinted at in her presence. Ladies simply didn't speak of such things.

Mattie had at first felt mortification at his telling, but a niggling sense of jealousy grew slowly to anger and soon edged out her embarrassment. "Truly it's amazing the knowledge you possess on the intricate workings of the female body." Her lip curved into a sneer. "One wonders if you're not a man of medicine in disguise."

Callahan smiled, aware of her reaction. Happily and correctly, he put it to a spurt of jealousy. Wisely he led her thoughts to other directions. He held her close and insisted. "Mattie, it's common knowledge."

"You mean everyone knows but me?"

"Had your mother lived, you'd know as well."

Mattie digested this information in silence. Perhaps she had jumped to conclusions. Perhaps he had not come by this knowledge firsthand. Fool, of course he had, she reasoned correctly. Just look at him. Her heart fluttered as her chocolate gaze took in his tanned, bearded face. The straight nose, the laughing blue eyes, the even white teeth. What woman could resist? And this man would not have ignored a come-hither glance. Silently she wondered how many women had come before her. Many, if his expertise was any proof.

Mattie strove to maintain indifference. What matter was it to her, after all? They were nothing to each other. Nothing more than two adult human beings reaching out for a stolen moment of pleasure. Mattie was positive he would see it that way, she only wished she could.

Suddenly she asked, "Do you possess equal knowledge of the male species?"

Callahan chuckled. "Being not half so mysterious, or alluring, there is less to know."

"Do you think so? I don't agree."

Callahan raised his brows, silently waiting for her to continue.

"You appear mysterious to me."

"Do I? Why, I wonder?"

Mattie shrugged. "I've never felt a man's body before. You're hard and scratchy. Do you all feel this good?" Mattie asked as she deliberately and most suggestively slid her body over his.

"I don't know. I've never rubbed naked against a man."

Mattie giggled. "I promise you, you're missing something."

Callahan laughed. "I'm afraid the notion does not entice, no matter how you might swear to it."

Mattie slipped to his side and ran her hand over his chest and stomach.

Callahan groaned and looked down his nose at her sparkling eyes. "You could get arrested for that."

Mattie laughed, her hand stilling, burning hot against his flesh, even motionless, driving him out of his mind. "In that case I'd better stop. I don't fancy spending time in jail."

Callahan's hand came to cover hers. A wicked smile teased the corners of his mouth. Slowly he began to guide it lower over his flat stomach and lower still, while suggesting, "You could always deny the charge."

"I guess I could," Mattie answered in agreement, her eyes twinkling with mischief. "But who would believe me? They'd think me a liar or insane to resist this."

Callahan groaned as her hand closed boldly around him. He rolled over and pinned her beneath him. "Mattie," he breathed on a sigh. "Mattie, God, do you know what you're doing?"

Mattie smiled. "I've no further knowledge of your body than I do mine. But I suppose you could tell me."

"Why don't I show you instead."

Her smile was slow and dreamy. "Why didn't I think of that?"

Callahan had never felt so exhausted in his life. He'd been a boy of fifteen the last time he'd taken a woman three times in one night. He wouldn't have believed he possessed the strength or the inclination. But she had proven his thinking wrong. Callahan sighed as he felt her cuddle against him. His heartbeat picked up a pace. Barely over their last encounter and he was seriously considering yet another time around. Later, he silently cautioned himself. You're apt to suffer some permanent damage if you keep at it like this. Forcing his mind from the helpless responses of his body, he commented, "You didn't answer me before. Why did you lie? Why are you going to California?"

"The lie was my excuse to go. The reason is none of your business."

"Mattie," he warned.

"Don't bother to threaten me, Callahan. I have to go to California. The why's are not important to anyone but myself."

"What are you going to do once you get there?"

"Why?"

"How will you live?"

Mattie shrugged. "I'll find a job, I guess."

"Doing what?"

Mattie gave a wicked laugh, rolled to her back, and stretched alluringly, her arms above her head, her leg bent in an all too enticing pose. "Well, now that I know . . ."

"Don't even think it!" Callahan felt a blinding flash of pure rage. He rolled upon her, roughly pinning her beneath him. His eyes were hard and cold, his mouth contorted in fury.

Mattie stiffened at his attitude. Of course she had no intention of plying a trade with her newfound knowledge. He seemed not to realize she had been teasing. Mattie had no idea what had suddenly come over this man, but she wasn't about to take his fury in stride, nor cower before it. "Don't think you can tell me what to do, Callahan."

"I'll tell you anything I damn well please."

"Fine! But I won't listen to a word of it."

"Oh, you'll listen all right. You'll listen and do exactly what you're told."

"God!" she grunted in exasperation. "Who do you think you are, my keeper? I've done just fine till now. I don't need you or any man telling me what to do."

He wanted to thrash her. Never in his life had he come so close to striking a woman. All he could think, all he could see were her arms and legs around another man, her body responding as she had to him.

Callahan shook his head as haunting memories of Beverly came to mind. That was how he would always remember her. Always with her legs around the man. Always the bastard's body driving into her.

Callahan didn't stop to think that he was blinded by raging, almost insane jealousy. All he knew was he'd kill her if she even looked at another. He'd never let her go. She thought she was staying in California, but he was taking her back. Kicking and screaming, if need be, but back she was going. "I'm not going to argue with you. The moment I deliver . . ." Callahan cursed at the slip. The damn woman had him so upset that he had almost blurted out his mission. He had nearly forgotten the possibility she might be an agent.

He gave a mental shrug. Shit! He didn't care if she was or not. She wasn't getting the chance to do a damn thing about it. "The moment we get there, we're booking passage for New Orleans."

"The hell we are!" Mattie gasped with shock. "Are you out of your mind?" She shoved him off and grabbed a quilt to cover herself. "Do you think I've suffered this trip only to turn around and go back the minute I arrive?"

"I have to go back."

"Why?"

"I have to go back," he repeated, offering no explanation.

"Well go then, damn it. I don't care what you do."

Mattie gave a silent groan as she pulled a nightdress over her head and adjusted a number of quilts in the far corner of the wagon. God, why had she allowed this to happen? Hadn't she suspected he would try to stop her? He hadn't an idea of the truth behind her need to go west and already he insisted she go back with him. Mattie trembled at the consequences were he to guess the truth, but forced aside her fears as insignificant.

It mattered not what he said, thought, or did. He wasn't her husband, after all. Mattie shivered at the totally obnoxious thought. Who did he think he was to order her about? Her life was her own, not his to control.

Mattie slid beneath the quilt and turned her back to the man, who no doubt still fumed, at the opposite end of the wagon. Well he could rant and rave to his heart's content. She was going to do exactly as she pleased. And if it meant she was forced to sneak away in the dead of night and hide until he gave up his ridiculous notion, she'd do just that.

Callahan lay where she had left him, his mind conjuring one plan after another to ensure her cooperation. Like it or not, she was going back with him. The only problem was how he could manage it.

He could force her at the point of a gun. Callahan shook his head, knowing the impossibility of the notion. Even if he could keep a gun trained upon her till they boarded a ship, she knew him well enough to realize he'd never shoot.

He could insist she was his runaway sister. His runaway wife? No, if she pressed the point and she no doubt would, that would require some proof.

He could bind her to him. Callahan smiled at the delicious thought. He had handcuffs packed somewhere among his belongings. He could claim she was a criminal and he was taking her back East to stand trial. After all, he was an agent of the Justice Department. He could show proof of that, should any question his actions. He almost laughed aloud at the impotent rage she would surely know. No doubt, she'd be ready to kill him for that.

Suddenly he smiled as he realized her newly awakened passion might be all the persuasion needed. Callahan stretched comfortably upon the thick quilts, his hands cupped beneath his head. Had he anything to say of the matter, her actions tonight would eventually prove to be her undoing. Soon enough she'd be wanting another sampling of what raged between them. Callahan hid a confident chuckle behind a cough.

Suddenly a niggling doubt persisted. Callahan was suddenly positive her stubborn nature wouldn't allow her to give in to this need. No matter, he shrugged, he was more than willing to make the first move. She wouldn't turn a cold shoulder while in the midst of sleep. Yes, she'd become a willing partner in the ecstasy they shared, no matter how she might rage the next morning.

His grin broadened. And if she should become with child, it would do naught but ensure her complacency. Surely she would then see the need to stay with him. Callahan forced aside a nagging doubt. She wouldn't imagine it possible to care for an infant alone, would she? No, she'd admit to needing him then. Callahan closed his eyes and smiled in contentment as one pleasurable picture after another came to his mind. She didn't know it yet, but they were going to spend many hours making these thoughts into reality.

In bare feet, a folded blanket clutched in her arms, Susie O'Conner left her wagon and slipped into the darkness. Her father's snorting, irregular snores sounded sharply above the chirping of crickets, the croaking of bullfrogs and the rustling of wind in the tall grass. Susie only hoped the snoring wouldn't grow so loud as to wake him up as it sometimes did.

Gooseflesh slid up her back when she remembered the last whipping he'd given her. God, but he had been brutal, breaking the skin in a dozen places. It took her near a week before she could walk without pain again.

After the beating, her father had asked if she'd learned her lesson, and Susie had told him, in all honesty, she had. Never again would she entice someone into a bed that fairly shrieked against what she considered a most necessary movement.

Susie shook her head with disgust. That was Tommy Denning's fault. Stupid boy. He had insisted the barn was too cold in April. She should have reminded him she'd make him warm enough.

Within a month of that night, her father had sold the farm and packed their meager belongings into a small wagon. They were heading west, he said, somewhere where no one knew of her shame. Susie shrugged. It didn't matter. Not really. There were men everywhere and she'd heard those out West were more prime for the picking than anywhere else.

Surely she'd find her happiness there. After all, what was it she asked out of life? She looked for no riches, no jewels. She longed for no home, no children, and definitely no husband. All she wanted was a man, and if she sometimes had more than one at a time, what was the harm?

Susie grinned as she approached the meeting place. She couldn't wait. She could feel herself growing all hot, just knowing what would soon happen. God, but she hoped he was ready. It had been days since she last had a man.

Susie came to an abrupt stop. Her eyes widened with surprise. It was late. Everyone should have been in bed long ago. Who the hell was talking? Two people, perhaps more, stood behind one of the wagons, their voices low as they whispered. Susie stopped and waited for them to leave. She didn't want to be seen near his wagon. After all, he was married, no sense in causing a fuss when you didn't have to. She tapped her foot impatiently, hoping they'd hurry along.

The smallest of sounds came from behind her. She smiled in anticipation, believing it was her lover, and turned only to find eternal rest.

Poor Susie, whose only crime in life was to satisfy the flesh, died at the age of fifteen, her body flung carelessly aside after her murderer took her for the very last time.

Mattie stepped from the wagon the next morning, her expression wary. A sigh of relief slipped past her lips when she realized their small campsite was empty. Callahan's horse was nowhere to be seen. Perhaps he had gone hunting as was his usual habit most Sunday mornings. Mattie only hoped he'd be gone all day. The less she was forced to bear his company the better.

But it seemed Mattie was not to get her wish this fine sunny day, for Callahan, Jake, and Jim Stables came charging into camp only moments after she finished her coffee.

Mattie never noticed, for she purposely turned her back to the man, but Callahan only had eyes for the wagon master. It wasn't long before Cassidy was located and the news of their recent discovery imparted. Moments later the camp was abuzz with the news.

Susie O'Conner had been found dead, without a stitch of clothes, her body obviously abused. What was once a pretty face was now shivered upon at first sight.

Later that same morning, the body was dressed in a flowered gown and wrapped in a blanket. She was interred in a shallow grave, while Mr. O'Conner stood helplessly by, shrunken, eyes hollow, face gray, and watched shovel after shovel cover the last of his family. The man was obviously in shock. He said nothing to those who offered their condolences. No doubt he never heard them. Though many tried, no one could find the right words. There were no words to soothe this torment.

Mr. Cassidy read from the Holy Book and then, careless of the girl's father, took it upon himself to deliver a sermon on the wages of sin, promising the girl got what she wanted.

Mattie was astonished that the man should show such callous disregard of the grieving father. Didn't he realize Mr. O'Conner's suffering?

Mattie watched Callahan's face darken with fury and knew his feelings matched her own. Believing it wasn't her place, she wasn't about to speak up, but when one or two of those good Christian folks, standing by, called out their agreement, Mattie couldn't seem to help herself. She never thought of the possible trouble that might ensue.

"Excuse me, Mr. Cassidy."

Cassidy stared at the tiny woman who dared to interrupt. And he was going at such a fine pitch. Why, a minute or two more he would have the crowd in the palm of his hands. From past experience he knew there was nothing half so exhilarating.

Mattie took strength from Callahan's arm as it suddenly came around her waist. "I'm afraid you've made a mistake. No one wants to die. Especially not a death as horrible as Susie suffered."

"Are you condoning fornication, Mrs. Callahan?" Cassidy asked with a sneer.

"Certainly not, Mr. Cassidy. But I can neither condone your judgment of the girl. After all, the Bible says, 'Judge not, lest ye be judged.' "

Cassidy's eyes bulged with outrage. His pasty white face mottled with fiery color. "I'm not judging her, Mrs. Callahan," Cassidy snapped, almost shaking with anger. His lips thinned into a cold, hard grimace. "I leave that in God's capable hands. I'm simply remarking on the evil within us all. No one here is free of sin. You don't claim to be, do you?"

And at Mattie's shocked silence, he grinned. "No, I

185

thought not. You are indeed a sinner, like the rest of us." His grin turned suddenly leering and his eyes dipped to the bodice of her dress. "Perhaps your sins go far deeper than any would suspect. Why else would you defend a jezebel?"

Callahan sucked in his breath at the man's audacity. An instant later he was holding Cassidy by his shirt-front, careless of the fact that the man's legs dangled helplessly above the ground. Cassidy's eyes were bulging again, though this time from an entirely different cause. His sickly white skin grew decidedly blue, his air supply apparently greatly lessened. "If you dare talk to my wife like that again, I promise you there'll be another grave to dig." Callahan gave the man a shake before he went on. "Had you, as does my wife, any regard for your fellow man, you'd worry over Mr. O'Conner's feelings and less your own insane rantings." Callahan nearly threw the man on the ground and walked away.

But if Callahan thought that was the end of it, he was mistaken. "Mr. Callahan," Cassidy called out as he came to his feet and brushed off his black coat. "You were seen on numerous occasions to visit the O'Conner wagon. Could it be you have something to hide?" Cassidy grinned as Callahan stopped short and turned to face him.

"I was with my wife last night," Callahan defended.

Cassidy laughed. "So you say. Are there any to prove your words?"

"I will."

"Mrs. Callahan, I don't mean to doubt you, but how can you know what happened after you went to sleep? How can you be sure your husband didn't walk out for," he hesitated knowingly, "shall we say a breath of air?"

"He did not."

Cassidy chuckled, knowing the impossibility of her statement. He had her now. "And you can swear to that? Swear it on this Holy Book?"

Mattie's face turned crimson, but she forced herself to speak. "Mr. Cassidy, it is apparent you've never married, else you'd know honeymooners rarely sleep."

Callahan's eyes widened with respect, while the smallest of smiles teased the corners of his mouth. A few of the men snickered. A few of the women gasped. Jake grinned. Nora laughed out loud. And Mattie wanted to find a hole and crawl in.

Chapter Fifteen

If he said one word, just one word, she wasn't going to be held responsible for what she might do. At the very least she would likely run off into the endless stretch of prairie screaming like a madwoman.

Mattie reluctantly and in stiff silence bore the beast's arm around her waist, all the way back to their campsite. God, but she hated this brute. She knew he was laughing, albeit in silence, but laughing nonetheless. And she hated him all the more that he should find humor in her humiliation.

If she allowed herself to think on it, she hated him for countless reasons, in truth, this episode being the least important. She hated him for the shiver he caused when he looked at her. For the weakness he brought to her knees at a kiss. For the trembling ache that tightened her belly and the thunder caused to her heart at the sound of his whispers. But she wouldn't allow herself to think on it. He, of all men, simply wasn't worth the slightest thought.

Callahan released his hold as they neared their wagon. "Thank you, Mattie. I know that took a great deal of courage."

Mattie gave a silent curse. What had come over her that her heart should thunder in her breast at the gently spoken words? Mattie forced aside the errant emotions he seemed so easily to instill. She wouldn't notice the tenderness in his voice. She wouldn't look at him. She didn't dare lest she fall helplessly under his spell yet again.

This man couldn't be allowed such control. It was out

of the question. She had a mission to fulfill. He had no place in her life.

"Whatever you are, Callahan, you're no murderer."

Callahan chuckled at the reluctant words that seemed to be torn from her throat. "And what am I, do you think?"

It was the laugh that did it. She never would have raised her hand had he not laughed. But her mortification seemed to come back tenfold at the sound of his merriment. Her fingers curled into a fist. She pulled back her arm, expecting to land a clean, totally unexpected, blow to his midsection.

But Callahan saw the coming punch and pulled her sharply against him. Mattie felt her breath leave her lungs as her body slammed against his. "That won't accomplish anything."

Mattie struggled to free herself. "Don't laugh at me, damn it! I won't have you enjoying my humiliation."

Callahan ignored her attempt to create some space between them. His arms held her tightly against his body as his hands raced in soothing strokes over her back. "Is that what you think?" And when she refused to answer, indeed refused to look at him, he gripped her shoulders and gave her a gentle shake. "Is it?"

Mattie yanked herself free of his hold. Bravely she stood her ground, her head tipped back as she glared into blue eyes. "I think you are the cruelest beast. Heartless and mean. Arrogant and uncaring of others, especially their feelings."

Callahan's lips split, his black beard emphasized the flash of white teeth. Mattie thought his grin despicable, one of pure male confidence as he hooked his thumbs into his belt, leaned his shoulders against their wagon, and crossed one foot over the other. "And what about making love, Mattie?" His eyes darkened with remembered pleasure. "How do I rate in that quarter?"

Mattie felt her whole body quiver. She couldn't answer him. She dared not utter a word.

"I can tell you how you rate," he continued on, his

voice growing silky, sending unwanted shivers up her spine.

"I don't want to hear it." She choked a breathless dry whisper.

"Why? Are you afraid I might have found you lacking?"

Mattie mumbled something quite unladylike under her breath and Callahan laughed.

"You know I didn't, Mattie. You know something very special happened between us last night. Something neither of us could easily find with another."

Mattie closed her eyes for a long moment. She wouldn't let his softly spoken words weaken her resolve. God, she almost moaned aloud, when had she ever felt such confusion? She couldn't begin to understand the need he so easily brought to surface. This was a new Mattie, someone she'd never before known.

And this complicated man! One moment he was sweet and gentle, while the next raging and wild. He might spout tender words, but the truth of it was, he offered her nothing but physical pleasure. And you want more, came a voice from the back of her mind. No! she vehemently denied. Determination straightened her shoulders, as pictures of Melanie's torn body flashed suddenly in her mind. Her mouth thinned. She had a job to do. This man had no place in her life. She wanted nothing from him. She didn't! Nothing but to be left alone. "Well, since it won't be easy, I'd best get at it, hadn't I?"

Mattie had felt a moment's disappointment at Callahan's laugh. She had suspected her outrageous statement might provoke him into an argument. It was a great deal easier to withstand his allure when angered. The silly comment she had made last night had triggered his anger fast enough. And yet now he seemed totally in control, her nonsensical words easy enough to shrug off. "What are you so afraid of?"

Mattie stared, fighting with every ounce of control not to fall into his arms and accept his soothing comfort. Her throat closed. It would be so easy. Maybe he could even help her? No, she didn't trust him. He wouldn't see the need as she did. Mattie swallowed. She could hardly speak. "I'm not afraid of anything."

Callahan's smile was so tender, Mattie had to fight against the sudden urge to cry. "Oh yes you are."

"I'm not!" she denied.

Suddenly, and to Mattie's surprise, he shrugged his shoulders, and walked away. "Have it your way."

Mattie blinked. Was that it? Was that all the effort he was going to put into the relationship he'd hinted at wanting? Mattie cursed the feeling of emptiness and crushing disappointment and groaned out her self-disgust. Good God! she'd be a raving lunatic by the time they reached California if she didn't manage some control. She had to steel herself against this man, or all her plans would be for naught.

Mattie watched as he went about the chore of feeding the oxen. His words might have torn into her soul, but he had apparently forgotten her existence. His obvious lack of concern only went to prove her opinion of him justified. "Don't let a softly spoken word influence, Mattie," she whispered softly. "The man is out for all that he can get. He is a beast. There is simply no other word to suit him."

Callahan breathed a deep sigh as he forced his body to relax. Jesus, but this woman could drive the best intentions clear out of a man's mind. That remark she made about finding another was enough to drive him mad with jealousy. It took every ounce of willpower he possessed to shrug and walk away, for he had sense enough to realize she was purposely trying to rile him. Perhaps she hoped to insulate her feelings in reciprocated anger. Callahan shook his head, his mouth twisting into a grimace. The woman had no idea just how dangerously close to the fire she played.

He knew she had suffered no little degree of embarrassment. And when he tried to ease her suffering, what did he get? An attempted punch in the stomach!

God, what had he ever done to deserve this torment? Why couldn't he have chosen another to love? Callahan moaned almost as if in pain as he recognized, for the first time, the emotion that had been twisting his guts for weeks for what it was.

God, but he was going to have a time of it, taming this shrew. Callahan suddenly chuckled at the thought. If handled correctly, the chore might prove interesting, especially at night. Callahan's mood brightened considerably. Yes, it might very well prove to be most interesting at night.

She had barely spoken a word to him all day. Even at dinner she had sat silently across from him, finding the stew on her plate enough in the way of company.

Callahan grinned into the dark as he patiently waited for her sleep to grow deeper. It didn't matter, her obstinance. Soon enough his lovemaking would bring her around. Soon he'd have her crying out her need, pleading with him to take her and end the torment. Tonight, he vowed, he was going to hear those words. The rest of what she said meant nothing. And he'd wait, no matter how long it took, for what she'd so far refused to say.

He could hear her breathing. Slow, steady, and deep. It was time. Silently he came to his feet and moved toward her. It took him some time to find her in the dark, since he dared not light a lamp, lest she awaken. Finally he managed to slip beside her without crushing her beneath his feet.

Callahan smiled, for the moment he lay down she snuggled her rump against his stomach. She might profess her dislike, but her body seemed to like his well enough. Callahan gasped as moments later she turned into his arms. Indeed, her body seemed to more than like him.

Mattie sighed. He was beside her whispering beautiful loving words. Her heart melted at the sound. God, how she wanted this man. Wanted him for all eternity.

If only, if only . . . Don't spoil it, Mattie. Don't think. Enjoy this moment. He was telling her he loved her. Mattie sighed, her heart swelling with joy. He was saying it with softly murmured phrases. He was saying it with his hands, with the texture of his mouth against her flesh. Mattie smiled. Life was so simple in sleep. In sleep, dreams were enough.

Mattie moaned as the warmth of his moist breath brushed against her neck. She gave a small giggle. Even in dreams his beard felt wonderful. Would the rest feel as good? Oh please, she didn't want to wake up. She didn't want to lose this pleasure to reality.

The buttons of her gown opened as if by magic. Dreams allowed magic, didn't they? His mouth nuzzled her throat, sliding closer, closer to her breast.

She arched her back, giving him greater access to flesh that ached for his touch. Mattie groaned and listened with some surprise as the sound was answered by a deep murmur of pleasure.

Callahan growled. His hand slid beneath her night-dress and found her wet and lusciously hot, ready for him. Her legs parted, silently inviting more.

Mattie eyes blinked open. Her body stiffened as she realized this was no dream. He was . . . "Callahan!" she gasped. "Callahan," she moaned only a second later, but the pressure of his mouth cut off any objection she might have uttered.

Mattie shivered and moaned as his fingers slid into the warmth of her body. It was too late. He had caught her unaware. She couldn't resist. Her body was already on fire, begging for more of the ecstasy only his touch could bring.

Callahan's body shook, his hands trembled. Desperately he tried to stay his passions, even as his soul reveled in her warmth. Last night he had taken her until they both lay exhausted and gasping for their next breath and still he had not had enough. Idly he wondered if ever there'd come a time when he would.

Last night he had shown her the most tender torment. But not tonight. Tonight he felt not the slightest need but to stake his claim, to make her his forever.

His mouth covered her own. Feeding on her taste, drinking of her scent, taking all he could of her warmth until he tempted madness should he go on. And yet once started he couldn't stop. He'd have her now. Again and then again and yet again, until she had not the strength but to cling to him for all eternity.

There was little time for preliminaries. To know her body was ready and willing to accept him was enough to drive him beyond all reasonable thought. It might as well have been their first time for all the restraint he felt. That she could bring him to madness, after last night, was a terrifying truth.

Callahan swung his body over hers. He never heard her soft murmur of delight as his flesh brushed hers. Her legs parted and her sigh of relief became a gasp of blinding pleasure mixed with pain.

Callahan groaned as he lifted her hips and guided himself deep into her moist, heated depth. "Mattie, Mattie," he choked, starved for her, his hands straining to bring her closer.

But he needn't have worried at Mattie's not being ready. His low groans and the already familiar worshiping of his lips to her flesh set her nerve endings on fire. Indeed she reached greedily for him, hungry to bring him closer to her need.

Mattie's moans built to a feverish pitch. The sensual brush of his beard against her flesh was driving her out of her mind. She couldn't bear much more. She tried to pull back. She was melting in the heat and yet growing tighter with every second that passed. It was too much, too much. "No," she murmured, almost drunkenly, unwilling to see this powerful moment to its frightening end. "No, I can't."

But Callahan wasn't about to allow her retreat. His voice was low and breathless. "You can and you will, Mattie," he insisted as he deepened his thrusts to mind-boggling proportions.

Callahan felt as close to losing control as ever he'd come. Nothing, no one had ever driven him to these heights. All he could think was to bury himself deep inside her body. All he could want was the delicious feel of her warmth surrounding his aching, throbbing need.

He lifted himself to his knees, his hands on her hips holding her body to him.

Mattie's cry of exquisite pleasure caused him near insanity. Her wildly entreating words and silken touchings were more than his mind could endure. He couldn't stop the pleasure from building. He couldn't stop . . . Couldn't stop.

He was taking her breath, her soul. There wasn't anything left and she didn't care, for just as he took all she had to give, she claimed him in return until neither gave but received. Her nails dug deep into his back and just when she thought she'd surely die if he didn't soon end the torture, her body stiffened and pulsed with life, throbbing with wave after crashing wave of delicious, aching relief.

Callahan absorbed her low, keening cries of pleasure into his mouth, the sound robbing him of the last of his control. His body stiffened for endless agonized seconds. His eyes closed as the ecstasy suffused his entire being. And then finally a shudder and unbearable release. Callahan breathed a deep groan as he fell exhausted against her breast.

It took a few moments before he heard anything but the pounding of his heart but finally smiled as he listened to her softly muttered "Wretch." She might have pushed him away but seemed to have forgotten her words the moment they were uttered, for her arms came around him and held him securely against her.

"I waited too long," Callahan gasped, his breathing still uneven, his heartbeat not yet returned to its normal rhythm.

A low, rumbling chuckle came to her lips. The man was impossible and so appealing she knew she didn't have a chance against his charm. What was the use?

There was no denying the fact that she wanted this man. Why should she torture herself with denials? Once they reached California it would end. Why not enjoy what she could now? "And you consider from last night to now too long of a wait?"

"I mean I waited for you to fall asleep. You took so damn long."

"That was because I knew you were awake. I was listening to you tossing and turning."

". . . And waiting."

"So you could sneak up on me?"

Callahan chuckled his agreement. "I was thinking about this all day."

"I imagine it's useless, in the future, to make up two beds."

"Especially since we'll be needing only one."

Mattie nodded. "I suppose it doesn't matter my objections."

"You have objections?" he asked in feigned innocence.

Mattie laughed low and silkily. "You are a wretch, Mr. Callahan."

"Oh God," Callahan groaned. "Don't call me mister."

"Why?"

"It's a sure sign of your anger."

Mattie's eyes widened with surprise. A smile curved her full lips. "Is it? I hadn't realized."

"I'd wager there are many things you haven't realized."

"And you are going to correct that oversight by telling me. Am I right?"

Callahan chuckled, his arms pulling her with him as he rolled to his side. "Do you know you cry out the most delicious sounds of delight when I'm pleasuring you?"

"Callahan," she groaned, mortified, her face growing crimson even under the cover of darkness.

He gave a tender laugh as his hand roamed at will over her back and hip. "There's no need to be embarrassed." His mouth nuzzled her temple and cheek, feeling the warmth of her skin and realizing correctly her blush. "You can't know how it heightens my pleasure."

Mattie groaned as she buried her face in his neck. "You are a beast to torment me. Stop it."

"You might be right."

Mattie glanced up into his shadowed face. She couldn't tell his expression in the dark, but his words and the movement of his hands left her without a doubt as to his intentions. "There are more pleasurable ways to bring torment."

Mattie hummed a happy tune as she unfolded the quilts stored neatly each morning in the corner of the wagon and arranged them into comfortable bedding. Her eyes were bright with pleasure and an ever-present smile, the same smile that had curved her lips for the past week. She shivered as her mind wandered back to this morning and the utterly complete happiness she'd found waking up in Callahan's arms. Her chocolate-brown eyes glittered with expectancy remembering Callahan's bold look and hungry kiss just before he left for his turn at the watch. He had told her not to wait up and whispered his promise to awaken her when he returned. She knew what this night would bring. Mattie laughed softly. This night and every night until they reached California.

Once she had realized the inevitability of their situation, she had made herself a promise. She wouldn't think of the future, nor of the right or wrong of her actions. She wouldn't worry of their eventual parting. She'd take what he offered, enjoying the present, until the time came when she'd do what she must.

Mattie's gaze fell upon the barrel of flour, or what was left of it. She worried her bottom lip and cursed her lack of ability. Perhaps she should tell Callahan they were running dangerously low. If only she hadn't made so many mistakes, they would doubtless have twice as much left. Her eyes crinkled with merriment as she

197

remembered her first attempt at making biscuits. It had taken many tries before they were at least edible.

No, she wouldn't worry Callahan on that score. He had enough to think about. She could only hope they'd reached a settlement before the last of it ran out. If not, she hoped she could borrow some from her neighbors.

Mattie's gaze swept the crowded wagon. Had Callahan stored another barrel, maybe behind those crates?

Mattie looked with disgust at the long wooden boxes that took up so much room. She and Callahan had argued over what she considered a great inconvenience. Granted he was being paid handsomely for transporting the farming materials, but it was her wagon and her right to expect some little comfort during this most uncomfortable trip. And that didn't mean tripping over these damn things every time she tried to move around.

Mattie leaned over one of the crates. A lantern in her hand, she tried to see beyond it. Nothing, she sighed. Nothing but another exactly the same size and still another beyond that. As far as she could tell, there were near a dozen. Mattie grimaced. She ought to have insisted Callahan pay her half his fee. After all, it was her space he was using.

Mattie shrugged with annoyance. There were no barrels. She sat upon one of the crates and reasoned they'd not likely starve. They still had the cow, so there was plenty of milk, so much so that she had to give most of it away. Plus the half dozen chickens laid with fair regularity and Callahan kept them well supplied with meat. She really had no need to complain. The only thing she longed for was fresh vegetables and perhaps fruit. Her mouth watered as she imagined a juicy orange.

Mattie shrugged away the thought. It wouldn't do, this hungering for what wasn't possible. Ungrateful wretch she was. Why was it so hard to be satisfied with what she did have?

As she came to her feet, the heel of her boot scraped

198

against the corner of the crate and Mattie noticed it had come loose. No doubt her constant kicking as she passed had done little toward keeping it secure. Mattie leaned down and hit it back in place, only to watch it fall to the wagon's floor. With a sigh Mattie crouched down, prepared to put it back and find something with which to secure it.

Mattie gaped with stunned disbelief as she knelt at the opening to the box. She wasn't looking at guns! Surely the dim light cast off by the lone lantern played tricks on her eyes.

Mattie's fingers shook as she brought the lantern closer. A moment later she closed her eyes and gave a moan that bespoke of budding horror. She had not been mistaken. The crate was filled with guns, rifles to be more exact. Good God, why? Why were they transporting a near arsenal across country?

There wasn't a doubt in her mind that Callahan had been aware of the contents since the beginning. He had lied to her. Why? Mattie couldn't think what he was about.

If they belonged to the Army, wouldn't the shipment have been accompanied by a troop of soldiers? No one owned these many guns, nor hid the fact unless they were doing something illegal.

That was it! He was doing something illegal. He was obviously selling them, or transporting them for someone who was. But who would buy guns? Who would need this many?

"Oh my God!" Mattie groaned as she came to the only conclusion possible. He was selling guns to the Indians. And his friends? Were they doing the same? Of course they were. How many others were involved? Surely no one made this arduous trip with only one or two wagons with which to deal.

Mattie shivered with self-disgust as her actions came back to haunt. She had lain with a man with the morals of a snake. He was selling guns to Indians who, in turn, would use them to kill white families. Babies, women, young children, no one was safe from their reported cruelties. And this beast, with whom she had imagined herself in love, was their supplier.

Mattie searched for a hammer. She found a steel bar Callahan used to repair the wheels. It didn't take much effort. In minutes she had three more cases opened. All were filled with rifles. And upon closer inspection, she noted they were the property of the United States Army. Mattie felt a wave of disappointment so great that tears glistened in her eyes. So he was a thief to top it off.

Numb with her discovery she sat amid the dozens of rifles and awaited Callahan's return.

Mattie heard his footsteps and watched with no emotion, at least none she'd dare name, as he entered the wagon.

Callahan smiled. "Still awake? I thought you'd . . ." Callahan's words stopped in mid-sentence as he surveyed the opened crates and the rifles that were scattered upon the floor.

". . . Be sleeping?" she finished for him. "I'm afraid not," Mattie returned in a voice that was horribly flat, totally devoid of emotion.

"Mattie, it's not what you think."

"What am I thinking, Mr. Callahan. Perhaps you might be so kind as to tell me."

Callahan felt trapped and the feeling brought an instant anger to the surface. He wasn't used to being forced to explain his actions. She didn't have the right to question him.

Jesus, why hadn't he been prepared for this? Why hadn't it occurred to him that she might come across the weapons? Stalling for time, hoping for inspiration, he wracked his brain for a believable story. Finally he flung his hat upon one of the crates and ran his fingers through his black hair. "How the hell am I supposed to know what that mind of yours has conjured up?"

"Are these yours?" Mattie asked, her gaze sweeping the hundred or more guns she had dumped carelessly to the floor.

"Who the hell do you think they belong to?"

"You were going west before I approached you. Weren't you?"

And when he didn't answer, she repeated, her voice noticeably louder, "Weren't you?"

"Keep your voice down!"

Mattie laughed, the sound holding not a trace of humor. "Of course. We wouldn't want the camp to know of your little business venture, would we?"

"Trust me, Mattie."

Mattie grinned, showing for the first time a touch of real humor. "When all else fails, it's 'Trust me, Mattie.' Can't think of an appropriate lie, is that it?"

Callahan flushed with the truth of her words, for they both knew he had been trying to do just that.

"You're going to dump these rifles tonight." It wasn't a plea. It wasn't a question. Mattie stated a simple fact.

"I can't."

"You will."

"Mattie, you don't know what you're saying."

"Don't I? Tell me you're not selling these guns to the Indians," she dared.

"I'm not. I swear it."

Mattie shot him a look of disbelief. "But you won't tell me to whom you're selling them?"

Callahan shook his head. He couldn't tell her. He hadn't the right. Orders were orders. This was supposed to be a secret mission. He hadn't the authority to tell anyone.

"And I'm supposed to believe you?" Mattie grunted, her lip lifted in a sneer. "Give me a reason why I should. What have you ever done but lie to me?"

Callahan's eyes widened. Good God, the woman possessed incredible audacity. His mouth tightened in outrage. "Lies? Are we talking lies here? You? Who's proven herself the master of the art? You dare to accuse me?"

Mattie made a sound as if to protest his accusations, but held her tongue at his warning glare.

With some effort Callahan managed to control his rising anger. He hooked his fingers into his belt and bestowed upon her a humorless smile. A common reaction to those accused of wrongdoing is to stage a counterattack. Callahan didn't consciously plan this maneuver, but struck out defensively and pressed home his point. "Oh, I forget. You'd never lie. Not the *virginal* Mrs. Trumont."

Momentarily flustered, Mattie appeared at a loss for words, but it didn't take a minute for her to realize what he was about. Her lips twisted with scorn. "A very neat trick, Mr. Callahan. Turn the tables on your opponent, thereby exonerating yourself."

Callahan's brows rose with surprise as he realized he'd been doing just that. Damn but she didn't miss a thing. "Tell me why you're going to California," he demanded, his voice taunting her to tell the truth at last. "If you don't lie, it should be easy enough."

Mattie looked at him a long moment before she finally shrugged. What difference did it make? He'd never know who her intended victim was. He'd have to kill her before she'd tell him Ellis's name. A touch of the shock she'd suffered might be just what he deserved. A hard smile curved her lips as she stated simply, "I'm going west to kill a man, Mr. Callahan."

Callahan almost laughed at her absurd reply. This tiny woman whose head barely reached his shoulder, who exhibited nothing but gentleness, who even in anger had never shown the slightest viciousness or cruelty was speaking of ending someone's life as calmly as if discussing an afternoon tea. Ridiculous. Callahan nodded his head and gave a knowing sneer. "And you don't lie, am I right?"

"You are quite right, Mr. Callahan," Mattie stated simply. "Now, shall we get back to the matter at hand? To whom are you selling these guns?"

"You can't be serious! You can't expect me to believe this nonsense."

"Mr. Callahan," Mattie sighed wearily. "It matters little to me whether you believe it or not."

"Why?" Callahan's eyes widened with alarm as the possible truth of her statement began to dawn. It was outrageous. It was impossible, but . . . "Why would you want to kill someone?"

"Not just someone, Mr. Callahan. The man who abused and murdered my sister."

He gave her a long, hard look, trying to see beneath her bland expression. "If that's true, why didn't you report it to the authorities?"

Mattie laughed. "Oh yes, the authorities. You see, there was bit of a problem there," she said, not bothering to disguise her sarcasm. "The man who had chosen to bestow his attentions on my sister was a Yankee captain." One eyebrow lifted at her pointed look, remembering the blue coat he wore at their first meeting, and Callahan felt an almost irresistible impulse to apologize for his very existence.

"Later, when complaints were made, I was told by our illustrious occupiers," her voice filled with hatred, "that 'These things happen in times of war, miss.'" Mattie sent Callahan a smile that chilled his spine. "See how the authorities handled it?"

"So you intend to take the law into your own hands?"

"Didn't he do as much?"

"He didn't obey the law at all, Mattie. You know it's not the same."

"Oh but it is the same," she countered ever so sweetly, her bitter smile belying her softly spoken words. "Only, like him, I'll probably not get off scot-free."

"And it doesn't bother you, knowing the consequences you'll no doubt suffer?"

"You mean when I'm caught?" Mattie nodded. "It bothers me, Mr. Callahan, but not near enough to stop me."

"Jesus Christ!" he raged. "How can you be so damn

calm about this? Can't you see you're throwing your life away?"

"It's my life, isn't it? And my business."

"Who is he?"

Mattie laughed and shook her head. "So you can warn him?"

"I'll never let you do this."

Mattie lifted her chin a notch. Her smile was icy cool. "Pray tell?" She laughed softly. "I'm afraid you have little choice in the matter."

Callahan ran his fingers through his hair in frustration. Suddenly a thought occurred. "How do you know the man's identity? You couldn't have been there, or . . ." He left the sentence unfinished, a sudden helpless rage at what surely would have happened to her tightened his throat and forbade another word.

Mattie lowered her eyes and her cheeks darkened as if in shame. Her voice was barely above a whisper when she said, "I was there, Mr. Callahan. I was hiding in the cellar. I heard the screams. God," she breathed a shaky sigh, "I think I'll always hear the screams."

Mattie lifted her gaze from the wagon's floor and faced him squarely. "After they left, I found my sister. She told me who he was just before she died."

"They? There was more than one?"

Mattie nodded, her voice dull and lifeless. "Six. The man I'll kill was the leader."

Callahan's knees almost wobbled in his relief that she should have escaped such horror unscathed. He took a deep, calming breath, forcing his mind to the here and now. "And you feel a measure of guilt that she suffered while you hid."

Mattie shrugged. "I did for a time."

"You still do or you wouldn't insist on avenging her death."

Mattie gave a brittle smile. "You might be right." She shrugged. "What does it matter, my reasons? I must do what I must do."

Mattie straightened her shoulders. "Now if you are

quite finished, I'd like to get back to these guns."

"We are far from finished, Mattie. You don't think you can calmly state you're going to kill someone and I'm going to do nothing about it."

Mattie smiled. "What can you do?"

"I'll . . . I'll . . . Damn you, Mattie! You can't do this." Callahan punched his leg with frustration.

"Who are you selling the guns to?"

Callahan almost groaned knowing the fruitlessness of continuing his questioning. After a long hesitation, he finally replied, "I can't tell you."

"You won't tell me," she corrected.

Callahan shrugged. "If you say so."

"Very well." She nodded. "Since you won't tell me, Mr. Cassidy might have greater results."

Mattie made to move toward the end of the wagon, but was stopped in her tracks by words so ominous, so clearly filled with warning, she felt her heart shrivel with dread. "I wouldn't."

She turned to face him, her eyes narrowing as she studied his expression. "What do you mean, you wouldn't?"

"Mr. Cassidy's death. You wouldn't want that on your shoulders, too."

Mattie gasped, her eyes widened with fear, and Callahan felt a crushing pain almost double him in half that she should direct such an emotion toward him. "You'd kill him?" she asked, her voice barely above a whisper.

Callahan forced an indifferent shrug. "I'm afraid you're giving me no choice."

This was a nightmare! It couldn't be happening. She felt like a caged rat. She couldn't keep this information to herself and yet she couldn't take the chance of finding out if Callahan's threat would be proven true.

"Do you intend to kill me as well, now that I've found you out?"

Callahan almost laughed at the absurdity of the notion. Kill her? Kill the woman he loved more than his own life?

With some effort he managed to control his expression and replied in a voice as cold as he could possibly manage, "I don't believe that's necessary." And then, helpless to resist, he added, "I'm sure I can trust you to keep our little secret."

Mattie shivered at his chilling, underlying threat. How could Mr. Kyle have imagined this man to be a good sort? He was nothing but a cold-blooded murderer. God only knew how many he'd already killed.

Mattie shivered with disgust thinking about his murderous hands touching her. She didn't for a moment doubt his words. There was no way she was going to tell Mr. Cassidy what she knew. No matter that she could hardly stand the man, she wouldn't be able to live knowing she was responsible for his death. But what was she to do? Could she simply forget what she'd seen? Could she allow Callahan to proceed with his dirty work?

Suddenly a wild idea dawned. Could she? She was bound and determined to kill Ellis. What did it matter if yet another received his just reward at her hands.

Callahan easily read her fear and then her fierce determination. There wasn't a doubt as to what she was thinking. The only question was could she go through with it? He didn't think so, but he wasn't going to lie awake each night wondering if he'd trusted her too far. He had to make sure. He had to know. If he wanted to turn his back on her, he needed to know. "If you think you can kill me, thereby doing away with this problem, do it now." Callahan took his gun from the holster on his hip and handed it to her.

Mattie swallowed as her gaze met his. The cool metal was heavy in her hand.

Callahan realized her inexperience by the way she held the weapon. "Do you know how to use it?"

Mattie shook her head.

"How do you expect to do away with your intended victim? Beat him to death with your eyelashes?"

Mattie shrugged, ignoring his sarcasm. "I haven't thought that far ahead."

Callahan nodded. He straightened the gun in her hand, showed her how to cock it, and explained the delicacy of the trigger. When he was finished, he stood directly before her. "I'm only going to say this once. I can't tell you where these guns are going, but I swear it won't be to Indians."

Callahan turned his back to her and knelt on the wagon floor. From the looks of him, he might have forgotten her existence. Completely at ease, he began to pack the rifles back in their boxes, all the while berating himself for his lack of common sense. Never in his life had he acted so irresponsibly. And yet he found himself helpless but to take a chance on her.

Months of traveling still loomed ahead before their journey would be completed and decades, if he had his way, before she'd see the last of him. The problem was, if she was frightened enough or suspected him of lying, it might be the last chance he'd ever take. Fool that he was, he knew he should have somehow emptied the gun before handing it over.

Callahan prayed his instincts were correct. She might intend to kill a man, but he didn't think she had what it took to perform such a cold-blooded act. Sweat trickled down his back as he wondered if he was right. He could hear her breathing behind him. He sensed her hesitation and breathed a sigh of relief when her small hand reached before him and laid the gun atop the box.

Chapter Sixteen

"We have a complication."

"What happened?"

Callahan watched the barely perceptible tightening of his friend's jaw. Jake's expression closed, his whole body tightened as he awaited Callahan's next words, while his seemingly nonchalant attitude grew more purposely pronounced. He leaned back against his wagon and idly fingered the handle of his gun.

"She knows what's in the crates."

Jake's eyes cleared and he shot Callahan a surprised look as if he had expected him to say something else. Callahan could have sworn Jake released a deep breath of relief, but shrugged aside the notion. His imagination was playing tricks on him. His mind was in a constant state of turmoil and he could lay the blame on that nasty-mouthed brat he was stuck with.

"I imagined that would happen eventually."

Callahan silently raged at his own stupidity. Was he the only one who hadn't thought of the possibility? He cursed under his breath. Had he no objectivity when it came to this woman?

"Bad?"

Callahan shrugged. "It was touch and go for a while." Callahan traced an indistinguishable pattern in the dirt with the tip of his boot. Finally he raised his gaze to his friend's amused expression. "I think we can safely assume she's not an agent. She accused me of selling guns to the Indians."

Jake's lips curved into a smile. "Nora told you, didn't

she?"

Callahan nodded. "I'm afraid there's more."

Jake looked at his longtime friend and purposely laughed. For all the camp it looked like the men were sharing some sort of joke. "What?"

"I'm going to need some help keeping an eye on her, especially once we reach California."

Jake nodded, as he waited for Callahan to continue.

"She told me she's going to kill the man who raped and murdered her sister."

Between his teeth, Jake hissed a long, low whistle, and forced a smile for the benefit of any who watched. He'd been in the business too long and seen too much to feel more than a smattering of surprise. "Well, now we know why she's on this train. Do you think she'll do it?"

"What's important is she thinks she will."

"But you know she can't."

"That doesn't matter. She's sure to get herself in one giant mess if she tries it."

Jake nodded. "What are you going to do? You can't keep her under lock and key while we're delivering the supplies. It might take us a week or more."

Callahan shrugged. "What I feel like doing is strangling her."

Jake chuckled. "I have to hand it to you, Callahan, you always did know the way to a woman's heart."

"Yeah," Callahan returned, clearly upset. An idea dawned. After a moment he realized it was the only way. Callahan groaned, feeling himself sink deep into despair, knowing what he planned just might doom any chance the two of them might have had.

"Got you scared shitless, doesn't she?"

Callahan muttered a round of vicious curses directed at the world in general as he walked away from his laughing friend.

Her lips tightened and she darted a quick look at her husband. Yes, his eyes were greedily taking in the rounded backside of the little beauty bending over the small fire. She didn't like it. She didn't like it one bit, but forced herself to shrug away her concern. A man was a man after all, and hers, she supposed, wasn't any different from any other.

A man would always look. It didn't mean anything, she silently professed. But down deep she knew it wasn't the looking that bothered her. It was what always happened after.

Mattie Callahan wouldn't give him the time of day, in any case. All she had to do was look at the young woman to know she was madly in love with her husband. And by the way Mr. Callahan boldly returned her shy glances, it was obvious the feelings were mutual.

She breathed a long, weary sigh as she remembered how her husband had once looked at her. Why couldn't it always be that way? Why did interest have to wane over the years? Maybe a man just didn't have it in him to remain faithful. She shook her head. That wasn't true. She knew many who had kept their roving eye to their own bedroom.

She shrugged. It didn't matter. Not really. In the end he always came back to her. He needed her and always would. He wasn't a saint after all. What did she expect when one of those loose women flaunted herself in front of him? It wasn't his fault. He was a good man. It was the drink that did it. Besides, wasn't he always sorry? And later wasn't it always the best it could be?

Callahan watched her as he moved into their small camp. Jesus, he could feel his body stir with only a look. What would he do if they accidentally touched? How the hell was he supposed to finish out this trip without taking her to bed again?

Damn it anyway. How did she get to hold all the cards? Who was she to make the decisions? Shit, but he'd been a fool to have given in to her demands. After some nasty remarks and veiled threats, they both realized a truce of some sort was indeed imperative. Between them they had managed to strike up a bargain. She would keep his secret, while he would keep himself out of her bed.

Callahan moaned. From the moment he had nodded his reluctant and decidedly unhappy consent, he knew it was a mistake. This stubborn little runt would never go back on her word.

At first he had insisted on his secret for hers.

Mattie had laughed at the notion, "If you didn't believe me, why would they?"

Callahan's lips tightened into a thin smile. "Word could always leak out of the truth of our marital status," he warned, not even bothering to hide his evil smirk.

Mattie nodded knowingly, her chocolate eyes darkening with anger. "Blackmail, Mr. Callahan?"

"Indeed no!" he had replied, seemingly aghast at the suggestion. "I simply worry for your reputation."

"I'm sure you do," she had sneered in obvious disbelief. "But I wouldn't worry overmuch. If word gets out and Mr. Cassidy asks us to leave his train, I'll just have to tell him and all the rest of our traveling companions exactly what you're carrying in those boxes. Certainly you couldn't kill them all?"

Callahan bit his lip. Damn her anyway. She always had to go him one better. Never had he felt so utterly under another's spell, so helpless against her ragings. "And you expect to keep your secrets and me out of your bed with that one threat?"

Mattie laughed, stretching her arms above her head in an effort to appear confident. "It's a matter of who possesses the greatest weapon, don't you think?" She smiled, flung a few quilts in his general direction, turned her back, and said. "Good night, Mr. Callahan."

Callahan's thoughts returned to the present as he watched her bend over the fire and mix something in a black pot. Suddenly angry that she should have such a hold over him, he moved directly behind her and snarled, "Is that show for my benefit or our neighbors'?"

Mattie gasped at the sudden unexpected sound of his voice and spun around, almost falling into the fire as she did. Callahan reached out a steadying hand, the warmth of his touch penetrating the thin cotton of her dress as he held her small waist. Her heart was pounding in her throat as she glared her resentment. "Was that necessary? Did you have to sneak up on me like that? And what are you talking about?"

"I'm talking about the way you stick your rump out when you bend over. Everyone is getting quite a show."

Mattie's cheeks colored beautifully, but a timid glance around told her no one but this despicable oaf was paying her the slightest attention. Her top lip curled into a sneer. "And what am I supposed to do about that? How can I cook over the fire without bending?"

Callahan knew the truth of her words, but for the life of him he couldn't force his mind to reasonable thought. "Other women cook without looking like they're asking for a roll in the hay."

Mattie gasped at the unfair accusation. "Beast!" She flung the spoon she was holding to the ground. "Get your own damn supper. See if you can do it without bending over," she muttered just before she turned her back to him and stomped off in the direction of the river.

Callahan sighed as he sat before the glowing flames and watched his supper burn before his eyes. He didn't care. The last thing he wanted was food. Right now it wouldn't have bothered him if he never ate again.

One thought came again and again to haunt. He wasn't going to make it. It had been less than a week since last he touched her and he was aching so bad, he was near out of his mind with the need to hold her in his arms. She was becoming every day more of an obsession. A wry smile twisted his lips. By the time this train got to California, he'd be a simpering idiot, begging for the honor of kissing the hem of her skirt.

The worst of it was their estrangement was showing in his temper. Each day it grew harder to control his rages. He growled at nearly everyone, including the woman he wanted the least to alienate.

Callahan shook his head. Once upon a time, before this termagant had entered his calm and orderly life, he had been a happy man. Maybe he hadn't even known it at the time, but he was. Idly he wondered if he'd ever again be blessed with that emotion.

"Leave it to him!" Mattie grumbled as she stomped over the uneven countryside toward the river's edge. Who else would have a mind so repulsively degenerate as to imagine obscenity in so innocent a pose. She was cooking, for God's sake! How else did he expect her to stir the food, but to bend over? Should she have lengthened her arms to suit his evil mind? God! but the man was simply too much to bear.

In her anger, Mattie sat without thinking and then groaned at the shock her abrupt action lent to her spine. Great, Mattie, cripple yourself. That would solve all your problems. Then the beast would really have the upper hand.

She gave a weary sigh, her hands came to cup her face. What was she going to do? She couldn't stand much more. Never did he say a pleasant word to her. When he spoke at all it was usually a growl.

God, but she was so tired of fighting, of being forever on edge, always waiting to come back with a nasty reply. Why couldn't they simply get along?

Mattie, so caught up in her thoughts, was more than

a little surprised to find darkness had fallen. She knew she shouldn't be out by herself. She had been warned a number of times of the dangers that lurked on these prairies. With a great sigh she came to her feet and brushed at the dried grass and dust on her skirt.

Mattie gave a sudden shiver. She had the oddest sensation that someone was watching her. Of course she was mistaken. The moon hadn't yet risen. The stars alone cast their meager light upon the earth. She couldn't see two steps in front of her and only knew her direction from the campfires burning in the distance.

No one could be watching her. No one could see any more than she.

But Mattie was wrong. Dead wrong if he had his way, for he wasn't leaving anyone alive to tell what he'd done. He'd wanted her for a long time. From the first moment he'd seen her, but she was never alone, at least not as far as he'd noticed.

She was a lady this one, not like that dirty little whore, Susie. God, that bitch had probably given it to every man on this train except him. His face grew flushed with remembered fury. She had laughed when he told her he wanted his share. She was nothing but white trash. Who did she think she was to laugh at him?

He wouldn't have had to kill that one, except that she'd gotten him so mad. He didn't always kill them. Not when they were real willing. He shuddered at the memory of the last one back home and all that blood. That was a messy affair, but his woman had covered for him. Thank God.

The need, as always, was uncontrollable. He'd felt it before, but never this strong. He knew his wife didn't like it. Most times he didn't care if she liked it or not, especially when he was drinking. Both of them knew he couldn't help himself. Who could resist a slender waist and full breasts? His mouth watered as he imagined this one struggling beneath him. Her skin would be soft

214

and yet firm. God, his eyes closed in imagined pleasure. There was nothing like a firm young body.

Callahan was sitting alone before the fire, brooding as he sipped thick black coffee. He wouldn't go looking for her. It was dark and she should have been back long ago, but he'd be damned if he was going to run after her again. He'd played the fool enough. He didn't care that she could be in danger. He didn't! he insisted. He'd had enough of her. What good was loving someone when all it caused you was pain? He didn't want to love her anymore. As of right now it would stop. He absolutely refused.

Callahan came to his feet. He was going for a walk. Steadfastly he denied this sudden need for exercise had anything to do with Mattie. He wasn't worried. Not about her. Pity the poor fool, man or beast, who dared to cross that woman's path, he thought crossly.

She could take care of herself. God, that was clear enough. Besides, he didn't love her, not anymore. And she was no longer any of his concern.

Callahan was halfway to the river when he heard the scream. It was her. His heart thundered in his chest, pounded in his ears, almost choking off his ability to breathe. It was Mattie! Instantly he was running, his long legs covering enormous distance in a flash. A prayer mixed wildly with curses as he unconsciously sought aid from above. How was he to find her? Here in the vast wild prairies, on a night so ominously dark?

Callahan groaned as visions of Susie's abused body flashed in his mind. Contrary to what most believed, there was a murderer on this train.

After some amateur detective work, folks came to the conclusion that an Indian must have done the young girl in. The guard had been doubled to ward off any future attacks, much to the satisfaction of many a nervous traveler.

But Callahan knew better. An Indian might very well come that close to camp. If the spirit moved him, he might even take an unprotected woman. But never would he chance discovery by taking the woman and using her within calling distance of help. No, Susie had gone with her killer or killers of her own accord. Of that he was certain.

There was a clump of low-lying bushes along the river's edge. Callahan headed toward the place most likely to provide a hiding place for an attacker.

Mattie walked back to camp while grumbling at her nervous-nilly actions. That stupid possum had taken her completely by surprise, just as she'd come to her feet. Instinctively she had jumped back, never realizing she was off balance. Not until, arms flaying and legs wobbling, her bottom splashed in the river. God, was that water cold! Mattie shivered, and quickened her pace. She'd better hurry and change if she didn't want to come down with something.

Suddenly she gasped and jumped aside, her wet skirts hampering her every movement, nearly causing her to fall again. Mattie breathed a sigh of relief, for at the last second she had managed to avoid a collision with Callahan's racing figure. She turned around, watching with wide, startled eyes as he raced on by. Where in the world was he hurrying off to?

Callahan, almost blinded by fear, ran right by her. He hadn't expected to see Mattie walking back to camp. What he was looking for, dreading to see, was her lifeless body sprawled somewhere along the shore of the river.

Callahan came to an abrupt stop as his mind registered Mattie's startled form. He spun on his heel and retraced his steps. A second later he was holding her drenched body in his arms, squeezing her against him with a strength and determination that dared the world to separate them again.

"What are you doing?" Mattie asked with no little surprise to find herself suddenly engulfed in his arms. Finally came a breathless whisper as his hold tightened to near pain, "I can't breathe."

It took a long moment before Callahan came to his senses. And when he did his relief instantly vanished, replaced by an anger so intense his fingers shook with the need to pull her over his lap and smack her bottom until she begged him to stop.

His hands at her shoulders, he held her from him. "What the hell are you doing out here?" And when she didn't instantly answer, he shook her until her teeth rattled. "Why did you scream?"

Mattie was dizzy; the tiny stars above were spinning helplessly around her. Finally able to brake his hold, she staggered back and fell with a whooshing sound upon her rump. "You beast!" she snapped as her hand moved to push her wet hair from her face. "What do you think you're doing? What is the matter with you?"

"Me?" Callahan raged. "Didn't you scream?"

"Oh," Mattie murmured as she remembered the small animal that had darted across her path. "I think I saw a possum."

"A possum! Jesus Christ! A possum?" He ranted on. "And for that you screamed?"

"Well, it scared me," Mattie countered defensively.

"Lady, you don't know what the hell it is to be scared," he grunted as he reached down, brought her roughly to her feet, and suddenly flung her over his shoulder.

Mattie gasped, unable for a second to realize why she should be looking down at the earth. "What?" she squirmed instinctively. "What are you doing?" And when he gave only a grunt for a reply, she hit his back with small fists. "Put me down!" she demanded. "Put me down this instant!"

But her efforts for freedom were in vain, her punches

apparently lost in the relief that filled his being. "She's all right," Mattie heard him explain to someone. Her face turned red. How dare he calmly walk back to camp with her flung over his shoulder like a sack of flour? Who did he think he was? God, she was going to kill him the minute he let her go.

Mattie closed her eyes. She wouldn't raise her head and look at the smirking crowd. She could hear the low, snickering sounds of barely held laughter. Damn him. Damn him to hell!

Callahan nearly threw her into their wagon. Mattie staggered, fell to her knees, and came to her feet before Callahan jumped inside. For the first time he realized she was soaking wet. "How did you get wet?"

"Drop dead!"

"I asked you a question, lady."

"And I told you to do something." As tiny as she was, Mattie managed to look down her nose at him. "Now run along like a good boy and do it."

Mattie's voice shook, but it wasn't from fear or even the rage that filled her. She was shaking all over. The river water had been a cold shock against her skin, and the chill of the night air did little toward replenishing her warmth.

"You're shaking like a leaf. Get out of those clothes."

"Go to hell!"

Callahan grinned. "Drop dead? Go to hell? My my, we are becoming quite a linguist."

"I hate you," Mattie fumed, her anger growing by the minute. "I hope you rot in hell."

Callahan laughed. "Now we're becoming redundant, sweetheart, wouldn't you say? Go to hell? Rot in hell?"

Mattie fought for control. In a minute she was going to lash out at the monster and tear him limb from limb. And in her present state of anger, she hadn't a doubt she possessed the strength to do it. Her eyes were deadly cold, but her voice grew suddenly so soft, so silky smooth, Callahan felt a shiver of excitement race up his spine. "It's late. You must be tired."

He looked at her with some puzzlement, amazed at the sudden turn in conversation. His eyes narrowed, not trusting her in the least.

"Why don't you lie down and sleep?" she asked, her eyes glowing with a fury even the dim light cast by their campfire couldn't hide. He knew very well what she wanted to do to him, hoped to do to him should he relax his guard.

For the first time in a week, Callahan burst out with happy laughter. Oh God, but he loved this woman. No amount of denying it would ever change that fact. He loved her and no doubt would continue to do so until the day he died.

Mattie's lips twitched at the corners. Laughter really was infectious, even if she was beside herself with rage, even if it was directed at oneself. She took a long, steadying breath, stubbornly unwilling to let him believe she had forgiven his outrageous actions. "Callahan, go away so I can change."

Callahan moved toward her instead. "Do you know how delightful you are?" he asked as he took her in his arms.

Mattie grew instantly stiff. She didn't want this. She couldn't afford the luxury. No matter his appeal, she wasn't going to ever again give in to this temptation.

Callahan felt her spine straighten and whispered, "Don't worry. I remember our bargain." His cheek rested for a second against her wet hair and he breathed in the dizzying clean, sweet scent of her. He began to shake and couldn't tell if it was delayed reaction to finding her safe, or the need to take her to bed. Perhaps a combination of both. "Only I never said I wouldn't touch you or kiss you, did I?"

"Callahan, don't."

"I won't," he promised just before his mouth lowered to hers.

219

"You're involved in it too, aren't you?" Mattie hadn't seen Nora or Jake in close to a week and a half. "I suspected you might be, but when you didn't come near me all this time, I knew it to be true." Mattie sighed and raised her hand as if to ward off the coming denial. "No, don't bother to say anything. I don't want to hear lies."

"Why do you think I would lie to you? Aren't we friends?"

Mattie sighed. Long moments passed before she spoke. "Looking back, I remember my life was not far from that of a fairy tale. I was so loved and protected. My brother and father did a good job of keeping us ignorant of the outside world. Then the war came and they were killed. Just before it was over my twin sister was murdered." She laughed bitterly. "After the war, I lost my home, and was literally thrown into the real world. I suppose I never really knew anything of relationships till now." Mattie continued to walk on, keeping up with the steady but slow progress of the wagon.

"I always believed things were either right or wrong. I imagined . . ."

"What did you imagine, Mattie," Nora prompted at her hesitation.

Mattie sighed and then shrugged. "I imagined friends were someone you could trust."

"And you can't trust me, is that it?"

"You're Callahan's friend."

"And I can't be yours, if I'm his?"

Mattie looked into Nora's clear gray eyes. She felt so confused. How could people like her and Jake, and Callahan, for that matter, act so normal, be so nice, and yet do whatever it was they were doing? "I guess I'm no judge of character," she finally admitted with a shrug.

Nora smiled. "I think you're right on that score."

Mattie shot her an expectant look, waiting for her to go on.

"You think Callahan's some sort of demon, don't you. Well I'd say you've made a whopper of a mistake in judgment there."

Mattie smiled, her disbelief apparent. "I'd expect you to be on his side."

"Mattie, why do you imagine his business to be illegal? Why do you always think the worst of him?"

"Why is he hiding the guns if it's not illegal?" she shot back. "Why won't he tell me what he's doing if there's nothing wrong?"

"Why can't you take the man on faith, Mattie? He did as much for you."

"When? What do you mean?"

"He knew from the first you weren't exactly who you said you were."

Mattie smiled sadly. "So, he told you that too, did he?" Suddenly her brow creased with confusion. "How could he have known that?"

"Does it really matter? He knew. And yet he believed, wanted to believe you were not what all the evidence pointed to."

"Evidence? What evidence? Nora, you're talking in riddles."

"I guess I am." Nora sighed. "I missed you. I missed our talks. I wanted to clear up this mess, but I see it can't be done. Not yet. I promise you, the minute I'm able, I'll tell you everything. That is, if Callahan doesn't beat me to it."

Mattie gave a humorless laugh of disbelief.

"He wants to, Mattie. It's tearing him up that he can't tell you."

Mattie laughed again. "No doubt."

"You'll never meet a man more worthy of your love, Mattie."

Mattie gasped and stopped short. "Love! Who said anything about love?"

221

"Don't you think everyone knows what's going on between you? Mattie, it shows every time you look at each other." Nora laughed at her look of astonishment. "No, I can see you didn't know it."

"I'm not in love with anybody," Mattie stated with a determination she didn't come close to feeling.

Nora nodded and dropped the subject. "Take care, Mattie," Nora said as she hurried ahead to her own wagon, "and remember, whether you believe it or not, we're all your friends."

Mattie grumbled as she walked alongside of the wagon. "All your friends." She'd have to be insane to believe that. Granted, she was coming to believe relationships were complicated. Much more complicated than she had first assumed, but one didn't base a friendship on lies. No matter how much they insisted, she'd never believe it.

If they truly believed her their friend, they would have told her what they were about. And Callahan, if he really felt more for her than a warm body to share his bed, wouldn't he have done the same?

Mattie sighed. She might be young and inexperienced, but she knew without honesty and trust, there could be no relationships of any sort.

Mattie glanced toward Callahan sitting high upon the wagon's seat. Nora had hinted at love. Could she mean . . . ? No! Mattie wouldn't allow the thought. They were just trying to get her on their side. Another trick. She wouldn't believe it. Would never believe a man could love a woman and keep a secret, even though it was sure to tear them apart.

"Do me a favor, will you? Keep the hell away from her."

"Callahan, I was just trying to . . ."

Callahan glared at Nora, his lips tightening to a thin line of anger. "I don't give a damn what you were trying to do. Stop meddling!"

"Hold on," Jake interrupted in a low, soothing voice. Before their words turned into a shooting match and caused attention, he turned toward them, trying to calm down the two of them as they stood toe to toe and raged at each other. "What happened to set you off?"

"Nothing happened, that's what. Except I can hardly get her to talk to me now." Callahan nodded his head toward Nora. "This big mouth here, thought she could set the world to rights. Well, she can't." He turned to face Nora. "And I want you to stop."

Nora fumed as Callahan stomped off toward his own campfire. "Stupid, ignorant bully. No wonder she's giving him such a hard time. It's beyond me what she finds so appealing in the man."

Jake chuckled as he listened to Nora's mutterings.

"Unlike myself, of course." Jake grabbed Nora's stiff body and pulled her down to his lap. He grinned as he ran his finger over her pouting mouth. His eyes shone with aching tenderness. If only he could tell her, if only he could be sure she'd want him still. Jake forced his dismal thoughts aside, determined to enjoy the moment and the lady in his arms. What would come, would come. Thinking about it made no difference. "I'm far from stupid. Well educated and haven't a bullying bone in my body."

Nora giggled. "Bullying? Are you sure there's such a word?"

"Positive. Didn't I just tell you, I'm well educated?"

Nora smiled. "Well, since you're so perfect, I'd be a fool to let you slip through my fingers, wouldn't I? Are you going to marry me or not?"

Jake grinned, his eyes widening with delight. "I thought the man was supposed to do the asking?"

Nora gave a slight shrug. "If a woman doesn't mind waiting until she's old and gray."

223

"Are you telling me I'm a bit slow getting to the point?"

"You might say that."

"Well, let's see," Jake teased, appearing to think on the matter, his blue eyes studying her face.

"What?" she asked as her teeth worried her bottom lip.

"I'm trying to think if you are everything I want in a woman."

"Of course I am. Why, any man would be thrilled to have me," Nora answered and began to enumerate her qualities as she counted on her fingers. "First of all, I'm reasonably good-looking. I'm easy to get along with. I have all my teeth. See?" She clamped her jaws together and opened her lips.

Jake tried but couldn't hold back the laughter. "Very romantic."

Nora shook her head, brushing aside his remark. "We're not talking romance here. We're talking qualifications." Again she began to count on her fingers. "My health is excellent. I'm great in bed." Nora gave him a knowing grin as she rapidly raised and lowered her brows. "And last, but certainly not least, I'll always remain faithful."

Jake laughed. "Just like a puppy?"

Nora grinned and poked his chest with her finger. "If you mean you can treat me like a dog and get away with it, forget it."

Nora tried to get up, but was held in place by Jake's arms. "Come to think of it, there is one thing I like about you."

Nora blinked. "One thing? Only one? What?"

Jake's mouth lost its humor as his lips lowered toward her own. "Let's go inside and I'll show you."

Nora sighed as he released her mouth after a long breathless kiss. "Now why can't they solve their problems as easily?"

"Maybe they don't love each other."

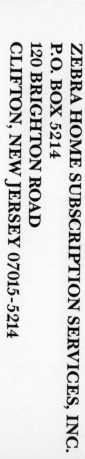

ACCEPT YOUR FREE GIFT AND EXPERIENCE MORE OF THE PASSION AND ADVENTURE YOU LIKE IN A HISTORICAL ROMANCE

Zebra Romances are the finest novels of their kind and are written with the adult woman in mind. All of our books are written by authors who really know how to weave tales of romantic adventure in the historical settings you love.

Because our readers tell us these books sell out very fast in the stores, Zebra has made arrangements for you to receive at home the four newest titles published each month. You'll never miss a title and home delivery is so convenient. With your first shipment we'll even send you a FREE Zebra Historical Romance as our gift just for trying our home subscription service. No obligation.

BIG SAVINGS AND FREE HOME DELIVERY

Each month, the Zebra Home Subscription Service will send you the four newest titles as soon as they are published. (We ship these books to our subscribers even before we send them to the stores.) You may preview them *Free* for 10 days. If you like them as much as we think you will, you'll pay just $3.50 each and *save $1.80 each month* off the cover price. *AND you'll also get FREE HOME DELIVERY.* There is never a charge for shipping, handling or postage and there is no minimum you must buy. If you decide not to keep any shipment, simply return it within 10 days, no questions asked, and owe nothing.

Nora's heart swelled with joy. Tears glistened her eyes, causing them to glow like polished silver in the firelight. Her fingers touched his jaw, and for the first time in her life, Nora felt shy. "You mean like us?"

Jake nodded and then kissed her again.

"I think they do," Nora whispered as she tugged on his ear with her teeth. "They just don't know how to go about showing it."

"Shall we give them a few lessons?" he asked, his lips nuzzling her neck.

"It's an idea, but I think we should get it perfect first." Nora's weary sigh belied the merriment in her eyes. "And you know what that means."

"Mmmm," Jake returned. "Let's go practice now."

"I said I'll do it! For God's sake what do you think I'll do, slice your throat?"

Callahan looked down at the tiny woman standing before him. One dark brow rose and an arrogant grin curved his lips. "The thought has crossed my mind."

Mattie's annoyance was obvious in her flashing eyes. She couldn't explain the sudden leap in her chest, or the resulting aggravation the flash of white teeth against his black beard seemed to have caused. All she knew was if he kept smiling like that she'd give him cause to worry all night. "If I didn't finish you off when I had the chance, what makes you think I'd do it now?"

"Why are you so anxious to help me?"

Mattie shot him a look of disgust. "I'm not in the least anxious, Mr. Callahan. If you want to chop your hair up, it's certainly your privilege."

Mattie couldn't explain her actions. She had offered to cut his hair before she even knew she was going to say the words. And his obvious suspicion only seemed to further her insistence.

Callahan almost smacked the scissor into her hand. His legs spread wide. His fists planted on his hips. His

225

eyes dared her to do her worst.

Mattie glared in return. "What should I do now? Go find a ladder?" she snapped as she turned and walked toward the fire. Mattie pointed to a nearby rock and ordered, "Sit."

It wasn't as if she hadn't cut hair before. She had often done this for her father and her brother. So why was she so nervous? Why were her hands shaking? Mattie refused to search for an answer. It didn't matter. She was simply doing for him what any wife would have done for her husband. And he was supposed to be her husband, wasn't he? Certainly anyone watching him struggle to cut his hair would grow suspicious at her lack of concern.

Mattie pulled her fingers through his hair and gave a silent gasp at the sudden ache that came to her chest. How could she have been so foolish as to not remember, not think of what touching him would do to her insides? Mattie took a step back and tried to stop the trembling that had suddenly overtaken her.

Callahan, unsuspecting of her extreme reaction, shot her an expectant glance.

Mattie took a deep breath and steeled herself for the torture she was sure to know. She swallowed and forced herself to lift a shining lock from his scalp. Mattie marveled, secretly luxuriating in the heavy silky texture. She had forgotten just how soft and thick it was. How pleasant to the touch. The scissor snipped the curl and it fell to his lap.

Automatically, Mattie reached for it, intending to brush it to the ground. Her hand stopped in mid-air, her cheeks grew pink as she realized exactly where it now rested.

Callahan grinned at her hesitation, his hips seemed to lift ever so slightly, daring her to touch him. "Go ahead. I don't mind."

Of course he would enjoy this, Mattie raged, her lips tightening with annoyance. There was little she could do that he didn't find reason to tease and taunt. The simplest, most innocent of actions became provocative in his eyes.

Callahan grunted as she again reached for his hair and gave a sharp tug. And yet the laughter never left his eyes. "Sorry," he said, and they both knew he didn't mean it.

Mattie's concentration on her task soon cooled the fire that had grown instantly to life at the touch of him. Before long she wasn't even conscious of his nearness, or of the fact that her leg leaned against the inside of his thigh, or that her breast brushed against his shoulder as she worked.

Callahan stiffened and Mattie giggled as she lathered his neck and reached for his straight razor. "Trust me, Callahan." She taunted him with the ominously familiar words.

Callahan turned to face her. For a long, endless moment their eyes met and held. Finally he nodded and turned his back.

Mattie's heart thundered in her chest. What did it mean? Was he telling her he'd trust her, but she didn't have it in her to do the same? But it wasn't the same. He knew she wouldn't do him harm. But what did she really know of this man? He had told her he'd kill anyone she told. Had he meant it? Or was he only trying to frighten her into silence?

Mattie sighed as she finished, listened to his stiff thanks, and watched him join his friends for a few moments of conversation before he went to bed.

Bed! Bed! Bed! Is that all there was to a relationship? Mattie grimaced and glared at his retreating back. Apparently it was, in his mind at least, for if he couldn't have her in his bed, he found little reason to waste his time in her company.

Mattie shrugged and allowed a heavy sad sigh. It was just as well. She was better off alone, better off by far. They did little but fight when together anyway.

227

"Soon, soon," Mattie murmured as she climbed into her wagon and prepared herself for bed. "This will all be over soon and you can forget his very existence."

Mattie turned, wriggling herself into a comfortable position among the quilts, all the while repeating as if a litany, "You'll forget. You'll forget." The only trouble was, when would she believe it.

Chapter Seventeen

Mattie clapped her hands. The delightful sound of her laughter floated on the air as she extended her hand toward the shy child and invited Clay Benson into the merry circle. Much to the delight of a dozen or so children, she was then pushed into the circle's center. The children giggled as she surveyed the lot with supposed fear. "Don't let him get me," she pleaded to their uproarious laughter and then screamed in mock terror as little Tommy Carson, grunting like a bull, tried to break through the circle of hand-holding children and tag her out.

When sheer force got him nowhere, he ducked beneath a pair of joined hands and raced for her. Mattie screamed again and charged out of the circle. But not in time. She was only an instant from safety when the little boy touched her back.

Mattie laughed as the children cheered. Obviously the thrill of winning out against an adult was something to savor. She was again part of the circle, when a harsh, deep voice brought the noisy, laughing children to a deadly silent stop.

"Clay," the slightly slurred voice rang out. "You goddamned useless bastard. Didn't I tell you to water those beasts?"

Clay Benson's face turned white with shock and then red with embarrassment. This wasn't the first time Mattie had heard the boy's stepfather lash out drunken obscenities. Mattie sighed with pity, although she knew better than to allow a flicker of the emotion to show, lest she add to Clay's growing mortification.

"I ain't no bastard," Clay answered sullenly, no doubt feeling forced to defend himself among his peers.

"You ain't, eh?" Martin Black chuckled, a mean-sounding laugh. "Well, I say you are. What are you going to do about it?"

Mattie's eyes widened with amazement. The man was actually goading his stepson into rebellion, no doubt hoping for an excuse to lay his strap into him.

Mattie's hand tightened on the boy's, hoping to dissuade the youngster's obvious impulse to fight back. But Mattie hadn't taken into consideration the matter of honor. In some respects, already years beyond the tender age of nine, Clay believed, no matter the indignities suffered, he had to defend himself and his mother, or forever lose face.

The children stared wide-eyed at the shivering nine-year-old, waiting for his next word, his next move. "My mother married my father," the boy said in a voice filled with pain and fear.

Martin Black threw his head back and laughed. "She told you that, did she? Well, she's a liar, just like her little bastard."

Mattie gasped with surprise that the man should so defame his own wife. Her mouth dropped open and her cheeks burned with humiliation as the thin woman in question came around the side of the wagon. There wasn't a doubt in Mattie's mind, Ada Black had heard everything he said and yet she gave not a flicker of acknowledgment. Her eyes lifted to her husband in a silent plea. Her hands raised as if to beg forgiveness for her very existence. "Martin," she said, her voice soft and sweetly southern, "the boy doesn't mean nothin'. Please."

"Shut up, woman. This is between me and your son."

Ada Black continued on, knowing as sure as she took her next breath what the outcome of this confrontation would be. It always ended this way. Every time the man took to his drinking, it came to violence.

"Martin, please," Ada continued as she moved closer.

Mattie watched with amazement. It was easy enough to see what the woman was doing. She was offering herself up, almost like a sacrificial lamb, in place of her son.

As if on cue, the boy broke free of Mattie's hold and raced to protect his mother. Mattie saw the punch coming and screamed as the man's fist contacted with the small boy's jaw. Clay Benson's thin legs crumbled and he fell to the ground.

Ada began to wail out her torment, only to receive a sharp slap and an ominous warning from her husband. "Shut your whining, woman."

It might have ended there, were it not for the fact that Ada ignored the blow she took to her head and tried to get to her unconscious son. Martin Black, even through his alcoholic haze, seemed to suddenly realize his form of punishment had had no effect. Apparently this left him decidedly unsatisfied. So he hit her again. And then again.

Silently, on flying feet, the children scattered, each back to the safety of their wagons and family while Mattie stood in helpless stupefaction and watched the scene unfold. Strangely enough, it seemed to her it had been played out before. Everyone appeared to know their parts and played them to the predestined finish.

If it weren't for the fact that Ada Black was taking a terrible beating, Mattie might have believed the whole thing staged. Even the cursing sounded without depth or any real emotion.

But Mattie couldn't deny the blood that spurted from Ada's often broken nose and split lip. Or the terrible almost animalistic groanings that filled the otherwise silent air.

Mattie looked wildly around her, desperately searching for someone to help. Although many stood by, she realized, almost at once, not a man among them would even raise his eyes to the goings-on. Mattie raged and silently branded each and every one a coward. Her dark eyes glared her disgust.

A huge stick, in truth more a small log, lay half burned upon a now-dead fire. Mattie grasped the stick with both hands and ran toward the screaming, helpless woman. With a grunt, Mattie swung the huge stick and contacted the blackened end, with no little force, upon the despicable man.

Martin Black would be sore the next morning, but for now the blow he had taken to his shoulder merely startled him. He turned to face his attacker, holding the limp form of his dazed and bleeding wife in one arm.

"Leave her alone," Mattie dared to order.

"This ain't none of your concern, missus."

"I said leave her alone," Mattie repeated as she held the stick menacingly before her. She prayed her fierce expression would leave him without a doubt that she was prepared to hit him again, should he continue his abuse.

Martin Black snarled at the nerve of this twit. "If you don't mind your business, I'll make you sorry."

Mattie laughed at his threat, and if her voice shook, he seemed not to notice. "You forget, Mr. Black, I'm neither a child nor your wife. I'm not afraid of your threats."

"So you're not afraid of me, eh?" he grinned, his eyes taking in Mattie's tiny form. His eyes widened with appreciation as he openly enjoyed what he saw. Particularly it was her bravery that appealed, for he had never before witnessed such in a woman. His grin grew wider, exposing rotted teeth, his eyes leering. "Maybe if I'd a married someone like you, I . . ."

"You'd already be dead, Mr. Black."

Martin Black threw his head back and laughed. "So you would have done me in, would you?" His expression grew more obviously leering. He licked his lips and Mattie fought against the shiver of disgust that ran through her.

But some part of his drunken mind remembered a huge, always lurking nearby husband. A husband with an evil glare that promised untold suffering should anyone dare come near his cherished wife.

Wisely, Martin Black forced aside the enticement she offered. No woman on earth was worth facing a husband like that. He shrugged. "Go away, lady. This ain't none of your business."

"I'm making it my business. Let her go."

Martin Black turned away from Mattie and faced his wife again. His disgust was clear as he gave her limp body a hard shake and taunted, "Who this bitch?" And just before he released her, he gave her another hard slap, snapping her head and laughing at the weak groan he had forced from her bloody, slackened lips.

Mattie heard the low roar of anguish come racing from behind her. She caught a blur of movement from the corner of her eye and watched as Clay ran smack into his stepfather. Of course there was no contest between the two, and a moment later Clay was taking much the same punishment his mother had suffered.

Mattie never thought of her actions, nor of the consequences they would no doubt bring. All she knew was someone had to stop this animal. She swung the stick again, this time taking careful aim and using all her strength. Her feet actually left the ground, so hard did she deliver her blow. She grunted with satisfaction as the stick bounced off his head. This time the man felt more than surprise. He turned, blinded with pain, shoved Clay aside, and lunged at his attacker.

But the vicious thrust of a meaty fist never contacted with Mattie's still form, for the instant before her jaw was to explode, she was whisked from harm's way and flung carelessly to the ground.

Callahan's fisted hand shot out and contacted with a clean sharp snap to the raging man's twisted face. Mattie watched, stunned into immobility, as Callahan landed another and then another. The man's eyes rolled back until only the whites showed. A second later he too was sprawled upon the ground.

Mattie was yanked to her feet by less than gentle arms. His hand clamped to her arm in a manacle hold and a minute later Mattie was stumbling behind a silent Callahan as he nearly dragged her back to their campsite.

In the comparative privacy of their campsite, he pulled to a sudden stop, spun around, and caught her by her shoulders. Mattie's bonnet fell to the ground. Pins flew every which way, hopelessly lost in the tall grass as he shook her shoulders with such intensity as to nearly snap her neck.

"Fool!" he ranted. "How dare you interfere between a husband and wife?"

Mattie wrenched herself free of his hold and reached out to the wagon in an attempt to steady her shaking legs. Bravely she faced him, refusing to cower before his rage. "How dare I not? The man was beating his family. The cowardly lot on this train simply stood by and watched."

"So you became their protectors?"

"Someone had to do it. I don't remember seeing you rushing to their aid."

"Because I know my place, lady. No one comes

between a man and his wife."

"Has he the right to abuse? Will all the world watch and not lift a hand?"

"You know the way it is."

"I don't care how it is. I'll never stand by and watch while a bully beats those weaker than him."

"What would you have done if he hit you?"

"I'd have hit him back."

"Just like that?" he asked incredulously.

"Just like that," she returned with a fierceness she'd never before suspected herself capable of.

Callahan laughed a mean sneer, knowing the ridiculousness of her intent. If the man had hit her, he would have had to kill him. Callahan's hands shook, so bad did he long to do the man harm. And why? Because a little smart-mouthed brat couldn't keep her nose from other people's business. "It seems to me you need a lesson in minding your own business, lady."

Mattie's jaw tightened at the thinly veiled threat. Callahan had taken much abuse from this woman, but she put his manhood on the line when her lips curled into a sneer. "And who do you think man enough to give it to me?"

Mattie knew she had gone too far, but she didn't know how to get out of it. Now that she had let her tongue rattle on, she was at a loss as to how to take the words back.

Callahan's mouth became a thin line of anger. He paled beneath his tan at her insult. "Why you . . ." His hands reached for her. "The day I can't handle a little runt like you . . ."

Mattie gasped. Even in cold rage, she had never suspected he would lay a hand on her. A moment later she grunted when she landed inside the wagon, her backside smarting painfully as it contacted with the wagon's unyielding floor.

Callahan pulled himself up behind her and loomed

menacingly above.

"What do you think you're doing?" she asked, and gave a silent curse at the trembling in her voice.

"I'm going to show you exactly who is man enough."

"Callahan," she warned, "if you touch me, I'll . . ." But when her warning only caused him to move closer, she scrambled away and instantly changed tactics. Instinctively she knew no amount of threats would waylay his intent. And that he was about to deliver a certain amount of abuse was indeed apparent. Her mind worked quickly toward self-preservation. And before she allowed her pride to step in the way, she blurted out, "I apologize. I didn't mean it."

The words were like a splash of cold water and seemed to instantly deflate his anger, at least the worst of it. In truth, he had no intentions of striking her. What he meant to do was to scare the living hell out of her, and perhaps shake her until her teeth rattled.

Callahan waited a long moment before he dared to ask, "No? What did you mean then?"

Mattie gave the tiniest of shrugs and nodded. Her words were stiff, barely audible when she spoke. "I didn't mean to insult you. I was upset."

Callahan grinned. He knew she was conducting a full-scale war against the urge to rail at him, no matter the consequences, but her common sense had taken firm hold. Obviously she considered it wiser to give in on this point, rather than risk the possible effects of a carelessly spoken word.

"You will, in the future, mind your own business, I take it."

"And if I can't?"

"You can and you will. I want your promise, Mattie."

Slowly she shook her head. "Callahan, I can't."

"Your promise," he insisted. "Right now."

"Or what? Will you beat me if I refuse?"

236

Callahan smiled. How little she knew him. Callahan couldn't imagine a time when he'd ever raise his hand to her, but she didn't have to know that. No, it was best if she never knew that. "If I must."

Mattie came to her feet. To apologize for a careless remark was one thing, but to allow this man control over her future actions was quite another. She didn't care what he said. She'd never allow abuse if it was within her power to stop it. Bravely she faced him, her stubborn chin raised as she awaited his reaction. "You might as well start."

Callahan never expected her answer and blinked with surprise. Damn her! She wasn't the least bit afraid, or maybe she was. He studied her eyes. Yes, fear lurked in their depths, but she had pushed what she could of it aside, believing herself right in her actions. Callahan couldn't stop his smile of admiration and the glowing warmth that entered his eyes.

"Mattie, your bravery could someday get you into a lot of trouble."

Mattie gave him a soft smile. "It's not bravery, Mr. Callahan. I was so scared, I couldn't move even when I saw his punch coming."

"And yet you'd do it again?"

"How can I not? How can anyone watch a woman beaten until she was bleeding, or a boy brought down with the power of one punch."

"The law is not on your side, Mattie. A man has the right to do what he will to his family."

"Then the law should be changed."

Callahan smiled at her simplistic reasoning. "Perhaps it will be someday, but for now . . ."

"For now," she interrupted, her heart pounding, for suddenly his tender smile was more terrifyingly dangerous than Black's drunken rages ever could be, "I think it's best to get dinner started."

* * *

Mattie heard it again. It wasn't her imagination. Someone was crying. She glanced around, an automatic reaction, but foolish to be sure, for here in the dark, outside the circle of wagons, she couldn't have seen her hand held before her eyes.

The sky had been overcast all day, the clouds heavy with the promise of rain and the night offering no relief or safe harbor from the coming storm. The stars and moon were covered with thick, low-lying clouds that allowed not a glimmer of light to pass through.

Alternately Mattie raged at the lack of light, since she often stumbled like a drunken fool over the uneven landscape of the treeless plains and then blessed the cover of darkness, which offered her the only privacy she was likely to get.

Mattie shivered in the cool, moist air and pulled her wrap closer around her slender body. For a long moment, she stood perfectly still and listened. She heard a sniff and then a soft sob. Her cheeks grew pink as she realized just how close the sound was. It was the middle of the night. She had come out here to answer nature's call, no matter Callahan's insistence that she remain inside at night and use the chamber pot and she'd never expected another to be about.

Mattie felt a moment's pity, for the poor soul sounded as if the world had come to an end. Clearly the cries were not that of pain but of sorrow.

"Who's there?" Mattie called out, only to receive silence for an answer.

"I know someone is there. I'll call the guard if you don't answer."

"It's me" came a small, watery voice.

"Where are you?"

"Here" came the answer.

"Great," Mattie mumbled to herself. "Me and here. That's a big help."

238

Mattie moved toward the sound of the voice. It was a child, she knew, but what was he or she doing out at this time of night? Suddenly she realized he must have been about the same business as she. "Have you fallen? Are you hurt?"

"No" came a shuddering sigh.

"Then what are you doing here?"

"Nothing."

Mattie scowled. Nothing. Definitely a child.

"Who are you? I can't see!"

"It's Clay, Miz Callahan."

"Oh," she responded. "Are you crying, Clay?"

"Uh uh" came the answer.

Mattie smiled. Of course he would deny it. That was a stupid question. Mattie found him at last. Actually they found each other and sort of banged into each other as they groped in the dark. "You didn't fall, or hurt yourself did you?"

"No."

Mattie sighed. "Well, I guess everything is all right then."

"I guess."

"I thought I heard someone crying. Did you hear it?"

No answer. He was probably shaking his head.

"Why don't we sit down and talk for a minute," Mattie invited. She knew he sat at her side only because his booted foot kicked her in the ankle. After a moment of silence, she said. "You know, Clay, if a person feels bad, it's okay to cry. It doesn't matter if he's a boy or a girl."

Silence.

"Do you believe that?"

"No. Only sissies cry."

"Who told you that rubbish?" But Mattie already knew.

"My stepfather."

239

Mattie grunted. "Does he always tell the truth?"

Mattie imagined the boy shrugged. No answer.

"So why do you believe him?"

"He's a man. He doesn't cry."

"I'd wager he'd cry fast enough if somebody beat him up all the time."

"Oh I wasn't crying because of that," he said so bravely that Mattie felt her heart like to burst.

"You weren't?"

"No."

"Why then?"

"It's just . . ." A long hesitation. "Things."

"You know, I might be able to help, if I knew these things."

Clay breathed a long sigh and was silent for endless moments. Mattie was about to give up, believing his long silence a refusal to take her up on her offer, when she finally heard his hesitant reply. "The kids. They make fun of me. 'Cause of what he says."

Mattie silently called the man every name she ever knew plus the few she had learned since starting this trip. "And that bothers you, does it?"

"It bothers me some. But mostly it's my mother. They say bad things about her."

No doubt, Mattie silently remarked, knowing children to possess their own particularly cruel form of inhumanity.

"She married my father, Miz Callahan. I swear it! He died in the war. I ain't no bastard and she ain't no . . ." He broke off and Mattie could only imagine the effort it took not to cry again.

Mattie felt the pain stab at her chest. She longed to take him in her arms and cuddle him close to her breast, but she didn't dare. Somehow she knew if she touched him he'd close up and probably run back to his wagon. He already had a mother, what he needed now was a friend. "Clay, you don't have to swear it to

240

me. I believe you. Besides, it isn't anyone's business but yours.

"Look," she went on, "I don't take to violence. As a matter of fact, I'm the first one to say keep your hands at your sides. But if anyone ever," she repeated and emphasized the word, "ever called my mother names, I'd give him a shiner the size of Missouri."

Clay giggled. God, he was so young. Mattie shook her head, wondering why life was so unjust.

"You think I'll get in trouble?"

"I think whomever is mean enough to say such a thing won't dare tell his father why his eye is black and blue."

Mattie could just feel his smile.

"One thing, though," she offered as a warning. "I wouldn't do anything if others were around. If your father got word of it, he might . . ."

"He ain't my father!" Clay almost shouted. And then finished in a softer voice, "But I know what you mean."

They sat for a time in companionable silence. "Feel better now?" Mattie finally asked.

Mattie grinned. Apparently he nodded his head again.

"I think we should be getting back. Someone might notice one or both of us gone."

Together they walked back to the camp. In the light of the low-burning fires, they whispered their goodnights.

Mattie smiled as she watched him walk toward his wagon. For the first time since she'd known him, his back appeared straight, his walk almost a swagger. Mattie shook her head. She couldn't believe she had actually told him it was all right to beat up somebody. Probably the worst advice she'd ever give, she mused. Still, she had no other answers. She only wished she did.

Mattie stifled a startled scream as Callahan came

241

around the wagon, a rifle in his hand. "Where the hell were you?"

Mattie's face turned red. It was impossible for her to talk about such personal things with this man, even though he seemed to take the private workings of the human body so casually in his stride.

"I went for a walk."

"Right, you don't get enough exercise during the day." Callahan brushed aside her explanation. "I know why. What I want to know is what took you so long? I've been out there searching the grass for your body."

Mattie's cheeks flamed. Good God! Imagine if he had come across her in the midst . . . She couldn't finish the thought. Her body gave an involuntary shudder.

Callahan shot her a look of disgust and shook his head. "Lady, do you think you're the only one? We're all human beings on this train. If you eat you gotta . . ."

"Mr. Callahan!" Mattie interrupted, her voice rising dangerously close to a shriek. She hadn't a doubt as to what he was going to say and she definitely did not want to hear it. "The next time I leave the wagon at night I expect you to honor my right to privacy."

"Why? I haven't so far."

"What?" she squeaked, aghast at the mere thought.

"I followed you every time."

"Good God! Why?"

"To make sure you got back here safe. What do you think? I like to watch?"

"You don't." Please God, let him tell her he never watched her.

The wicked thought, to tease her, did cross his mind, but Callahan, realizing correctly her horror, quickly relented. "No, I don't." He grinned at her obvious sigh of relief. "I just stand close enough to hear if you scream."

Callahan looked over his shoulder at the Blacks' wagon and watched Clay roll himself into a blanket beneath it.

"What were you doing with the kid? Was he lost?"

"No, we were talking."

"Yeah?" he asked, obviously making it his business to find out about what.

After a few moments Mattie shrugged. "I just told him to blacken the eye of the next person who made fun of him." Mattie shot a grinning Callahan a meaningful glare. "Good advice, don't you think?"

"If you're big enough to do it," he said innocently enough, but Mattie knew, from the glitter of merriment in his eyes and the trembling of his lips, he had just issued an out-and-out dare.

Refusing to be drawn into his teasing, Mattie remarked, "Oh, I don't think size has all that much to do with it. Determination will win out, wouldn't you agree?"

Callahan's arm circled Mattie's waist as he walked her to the back of their wagon. "You might be right. A man might achieve everything he wants with enough determination."

Mattie gave a silent groan. He had done it again. Of course he was talking about their relationship, or more to the point, their lack of one. How did he always manage to shift the conversation along these lines?

Mattie shot him a look of annoyance, just before he slid his rifle inside, jumped into the wagon, and pulled her up behind him. "As might a woman, Mr. Callahan."

"Ah yes," he whispered, his hands refusing to relinquish his hold at her waist. "But suppose two are of equal mind, and yet their objectives differ? What then?"

"Equal determination, you say?"

243

Callahan nodded. "What then?"

Mattie sighed, knowing full well his attempt to trap her. "Then it's in the hands of fate, don't you think?" Mattie pulled herself free of his arms and walked toward her bedding. "Good night, Mr. Callahan."

Callahan's answer was a low silky chuckle that raised the hackles at the back of her neck, for he knew she hadn't taken into account the many times a man could take charge of his own fate.

Chapter Eighteen

"He's never ridden a horse. Can you imagine?"

Callahan nodded as he pulled the girth tight under Thunder's belly. Effortlessly he threw the heavy saddle over Apple's broad back. "I guess that's not unusual for a city kid."

Mattie shrugged her agreement. "I never thought his father would let him go. How did you ever get him to agree?"

Callahan glanced up as he bent to tighten the saddle and grinned. "I threatened to turn my wife on him again. Believe me, the man isn't as stupid as he looks."

Mattie grinned and turned shyly away. No doubt Callahan would forever remind her of her attack on the man, something she would obviously prefer to forget.

A gentle breeze pressed the loose shirt she wore against her slender back and shapely bottom. "You know, I'm beginning to think you were right. Trousers are definitely more appropriate for riding."

Mattie turned back to face him, one brow lifting skeptically. "Why the sudden change of heart?"

Callahan's almost insolent gaze moved over her slim form. He shrugged. "I can see you have greater freedom. I'd just prefer you to wear them only when we are alone."

Mattie shot him a scathing glance. His possessive

attitude didn't sit at all well with her. "A pity then, you have so little to say about it, isn't it?"

Callahan grinned. Soon enough, my lovely, he promised himself. The day isn't far away when I'll have everything to say about what you do. He gave a casual shrug. "The shirt helps."

Mattie glanced down at the oversized shirt she had borrowed from Callahan that morning and scowled. It came nearly to her knees and hid every curve of her body from view. "Helps? I think it hides more completely than does a nun's habit."

They had argued earlier when it became clear she wasn't going riding in skirts, but intended to wear the borrowed trousers. After a heated discussion, Callahan finally suggested she wear his shirt as well. Rather than prolong the argument, Mattie gave in to his request and both appeared pleased enough at the results, Mattie, because her comfort was ensured, and Callahan, because she wasn't shaking her beautiful bottom for the appreciation of every male eye.

"Here he comes."

"Did you pack our lunch?"

"Right here." Callahan nodded as he patted the saddlebags.

It was decided that until Clay had grown used to the feel of the back of a horse, he would ride double with Callahan. If all went as planned at their picnic, he would have his first lesson at riding alone.

Later, Mattie smiled as she stretched out upon a quilt, the remains of their lunch already packed away. She watched Callahan lead Apple in large circles, with Clay clinging to the saddle horn.

Shouts of laughter bubbled from the young boy and mingled sweetly with the gentle murmur of a summer breeze as it whispered through the tall grass. Overhead the sky was bright blue, while white puffy clouds swirled happily upon the far-off horizon.

Mattie returned the boy's wave and smiled at his apparent ecstasy just before she closed her eyes against the bright warmth of the sun and began to drift into a light doze.

Callahan suddenly flung himself beside her with a loud groan. "How come you get to lie here while I do all the work?"

Mattie gave a low, wicked laugh as she glanced at his smiling eyes. "That's easy. You're the man."

"So?"

"So, you're bigger and stronger than me."

"If that's the case, why aren't I making you do it while I rest?"

"Because you're gallant and know I'm tired?"

Callahan shook his head.

"Because you're kindhearted?"

Callahan grinned. "Try again."

"A gentleman?"

"I doubt it."

"Mmmm, me too." Mattie giggled at the warning glare that shot her way. "Why then?"

"Because I'm not as smart as you."

Mattie laughed. "It does wonders for the soul to admit the truth, doesn't it, Callahan?"

"Does it?"

"I know it makes me happy."

Callahan rested his weight upon his elbow as he looked down at her. His eyes darkened as his hand toyed with a lock of her hair and watched the raven curl twist around his finger. "Are you happy, Mattie?"

Mattie gave a soft smile as she watched the flight of an eagle in the far-off distance. Her thoughts

247

returned to the happiness she had known as a child and young girl. Her eyes clouded with pain as she remembered the war and everything it had taken from her. Mattie sighed. At least the war was over along with, she hoped, the worst of her suffering. For that she could be grateful. Finally she shrugged. "I'm not terribly unhappy. I guess that's good enough."

"Is it?"

"What more can anyone expect?"

He shrugged. "Some people are lucky enough to find real happiness."

Mattie shrugged. "Those who are more blessed, I imagine."

Callahan shook his head. "No, not more blessed, just smart enough not to throw their chance away."

Mattie shot him a look of suspicion. "I assume you're telling me something."

Callahan lay down upon his back, his hands beneath his head. His mouth curved into a decidedly secret grin. "I told you you were smart."

Callahan twitched his nose. His eyes remained closed, as he listened to the soft giggles coming from somewhere behind him. Again something touched his face. Pretending to still be asleep, he moaned and turned his face.

Again the giggles.

Callahan opened his eyelid a crack. A feather tied to a string, tied in turn to a thick reed of grass danced just above his face. He closed his eyes and forced himself to give no reaction when it again descended.

"Maybe it fell off."

"It didn't" came Mattie's conspiratorial whisper. "It ain't doin' nothin'."

"It will."

Again the feather touched his face. Callahan held back his grin and waited.

"It must've fallen off."

"Hold the stick. Wait here and I'll look."

Callahan heard her noisy shuffle among the tall grass. He waited patiently for her to come nearer.

Mattie bent down and grinned as she watched the feather dance across his skin. She glanced behind her to see Clay peek his head out of the grass.

Suddenly she screamed as Callahan gave a mighty roar and sprang to his feet in almost one movement. In an instant she was running, but it was too late. Already his hands reached for her waist. Effortlessly she hung at his side, bouncing against him as he started after Clay.

The three of them were gasping for their next breath by the time he caught the boy and flung the two of them to the ground. Menacingly he stood above his prisoners and watched Mattie and her cohort dissolve into giggles.

"Whose idea was it?"

Each of them pointed to the other, their answers adding to their laughter.

"His."

"Hers."

It took some effort, but he managed to keep his grin at bay. Callahan rubbed his chin and began to pace the ground at their feet. "I see. Both equally guilty. Now what punishment do you think just?"

Clay's eyes darkened, but his moment of fear quickly dissipated at Mattie's happy giggle. "There are two of us and only one of you."

Callahan nodded. "Granted. But I'm the man, remember?" he asked, apparently referring to their earlier conversation.

"Right, but I'm smarter." Mattie lunged to her feet the moment Callahan's back was turned, and was yards away before he managed to catch her again.

She was laughing, as his arms held her securely against him. Her body grew soft and yielding as she forgot the enforced distance she had recently maintained and collapsed happily against him.

His blue eyes darkened as he greedily absorbed the beauty of her. He couldn't imagine anything lovelier, and silently promised to give her laughter for the rest of their days together. And that they would spend them together, he had no doubt.

Callahan's heart swelled with a love so achingly pure he was helpless but to tremble beneath its mighty force. "But not smart enough to ever get away from me," he promised just before his lips claimed hers in a smoldering kiss.

Mattie's laughter turned instantly to sensual pleasure as his mouth and tongue worked its magic. A soft sigh of delight slipped from her throat as his lips lingered and teased her sensitive, moist flesh.

Only the sound of Clay's young voice, heavy with disgust, caused them to remember they were not alone. "You all always do that junk?"

Mattie giggled as she watched Callahan's mouth silently repeat the word "junk," his expression clearly showing his astonishment.

A grin twitched at his lips. "All right then, what do you think I should do to her?"

Clay shrugged and then remarked hopefully, "You could tickle her."

"No, he couldn't," Mattie announced with absolute finality. "Think of something else."

Callahan's brows rose and fell in rapid succession "Personally, I like the boy's idea."

"I'm sure you do." Her eyes glared a warning.

"Think of something else."

Callahan's sigh told her just how much of a spoil-sport he thought her. "What do you think, Clay? Should we make her eat a worm?"

Clay laughed with childish delight as he danced in a circle and clapped his hands. His eyes widened with excitement. "And then could we watch her throw up?"

"I thought you were my friend?" Mattie asked, her eyes wide with indignant surprise. She shot Callahan a look of disgust and elbowed him in the stomach, in an effort to stop his laughing.

Clay gave her a blank look, wondering what being her friend had to do with anything?

"Besides, how did I become the villain here? What about him?" She nodded toward a giggling Clay.

"Tsk, tsk." Callahan shook his head. "Trying to shift the blame to a helpless child, lady? We both know you were the brains behind the crime." His gaze returned to the small child. "This poor lad, like most of the male species, had no chance against your feminine wiles."

While laughter danced in his eyes, he gave her a long, searching look and suggested, "Maybe she could give us piggyback rides?"

"Naw, she's too small," Clay returned, his tone clearly implying her to be of little use because of her diminutive size.

"What then?"

Clay shrugged. "I guess you could kiss her again. That's disgusting enough."

Callahan grinned, his eyes alighting with absolute approval. "You heard the man."

Mattie moaned. It was getting worse. The man never touched her that her world didn't tip at an alarming angle or shift dangerously out of focus.

Now she could literally feel the ground shaking beneath her feet. Mattie pulled her mouth free of his kiss when something hard bounced off her head. For a second she thought Clay was throwing rocks.

"Ow!" she grunted as another hit her shoulder. "Clay, what are you . . . ?" Maggie never finished the sentence as Callahan stiffened and pulled abruptly away. His eyes scanned the horizon. The sound of thunder rumbled somewhere in the distance and a flash of lightning split a jagged line across a sky that had somehow separated into two distinct halves. One blue and clear, the other alarmingly dark and menacing.

Mattie stared in amazement, her hands reaching automatically to protect herself against the fist-size hail that suddenly beat upon their heads. What in the world was happening?

Callahan's heart pounded with fear. In the far-off distance came a thick, black, speeding funnel of death. There was no sense in trying to make it back to the wagons, for those on the train stood no better than he against this monstrous force of nature.

Callahan dropped to his knees and began to dig at the ground with his bare hands.

"What are you doing?" Mattie asked, her eyes wide with confusion and dawning fear. She'd have to be deaf and blind not to have noticed his anxiety. What in the world was the matter?

"Don't just stand there. Dig, damn it!"

Mattie never thought to argue. She didn't know why, but she knelt across from him and joined him in his efforts. "Why? Why are we doing this?"

"Hurry," Callahan ordered.

"What's happening?" Mattie insisted as she flung soil from the opening he had begun.

Callahan glanced over his shoulder and cursed at

252

the oncoming cloud. Mattie's gaze followed his.

TORNADO! The word chilled her heart, causing her to waste precious seconds in frozen panic. But an instant later, Callahan's loud curses filtered through her fear and clumps of dirt began to fly from the ground. Faster, faster she worked, never feeling her nails break, nor the deep scratches caused by small sharp rocks. Terror froze her blood and brought a breathless pounding to her chest as the dreaded sound began to wind itself over the tall grass directly toward them. The sound at first was so low she had mistaken it for rumbling thunder. But it wasn't thunder. It was a deep, almost groaning but continuous lament of death, that grew louder as every second brought it closer.

"Clay!" Callahan yelled. "Get over here."

But Clay couldn't move. Open mouthed with shock, he watched the enormous black cloud brush the earth and head right for him. And still he couldn't move. He tried, he really did, but his legs just wouldn't work. Tears blurred his vision. He didn't think about dying. He only knew he was afraid. More afraid than ever in his life.

Callahan cursed. "Don't stop!" he ordered as he left her to fetch the boy.

The sound was growing in strength. The earth literally trembled as if cowering before a force of such might. Mattie's hands moved faster than she'd ever known possible. The wind whipped her hair wildly around her face, and brought tears to her eyes until she could see nothing. But she hadn't even the time to wipe them away. Without thinking, she knew every second wasted was a second closer to death. By the time Callahan returned with the boy, a ditch had been cleared. Callahan dumped the boy inside and yelled, "Don't move."

"Hurry, Mattie, God, hurry," Callahan muttered, but it was too late. She couldn't hear a sound over the roar. It sounded like the train she had taken to Independence, only louder, much louder.

It wasn't nearly deep enough, but they had run out of time. Callahan pushed Mattie almost face first into the pit, alongside a shivering Clay. Mattie landed with a dull thud, but rolled instantly to her back, more afraid not to see. Callahan almost jumped on top of her, knocking the breath from her with the force of his weight. His arm circled the boy, and the three huddled together, helpless against nature gone berserk.

"Close your eyes," he yelled, his mouth only inches from her ear and yet she was barely able to hear him.

Mattie's arms went instinctively around him, holding on for dear life. She buried her face in his neck, unable to stop the screams as the funnel ripped the sound from her throat.

It was upon them, bellowing, louder, louder, screeching, screaming until Mattie wondered if they hadn't died and gone to hell. The roaring, thunderous winds tore a wide path across the earth. It wrenched anything at ground level, scooping plant and animal alike into its slender, ever-moving, ever-blackening cone. Gusts of wind sucked away all sound only to instantly replace it with ear-splitting howls. Howls that ominously resembled mocking laughter, screeching its joy as if to ridicule their shivering terror.

Mattie felt his lips on her cheek. She felt rather than heard his words. He was speaking to her, but she couldn't hear anything above the horror that circled them. Her arms pulled him tighter to her. Dust filled her every breath. She began to choke, searching suddenly for air. On the verge of panic, she began to fight his weight, which only seemed to further inhibit her breathing. Callahan pulled her more firmly beneath him, pressing her face into his chest.

And then even the dust was gone. There was no air. Everything, including her breath, was sucked into the greedy wild cavern of black death.

Mattie moaned out the last of her panic as the steady beating of his heart finally brought a moment's sanity into a world gone suddenly insane and eased the terror that threatened to overtake her.

And just as it came, it began to recede. The sound of a thousand locomotives raced off to distant lands, leaving an empty, eerie silence in its wake.

Callahan shifted, his arm still around the silently sobbing boy. Gently he patted Clay's rump. "You all right?"

Clay nodded.

"Go check the horses, will you?"

Clay moved from their side, wiping away the telltale sign of his fear with the backs of his hands. Within moments he forgot the terror he had known. It wasn't as if he hadn't been afraid. He had been. But more than fear, he had felt excitement. With childlike innocence, Clay had believed himself protected in the company of Mr. and Miz Callahan and wouldn't realize for years to come the frailty of human lives.

Callahan shifted his weight, leaning on his elbows. "How about you? Are you all right?"

Now that the danger had passed, Mattie began to shake. Her lips quivered when she tried to smile and tears streaked her dust-covered face. Mattie couldn't talk so great was the urge to cry.

Callahan had to fight against the need to whoop

and yell, as a wave of joyous relief flooded his being. Suddenly he felt an almost overwhelming urge, so powerful it nearly rivaled the tornado in strength, to take her in his arms and reaffirm the life to which they had so desperately clung in the most basic of ways. And had they been alone, he would have done just that. A smile curved his lips and twinkling light entered in his eyes. "I didn't hurt you, did I?"

"No," she answered, as yet too shaken to even notice his exhilaration.

"Nothing broken?"

"I don't think so."

"Perhaps I should make sure."

His hands moved over her neck and shoulders, down her arms. He touched her waist and slid his fingers beneath her shirt under the pretense of examining her ribs.

Mattie's gaze rose to meet his, her heartbeat growing erratic, her breathing shallow. A thrill of excitement shivered down her spine. She desperately needed this moment. She felt as if she'd burst into a million pieces if he didn't wipe away the fear. His hands moved over her diaphragm, growing daring, moving higher, higher. She gasped as they touched and lingered with bold possession at the soft flesh of her breasts.

"Mmmm." His teeth flashed white against his dark beard. "Everything seems to be working properly."

Mattie knew she should have raged at his outrageous behavior. She even managed a sneer of sorts, but her lips refused to continue their show of distaste. Abandoning her attempt, she shook away what should be and laughed with pure enjoyment. "And you insist you are only checking to make sure nothing is broken?"

"Of course. What else do you think?"

"Callahan, I don't recall ever having bones there."

"Here?" he asked as if surprised by this newfound knowledge. He flicked aside the straps of her chemise, cupped the soft flesh, and gently rolled the sensitive tips between his thumbs and fingers. "Are you sure?"

Mattie almost, but not quite, held back her groan. "Positive."

"What ever made me think you did?"

"Callahan, you are a beast to take advantage of a lady."

"Am I taking advantage of you?"

"You are."

Callahan grinned. "You only have to tell me to stop, you know."

Mattie was growing decidedly more breathless by the moment. "Is that all I have to do?"

"That's all."

"Then perhaps I'd better." Her breathing was no more than a shuddering sigh. She couldn't help it, her hips lifted automatically toward him.

"Shall I say it now?" Her eyes fluttered closed.

Callahan groaned and then shuddered with pleasure as she moved again. "You could wait a minute or so."

"Mmmm. Do you imagine any harm could come of it, should I take your advice?"

"None that I know of."

"Apple's missing! I can't find her anywhere!"

The mood was shattered in an instant. Callahan's lips tightened with dread as he rolled to his feet and helped Mattie out of the shallow ditch.

It only took a second for them to realize the boy was right. Apple was gone. Mattie could only pray he had run for safety. Callahan could only hope he didn't know better.

"What are we going to do?" She spoke to Callahan's back as he bent down to examine the bloody gash in Thunder's flank. Blood ran the length of his leg.

Callahan's mouth was grim, his eyes dark with emotion when he faced her at last. "Walk."

"Is it bad?" Mattie asked, nodding toward the horse.

Callahan nodded. "He was hit with something. Cut him to the bone. Later I might have to . . ." He let the sentence hang. "We'll see."

This time they heard it together. Mattie gasped. "Not again!"

Callahan shook his head. It couldn't happen, could it? A twister could easily turn course, but did they ever turn back? He couldn't remember hearing of such a thing. His eyes searched out the horizon for a reappearance of the long funnel. He was looking up and almost missed the dark brown wave of motion that streamed over a distant, low-lying hill. His body stiffened with shock.

"Jesus Christ, NO!"

Desperately he looked around him, not at all sure which direction to run, not at all sure either way would make any difference.

Callahan grabbed his rifle. He should put a bullet between Thunder's eyes. It would be more humane than to leave the animal helpless against a stampeding herd of buffalo, but he knew he might need every bullet the gun held.

He looked to his left. To his right, his mouth twisted with indecision. They had only one chance. He couldn't afford to hesitate. Quickly he scooped Clay into his arms and gave Mattie a hard shove. "Run!" he yelled. "Mattie, run!"

The herd appeared to be perhaps five miles away,

258

but stretched over an ominous mile wide. And Mattie and Callahan were running directly across its path.

From the side of her eye she could see it coming nearer. Her heart pounded in her ears, mingling with the sound of thundering hooves. Sweat poured into her eyes and burned, almost blinding her. A throbbing pain began in her side, but Mattie refused to give in to it. Later, she promised herself. If she made it, later.

It didn't seem to matter how hard she ran. She couldn't escape it. The herd was coming closer, their hoofbeats nearly drowning out the gasping sounds of her breathing, the pounding of her pulse in her ears. Blinded by fear, set off no doubt by the twister, the buffalo ran on, their every step bringing the three of them closer to certain death.

It was obvious they weren't going to make it. From somewhere in the back of her mind she knew they were going to die. They had come nearly to the edge of the herd, but she could see it was too late.

Callahan stopped and flung Clay into Mattie's arms. Her knees almost buckled with the added weight. "Keep running," he yelled. And when she hesitated, suddenly unable to leave him, he bellowed, "Run, damn you!"

Instinctively Mattie did as she was told. Everything was happening so quickly, she hadn't time to think on her motives. But the natural instinct to survive was too strong to disobey his orders.

Mattie glanced over her shoulder. Callahan was holding the rifle up as if taking aim at the sun. He fired a shot, and Mattie prayed, never looking back, that the wild-eyed beasts would turn in the hoped-for direction. If they didn't, not one of them was going to live to tell about it.

He fired another shot and then another. All of a sudden they veered off as one and turned from their human target. They weren't out of danger yet. Most of the buffalo followed one after another, but all they needed was one to move off course and those behind it would follow.

Mattie was some distance beyond the herd before she finally stopped. The pain in her side was so severe as to bring her to her knees. Each gasping breath only seemed to add to her agony as air singed her starved lungs.

Callahan was beside her, his arms around her, Mattie, sobbing with relief, turned into his embrace. She clung to him, breathing deep into her lungs the delicious scent of him. Her hands moved with desperate strokes over his shoulders and back as if to reassure herself he really was there.

"I didn't think we were going to make it." Her voice shook as tears rolled down her cheeks.

"It was close. Too close," he soothed as he ran his hands over her back. "You are all right, aren't you?"

Clay sat nearby, watching the herd speed off into the distance. Now that the danger had passed, his eyes filled with excitement. Boy, was he going to have stories to tell the kids. They wouldn't make fun of him after this. Suddenly his attention moved to the two clinging adults. His eyes widened with undisguised awe. "Do you always have this much fun on a picnic?"

"I don't think we came this far. Are you sure we're going in the right direction?"

Callahan shot her a look of annoyance. That was about the tenth time she had asked the same question. Combine her nagging with the heat of the day and he had a ways to go before improving his humor. It was almost dusk, and only now did the sun begin to ease its blazing heat. The fact that they were dangerously low on water and had to ration what they had left, didn't help matters any either.

After the buffalo had disappeared over the horizon, they had returned to their picnic site, and from a badly mangled Thunder retrieved water, saddlebags, saddle, and blankets.

The canteen had been crushed almost flat, but amazingly still held enough fluid to see them back to camp. Only they weren't going to make it tonight.

Mattie sighed. "There's no need for you to give me evil looks. I just want to make sure."

"I'm sure," he snapped, his exhaustion making quick work of his patience. "Take my word for it."

Mattie fought back the tears. He hadn't really hurt her feelings. She was just tired, and near anything was apt to make her cry.

A half hour later, Callahan said, "It'll be dark soon. We'd better make camp."

"Here? Alone?"

Callahan lifted one brow and remarked sarcastically, "If you want to invite company, go right ahead."

"You know what I mean. It's not safe out here alone. You told me that about a million times."

"I know what I said. But we have no choice."

"Why don't we just go on?"

"And end up walking in circles?"

"Can't you read the stars?"

Callahan grinned. "As a matter of fact I can. But I'd need a mighty tall ladder to do it tonight."

Mattie gazed at the darkening sky, noticing for the first time the thick, low clouds and sighed as she slumped to the ground. "Will it rain, do you think?"

Callahan shook his head. "Not for a few hours. By

then someone will come looking for us."

Mattie laughed. "If you're waiting for Mr. Cassidy to send out a search party, forget it. He'll be just as happy to never see us again."

"Someone will come."

"Your friends?"

"They could be yours too, if you wanted."

"How can I . . ."

"Let's not go into that again," Callahan interrupted. "I told you I'll tell you everything as soon as I can." He looked around and shrugged. One place was as good as another. They might as well camp here.

No doubt after it was too late to stop whatever it was he was doing, Mattie remarked silently. Mattie strove to find her anger, but failed dismally. She couldn't hate him anymore. She didn't have the strength. All she wanted to do was lie down and sleep.

Dried buffalo chips were gathered and Callahan soon had a fire going. There might not be much in the way of supper, but at least they'd be warm until help came.

Mattie's stomach growled. They had eaten the remains of lunch, what there was of it, but she was still hungry, and more than that, she was thirsty.

But her hunger and thirst were nothing compared to her need for sleep. Mattie had never slept outside before. Her fears of all things slithery and crawly didn't even enter her mind. Minutes after she finished their meager supper, she was fast asleep.

Deep in exhausted sleep Mattie never felt him slide into the warmth of her blanket. She murmured something incoherent and fell instantly back to sleep as she snuggled close against him. A soft sigh escaped her lips as she rested her head upon his arm.

In the light of the fire, Callahan had watched for a long time, before giving in to the need to join her. Clay was asleep, snuggled deep inside the horse blanket, while Mattie had taken the quilt used earlier at the picnic.

Holding her close against him, Callahan reviewed the events of this wild day. He shuddered as he realized how easily her life might have been snuffed out, lost to him forever.

His arms tightened. His face nuzzled against her silky hair. A deep, shuddering sigh slipped from his lips. He had tried not to love her. Fearing for his very sanity, he had tried not to get involved. But he might as well have tried not to breathe, for that effort would have brought about the same results. It could not be done.

That he loved this woman, above his very life, he couldn't deny. And love her he would for all time. What he needed now was to convince her to love him in return. Callahan was a man of the world. He knew when a woman felt a measure of attraction for him. But damn this stubborn woman, if she didn't control those feelings past all endurance.

Callahan smiled as he breathed in the scent of her hair. She wouldn't control those feelings for long. He'd make sure of that. No matter his promise, he vowed to drive her crazy with wanting him. Crazy enough for her to put aside the one obstacle that stood in the path of their happiness.

Callahan awoke from a light doze and realized at once that she had, in her sleep, slid her hands beneath his shirt and was now resting burning palms against his chest.

His body stirred with need, despite his effort at control. Callahan grinned. Certainly it wouldn't hurt

263

to return the favor, he reasoned. And if he accomplished what had suddenly come to mind, before she fully awoke, he doubted she'd object overmuch. If luck was with him, she might, in fact, show her gratitude at some later date.

No, he wouldn't make love to her, not here. Too much was at stake to risk losing control. At any second, he expected to hear Jake's horse come charging into their campsite. He would not put Mattie in such an awkward position, as he easily imagined the embarrassment she'd know were they to be interrupted at a most inopportune moment.

Still, he felt an overwhelming need to prove to her she was as helpless as he to combat the hunger that raged between them. And if he kept his wits about him, how could she find fault?

Callahan easily opened the buttons of the shirt she wore. She never stirred when a moment later her trousers lay open as well.

Warm hands moved over silky skin, gently moving aside the cotton chemise that blocked the treasure he sought. His mouth dipped and slid hot kisses along her cheek, her jaw, the length of her throat, even as his hands moved over her rounded belly to the juncture of her thighs.

Mattie turned to her back, unconsciously giving him greater access to her most secret places and sighed, believing this yet another erotic dream, like the hundred or more that had haunted her sleep for weeks. Her trousers slid down her thighs as the teasing movement of his fingers caused her to arch her back.

"Callahan," she murmured sleepily, realizing at last this was no dream. Her eyes blinked open with surprise. "You shouldn't." But her whispered words fooled no one, not even herself. She wanted him to

continue. Indeed, her arms slid around his ne[...]
held him in place lest he have second thoughts and
leave her wanting.

"I know, sweetheart." He smiled, his mouth releasing its rosy-pink prize as he looked up into dark eyes
already dazed with passion. "Let me give you this
pleasure. I won't ask anything more."

His body shook with the need to take her, to make
her truly his. He felt an overpowering urge to taste
her everywhere, to search out every luscious hidden
morsel and rediscover with mouth and tongue every
delicious inch of her creamy white skin. But he dared
not, lest he lose the last of his control. So he held
back, satisfied for the moment to taste of her breasts
and feel the hauntingly stirring, hot, moist flesh at
her thighs.

Mere minutes passed before he realized he never
should have started this. It was killing him to hold
back, to refuse to give in to what he most desired.
He listened to her moans, knowing her every soft cry
of pleasure was slowly driving him out of his mind.

Mattie's hips lifted as she strained toward the
ecstasy that awaited. Her body grew tight. Tighter
than she'd ever known. She was gasping for breath,
her hands straining to bring him closer. "Oh, God,"
she moaned, her body tensing, growing harder, aching for more, starved for his touch. "God," she cried
again. "Callahan, please, please," she murmured, delirious with aching pleasure, as she pulled his mouth
to hers.

The heat of his mouth boggled her mind and sent
to flee the last of her reason. Her arms tightened
around his neck and she groaned as his tongue
searched out her sweetness and took into his mouth
her haunting essence. It was more than she could
bear, and she cried out her pleasure just before the

shuddering waves of blinding ecstasy shook her to her very core.

Callahan groaned as he pulled her tightly against him. He was shaking with the need to take her here and now. It took some time, but long, deep, calming breaths finally eased much of his torment.

His voice was low and husky when he spoke. "The next time I do that, I'm not going to stop."

Mattie sighed as she settled comfortably against him. "Never?" She grinned. "Now that's an enticing thought."

He chuckled. "I'm going to drive you wild."

"You've done that."

"Wilder then."

Mattie's finger traced his smiling lips. "I think you like it when I'm lying helpless beneath you."

Callahan grinned and looked down his nose at her. "You might say that."

"What happened to our bargain?"

He smiled as he pulled her face against his neck and nuzzled his mouth into her hair. "You could have stopped me at any time."

Mattie glanced up. "In my sleep?"

He shrugged. "After you woke up then."

"It was too late by then."

Callahan smiled.

"But you'd know that, wouldn't you?"

He shrugged. "I suspected as much."

"I won't marry you, you know," she warned.

Callahan's eyes widened with surprise. You won't, eh? Well, we'll just have to see about that, won't we? "Have I asked you?"

"No, but I'm giving you fair warning just in case you should get the crazy notion into your head."

"Don't worry. It never occurred to me," he lied.

"I'm going to do exactly what I set out to do," she

266

insisted.

"I know."

"And you can't stop me."

"Have I said I would?"

Mattie shook her head, not believing his docile attitude for a minute. "Your word, Callahan. When we reach Sacramento we part. You go your way and I mine."

Callahan laughed at the absurd notion, for he'd never let this woman go. "Yes, I can see us standing on the street shaking hands and wishing each other well."

"Callahan," she warned.

"And if I can't give you my word on it?"

Mattie sighed and bit at her lip, while a definite gleam began to grow to life in the depths of her dark eyes. "If I promise to give you anything you want for the remainder of this trip, will you then give me your word?"

Jesus, this was too good to resist. He'd promise her anything, anything, to have her come willingly to his bed. And if, in the end, she still insisted on finishing the insanity she'd started, he'd just have to convince her otherwise. His voice broke as he imagined the next few months of pleasure that awaited them. "Anything I want?"

Mattie nodded, her eyes never leaving his. Her heart thudded in her chest as she awaited his answer. In truth it didn't matter if he agreed or not. Although his agreeing would make it easier on both of them. Mattie's mind raced on to the possible complications he might cause. No, it wouldn't be easy, but she would do as she must. He had to return back East, or so he had said. She knew he wouldn't have the time to search her out, should she suddenly disappear.

"How about a hundred thousand dollars?"

Mattie shot him a stern look of disapproval. "Stop teasing. Anything in my power to give. Do I have your word on it?"

"You have it," he said, not willing to chance his luck by pushing her further.

Mattie smiled. "Now," she breathed with relief. "Tell me what you want."

Callahan grinned and gave her a light kiss on her nose. "For now, I want you to stop talking so I can sleep."

Chapter Nineteen

Every muscle in her body trembled. She couldn't take another step. If it meant her life, and it probably would, she just couldn't. Mattie had never known exhaustion to equal this. Even the first days on the train were as nothing compared to now.

Sweat poured down her face, stinging her eyes, often blurring her vision, and yet she couldn't find the strength, or will, to wipe it away.

Mattie shot Callahan a halfhearted look of fury, too tired to allow the emotion full rein. Damn the man. Didn't he realize the fatigue she suffered? Didn't he care? Since the first glimmer of light they had been on their feet. Hours had passed since they'd finished the last of their water and her mouth felt as though filled with cotton. The sun was high now. No doubt the noon hour had come and gone and still, curse him, they walked.

A soft sigh escaped her parched lips as she sank wearily to the ground. Mattie actually prayed for him not to notice. Perhaps he'd go on for miles and then it would be too late. She couldn't take any more of his badgering. All she wanted was to sleep.

Suddenly he was standing almost directly over her, his legs wide-spread, his voice filled with annoyance. "Mattie, get up! We have to keep going. The train might very well leave without us."

"I don't care."

"You'd care, all right, if we're left out here to die."

"We're as good as dead anyway," she mourned as

she lay flat to the ground and stared up at a beautiful blue sky dotted with light puffs of white clouds. "The train, if it escaped the tornado, is already gone. You know as well as I, Cassidy leaves at dawn, no matter what. We'll never find it."

"Get the hell up!"

Tears of exhaustion misted her eyes. "Leave me alone."

"I'm not carrying you and I'm not leaving you out here to die."

"You know, I really hate you. You haven't a compassionate bone in your body. And I'm sick to death at hearing you yell. Leave me the hell alone!"

Callahan hunkered down at her side, forcing aside the tenderness that sprang to life at her obvious exhaustion. Purposely he hardened his voice. "You don't hear Clay whining, do you? Stop acting like some goddamned spoiled brat and walk!"

"Bastard! I'll give you a spoiled brat," Mattie grunted as she came to her feet and gave him a shove, knocking him to the ground. Her exhaustion forgotten as her hands knotted into fists, her mouth curled into a vicious snarl, while murder flashed in her eyes.

"That's better," he grunted, coming to stand at her side, almost smiling at her show of violence, knowing her anger would sustain her for a time. He gave her a not too gentle shove. "Let's go."

They walked for near another hour—it felt like five—before Mattie realized the two dots of dust in the distance were actually riders. Callahan's sharp whistle brought their position to the riders' notice and Mattie almost cried out her relief to see Jim Stables and Jake finally draw their animals to a halt before them.

Never in her life was she so happy to see another

human being, although Callahan couldn't honestly say the same when he watched her throw herself into Jim Stables's arms, babbling out her gratitude.

That the man appreciated Mattie's close contact was all too obvious, by the look of pleasure that came to life in his eyes. Callahan had to force his hands to his side as he watched Jim's arm circle her waist almost possessively while she offered sips of water to Clay and drank her fill.

Callahan felt a niggling sensation he couldn't name lift the hairs on the back of his neck. He and Jim had gone on many a hunt and had often as not shared a campfire at night. Why then did he suddenly feel this odd sense of distrust? Why was he seized with a distinct dislike for Jim Stables?

With a scowl that silently bespoke his self-disgust, Callahan cursed his jealousy. It wouldn't have mattered who was holding her, he'd have felt the same. He had to learn to control this insane desire to smash the face of every man who touched this woman. Determinedly he forced his attention away from Mattie and the solicitous care she was being given. "How bad?" he asked his friend and partner.

"We lost two wagons and everybody who was in them." Jake's mouth twisted with disgust. "Cassidy never realized it was a tornado until it was too late. The folks were hiding inside the wagon instead of under them."

Callahan shook his head, realizing the waste. Cassidy should have known better. This wasn't the first train he'd taken west.

"Cassidy's sent most of the men out to find the remains." He shrugged. "So far, nothing."

Mattie blinked in wide-eyed astonishment when an hour later they returned to the train. She couldn't believe it. Apparently the tornado had cut a narrow

271

path directly across the huge circle of wagons. It was as though a giant hand had reached down from the sky and neatly snatched two, leaving each wagon on either side of the now empty places with not a scratch.

The immigrants were at best a subdued lot, the women teary as they went about their chores, while nearly all the men had left the train on their gruesome search for bodies.

One woman had lost her sister and the sister's entire family, while another immigrant his brother and wife. Mattie shivered, desperately wishing she could offer a word of hope. But after yesterday she knew nothing and no one could survive once absorbed into that black funnel of death.

Now what kind of a game was he playing? Damn, but the man was about to drive her out of her mind. She knew he wanted her. It couldn't be more obvious every time he looked her way and yet he held back, refusing to take the first step that would bring them together.

What did he want?

It had been more than a week since they had struck up the bargain. And since that day, he hadn't once taken advantage of her offer. Why?

Mattie stared up at the darkened canvas roof of the wagon. Her hands cupped the back of her head as she lay upon her bed of quilts. She sighed in confusion. If she could only talk to someone. Maybe she could understand what was going on.

Mattie grinned as she imagined asking another how to go about solving this problem.

"What's the matter?" came a deep voice from the other end of the wagon.

"Nothing," Mattie responded. "Nothing at all. Why?"

"I heard you sigh."

"Oh that. I was just thinking."

"About?"

Mattie gave a silent groan; her mind raced on. Did the man have to know everything? Was she allowed no secrets, no privacy? "Things," she answered finally.

"What things?"

"Callahan," she returned, a slight edge to her voice.

Callahan grinned. So she didn't want to tell him what was bothering her. Not that he couldn't guess. "If you tell me, I might be able to help."

Oh, you could help all right. You could do a lot more than help. "I'm hot, that's all."

Automatically he answered, "Then take off your . . ." Oh God, what was he saying? Had he finally lost what little mind he had left? How could he ever sleep knowing she was lying naked, not two yards from his reach? "Covers," he finally choked out.

The silence that filled the wagon was thick, almost suffocating as she realized what he had been about to say. What would he do if she stripped off her gown? Would he remain unconcerned? Would he simply ignore the fact that she was naked and obviously all too willing. Would he fall asleep?

Mattie bit back a low, mocking laugh. The ultimate insult. Why was he doing this? She knew he wanted her every bit as much as she wanted him. Why was he denying them both? What did he want?

Mattie's eyes widened as a thought came. Could it be? Did he want her to make the first move? Did he? Oh God, she wished she had more experience along these lines. She wished she knew what do to.

Her voice was gravelly and stilted as she forced the words. "You don't mind if I . . ." God, she couldn't

273

finish. This was too humiliating. What if he said he didn't give a damn.

"What?" Callahan asked, clearly on edge.

"My gown. Would you mind if I took it off." Mattie felt her cheeks burn at her daring. She squeezed her eyes closed, dreading his reply.

Callahan's heart was about ready to burst through the wall of his chest. Jesus, had a man ever known such suffering, such longing? Another minute of this and he wasn't going to be responsible for what he might do.

"No" came his strangled reply.

Callahan watched her. After a moment's hesitation she came to her feet. Her hands shook as she untied the ribbons at her shoulders.

The low-burning fire at their campsite brought just enough light to filter through the canvas for Mattie to see the glitter of his eyes. He was watching her every movement. Her body trembled, her breathing grew shallow and labored. How could she ever find the nerve to go through with this? Would he reject her? Would he turn away?

Callahan's breath caught in his throat as he watched the cotton gown slide down the length of her. He never heard the low groan he uttered above the wild pumping of his heart. A roaring came to his ears. He couldn't think. He couldn't breathe. He dared not blink lest this vision disappear. God, she was the most beautiful woman he'd ever known. Callahan was amazed at his reaction. Yes, he had seen her naked before, but for some reason he never quite remembered the full extent of her loveliness, and each time found himself thunderstruck again at the sight of her.

His heart swelled with pride, with joy, for he knew she was his for the taking. His to forever love and cherish. Never would another man know this pleasure.

Mattie stood for a moment, her hands twisting nervously before her. She waited for him to say something, anything, but nothing came out of the silence, nothing but the sound of his labored breathing.

So she had imagined this great longing. He really wasn't interested. Mattie bit at her lip. Tears felt dangerously close, and a lump was forming in her throat. He didn't want her after all. How could she have been so stupid not to have known?

Mattie wanted to die. She turned, shrinking back, bending for the gown she had just dropped to the floor. "Maybe I'd better not. It's colder than I thought," she muttered, her face flaming, knowing in her heart she'd never know a more mortifying moment.

Callahan saw her move and knew he had pushed her as far as she was able to go. She wouldn't come to him, at least not yet. Not until she came to know the true depths of her feelings. That she loved him, he hadn't a doubt, but he knew she hadn't recognized the truth, or at least admitted it to be so. He knew this as fact, for Mattie might possess great passion, but her morals would only permit total abandonment when she loved. Callahan shivered at the promise that lay before them and prayed she'd soon come to know her feelings.

"Mattie," he said as he sat. A moment later he was kneeling before her.

"Don't," Mattie choked, her voice tight with unshed tears. God, don't let him tell her he was sorry. If he felt pity for her she'd simply die.

"Don't what?" Callahan smiled as he took her face between his palms. "Don't look at you? Don't touch you?" He gave a soft laugh. "Impossible."

275

"Stand up for me. I want to see you. I want to touch you."

Mattie blinked her obvious confusion. She hadn't expected this, not after he had lain there so long. "I . . . I can't."

Callahan ignored her words and urged her to her feet again. "Yes," he whispered. "Yes, you can."

His hands were at her waist. Slowly they moved over her body. Mattie bit back the moan that threatened as his calloused palms moved up to lift and cup heavy breasts and then down to the flaring curve of full hips.

"Do you know what the sight of you does to me?" he murmured as his lips brushed against her skin, never realizing he had spoken out loud.

"Tell me," she implored, for she no longer trusted her instincts. She needed to hear it said.

Callahan chuckled. "What? Shall I lay my soul bare? Would you treat it kindly if you knew?"

Mattie moaned as he pressed his face into the softness of her rounded belly. "Oh God, Mattie, a moment doesn't pass that I don't think of you, want you, long to breathe your scent, taste your flesh." His calloused hands cupped her bottom and angled her hips toward his hungry mouth.

Mattie's knees wobbled, her sharp, indrawn breath filled the silent wagon as he buried his face in the warmth of her. Her hands clung to his shoulders as she sought to dispel the dizziness that always accompanied his touch. "I can't stand" came a breathless whisper as his tongue darted against her moist flesh and she gave up all hope of ever again knowing a world that wasn't tilted.

"Not yet," he groaned as he tore his mouth from her. "I'm rushing things."

"I don't mind," Mattie said without thinking, and

276

then flushed beet red as she realized his laughter.

"No, I imagine you don't."

His hands guided her to her knees. God, how he loved this woman. What possibilities lay ahead for them once she admitted her feelings for him? It had to be that she loved him. Callahan would allow nothing less. "I want to kiss you. You don't mind that, do you?"

Mattie smiled, growing more sure of her power over him as each second passed. "No, I don't mind that either."

Callahan brushed his mouth against hers, delighted as she eagerly invited him to deepen the kiss. Mattie's lips parted and she shivered as he took her bottom lip between his teeth and teased it with his tongue.

His hands came to her neck, his fingers threading through her long hair as he held her mouth still. "You have the sweetest mouth," he murmured, while leaving tender, short tantalizing kisses over her lips. "Do you know how long I've waited for this?"

Callahan groaned as his mouth fused hotly to hers, and his tongue, finding no obstacle to bar his way, plunged deep into her sweet mouth. Rediscovering the texture and taste, relishing in the ecstasy, he wondered if he'd ever find the strength to stop.

Mattie's whole world became the touch of his mouth, the scent and taste of him until she knew nothing but pleasure, sensation, erotic delight. "Why," Mattie gasped for air. "Why did you wait?"

"Your offer, you mean?"

Mattie moaned, unable to answer him. Her head fell back as Callahan licked at her throat and shoulder.

"It wasn't good enough. You had to want me equally as much."

"And you now believe I do?"

Callahan chuckled as he remembered her bold attempt to seduce him. If he lived a hundred years, he'd never forget how that gown slid to the floor and what it left exposed to his gaze. "Yes, you want me, lady. I've no doubt of it now." He nuzzled her throat, his tongue sliding over her collarbone and shoulder. "Tell me," he breathed against her skin, his warm breath sending chills down her spine. "Let me hear you say it. Tell me what you want."

Callahan's lips left the delicious warmth of her throat and brushed lightly at her mouth. He thought to tease her into admitting her need, but the wildly hungry response that met his lips left little room for thought. He forgot the question he'd just asked. He forgot he was awaiting her answer as he lost himself in her touch, her scent, her feel.

"I want you, Callahan." Mattie trembled, as he released her lips at last. "Oh God, I want you and everything you can do to me."

"Do you?" he asked as he guided her down to the quilts. "Do you want this?" he asked as he slid between her legs and entered her body with a mind-boggling thrust of his hips.

Callahan smiled as he listened to her helpless, mindless groan. His lips and tongue ravaged her mouth, thirsting for her taste, her feel, her very soul. He knew she was unable to answer him, unable to do more than accept his body and lose herself in the magnificent tremors of ecstasy that had already begun.

Callahan was surprised to feel the spasms close tightly around him. Her climax had been so quick. He hadn't known she was this near release. He closed his eyes as squeezing muscles brought an agony of pleasure and forced aside his need to take her right now. "No, not yet," he whispered as he felt her body soften and listened to the sigh that slipped tiredly from her slackened lips. "I'm not near finished yet."

Mattie's eyes widened with surprise. Every time she had lain with him had been an exercise in endurance, but he had never before pulled away. No, he had sometimes stopped to steady his heartbeat, to regain his breath, his strength, but had begun again within moments.

But this was different. It was too soon. She knew he hadn't reached his pleasure and yet he made sure to give her hers.

Mattie moaned as Callahan brushed his beard over her cheek, her throat, her chest, her breasts. She arched her back, bringing herself closer to his feathery strokes.

"Mmmm," Callahan smiled. "You like that, do you?"

Mattie grinned, feeling totally at ease and delightfully wanton. "You might say that."

"I love to watch them tighten for me. I especially love it when you're thinking of me and I see them tighten through your clothes."

Mattie laughed and gave a gentle shake of her head. "Shame on you, Mr. Callahan. Such wicked thoughts."

Callahan joined her in her laughter. "Aren't you glad?"

"Now I'd be less than a lady if I admitted to that."

"Ah, Mattie. Don't you know you are both a lady and enchantress?" He sighed. "No one but the most beautiful of witches could have cast such a spell over me."

Mattie smiled, her breathing growing decidedly uneven as he worked his way down the length of her body. His mouth was nuzzling her belly when she shuddered. "Have I?"

Callahan grinned. "I see the idea appeals. Shall I swear to it then?" he asked as he moved lower still, reaching his objective at last.

Mattie groaned as his tongue flicked out and sampled the taste of her.

"Shall I?" he asked again.

Mattie's hips rose instinctively toward the heat of his mouth. "I don't care what you do, just don't stop."

Endless, endless, endless. It went on forever. He hadn't lied. He was never going to stop. Mattie's skin was slick with perspiration and she groaned as her body tightened again. "No more. Please, no more," Mattie gasped. And then groaned again as yet another bout of shuddering spasms spread into wave after wave of demonic, aching bliss. "Oh God, you're killing me."

Callahan groaned as the taste of her filled his brain, his body, until he knew nothing but her. He trembled as he rose above her and slid deep into her moist warmth. Callahan's pulse throbbed, his breathing grew almost nonexistent. He squeezed his eyes shut, desperate to maintain control. Too late he realized he shouldn't have moved within her, not while she was in the midst of this throbbing pleasure, for the sensations that surrounded his body were almost unbearable in his present state. His heart thundered in his chest and he knew it was impossible to hold back any longer.

His hands grew almost vicious as he took her hips and held her fiercely against him. His control gone, he plunged deep within. His mind swam with delight, unimaginable sensation drove him past his limit. "Mattie," he groaned. "Mattie, my God," he choked as it began. "I can't . . ." He shuddered helplessly as his mind gave up its battle and his body surrendered to the final mind-exploding surge of ecstasy.

Mattie breathed the last of her strength on a sigh. She was numb. No matter what he did she couldn't have responded again. Callahan took her with him when he rolled to his back. "I think I died," she mumbled sleepily, unable to remember a time when she had ever felt so exhausted.

Callahan chuckled as he easily slid her damp body to lie over the length of him. "Consider yourself duly warned. That's what happens to ladies who take their clothes off in front of me."

"My God," she groaned, nuzzling her face into the moist mat of hair on his chest. "I'll wager it doesn't happen twice. I know I'll never do it again." Suddenly she raised her head. Her eyes narrowed as she looked into his smiling eyes. "What ladies?"

"What?"

"Have you done this . . ." She hesitated for a long moment, shrugged, then slumped against him again. "Never mind."

Callahan smiled, knowing how she was trying to control her jealousy. "Does the thought bother you, that there have been others?"

"Of course not," she returned, refusing to acknowledge the truth of the matter. "Why in the world should it?" she snapped almost angrily, her body growing stiff in his arms.

She tried to pull away, but Callahan held her to him. He couldn't stop the smile from forming. "Then why are you getting mad?"

"Me? Don't be ridiculous. I'm not in the least."

Callahan chuckled. "Yes, you are." His hands smoothed down her naked back, pressing her closer to his body. "Mattie, I haven't touched another woman since I first laid eyes on you?"

Mattie snickered her disbelief. "What about Lucy, or doesn't she count?"

"Not even Lucy," he promised with a tender smile, remembering now how it had angered him at the time.

"Why?"

"Because it was you I wanted." It's you I'll always want, he added silently.

"And Susie?"

"You saw me there every night. I never left the campfire."

Mattie grinned broadly, knowing he spoke the truth. "Why?"

"Because she didn't fight me near hard enough."

Mattie frowned. "Is it usual for you to easily tire of anything so freely offered?"

"You mistake my meaning. It wasn't only a body I wanted and that was all she had to give."

"What else did you want?"

"I wouldn't want this to get around," he whispered, his eyes scanning the wagon as if others were present and might overhear.

Mattie crossed her heart and giggled. "I wouldn't tell a soul."

"There is one woman who possesses the most lovely body I've ever known . . ."

Her brow lifted and she glared. "And you've known quite a few, no doubt."

Callahan wisely ignored her statement. "And this woman also has the snottiest mouth."

Mattie giggled, her eyes rounded with surprise. "You're not telling me . . ."

Callahan interrupted. "As much as the idea entices, a man cannot spend all his time in bed."

"In other words, you like to fight?" The idea was startling to say the least.

Callahan ran his finger down her slender nose. "I'd say there's some merit in arguing now and then."

"Is there?" Mattie grinned as she leaned back, her breasts swaying above his chest. "I wonder what that could be?"

Callahan toyed with a tempting rosy tip, a smile curving his mouth. "After an argument, people usually make up." His fingers rolled her nipples into tight buds and he listened with appreciation to her low murmurs of pleasure.

"Do they?" She laughed softly. "I take it you know this from firsthand experience."

"Let's say, I've heard about it."

"Have you heard how it's done?"

He nodded almost solemnly. His voice grew thick and low as he suggested, "Shall I show you?"

"Mmm, yes, please."

"I don't believe a word of it." She shot him a look of disgust at what she supposed was an outrageous story. "If it didn't kill you, it would at least have left a mark."

Callahan chuckled. "And you know for a fact that I have no scars."

Mattie blushed and lowered her eyes shyly.

Callahan's chest swelled with pleasure that this lovely woman could belong to him, for whether she knew it or not, she'd never know another. He shrugged. "I shot it in flight. It was already dead, or nearly so by the time it landed."

"And still you insist this mountain retreat of yours to be paradise? In truth, the picture you paint leaves much to be desired. What about bears?"

Callahan ignored her question and went on to elaborate the qualities of his mountain home. "I promise the air is the sweetest, the water clean and icy cold from the streams."

Mattie shot him a look of distrust. "I'd wager there's not much use for air or water, if a body is torn to ribbons by one of your furry friends."

Mattie shrugged as she walked at his side toward the stream. "No thank you. I think I'll brave the restrictions and population of a small town, where all the furry animals are friendly and tame."

"You could always look for yourself and then decide on its merits."

She shrugged again and gave a soft sigh. "If things were different."

Callahan knew she was talking about her plan to see justice done. He gave a silent curse. When the hell was she going to give up this ridiculous notion? Didn't she realize, if by some miracle she managed to find the man, she didn't have it in her to kill. And should the impossible happen, didn't she know she'd surely be caught? Perhaps even hanged? Callahan shivered at the thought. Never! Never would he allow this woman to put herself in such jeopardy.

They had reached the stream. Mattie and Callahan took off their shoes. With buckets in hand they waded a bit from the edge, in order to fill them without a trace of sand.

Callahan was bent over, filling the second bucket when he gasped at the icy deluge that suddenly gushed over his head. "Is your water colder than that?" Mattie asked on a laugh as she hurriedly splashed her way toward the supposed safety of shore.

"Why you . . ." came a dangerously deep voice, filled with the need for retaliation and all too close behind her.

Mattie screamed as she felt herself lifted and flung into the air, to land with a giant splash some distance from shore.

She giggled as she came to the surface and faced his dripping face. "Why did you do that? I could catch my death in these waters."

"Why did you dump the bucket over my head?"

"Me? Why on earth would I do that?" she asked with a giggle as she moved suggestively against him. Her arms reached around his neck in a supposed embrace. "Perhaps you were caught in a sudden cloud burst."

But Callahan wasn't the least fooled by her all too sweetly innocent attitude and grinned when the groaning pressure she put to his neck brought about no immediate results. Obviously she was struggling to dunk him. "What is it you think you're doing?"

Mattie smiled. "Why, I'm hugging you, of course."

"Hmm, hugging me with a choke hold? It's different, I'll give you that."

"Couldn't you have been a bit smaller?" she grunted as she hung from his neck. "Or weaker?"

"So you could take even more advantage of me? I shiver to think what your heartless soul might conjure."

"You're no fun at all, Callahan," she pouted beautifully as she pushed herself away.

"You don't think so? Shall I show you then how much fun I can be?"

Mattie shrieked with laughter as he pulled her against him and dropped beneath the water. "You beast! What chance have I against you?" Mattie gasped breathlessly as they came to the surface at last.

"No chance at all," he promised as his mouth swooped down and captured hers.

Mattie's jaw ached with the effort it took to stop her teeth from chattering as she hurriedly searched through her trunk for something dry. "Re-remind me ne-never to go near water with you again. You are obviously not to be trusted." She laughed as a balled towel bounced off her head.

"Hurry up and get those clothes off. I don't want you getting sick on me."

"Afraid you might have to do some of the work around here, Callahan?" Mattie's hands were shaking as she fumbled through her clothes.

"You know me, lady. I want my coffee ready and waiting after a hard day on the trail."

Mattie gave him a tender smile, knowing it was he who most often made the coffee. "I'm glad you found some use for me. You didn't think much of me at first."

Callahan chuckled as he moved toward her and hurried along the job of stripping away her wet clothes. "You're very much mistaken there. The first sight of you brought many things to mind." A moment later she was bundled into a thick quilt and she sighed with pleasure as he ran his hands over her back in brisk, warming strokes.

Mattie giggled. "I can imagine."

Callahan shook his head. "I doubt it."

"Doubt what? That I know what you thought?" Mattie smiled. "Shall I tell you then?"

"Be my guest," he remarked as he released her for the short time it took to finish undressing.

"You said to yourself. 'Who the hell is she? What the hell is she doing, paying me to take her west?' Am I right?"

"Don't curse."

Mattie laughed and held her hands up in a gesture meant to proclaim her innocence. "I was relating your thoughts, not mine."

"When do I curse?" Callahan took just that moment to stub his toe on one of the wooden crates and bestowed upon her still another word she could add to her growing knowledge of swear words.

Mattie's giggle turned into a warm smile. She opened the quilt, a clear invitation for him to join her. "Come and warm yourself."

Callahan quickly took her up on her offer and groaned the moment his cold body contacted with her now heated flesh. "Oh God, do you know what you feel like?"

"I know what you feel like."

"What?" he breathed, his face against her wet hair.

"An iceberg. I should have given you your own quilt."

Callahan laughed as he pressed his cold mouth to her neck. "Make me warm then, lady. Make me burn, like you."

Chapter Twenty

"Watch out! Oh my God! Oh God!" Mattie screamed as she lunged to her feet and swayed atop her wagon. Despite her calls of warning, the toddler, clearly half asleep and dazed from an afternoon nap, paid no attention. Unconcerned of Mattie's frantic waving and calls, she wobbled to the edge of the wagon that trudged on ahead. Mattie couldn't take her eyes from the little girl and moaned in helpless horror as Becky smiled and then suddenly tumbled, headfirst, out the back to hit upon a ground as hard as cobblestone.

From beginning to end, it was over in mere seconds, and yet the scene seemed to play out in agonizing slow motion, promising to forever haunt its only witness. Mattie knew she would never forget how the look of childish trust and confidence spread instantly into fear as the baby toppled over the wagon's tailgate.

Desperately Mattie pulled at the reins that held her six oxen in line. Her muscles bunched and strained. The leather straps sliced unnoticed into her hands and the oxen came at last to a stop.

Mattie was trembling with fear as she made to jump from the wagon. In her hurry, she didn't notice her full skirt catch firmly to the rough edge of the seat. The material didn't give at first and with some amazement Mattie felt her legs snap out from beneath her. Her weight caused the skirt to tear, at last, and with a heavy, bone-jarring thud, Mattie fell almost flat on her face.

She was dazed and shaken from the force of her fall. A cloud of choking dust caught in her throat and she began to cough as she automatically gasped for breath. Mattie only vaguely realized a searing pain as it spread its burning waves up her leg. She was trembling, conscious of the fact that she was hurt, but later would be soon enough to see to her injury, she hadn't the time right now to think on her own discomfort. She had to get to the baby.

She was covered with a fine silt of brown dust. Her wide-brimmed hat had fallen away. Her hair had come loose from its confines and swung free before her face as she crawled over the hard ground on hands and knees to the limp form, lying so dangerously close to the oxen's hooves.

Almost blinded by tears, Mattie reached the little girl and pulled her into trembling arms. "It's all right, darling," she muttered almost incoherently as she pressed her face to the gentle, warm curve of the child's throat.

Mattie never saw the long, deep gash along the baby's temple. She never realized the blood that gushed from the wound as it mingled freely with her tears and spread over both their faces.

From the wagons that had been following came her fellow emigrants. Slowly a small, pitying circle formed around Mattie and the child, while the wagons ahead continued on, for the moment blissfully unaware that a tragedy had taken place.

Callahan and a few of the men had been gone most of the morning on a search for missing cattle. Over the hushed, sympathetic murmurs of the crowd, Mattie heard the roar of Callahan's borrowed horse's hooves as they raced back toward camp.

A moment later he was out of the saddle and running to her side. Callahan's heart thundered in his chest, the sound deafening him to all. For a long second he couldn't draw or release breath as his wild gaze took in the blood that streaked Mattie's face.

Becky Thompson, a bright, cheery two-year-old, lay limply in her arms, but Callahan couldn't, for a moment, tell which one of them was hurt.

Kneeling down beside her rocking form, he finally managed in a strangely strangled voice, "What happened?"

Mattie looked toward the sound of the voice at her side but could see little of Callahan's concern through her blur of tears. "She fell. I yelled, but she didn't pay me no mind."

Mattie shuddered as the scene played out before her eyes again. "I almost ran over her."

Callahan read correctly the terror in her eyes, and gently insisted, "But you didn't."

An agonized scream started somewhere off in the distance and continued on until it was almost in Mattie's ear. Suddenly the child was torn from her arms by a hysterically sobbing mother, leaving Mattie suddenly chilled and bereft.

The crowd began to suddenly disperse, some muttering oaths of disgust that another should have joined the many who had already gone on to meet their maker.

Callahan wiped at the dirt, blood, and tears that covered Mattie's cheeks. Gently he took her in his arms, cradling her against him, much as she had the child and murmured almost the same soothing words. "It's all right, sweetheart."

"It's not all right, Callahan. How can it be all right

when babies die?"

Callahan had no answers. Indeed there were none. No one could reason away a child's life. All he could do was hold this precious woman close and pray she'd never suffer the agony that had befallen so many others, and if he could not in the future spare her the pain, at least he'd always be there for her to offer his comfort as best he could. "I know, but there was nothing you could have done. You couldn't have stopped it."

"If I could have gotten to her sooner."

"Mattie," he whispered near her ear, "I won't have you blaming yourself for this. The child was her mother's responsibility, not yours. It was she who should have been walking behind the wagon."

Mattie sighed. She knew he was right. If it were her child, she would never have left her unattended. But if only . . . Mattie forced away the useless thought, knowing it did little good to think of "if onlys."

"Are you all right?"

Mattie nodded, forgetting for the moment her injury. Callahan helped her to her feet. Only then did she realize the pain in her ankle. Through clenched teeth, Mattie sucked in her breath as she tried to put pressure on it.

Callahan cursed and lifted her into his arms. His face paled beneath his tan, his mouth tightened, white with anger. "Damn it, you're not all right. What the hell did you do to yourself?"

"I don't remember. I think I fell."

Callahan cursed again as he carried her to their wagon and sat her upon the opened tailgate. His mouth, no more than a grim white line above his black beard, twisted with dread as his gently searching hands found the swelling at her ankle. Mattie gasped as searing pain shot up her leg.

"You think you fell?" he snapped as his gaze took in her dust-covered clothes and an ankle swollen to almost three times its normal size. "Goddamnit, Mattie, look at your ankle."

"Stop yelling at me!" she yelled in return. "If this is how you show concern, I can live without it."

Callahan sighed and took a deep, calming breath. She was right, of course. She hadn't done anything but try to help an injured child, thereby hurting herself. He had to gain some control over this unreasonable impulse to lash out at her when she was hurt. But he couldn't seem to control his fear where she was concerned, and his fear almost always led to a rash outburst of anger.

Callahan quickly found a length of cloth and tied it securely around her ankle. "No doubt the doctor is with the Thompsons right now. I'll call him over in a few minutes. How does it feel?"

Mattie nodded. "All right, as long as I don't move it."

Mattie glanced down at her blouse. Her eyes widened as they took in the blood. "I'm covered with blood!"

Callahan nodded. "The baby's head was cut."

"Can you get me something?" she asked, suddenly shivering with disgust. "I'm . . ."

Knowing her needs, he responded, "I'll have to move you inside."

Mattie nodded and hardly groaned at all when Callahan lifted her again.

A few minutes later, dressed in a fresh blouse and skirt, she washed her face free of the blood, brushed her hair, and repinned it at the nape of her neck. The doctor came soon after and Callahan gave an audible sigh of relief as they were told her ankle suffered only a bad sprain. Mattie would be fine in a few days.

Mattie's glare clearly bespoke her anger.

Callahan gave her a sheepish grin. "You're mad at me, right?"

"Me! Why on earth should I be mad?" Mattie shot him a killing look. "Just because you're unreasonable enough to curse and scream at me while I'm in pain, I can't see why that's any reason to be upset."

"I wasn't cursing at you. I was cursing, period." Callahan sighed. "I'm afraid you'll just have to get used to it. I can't help yelling when I'm worried."

Mattie's gaze moved to meet his frown. "Were you worried? Why? I only twisted my ankle."

"Mattie, for God's sake, don't you realize what you looked like?" Callahan closed his eyes at the remembered fear. "I couldn't tell who was hurt, who was bleeding. All I could see was you sitting on the ground covered with blood."

Mattie gave a gentle smile. "And if I'm to bleed, I imagine you want to be the one to have caused it."

Callahan chuckled as he moved to her side. "You really are the most beautiful woman I've ever known. Now if I could only find a way to keep your nasty mouth closed, you'd be perfect."

Mattie smiled. "I think only the perfect can demand perfection, Callahan."

"And I have a long way to go, is that it?"

Mattie felt her chest swell with emotion as his finger gently traced her rounded cheek and firm jaw. Her lips quivered and tears filled her eyes. She was better off the object of his rages, rather than face his gentleness. She couldn't push back the ache in her throat that threatened to cut off her breathing, nor stop the tears from rolling down her cheeks. Finally, with a trembling small voice, she asked, "Do you think you could hold me for a little bit?"

Callahan almost groaned as he took her in his

arms. Not for a little bit? he silently promised. For ever, my love.

They were passing through Devil's Crater. Mattie shivered with disgust. It was easy enough to see why the name. Only rock and sand existed for as far as the eye could see. Nothing grew here. There was no water, nor would there be for another day or so, and then those who had come this way before promised it would be undrinkable, filled as it was with alkali. Here in this godforsaken place, almost midway between Fort Laramie and Independence Rock, little Becky was laid to rest.

Mattie sighed as she watched the last shovel of sandy earth dribble over the low-mounded grave. Mrs. Thompson had liberally drenched the baby and her clothes in camphor, in the hopes of reaching a settlement before they were forced to inter the body. But nothing could stop nature from proceeding on its due course, and at last the baby had to be buried along the road.

"Are they quite mad?" Mattie asked softly, standing a little away from the rest of the mourners. "Whatever possessed them to travel with small children and babies?"

Callahan's arm tightened around her waist. As he watched Lavinia Thompson being almost carried back to her wagon, her pitiful sobs of remorse were sure to soften the hardest of hearts. "No doubt they had no idea of how dangerous the journey would be."

"I'd never allow it. My husband would just have to go alone."

"Spoken like a dutiful wife."

"You can make all the fun you like, Callahan, but I mean it. I'd never jeopardize my children."

"It's not only children who die, Mattie."

"No, they're not the only ones. But they are often the first to go." Mattie shivered as she imagined a child of hers left out here, without even a marker for its grave, to rest forever alone, all but forgotten in this wretched wilderness.

Mattie stopped on her way back to the wagons and turned to watch as a team of oxen obliterated any sign of the grave.

She shivered at the deliberate desecration, but knew the reason behind this seemingly heartless act. How many graves had they come upon where white, sun-bleached bones had to be again interred? For an Indian, it seemed, found the temptation to investigate quite beyond his ability to resist and felt no disgust in digging up a body for its clothing. And if it wasn't the Indians, it was the wolves and coyotes. Mattie shuddered. Would they never get to California? Would it never be done?

Fort Bridger at last. The train was splitting off. Mr. Cassidy was taking more than half and turning north toward Fort Hall in Idaho and on to Oregon. Mattie wasn't sorry to see him go. The man gave her the shivers. She was happy to be rid of his constant condemning glares and relieved to be staying on with the obviously more steady second in command.

Mr. McMillen, a gentle, soft-spoken man, would now lead this smaller group more directly west toward California. Mattie sighed. Only the tip of Utah and all of Nevada and they'd be there. They were beyond the halfway point. Soon, soon, Mattie silently repeated almost as a litany as one day ran into another and then another, until she began to believe life held nothing more than walking, heat, and dirt.

Mattie blinked the dust from her eyes as the sparkling water glared back the sun's rays and snaked its lazy path across their trail. Was this but another mirage? If so, this imaginary picture held a new twist, for dark, almost shapeless buildings appeared to dot the far-off horizon.

Suddenly she gave a soft laugh as she watched the distant buildings steady themselves through the wavering haze of heat and come more clearly into view. Her heart filled with delight. She cast an inquisitive glance toward Callahan, who as always sat high upon the wagon, directly behind the oxen. He hadn't missed her smile or the twinkle of pleasure that lit up her eyes. "A mailing station and maybe a trading post," he offered to her unasked question. "We might be able to buy a few supplies."

The buildings proved to be exactly as Callahan thought, and Mattie wanted to dance with joy as she moved between row after row of supplies. Provisions were exorbitantly high and Mattie rightly reasoned Mr. Perrywinkle was cheating his clientele when she saw coffee at forty-five cents a pound, sugar three dollars, and flour thirteen a bag.

Callahan bought another horse, and the price was so high Mattie wondered if Callahan hadn't used the last of all he had.

But her need to remind the man of Christian charity, or at the very least fairness, disappeared like a puff of smoke in the wind when she eyed an orange perched alone upon his roughly finished counter. Her eyes softened as they held with clear longing to the prized fruit. Mattie sighed. How far had she come when the thought of biting into its juicy sweetness overcame all reasonable thought? But Mattie didn't long question her feelings, for Callahan had noticed her hungry glances and despite the cost of one dollar, bought it.

Mattie almost laughed aloud with delight. She would willingly have kissed Mr. Perrywinkle, thief that he was, for selling it. She did kiss Callahan for buying it and giggled as he held her close to his side and teased, "Enjoy it, lady. It's going to cost you more than one kiss."

There was an air of excitement when they camped that night. All who could afford it, and some who clearly couldn't, had nearly emptied Mr. Perrywinkle's store of supplies. The travelers were ready, or so they believed, to brave whatever future hardships this journey would bring. In truth one could settle no blame, for as so often happens, a full stomach leads to a faulty sense of security, and these innocents had no way of knowing their real hardships had barely begun.

The travelers were in an almost holiday mood. Many of the men played ball while the women, laughing with the simple pleasure of preparing the evening meal with enough water and supplies, went about their chores with obvious vigor and energy. It wasn't till dinner was finished and the men settled themselves down to talk and smoke around fires of dried sagebrush, that Mattie heard the rumors.

The train ahead had reportedly been attacked. Most of the survivors were so badly injured they could not travel the distance back for help and were forced to await help from another train. McMillen ordered the guard doubled and many sought the safety of their wagons earlier than usual that night.

Callahan was taking his turn at guard duty while Mattie was about to enter her wagon, when for the first time in weeks, Mr. Robinson came to their camp. He stood, with hat in hand, his eyes meeting Mattie's gaze in the light of the fire. "Do you mind if I

297

speak, ma'am?" Mattie nodded a silent assent and Robinson cleared his throat. "It's been a long time since you came over to Jake's fire. Nora misses you."

Mattie's lips tightened as she fought against the need his words instilled. The days were too hard and long to remain alone. The need to talk and confide in a friend was almost overwhelming, but the truth couldn't be ignored. They weren't her friends. They couldn't ever be. They were selling guns, or at least delivering them to someone who would sell them. If their business was honest, Callahan would have long ago told her. "I miss her too."

"Then why don't you . . ."

"I'm afraid you misunderstand, Mr. Robinson. This is not a matter of a simple difference of opinion. I miss her, but I don't trust her, or any of you for that matter. You people are doing something wrong, or you wouldn't be hiding it."

"And yet you trust Callahan."

"I love . . ." Mattie came to a sudden stop. Her cheeks grew red at her blunder. Whatever could she be thinking to nearly blurt out such a thing? It wasn't true in any case. She didn't love Callahan. She didn't! "I have little choice in the matter, Mr. Robinson. I need Callahan to take me west."

Robinson nodded. "And it doesn't matter that he's involved with . . . with us, as long as you get what you want."

"That's not it at all!" Mattie returned. "It does matter."

"And yet you're still with him."

"I told you, I had no choice."

Robinson shook his head. "I don't believe you. You could have left him and hired on with almost any one of these wagons. Extra hands are always needed."

Mattie knew he was right and yet she couldn't bring

herself to admit it. She stared silently into the red and yellow flames.

"I didn't come here to get you all fired up," Robinson sighed as he slapped his hat against his leg. "I only wanted to let you know you're welcome at the fire anytime. It don't matter none what you did, or what you're goin' to do. We don't judge anyone here."

Mattie gasped, her whole body growing instantly stiff. There wasn't a doubt in her mind that the man knew her plans. In all probability, they all did. Damn that Callahan! The minute she set eyes on him, she was going to kill him with her bare hands.

Robinson nodded his good-night and turned toward his camp, when a high-pitched shriek split the night and an arrow whizzed by Mattie's shoulder and lodged in the back of Robinson's leg.

Mattie was completely dumbfounded. She watched Robinson's leg buckle beneath him. She didn't even think to scream. Her worst fears were about to come true and all she could do was stand there and stare.

Suddenly a heavy weight crashed into her back. Mattie gave only the smallest of screams as she went sprawling forward and found, much to her surprise, her face pressed into the sand. Quickly, the weight shifted. She heard Callahan's curse above her and then a scream turn into a low groan. She tried to turn around, but only gasped, for the weight was suddenly upon her again, only this time it had increased twofold.

Mattie managed to lift her face from the sand at last. She turned her head to see what had happened, only to find herself staring straight into the sightless eyes of a dead man, with Callahan sandwiched between them.

But Mattie didn't at first recognize the fact that the man was dead. All she could see was his terrifying face painted in black with red lines running across it.

Her screams were lost in the melee that followed. At first it seemed everyone was screaming. Screaming and running. Shadowed figures dashed around, or leaped over fires. Some entered wagons dragging screaming women out by their hair.

Callahan rolled the Indian off them and shoved her under the wagon. Crouched low, he fired his rifle and an Indian fell.

Don't leave me, she wanted to cry. Please don't leave me. But the words didn't come, for in her terror her voice wouldn't work. Even if it had, Callahan couldn't have heard her among the screaming horror that filled the camp.

Mattie lay flat beneath the wagon, trying to make herself as small as possible, while praying no one would notice her there. She wanted to close her eyes and wish it all away, but she couldn't. She had to watch. It was all so much more terrifying not to be able to see.

She watched as Mr. Gould was shot. His wife Jane ran to his aid. Mattie gasped and whispered, "No, no, hide!" Her heart thundered with fear. They're going to see you! Hide! she screamed in silent agony. Mattie groaned, for she knew the woman never gave a thought to the danger. She was trying to turn her husband to his back, when an Indian ran right by her, and with a sickening slash of his knife, cut into her throat as easily as slicing into a loaf of bread. Mattie shivered as Jane's body crumbled soundlessly upon her husband's.

Mattie reached a desperate hand toward Callahan and noticed for the first time she was alone. So absorbed was she by the horror surrounding her, she hadn't seen Callahan leave. Her terrified gaze searched out the immediate area, but all she could see was an Indian laughing as he jumped from a wagon with a baby held, as if a trophy, high over his head. He was running, whooping, and hollering with some unnamed joy when he suddenly seemed to tire of the game and flung the baby into one of the fires. He stopped for a moment and laughed as he watched its clothes turn into flames, but his curiosity was short-lived. He soon turned toward the more interesting sight of a woman who had run past his line of vision.

Mattie never noticed the soft, moaning sound of pity that escaped her throat. She felt tears burn her eyes. Her lips thinned with rage that this animal should so heartlessly kill a helpless baby. Suddenly a calmness seemed to slip over her. It wasn't that she was no longer afraid. She was terrified, but her anger somehow relegated her fear to a weak second place. Suddenly she knew she couldn't lie here and watch this horror unfold. She had to do something. She had to try, or forever live with the shame of knowing she hadn't changed. She was still a sniveling coward.

What she needed was a gun. But in order to get one she had to get into the wagon. God, there were enough guns in there to supply an army, but she wouldn't take one of those. There was no ammunition for them, not in her wagon, at least. No, she had to get a hold of Callahan's other rifle.

Mattie turned and crawled on her belly to the end of the wagon. She gave a quick look around, came to her feet, and reached inside. Even in the dark, it didn't take but a second to find the gun. Callahan always kept both his rifles against the wall within easy reach from outside. A moment later she was under the wagon again, her body soaked with the sweat of fear. She breathed a sigh of relief to have managed it safely as she settled back into place.

Mattie listened to the helpless screams of those

301

hiding in tents and wagons. She wondered how in the world the women could stand their terrifying confines. She would be shivering with fear, knowing the thin canvas to be meager protection from the prowling shadows slithering just outside.

Mattie sighed with disgust, knowing even in the best of times, she was not what one would call a sharpshooter. And now, in her fear, she cursed the palsey-like shaking of her hands. Mattie raised the rifle to her shoulder and propped her arm upon the ground. It steadied her aim somewhat, but even so, she knew it would be a miracle if she managed to hit anything.

Mattie's eyes widened with shock as Lucy Stewart ran past her line of vision, a grinning half-naked savage hot on her trail. Mattie shuddered as the Indian reached out and grabbed a handful of hair. Lucy was yanked off her feet and flung to the ground in a cloud of dust. Mattie watched in amazement, for right in the open, careless of the obvious danger of being shot, the Indian pounced eagerly upon her.

He was tearing at her dress, trying to lift it over her head, her pitiful cries unheard, when Callahan suddenly lunged from the shadows. In an instant the man was pulled from the sobbing woman. A handgun was pushed into his belly and the man doubled over dead.

Callahan never saw the Indian behind him, but Mattie did. She took careful aim and pulled the trigger.

All the curses she had learned since beginning this trip whispered past her stiff lips as the bullet kicked up the dirt at Callahan's feet. Mattie shivered, knowing she had barely missed the man, when the one she wanted to hit was some two yards to his right.

Callahan grinned as he saw the tiny cloud of dust swirl at his feet and spun around to face his equally

302

grinning combatant. It was Mattie of course. He'd never known another to be quite so bad a shot. Obviously she had been trying to protect him. Once this was over, he was going to insist she learn how to shoot.

Mattie jumped, her heart pounding with fear as she listened to Mrs. Thompson's piercing scream. Suddenly it was cut eerily short. Mattie shivered. She didn't want to know the reason why. The Indian was howling like a coyote when he jumped from the Thompson wagon. Behind him stumbled a screaming Augusta, the Thompsons' eight-year-old daughter. Helplessly she fell to the ground, and was savagely yanked again to her feet by her hair.

Mattie cringed. By the glittering lust which shone clearly in his eyes, she knew what the savage was about to do. He was taking his prize of battle, dragging the girl away from the camp into the darkness, and no one had noticed. No one was going to stop him.

Mattie looked wildly about for help, but of course, everyone was intent on fighting the battle immediately at hand. They hadn't the time or the inclination to worry of one child. There were dozens still to protect.

Without thinking—indeed, she dared not, for she'd never find the courage needed should she think—Mattie slid from the shadowy protection of the wagon. She was out in the open now. The circle of wagons was against her back.

Godalmighty, but it was dark. Mattie wondered, for a moment, how she would find the girl in this huge expanse of blackness. But she needn't have worried. Augusta's cries were clear enough, the sound leading her on like a beacon flashing in the darkest night.

As it turned out, Mattie came across them quite by chance. Actually, she almost fell over them. She

303

tripped on something, a rock perhaps, and her finger closed automatically on the trigger. The gun went off purely by accident.

The Indian lifted himself off the sobbing girl, as if to lunge at his attacker, but, Mattie would realize later, the action was purely reflexive. Severely injured, he fell helplessly to his back. He was moaning at her feet. She could just see his writhing outline next to the stiller form at his side. Mattie's heart was thundering with fear. Had she killed Augusta in her awkward attempt to save her? "Augusta," she whispered. "Are you all right?"

"No" came her whimpering reply. "He ripped my clothes. He was trying to hurt me."

"We have to go back," Mattie returned, relieved to know she hadn't found her too late. Augusta was shaking so, Mattie wondered if she could stand. But there was no time to feel pity for the girl. She had to get the two of them to safety and she had to do it now! "Hurry," she urged as she reached for the small hand and pulled her to her feet.

Mattie was backing away from the now silent form, when another suddenly loomed before her. Augusta screamed and flung herself at her savior, almost knocking Mattie over in the process. Mattie's hand automatically lifted the gun and pointed at the Indian's bare chest.

Hawk watched her back away. That she was afraid was obvious, and the knowledge brought a stirring to his loins. He liked them to be afraid. Somehow their fear added to his strength. He would take this one, of course, as he had so many others, but this taking would be all the more special because of her show of courage.

For a moment Mattie thought he was going to let her go unassaulted, when he suddenly gave the most

304

bone-chilling smile Mattie had ever seen. It was dark. The night held only the gentle glow of stars. And yet Mattie saw everything that was evil and cruel in that smile. She gave an unconscious shiver and knew she'd gladly face death before allowing capture.

He bent at the waist, the movement so slight as to go nearly unnoticed. But Mattie was attuned to any action in this dangerous foe. She knew he was about to pounce. Indeed, she had been waiting for it. Mattie took a step back and raised the barrel of the gun a fraction. "Don't do it," she warned evenly, while silently marveling at the steadiness of her voice.

The Indian laughed, his dark eyes glittering with hate and lust. Slowly, insultingly, his gaze slid over her small frame. He smiled again, knowing his victory eminent when he saw her shiver of revulsion. He spit out the word, "Squaw."

Obviously he was telling her she was only a woman and therefore no match against an Indian brave. An unnecessary effort on his part, some rational corner of Mattie's near-hysterical brain reasoned, for she was already conscious of the fact. That he could best her was a foregone conclusion. Except for one important fact. She held an equalizer in her hands.

Her finger tightened on the trigger as he took a step toward them. When she didn't fire, he laughed confidently, believing he held her cowed in fear. But his laughter turned into a short, surprised gasp as the gun belatedly went off.

Mattie almost dropped the rifle, for she was far more surprised than he to hear it fire. Oh God, why hadn't she been able to master this thing? Mattie gave an unconscious curse as she fumbled, trying desperately to hold on to the weapon. She couldn't help her sigh of relief when an instant later she had her finger back on the trigger. She looked across the ten feet that separated them and wondered how she could have missed.

The Indian's teeth flashed white in a sneer of disgust that she should dare suppose to keep him at bay. There was no way Hawk would be bested by a mere squaw, rifle or no. He was going to kill her for her arrogance. And he was going to kill her slow.

From a band of rawhide tied around his naked thigh, Hawk pulled the longest knife Mattie had ever seen. Mattie pushed the sobbing, clinging girl away. "Run," she almost screamed. "Get help!"

Wild with fear, Augusta's feet fairly flew over the uneven landscape as she raced for the protection of the wagons.

Mattie continued to back away, her gun raised still, hoping to ward off his advance. She wanted to cry, knowing she couldn't hit anything more than a few feet away, and if she waited for him to get that close, it would be too late.

Mattie was shaking like a leaf when her back came up flush against a solid form. She almost groaned aloud, for Mattie knew it wasn't a tree, although she imagined a tree couldn't be any harder. She didn't want to look. She prayed it was Callahan, but knew she would have instantly recognized his touch. In any case, the gleam in her adversary's eyes left her little doubt that it was yet another grotesquely painted savage.

Still, some part of her refused to give up hope. Perhaps one of the other men from the camp? But her heart sank to the pit of her stomach with despair, when, seconds later, a dark hand reached around her and relieved her of the rifle.

Mattie tried to dash to her left, only to find herself suddenly and all too easily flung to the ground, her rifle thrown carelessly aside. In an instant the Indian she had faced off was upon her, ripping at her clothes, muttering obvious words of rage and hate.

Mattie's piercing scream was abruptly cut off as he landed a mighty blow to her mouth. Her lip split. She groaned from the pain and gagged as her mouth filled with blood. Mattie shook her head, trying to fight off both Indian and the threatening blackness that hovered about the edges of her consciousness.

She couldn't faint. To do so would only allow this animal free rein. She had to fight him, no matter she would likely be hurt all the more. She was too frightened to do otherwise.

Her nails bit into his cheeks and gouged a deep line down his face. He hit her again. This time the blow brought her closer than ever to darkness. She actually saw tiny flickering lights dance just behind her eyelids.

The savage lay heavily upon her. From somewhere above them, Mattie heard a sharp word. A moment later the two men were arguing, obviously over her. Mattie shivered, for it was apparent they were discussing the merits of taking her with them, as one pointed to some far-off unseen place, while the other grabbed at her breast and squeezed. Her attacker wanted her now. And from his vicious expression she knew he wanted her dead.

What was worse? Having your throat cut, or being forced to accommodate one or more of these animals? Throat cut, probably, she reasoned, but that left no chance for possible later escape. In any case, Mattie was destined to have no say in the matter. She gasped as she was yanked roughly to her feet. An instant later she was stumbling almost drunkenly, blinded by her hair, pushed and dragged over the blackened landscape.

Mattie was gasping for breath by the time they

reached the ponies. God, no! They were taking her away! How was she ever to find her way back?

In her struggles, Mattie kicked out and almost grunted with satisfaction to hear the low grunt as her booted foot contacted with his shin. She screamed again and yet again, her arms flaying wildly as she desperately sought her freedom. But freedom was not within her grasp on this night. She never saw the silencing punch come speeding toward her jaw nor realized that it left nothing but blackness in its wake.

Chapter Twenty-one

Mattie took a deep, silent breath against the pain that sliced through her brain. Her cheek and jaw ached, while her lips felt swollen to thrice their size. She tried to open her eyes, but thought better of the notion as the discomfort intensified to the point of agony. She felt the need to groan, but forced aside the impulse, knowing instinctively that something was wrong. Something was very wrong indeed, and she'd best continue to act as though asleep until she figured out what it was.

Beyond the pounding in her head came the usual sounds of camp. Dogs barked, children laughed as they ran on by. The sounds seemed much the same as she had awakened to every morning for the last five months. Only they weren't the same.

She heard not curses, nor the jingling of harnesses. No pots clanged as they were set upon morning fires. She couldn't remember why, but she knew she wasn't in her own camp.

What had happened? What had brought her here? And where was here?

Suddenly her memory returned, along with the accompanying grisly pictures of last night. It was last night, wasn't it? Mattie didn't know for sure.

She tried to think, but the panic that suffused her being left little room for calm reasoning. She had been taken by the Indians! Stories abounded of those unlucky enough to remain alive among the savages. Mattie shivered, knowing the abuse and beatings that were sure to fill her immediate future. Could she endure what lay ahead? Had she the strength? Would she ever be the same after this?

Mattie strove to ignore the most glaring reality of all, but even though she tried, she knew, in her heart, they'd not be satisfied to merely use her as a slave. Her whole being rebelled at the grotesque images that flashed through her mind and she knew a hopelessness never before felt. After last night she held no false hope. If they could take a child, nothing would stop them from taking her.

Mattie's body stiffened as she realized she wasn't alone. Someone was moving around behind her. She could hear their soft footsteps. Suddenly they stopped. Her skin tingled. Someone was leaning over her, she could almost feel them. She could definitely smell them. She waited for the attack she knew to be forthcoming. Amazingly, nothing happened. Perhaps whoever it was wished only to see if she still slept. Mattie controlled the unbelievable urge to bolt, and with a force of will managed to keep her breathing at a shallow, even rate.

Whoever it was seemed apparently satisfied that she would offer no immediate problems. Mattie heard a low grunt, that she supposed indicated approval, just before the footsteps moved away. A blinding shaft of light almost caused her a groan as it fell over her face, and then came the blessed dimness again.

Was she alone? Had the Indian left her for a spell? Could she use this moment to escape?

Mattie opened her eyes a crack, not at all surprised to find herself in a cozy enclosure. A teepee, no doubt. The train had passed many an Indian village in the five months of traveling. Mattie wasn't ignorant of the Indian's nomadic style of housing. Still, she had never before been inside one.

Someone had thought enough to cover her against the cool night air with a heavy buffalo skin, but now, in the warmth of day, the heat of her covers grew oppressive. Even though she was decidedly uncomfortable, she dared not throw the covering aside. She wasn't as yet positive as to her being alone.

Mattie turned her head, knowing she must, yet dreading what she might see. She breathed a sigh of relief as her gaze scanned the empty teepee.

Mattie forced aside the pounding in her head. She hadn't the time or luxury to think on pain now. Not when her life might very well hang on the quickness of her actions. Her mind set instantly to form a plan. Obviously she couldn't just walk out the opening, wish all she encountered a good day, and make her merry way unaccosted back to the train.

That, of course, would be pure insanity. A flicker of an idea made itself known. Mattie had heard stories of the terror the Indians held for those poor souls, driven mad with their fear. If indeed the stories were true, that was undoubtedly the only thing these savages did fear. But were they afraid enough to simply let someone clearly out of her mind go?

Mattie shook her head, unwilling to chance it. Besides, she had no guarantee they wouldn't simply do away with her, even if she had the courage and ability to pull off such a charade.

Annoyed with herself for dawdling, Mattie knew the only chance of escape was action, and there might never be a more opportune moment than right now. The only thing she could see to do would be to sneak out the back, under the hides, and make a run for it. With any luck she might lose herself in the hills and gullies that dotted this wilderness. Mattie wondered if she had any real hope of escape. No doubt the Indians would easily find her. Mattie pushed aside the truth of her thoughts, for she had to try or forever curse her cowardly inaction.

Moments later Mattie found herself faced with the first of her problems. There was no way she could crawl under the teepee. The skins were stretched so tight, they wouldn't move more than an inch above the ground. Mattie whispered an urgent expletive, all too easily adopted from the men on the train. She had to find a knife.

Her gaze moved frantically around the curved walls. No knives, but there were spears. Quickly she took one of the much decorated three standing near the doorway and sliced a line through the heavy skin, just opposite the front opening.

Mattie was out and running before she even looked where she was going. Indeed, she didn't care where she was going. All she knew was she had to get away. Without thinking, she jumped a small fire, nearly knocking down the old woman who was bending over it. Fire? It took a second, but she finally realized she wasn't struggling over uneven landscape. The ground was smooth and level, free of short grass and tumbleweed. The area wasn't an unbroken stretch of prairie, but held instead maybe a hundred brightly decorated teepees.

Mattie's steps faltered and she came to an awkward jerking stop. She looked around and found to her equal amazement and chagrin, she had run right into the center of camp. Her lips tightened with disgust and she shook her head in dismay at her all-so-obvious error. The teepee wasn't sitting at the edge of a camp, as she had imagined, but rather at its very center.

Mattie glanced at the surprised faces staring her way. It seemed to her all were momentarily frozen in place, for, like her, their astonishment couldn't have been more obvious. For a second she wondered why

312

no one had moved. But she realized they would no doubt come instantly to their senses should she dare to continue on and pounce upon her as a whole. Her pride rebelled at the thought of their enjoyment at her suffering, for she instinctively knew they'd find much to laugh at while watching her being dragged back.

Mattie instantly realized her alternatives. She could fight and scream as she was carried or dragged back to the teepee, or she could turn and retrace her steps, under her own power. She opted for the more dignified route.

Mattie wouldn't look at the smirking faces of the men. She heard the low chuckles, but wouldn't glance toward the sound. Silently, with back straight and eyes forward, she gave an arrogant toss of her head and walked back to the teepee from whence she had come. She entered it this time, not as she had left, but by the front opening. No one guessed how badly her knees shook, for she didn't collapse until she was out of sight.

"That's right, Callahan. Just leave me here to rot. Take your stupid guns where ever you're taking them. Don't worry about me. I'll be just fine. It won't take hardly any effort at all to fight off the whole of them.

"I don't need him," she continued on, her voice growing decidedly watery as she brushed aside hateful tears with the back of her hand. "I've made it just fine without him so far." Purposely she ignored the fact that she had done nothing of the sort, for without his help she would have been as capable as an infant on this journey. "I don't care that he left me behind. I don't!"

Mattie's tirade was brought to an instant end as the opening to the teepee parted. Someone entered, but Mattie didn't look up. Her whole body stiffened as she awaited the punishment that would surely come.

They had left her long enough. At least an hour or

more had passed since she had returned to the teepee. She supposed they had not forgotten her existence. Indeed, she believed they had left her to imagine the terrible things they were going to do to her. And in her enforced lonely prison, her imagination had run riot.

She trembled. She was terribly afraid. Desperately so, but she wasn't going to snivel and cry and beg for mercy. She didn't care what they did to her. Mattie knew that wasn't entirely true, but she wasn't going to ever allow another to cow her again. After all, what could they do to her? At the very worst all they could do was kill her. Mattie gave an almost imperceptible shrug. Certainly she had no wish to die, but how much terror could a body stand before she no longer cared? Mattie was to learn she had a ways to go.

She had been staring into the smoldering smokeless fire, centered directly beneath the opening in the teepee's roof and surrounded by a circle of flat rocks. She raised her eyes as a young Indian girl placed a large clay pot upon one of the warm rocks and silently left, but not before shooting Mattie a look of pure venom.

Mattie's mouth opened and she stared at her with surprise. Why should the girl hate her? What had she ever done except to pass through their country? If anyone had a reason to hate it was she.

A moment later an old woman, bent at the waist, perhaps permanently, stood inside the doorway. With a grunt she deposited a small cache of clothing at Mattie's side and motioned for her to put the articles on.

Mattie hesitated, but the woman grunted again and pulled at her own clothes, showing her with swift hand movements what she wanted.

Mattie nodded and reached for the clothing. It was obvious they wanted her to change. What she didn't know was why.

The old woman watched as Mattie unbuttoned her blouse and slid her skirt down her hips. When she reached for the clothes, the woman shook her head and again pulled at her clothes.

"Why?" Mattie asked, knowing the meaning of the gesture. "Why do I have to take everything off?"

There was no answer forthcoming, and Mattie sighed, knowing she would do as she was told.

Her fingers smoothed the soft buckskin dress over her hips. Mattie had to admit the dress was pretty, decorated as it was with fringe, if a bit short, for it came only to her knees. Comfortable too, she silently admitted. It gave a woman a certain freedom of movement. The whites could do worse than imitate their red sister's style of dress.

Moccasins were taken from the woman's pocket and extended toward Mattie. Mattie sighed, took off her boots and torn stockings, and put them on.

Next came a comb, carved from wood. And by the time the old women left the teepee, Mattie's hair was plaited into a long, thick, neat braid.

Mattie wondered if all slaves received this preferential treatment but knew instinctively they did not. The knowledge alternately lifted her spirits, in the hopes of being allowed her freedom, and plunged them into dark despair, knowing they weren't about to set her free, not if they wanted her to dress as one of them. Mattie's lips twisted with disgust, for the knowledge did little toward hampering her appetite. How could she think of eating at a time like this? Surely her one and only thought should be escape. But her stomach wouldn't listen to her thoughts. She heard the impolite growl as she breathed in the pleasing aroma emanating from the loosely covered bowl. Apparently, although the girl hadn't said anything, the meal was obviously meant for her. Mattie shrugged. At least they had no intention of starving her to death. And if she was ever to manage escape, she'd best keep up her strength.

She was just about to reach for the pot when again the opening to the teepee parted and another entered. This time Mattie's silent show of bravado disintegrated into nothingness as she turned to see an Indian brave, standing tall and menacingly over her. Mattie couldn't breathe for the terror that struck her heart. She watched as he silently took her by the shoulders and brought her to her feet. This was it. Mattie squeezed her eyes shut. Now the beatings would begin. She felt disgust at her cowardice, but couldn't suppress the small whimpering sound that came from her throat. Her fear was uncontrollable as she shivered, awaiting the first of many blows. But amazingly nothing happened.

Mattie opened her eyes and watched as he merely pointed toward what she had believed to be her meal. With some grunts and much hand waving, Mattie finally understood he wanted her to serve him his food. Mattie nodded, knowing the futility of refusing. If she didn't do as he wanted, he'd simply force her. In any case, there was no sense causing a ruckus over this simple order. No doubt she'd have many an occasion to deny him later. Mattie shivered at the ominous thought.

She sat behind him while he ate, a position she was nearly pushed into. Her stomach growled. It had to be mid-day, perhaps even later than that, and she hadn't eaten anything since the night before.

Mattie knew, under normal circumstances, she would have been embarrassed, especially since the sounds her stomach gave off were loud enough for any to have heard. But she wasn't the least embarrassed now. She was starving, and she didn't care who knew it.

"Very gracious, I must say," she mumbled, knowing he couldn't understand a word of it. "You know I've got to be hungry, but do you offer a morsel? Indeed you do not.

"I only hope to someday return your hospitality. Perhaps you might one day visit my home."

"But you are not visiting, woman. You live here now."

"Surely not forever," Mattie returned conversationally and then suddenly gasped. "You understand me?"

The man's back was to her. She saw the slight shrug of his naked back. "I've had white slaves before."

Mattie almost breathed a sigh of relief, but instantly realized she had little to be relieved about. The man understood English. So what? Did that make him any less a savage? She knew it did not. And yet, for some unknown reason, Mattie seemed to gain courage. It wasn't that she was no longer afraid, but rather that her fears were placed more firmly under control.

"Slave? Is that what I am?"

"It is."

Mattie shook her head. There was a time when her family had owned slaves. How ironic to now find herself in much the same position. She wanted to tell him that the practice had been abolished, that the war had set them free. She wanted to tell him the impossibility of it all. She wanted to tell him she'd never willingly submit, but she only asked, "Why? Why didn't you just kill me when you had the chance?"

The Indian grinned, but Mattie never saw it, as she was still talking to his back. "The chance hasn't yet escaped me, woman. I could kill you and will, if the need be."

Mattie shivered at his calm, almost nonchalant promise of death. Where is your bravery now, Mattie? she asked in silence. For someone who, not more than

317

an hour ago, believed death no great terror, you've certainly made an extreme about-face.

Mattie knew the best thing to do would be to remain as quiet as possible and pray for the chance to escape. She knew this, but her jittery nerves and fears wouldn't allow silence. She had to talk or start screaming like a mad woman, until the Indian ended her torture forever.

"What do they call you?"

"You will never address me by name. You need only know you belong to me."

"And if someone should ask to whom I belong?"

"You are a slave. No one will speak to you."

Mattie sighed. Is that the way of things here? Would no one ever speak to her because she was a slave? Aside from the abuse she was sure to suffer at his hand, Mattie wondered how she would manage to live out the rest of her life in silence? Finally she forced the thought from her mind as too gruesome to contemplate. "I'm hungry."

The Indian nodded.

"Are you going to give me something to eat?"

"You will not question me. You will eat when I finish."

Mattie's lips thinned to an angry line. She detested the man. It wasn't bad enough that he was a savage, but he was impolite as well. She almost laughed aloud at her ridiculous thoughts. Impolite? Yes, well, he was that and no doubt a few other things she hadn't yet begun to imagine. Suddenly the pot he was eating out of was thrust into her lap, its thick contents almost spilling out upon her lap as it tipped.

Mattie stared at the man, who was finally looking at her. For the first time, Mattie realized, this was the one who had stopped that vicious beast last night. Surely he wasn't as bad as she had first believed. He had saved her, hadn't he?

318

"Eat."

Mattie blinked with confusion. "Where's mine?"

"Nothing here is yours. You will finish what I leave."

"What? And eat out of your bowl?"

The Indian smiled, but said nothing, silently daring her to refuse his leavings.

Mattie shivered with disgust. It was he who had leaned over her while she pretended to sleep. The man smelled so horrible, she couldn't have mistaken him for another. The stench nearly took one's breath away. Since he had entered the teepee, Mattie had fought a constant battle not to gag. His skin glistened even in the dim light provided by the opening in the roof. He was covered with some kind of grease, no doubt the origins of the rancid smell. He had eaten with his hands. Even now he was licking the last of it from his fingers. Mattie's stomach rebelled. There was no way she could swallow something he had put his hands in.

Mattie shook her head and placed the bowl at her side.

The Indian grinned, knowing she wouldn't deny her hunger for long. He gave an uncaring shrug, came to his feet, and left her alone.

Mattie spent the rest of the day sitting alone and looking at the slowly congealing bowl of food.

There was some sort of ruckus outside. Mattie blinked her eyes with surprise. She hadn't realized she had fallen asleep and now winced at the pain as she tried to loosen the stiff muscles of her neck and shoulder.

It was night. Since the fire had gone out, inside, the teepee was completely black. Mattie crawled toward the sound and pushed aside the skin that hung over the teepee's opening, no small feat, since she couldn't see a hand before her eyes. She stepped outside.

It was lighter out here. Two fires blazed, almost side by side, illuminating all of the camp and the hundreds of people sitting and standing around them. Mattie breathed huge gulps of clean air deep into her lungs. She hadn't known how delightful an experience it could be until she had spent most of the day in that suffocating teepee.

Why hadn't she thought to come out before? Mattie stared around her. No one was giving her the slightest attention but for one young, huge brave who stood directly behind her. Mattie shrugged as she turned from his expressionless dark gaze. Her bodyguard, no doubt.

Mattie wondered what the commotion was about. She looked around. As best as she could figure the two men motioning toward an old man sitting at one end of the fires seemed to be the stars of the show.

Mattie was suddenly shoved forward, the force of the blow to her back almost knocking her to her knees. Behind her the Indian whose job it was to guard her was speaking to the same Indian girl who had earlier entered the teepee. That he wasn't pleased was obvious indeed.

Mattie knew the girl had shoved her. She already knew the girl hated her. What she didn't know was why?

"You hate me. Why?"

The girl's pretty face twisted into a silent, hateful sneer.

Mattie imagined she didn't understand and shrugged when the girl only continued to snarl at her.

"You are white. Is that not reason enough?"

So she did speak English. Mattie wondered just how many poor souls had been captured and used as slaves for these people. "No. It is not. Why do you hate me?"

"Black Bear will fight Hawk for you." Suddenly the girl spat in Mattie's face.

Mattie instantly saw red at the vile insult. Her fingers curled into claws that itched to rake the girl's smooth cheeks. And she would have lunged at the sneering girl had not some small part of her mind wisely called for sanity. Mattie realized little would be accomplished should she retaliate by attacking this girl. Mattie trembled at the effort it took to keep her hands at her sides.

She didn't need to ask. Following the direction of the girl's worried glances, Mattie knew without being told Black Bear was one of the two standing before the old man arguing his cause. She shivered as she realized the other was the man who tried to attack her. Mattie trembled with the knowledge that she should be forced to submit to either man. "One of them belongs to you?"

"Black Bear is my husband."

Mattie couldn't help herself, she laughed. The girl was jealous. Of all the ridiculous emotions to surface, that had to be it. Good God, if she only knew how little her reason. She'd give anything to be gone from here, to never have come here in the first place. And this silly girl was jealous!

Mattie wanted to reassure her, to proclaim her innocence, but knew any denials on her part would be next to useless. It didn't matter that Mattie had no interest in the Indian. That he wanted her was enough to instill hatred in the girl.

"If Black Bear dies, so will you," the girl promised, and Mattie shivered under the threat, not for a minute doubting her word.

Still, Mattie managed to keep her fears well hidden. She faced her antagonist without showing a flicker of the terror that chilled her heart. "If Black Bear dies, will Hawk let you kill me?" Mattie's sharp mind raced on, knowing instinctively that this girl, and the jealousy she felt, just might be her only means of escape. "And if Black Bear lives, but loses, will he stop wanting me?" she taunted deliberately. Mattie squared her shoulders and allowed her gaze to drift over the young girl. Her calm, insulting appraisal clearly told the girl Mattie believed herself without competition. "Both men want me."

The girl bared her teeth and growled. Mattie knew she was about to pounce on her. An instant later her show of temper was cut short by a few sharp words issued from Mattie's guard.

Mattie shot a glance toward the man hovering close to her side and prayed he didn't understand a word she spoke. She watched the girl finger the knife at her waist and knew she longed to plunge it into Mattie's body. "Help me get away and you will have no need for hatred."

Mattie held her breath and waited. At any second she imagined the silent Indian at her side knocking her senseless to the floor. Mattie breathed a sigh of relief when nothing happened. Obviously he hadn't understood.

A light of understanding grew to life in the girl's dark eyes. All of her problems would be solved if this woman was gone from here. She would have killed her herself if she didn't fear Black Bear's rage. That he wanted this woman was obvious. He didn't treat her as he had the others. He had covered her last night, while she slept at their side. Little Flower was astonished at the tenderness he showed. Black Bear had ignored her when she had asked why the woman tied outside, like the other slaves? But when she suggested the woman should be beaten, she had backed away with fear as Black Bear turned his anger on her.

Little Flower was desperate that Black Bear never touch this woman. She had seen the look in his eyes

322

while he watched the white one sleep. Somehow she knew it would never be the same between them if he did.

Slowly a plan formed. It wouldn't be so very difficult to arrange, Little Flower reasoned. Black Bear and Hawk would share the sweat lodge tonight to purify their spirits for tomorrow's battle.

For this night Lame Deer would be the woman's only guard. A sleeping potion in his water should take care of that. All they had to do was get past the guards, and she didn't care what happened to the woman. Actually she did care. She hoped the white woman would die before reaching help.

Mattie's spirits thrilled as she watched the girl smile at her. She thanked God that she had found an ally. No matter how this woman might hate her, she wanted to see her gone, if possible even more than Mattie wanted to go.

If he had any sense, he'd leave her right where she was. Damn fool! What kind of a woman runs off in the night in the midst of an Indian attack? God, he wanted to wring her neck, and that was exactly what he was going to do the minute he got her out of there.

Callahan's hands itched with the need to spank her until she screamed for mercy. But an instant later his intentions were forgotten. He pushed himself flatter to the ground as the Indian moved silently across his path. A film of sweat broke out over his body. He breathed a silent sigh of relief. That was close, too close. Another yard and the bastard couldn't have helped but see him.

He was out of his mind. That was it. She had finally done him in. Anyone with a lick of sense wouldn't be here alone. What he should have done was race back to Fort Laramie and gotten the cavalry.

And he would have done just that if he hadn't known what these bastards did to women captives. Callahan wouldn't let himself think what had probably already happened to her. What torture she must have suffered last night.

It didn't matter. He only wanted her alive. He didn't care how many men might have touched her. He'd make it all right for her. If it took forever, he'd make it all right.

The night held an air of excitement. Something was happening in the camp. Callahan wondered if Mattie might not be at the center of the commotion, but instantly discounted the notion. Surely the arrival of one more slave, no matter her beauty, would not cause this almost party atmosphere.

He didn't know what it was, nor did he care. All Callahan wanted was to get close enough to see where they were keeping her. Later, after everyone slept, he'd slip into the camp and take her out.

Callahan knew he had almost no chance of seeing his plans come to fruition. It would be a miracle if he managed to pull this off. No doubt he'd be dead by morning. Still, the almost positive knowledge did not deter. He had to try, for death could only be a blessed relief compared to the torment of living his life without her.

Callahan came to the edge of a small rise and almost screamed out his frustration. He wasn't nearly close enough and yet he dared go no farther. There was no cover. Were he to venture on, he was sure to be caught and to find himself captured before he managed Mattie's escape would gain him nothing.

His gaze moved over a camp alive with people. How the hell was he going to find her in this? Her hair was as black as any Indian's. Her size wouldn't distinguish her in a crowd. It was impossible.

Callahan felt the urge to give in to useless tears of

despair as his gaze desperately scanned the milling crowd below. He knew she was down there, but where? God, please! He had to know exactly where!

He had to get closer. There was nothing he could do at this distance.

Mattie was sitting outside the teepee. Her hands were wrapped around her raised knees in order to ward off the chill of the night air. She stifled a yawn and the tired sigh that followed, as she purposely blinked away the need to close her eyes and rest her weary head upon her knees.

She did sigh then, but the sigh was one of longing. God, what she wouldn't give to be able to go inside and lie down. Mattie wondered with some puzzlement at the constant need for sleep she was developing. You would have thought, after last night, she'd be well rested. Why then was she so tired?

Maybe she was coming down with something, she reasoned. Well, whatever it was, she hoped it wouldn't show itself until she got out of here. The last thing she needed was to get sick.

Mattie suddenly recalled the last few weeks of almost marathon nightly sexual encounters. She shook her head and gave a secret smile. It didn't take much thinking on the matter to understand her need for sleep. Actually, last night was the first good night of rest she'd had in weeks.

Right now the warmth and softness of the buffalo hides inside beckoned, but Mattie dared not heed to their call. Should she succumb to this temptation, she might never get out of here. No, she had to stay awake. Awake and alert, that was the ticket to tonight's success.

Mattie's eyes widened with surprise to hear the howling laughter spread into a roar of joyous excitement. The camp, which had begun to quiet down since Black Bear and Hawk had secluded themselves inside a hide-covered hut, was suddenly wide awake.

Mattie had expected at any moment to find the means of escape at hand, for one by one the Indians had entered their teepees. What in the world had happened to bring them all awake again?

She came to her feet, but found it impossible to see over the heads of the happily dancing mob. Damn, she groaned silently. Surely this commotion would have been the perfect chance. Just the diversion she needed, since it had caught the attention of everyone in camp. Everyone, that is, but for her silent, ever-watchful guard.

Mattie glanced at the man. He hadn't taken his eyes off her. Mattie knew the Indian girl was going to help her. Both knew it had to be tonight. Tomorrow would be too late. But how? How in the world was she to get away with this watchdog forever at her heels?

Suddenly, as if someone had given a signal that had somehow passed by her unnoticed, the crowd parted in total silence. The old man who had listened to the brave's earlier arguments came out of his hut and moved into the crowd.

Mattie gasped and her eyes widened with disbelief and horror. It couldn't be! Her knees wobbled as a silent moan of agony constricted her chest.

Callahan stood calmly at the center of the crowd. Flanked by two huge braves, his mouth was bleeding and a swelling was beginning to grow beneath his right eye.

Mattie gave a silent curse. How could he have been so stupid as to have gotten captured? Conveniently she ignored the obvious fact that she herself was also a captive as she silently berated the man for a fool.

Suddenly her eyes widened as a thought occurred and she almost smiled with relief. He was sure to have

326

brought help. He wouldn't be alone. Mattie hid the smile she couldn't control. It wouldn't be long now. Between Little Flower and the men Callahan was with, they were sure to get out of here.

Callahan watched the bent old man approach. He knew he'd be punished for spying on the camp. But that was the chance he took. Callahan sighed. It wasn't so much that he was afraid for himself, although he wasn't happy at the thought of what they were sure to do to him. It was Mattie who was the reason for the aching inside his belly. It was she who worried him. Where was she? What had they done to her?

Callahan knew a smattering of Arapaho, but these people were Cheyenne. Would they understand him? He gave a slight shrug. It didn't matter, for he knew they'd never believe his reasoning for watching their settlement, in any case.

There was no way he was going to tell them the truth. No doubt they'd take exquisite joy in torturing Mattie just to watch his pain. No, he was going to tell them he was a trapper, much like themselves. Depending on their mood, the Indian often left a lone man in peace to go about his work. It was the settlers they most despised, the ones who killed their buffalo by the thousands and appropriated their land as if it were free for the taking.

The discussion was short. Callahan used what little Arapaho he knew along with the common tongue of the plains, sign language, all to no avail. They did not believe him. From the beginning he knew the chance he took. He might have come upon them in the open. Then again . . . He left the thought unfinished. It made no difference now. Either way was a gamble. One he couldn't know the outcome of, unless he tried it.

The Old One, as Callahan realized he was called,

turned his back and walked back to his skin-covered hut. The crowd remained silent until the man entered, but only until then.

Once he was gone from sight, a roar came upon his ears the likes of which he'd never known. He was being dragged to the edge of their encampment where poles had been driven into the ground. There wasn't any use in fighting them. He had as much chance of winning had he pitted his strength against the force of the tornado.

Hastily he was tied spread-eagled between two of the poles. His torture began immediately thereafter.

Mattie looked out the hole in the teepee's roof and wondered how much longer before dawn. Little Flower was sitting across the small fire, almost opposite her. Her guard was still outside.

The camp had been quiet for some time now. Mattie tried again and again to ask the girl what she was going to do, but her every attempt was met with a stony cold look of hatred. Was she or wasn't she going to help her? God, but she couldn't stand this not knowing. More than that she couldn't stand what they had done to Callahan.

At last glance he was tied still at the poles, his body covered with cuts, his face a bloody pulp. She had to get out of here! She had to get him out!

Little Flower came suddenly to her feet. Silently she motioned Mattie to follow. Mattie's heart thundered so loud in her chest she wondered if the whole camp mightn't awaken at the roar. Now that the time had finally come, she was terrified almost into immobility. Mattie had to force herself to put one foot before the other. Suppose something went wrong? Suppose she didn't make it?

Just outside and to the right of the teepee's opening,

her guard sat snoring loudly, his head resting in sleep against his raised knees. Mattie knew Little Flower had given him something. Idly she wondered if the girl wouldn't be held accountable. Mattie shivered. She wouldn't want to be the one to answer for letting a prisoner escape.

Mattie breathed a sigh of relief. It was darker now. Both fires had burned down to smoldering embers and gave off only a minimum of light. Mattie glanced to her left. Two braves sat facing each other only a short distance from where Callahan hung. And hung was the right word, for although he was tied hands and feet to the poles, he had slumped forward in sleep. God, please, she prayed it was only sleep. Mattie wouldn't allow herself to think his relaxed position meant anything else.

Little Flower was leading her in the opposite direction, through the darkened camp. When they passed the last hut, she simply and silently shoved Mattie forward. Was this it? Was she to be given no horse?

Mattie shot the girl a puzzled look and watched in some amazement as her pretty face twisted into a goading sneer. She was silently daring Mattie to show her reluctance to leave on her own. To show a flicker of fear.

Little Flower had no idea Callahan had brought men with him to save her. But suppose she missed them in the dark? Was she to walk the miles that separated her from safety? Mattie's lips thinned with anger. Damn her and her childish actions. Didn't the girl realize that unless she got away, nothing was changed? Either Black Bear would take her to his bed, or wish he had, possibly for as long as she remained here. Mattie restrained the impulse to slap the girl's evil grin, knowing a show of violence would lead only to recapture.

Little Flower made to turn and leave, but Mattie

329

had other ideas on that score. She was leaving here, but she wasn't doing it alone. She was leaving with Callahan.

"Wait!" she whispered.

Little Flower hesitated and turned to face her, a knowing look in her eyes.

Mattie knew Little Flower expected to hear her ask for a horse, so she was pleased to see the look of confusion come into the girl's eyes when she said, "I'm not leaving without my man."

Little Flower's eyes narrowed with suspicion. "What man?" she asked, thinking, of course, of her own husband.

"The one they captured tonight."

"He belongs to you?" Mattie almost laughed at the astonishment that registered.

"He does, and you are going to help me get him out."

Little Flower shook her head. "I cannot."

Mattie's eyes hardened. "You will, or I'll tell Black Bear you helped me escape."

"No!" she gasped, and visibly shivered.

Mattie felt a moment's pity for the girl. No one should live with that kind of fear of her husband.

"He will . . ." Little Flower didn't finish her thoughts. She suddenly sighed and asked, "How?"

"There are two men watching him. Just talk to them." Mattie knew it was up to her to do something. The men that had come with Callahan couldn't simply ride to his rescue, lest they risk alerting the whole camp. No matter how many had come, she knew there wasn't enough on the whole train to thwart these people.

Little Flower shook her head. "If I talk to them they will know." A moment later she nodded her head. "I will bring them water."

Mattie nodded. Whatever it took. She watched as

Little Flower turned away again and thought of the consequences of her actions. Mattie didn't want to see the girl suffer, no matter the resentment between them. Mattie stopped her again with a touch to her shoulder. "Whatever you're using. Put it in everyone's water, or they'll suspect you."

Little Flower nodded her understanding and for the first time gave Mattie a real smile.

Mattie returned with the girl to the teepee and waited alone as Little Flower went about the chore. She fidgeted nervously, pacing back and forth, as she watched the dark night slowly grow light. Please, she prayed, hurry! Soon it would be too late!

It was almost light when Little Flower finally returned to the teepee. Mattie sighed with relief as the girl silently bade her to follow.

The guards sitting before Callahan were sprawled upon the ground in a deep sleep. Still, Mattie moved on silent feet toward the poles and its occupant. She was standing behind him, hiding actually, afraid at any second someone would walk outside his teepee to greet the new morning.

"Callahan," Mattie whispered. "Callahan, can you hear me?"

A low groan was her only answer.

"Callahan, damn it. Wake up. We've got to get out of here right now!"

"What?" he murmured, his voice dry and aching. Who the hell was bothering him. Why didn't they just leave him alone?

Mattie breathed a sigh of annoyance. There was a clear edge to her voice when she spoke again. "I said we've got to get out of here. Wake up, will you?"

Callahan forced his legs to support his weight and almost screamed at the pain that rushed into his arms and hands. They had gone numb, holding his weight for hours, but now that he had eased the pressure, the pain was nearly unbearable.

He groaned.

Mattie poked him. "Will you wake up? Have I done this for nothing?"

Callahan couldn't understand the words through the blaze of fire that raced up his arms, but the tone was unmistakably angry.

"What?" he asked, his voice growing clearer, his senses beginning to return.

"We have to go."

Callahan opened his eyes and looked around him. Almost directly in front of him were two braves sound asleep. Callahan smiled. Someone had been very busy tonight. He heard her whisper his name again. Where the hell was she? It was Mattie who was talking to him, wasn't it? "Where are you?"

"I'm behind you. We have to go."

"A very commendable idea, lady. Cut me loose and we'll get on with it.

Mattie glanced behind her. She was out in the open. Any one of the guards could see her by merely turning their heads. They had to hurry.

But perhaps they couldn't. Perhaps the men who had come for her had silently taken care of the guards.

"Where are the others?"

"What others?"

"You're not here alone?"

And at his answering silence she groaned. "Oh, that's just great, Callahan. You've got to be the most brilliant . . ." Mattie never finished her tirade.

"Shut the hell up and cut me loose," he interrupted.

"With what? My teeth?" she sneered.

"Lady, your tongue appears sharp enough."

"Unlike your common sense, you mean?"

Callahan strove to control his temper, not an easy accomplishment considering the degree of pain he suffered and the aggravation she managed to instill. But arguing with her was getting them nowhere. He sighed. "If we're finished insulting each other, perhaps you might get us the hell out of here. There's a knife in my boot!"

Mattie bent down and lifted the leg of his trousers, only to hear him growl, "My right boot, damn it!"

Mattie gnashed her teeth against the need to rail at him. How was she supposed to know which boot?

Chapter Twenty-two

Callahan groaned as a sharp rock dug into his inflamed chest. He was without a shirt, having had it torn from his body last night, and the sun's rays, while at first bringing a measure of soothing relief to his injuries, now burnt the exposed, damaged skin raw.

They were lying in a shallow natural gully Callahan could only wish was filled with water. He sighed as he imagined the cool, silky comfort spreading over his burning skin.

In the distance, the reason for their quick descent was a swirl of dust, caused by a dozen or more Indian ponies. Callahan didn't for a minute think the Indians would simply let them go. At any second he expected to hear the shrieks of satisfaction at having found them out.

It didn't matter that most were probably drugged, as Mattie had explained. There were bound to be many who were not.

Callahan groaned as he moved to peer over the edge of the incline. Hugging the ground, dirt stung the raw, open wounds of his chest.

"Are you all right?"

Callahan gritted his teeth against the need to groan again. He might be able to control the need to cry out against this pain, but to control his temper, caused by the pain, was another matter indeed. "Just fine," he sneered. "Never better."

Mattie, not in the best of moods herself, since she suffered much the same discomforts, as her companion, didn't take kindly to his snarling comment. Her lips tightened in anger. "You don't have to be so nasty. I was only . . ."

"You were only nagging again," he interrupted. "Why, it's getting so a body can't find a minute's peace and quiet around you."

Mattie muttered a low angry growl, while wondering why she had been so foolish as to have taken the time and effort to cut him loose? The man definitely deserved whatever the Indians had in store for him. Too bad she hadn't realized that at the time.

Mattie turned around and lay against the side of the gully. Surely she couldn't be any worse off by herself. At least she wouldn't have to listen to this beast.

Callahan breathed a sigh of relief as the distant cloud of dust moved off toward his right. Obviously, the Indians hadn't as yet found their trail. He had no doubt that they would. He could only pray their luck would hold and they would come across his horse before that inevitability came about.

He shot a glance toward Mattie and scowled. How the hell was it she'd come out of this with nothing more than a bruise to her jaw? From the looks of her one would never guess she'd spent time as a prisoner among savages. True, she was wearing their costume, but why wasn't she in rags? Why had they dressed her in the finest, and no doubt softest, buckskin? Callahan shrugged away the silent question. His gaze moved over her with obvious appreciation. Rather than take away, the dress only added to her appeal. Her slender arms and shapely legs were all but naked, and from the way her body moved, Callahan hadn't a doubt she wore not a stitch beneath it.

Why, if he didn't know better, he would have imagined she was being treated as an honored guest. An instant later he realized the only reason she would be dressed in such finery. What exactly had she done to be treated with such apparent care? Suddenly unable to control his anger as vivid erotic pictures flashed through his mind, he snapped, "What the hell is it with you and Indians, anyway? First White Cloud and now, who? Who was it who wanted you for himself this time?"

Mattie wasn't at all happy with his tone of voice. She glared at him for a long moment before she answered. "Black Bear and Hawk," she returned with some spite, and watched with no little satisfaction when his eyes widened with surprise.

Purposely she kept to herself the fact that both men—savages, she silently corrected, for she could not equate them with anything but the lowest form of beings—were equally repulsive to her. Hawk. Mattie controlled the shiver of revulsion his name brought about as she remembered the promise of hate that glowed in his black eyes, wanted only to extract revenge. Mattie had no doubt her death, at his hands, would have been too long in coming. And Black Bear, who, although he appeared somewhat gentler in nature, carried with him the gagging stench of his namesake. At least she supposed it was bear grease that covered his body.

"Two of them? Jesus," he muttered with disgust, "wasn't one enough for you?"

Mattie glared at him. They both knew she'd have had no choice had the whole camp wanted her. Her lips twisted with rage that he should be so unfair, and she growled between clenched teeth, "Why have one

336

when two are ever so much more fun?"

Callahan cursed. His body felt on fire and ached in places he hadn't known existed. To hell with her. He was in too much pain to continue this argument. Too tired and weak to stand a chance against her vicious tongue. Why the hell had he ever believed he enjoyed their arguments? Enjoyed her quick responses? He must have been mad.

Even though he promised himself to question her no further, he couldn't stop himself from sneering, "Were they?" Callahan knew he wasn't being fair. He knew she was merely retaliating in kind to his taunts, but, damn it, he couldn't seem to help himself. His aching discomfort left him not in the best of moods. Couple the pain with the frustrating fact that he had not been able to save her, and his self-esteem suffered a most debilitating, if not mortally wounded blow. Being forced to admit the truth of the matter, that if it wasn't for her he'd probably be dead by now, or very nearly so, left him far from happy.

He wanted to be the one to protect. He wanted her to lean on him for support, not the other way around. Knowing she was able to take care of herself made him feel unnecessary. And feeling unnecessary brought anger.

Callahan glanced a look to his right. Mattie was lying on her back, her face lifted to the sun, her eyes closed as if asleep. What was it about her that so appealed? Surely there were women more beautiful. So why was it she occupied his every thought? How had she become so deeply ingrained in his life that to live without her would not be living at all?

Callahan sighed. It was bad enough that he felt this pull. Why did everyone else have to feel it too? Since the beginning he had been far from ignorant of the admiring looks cast her way by nearly all on the train.

What the hell was he going to do with this woman? Would he be forced to keep her in seclusion, lest one horny bastard after another try to steal her away?

His father had been right. "Never fall in love with a beautiful woman," he had warned. Too bad Callahan only remembered the warning after it was too late. Too late he remembered the pain his father had suffered at his mother's betrayal. Too late he remembered his first wife. Callahan, suddenly filled with agonizing jealousy, couldn't control the impulse to continue on in the same vein. "Perhaps I should apologize for interrupting your fun. Maybe you prefer them over me."

Mattie sighed. The man was ridiculous. What in the world had come over him? Instead of being happy they had gotten away, a fact for which he had yet to thank her, he ranted on about the most nonsensical things.

"Maybe you should apologize, Callahan," she sighed again, having little heart to continue this argument, her statement pertaining only to the nasty comments he was making.

But Callahan took her words to mean his thoughts held some truth. She hadn't wanted to leave. He felt a rage the likes of which he'd never known. Not even finding his wife in the arms of another had brought on this near insanity.

"I could kill you," he said, his voice so menacing as to be almost unrecognizable. His hands clenched at his sides. He dared not move lest he lunge at her in violence.

Surprised at his vicious yet softly spoken words, Mattie glanced up at eyes glaring with barely controlled rage. Totally puzzled, she asked, "What is the matter with you? Are you sick or something?" She reached a hand to his forehead. "You've been acting crazy all day."

Callahan shook off her hand. Unable to help himself, he was suddenly upon her, his weight pressing her hard to the ground. His mind swore to ignore what he had suspected all along. She didn't have anything on beneath the thin dress, but the effort was doomed from the start. He almost groaned out his agony at the touch of her womanly softness. He fought for strength and finally managed to push aside the wild idea of taking her here and now. "Are you sorry?"

Mattie tried to twist out from beneath him, but Callahan caught her wrists in his hands and held them helplessly over her head, his body holding the rest of her in place. "About what?" Mattie bucked her hips trying to dislodge him while unknowingly bringing a mixture of pain and hunger to his aching body. "What is the matter with you? Let me go!"

Callahan chose to ignore the last of her comments. "About leaving the camp. Did you want to stay?"

Mattie's eyes rounded with surprise. Had she any sense she should have been afraid. Had she been with another, she would have been, but afraid of Callahan? Mattie found the idea ludicrous. She gave a short burst of laughter. "Is that what you've been thinking?" Mattie giggled at what he supposed was menacing silence. Slowly she shook her head, a smile teasing her lips as her body softened and she purposely snuggled up against his hard length. "Callahan, for such a smart man, you can sometimes be very dumb."

Callahan watched her eyes, knowing she spoke the truth. How had he ever imagined otherwise? God, he must be half out of his mind to have even suggested such a thing. It was the pain, he reasoned. The pain and exhaustion and thirst that allowed this agonizing jealousy.

"Mattie," he moaned, succumbing at last to the softness of her as he released her hands and pulled her
tighter to him, wishing they didn't have to move on,
wishing they were safe, wishing she would admit she
loved him, that she was already his wife, but Callahan
knew those wishes had best be laid to rest for the
present. What they needed right now was to find his
horse and get back to the train.

Callahan held tightly to the reins, his arms around
the woman before him shaking as if palsied. Actually
his whole body was shaking so bad, he wondered if it
wasn't Mattie who was holding him in the saddle. He
was sick. Really sick. He knew he was burning up
with fever. His mind began to waver not unlike the
whispery waves of heat that allowed solid structure to
move before one's eyes. His whole world became water. He could think of nothing else. In his imaginings
he could feel it, he could see it, he could even smell it,
but he couldn't taste it. God, how he wanted to taste
it. The little found in his canteen was quickly gone
and it hadn't been nearly enough.

In their endeavor to inflict supreme torture, the
Indians had done a masterful job. They had cut him
until there was barely a spot that lay unaffected. And
yet not one of the wounds was deadly in itself. All
were superficial, all inflicted to merely cause pain.
They had stung unmercifully at the time, but it was
only now that Callahan realized the knives had been
dipped in something, for his wounds were already
festering.

To touch him caused untold agony. He couldn't
remember a time when he hurt so bad.

Mattie laughed aloud as the riders came into view,
shaking Callahan from a dazed state. Even from a

distance, she recognized them almost immediately as Mr. Perry and Jake. Idly she wondered who was driving the wagons? Surely Nora couldn't manage but one, and Mattie doubted Robinson would have been of much help, if his injury was half as bad as it appeared. The last she'd seen of him was watching as he crawled under the protection of a wagon, clutching at his leg.

Callahan, on the other hand, wasn't half so pleased to see the men. "What the hell are you doing here?" he snapped. "Where are the wagons?"

"Nora's watching over them."

"What, all three?"

The two men looked suddenly taken aback. For the first time they seemed to realize what they had done. Guiltily they stared at the ground.

"She can't be driving them all, so that means you've left the train." Callahan began to curse at the danger they had put themselves in. "I hope we've only fallen behind one day."

Jake nodded. "We figured if we didn't find you right off, you'd have to find us."

"Well, don't just sit there staring like you've lost what little sense you've had. Get your asses back where they belong and move those wagons out!"

The two men mumbled a disgruntled "Yes, sir," and were soon racing back from whence they had come.

Mattie choked on the dust their horses kicked up and turned slightly in the saddle. "That was bright, Callahan. Both of them had water and you sent them away before we could get a sip."

Callahan almost groaned out his frustration. He knew she was right, but in his anger at their unprofessional actions, he had forgotten that fact. "They know they weren't to leave the shipment unguarded. I don't care what happened. They are to stay with their wagons."

"You left," she stated simply. "Why are you so hard on them when they did much the same as you?"

"I left my wagon in their care," Callahan returned. "And whether or not I'm hard on them is no concern of yours."

Mattie gritted her teeth against the urge to shove him off the damn horse. The man was a monster! His friends had come to his rescue and what did he do? He cursed them and ordered them away, without even thinking that she might be in need of a drink. Fool! she ranted on silently. How had she ever come to love such a man?

Mattie almost moaned at the truth of her thoughts. She gave a weary shake of her head and silently cursed the fact as truth. She had known and yet refused to accept that fact for a long time now. Why, she wondered, if she had to fall in love with someone, why did it have to be this mule-headed beast? Why couldn't she have found someone pleasant? Someone kind? Someone considerate to love? But Mattie knew the answer to those questions. Callahan might not be perfect, God, but that was an understatement, and yet there were times when he was all of those things.

She loved him despite his faults, or maybe because of them. Who could understand the reasonings of why one fell in love? All she could do was accept the fact.

Mattie wanted to cry out her despair. How could she have done this to herself? How could she have allowed the emotion precedence over her need for revenge? She had a mission. She had sworn to find justice for her sister. But she was suddenly aware of the fact that justice meant little compared to the love she felt. Indeed, the more one loved, the less the need for revenge.

* * *

It was evening by the time Callahan and Mattie caught up with the three wagons. Mattie almost cried, so wonderful did their campfire appear.

Her knees buckled beneath her as she slid from the horse into Perry's arms. Her voice was husky, her throat parched. "He's sick," she murmured to the man who held her steady.

Callahan watched their faces swim before him. He blinked again and again, trying to keep them in focus, but it was beyond his power to do so. He never gave up the struggle. It was simply taken from him as he finally slumped forward. He uttered a low curse, unable to stop the blackness from closing in. The last thing he remembered was the sound of Mattie's soft cry as he slipped unconscious from the saddle.

Perry had only that minute to realize Mattie's words. When he saw Callahan sway, he moved fast, but not nearly fast enough. Mattie cried out again as Callahan's limp body bounced heavily upon the ground.

Mattie had known almost from the beginning that Callahan was ill, but she never realized the full extent of it. She had felt his shivers. She knew the tremors in his hands, and yet the idea of him being as helpless as a babe never entered her mind.

She knelt beside him in the wagon and soothed his heated skin with cool, wet rags she had ripped from her petticoats. Callahan moaned as each compress was administered to his burning skin, but Mattie was relentless in her efforts to bring down his fever. She knew he was suffering. He shivered so badly she wondered if he wouldn't knock the wagon apart. He was burning up. Those red devils had done something to him. She didn't know what, but every cut was a festering wound.

Mattie wondered if a body could survive such fever. She prayed he had the strength.

Nora came to the back of the wagon. "How's he doing?"

Mattie shook her head. "Not too good. I wish the doctor was nearby."

Nora pulled herself inside the wagon and sat near Callahan's feet. "I doubt he'd do much better than you."

Mattie shook her head. She was fooling herself if she thought she was accomplishing anything. His fever would never go down, not unless they cleaned out his wounds. She remembered how her father had used whiskey. Pouring the burning liquid over an open wound often brought about amazing results.

"His wounds have festered and crusted over with dried blood. I think it might be poisoning him." Mattie lifted her eyes from his burning, limp form. "They're going to have to be cleaned out. Do you have any whiskey?"

Nora nodded and moved to fetch the needed supplies. She returned to the wagon with two bottles and an armful of soft toweling. Jake and Perry stood immediately behind her. "Maybe you'd better let Jake do it," Nora suggested.

Mattie shook her head. "I'll do it." She looked at the two men. "You're going to have to hold him down. This is going to hurt."

Mattie added a strong dose of laudanum to water. It took some time, but she finally got him to swallow most of it. Callahan appeared to be deeply drugged, but Mattie knew for what she was about to do, all the laudanum in the world wasn't going to help.

She took his knife, feeling some amazement at the steadiness of her hand, and cut into the hot, swelling sores that covered his chest. Mattie swallowed with disgust as they, one by one, emptied of all foreign matter.

Callahan groaned each time she cut into him and tried to push her away. Jake grabbed at his hands, Perry his thrashing legs. "Hold him," she warned. Tears filled her eyes as a scream of anguish was torn from Callahan's throat when she finally poured the whiskey over his chest.

His body stiffened from the blinding shock of pain and he struggled wildly beneath Jake and Perry's weight. The men were all but thrown off. Mattie stared in amazement as she watched Callahan buck. She couldn't believe his strength. Even dangerously ill, he had almost bested both his friends.

The process had to be repeated on his back. Mattie wiped away her tears as they finally turned him over and allowed him to rest. She prayed her labors had done some good and shivered at the horror of being forced to do this again.

Mattie shook her head and listened to the endless moans, clearly heard above the creaking of harnesses and grunting oxen as the wagon jarred horribly over the roughest ground Mattie could ever have imagined. Every mile clearly increased his torment, but all knew there were no choices in the matter. To remain alone in this wilderness would be to court death.

Each day they had driven farther than usual. They moved long into night in an effort to catch up. But they had been forced to stop often. Callahan needed care and all knew he would surely die unless he was constantly given water. Barring rain, they hoped to catch up with the train by tomorrow night.

They were a ragged lot at best. Callahan slipped in and out of consciousness. Robinson limped on his injury, while the rest were so exhausted they hadn't even bothered with a fire for the last two nights.

It had been four days and still there was no sign that the train was within reach.

Mattie's only consolation was that Callahan's fever seemed to have lessened. She couldn't be sure, since she was almost always at his side, but Jake swore the man felt cooler.

Mattie sighed as she pulled the wagon to a stop. It was night and their traveling was at an end for the day. Mattie longed to lie down. Her arms ached. Her back was stiff. All she wanted to do was sleep. If only Callahan would be quiet tonight, she might.

Again, the five travelers shared dried meat and water for supper and were soon in their wagons for the night.

Mattie awakened sometime later. She didn't know why, and her heart pounded in fear that Indians might have again come upon them and were moving about outside.

Callahan felt her stiffen against him. "Mattie," he whispered.

"What?" she returned, not realizing at first that he was speaking rationally at last.

"Where are we?"

Mattie lifted herself to her elbow, her hand reaching in the dark for his forehead. The joy that burst through her upon touching his cool, wet skin was not to be borne. Mattie laughed. "How do you feel?"

"Awful."

"Oh God, that's wonderful."

"It lends a soaring to the soul to know I can bring you such joy."

Mattie giggled and leaned a bit closer. "Do I have to put up with your nasty remarks again?"

Callahan sighed. "What the hell is so damn funny?"

Mattie was thrilled. She wanted to take him and hug him close, but she dared not, lest her touch add to his pain. She wanted to tell him what was so damn funny, but that would wait until a more opportune moment showed itself. "I thought I was the one who woke up grouchy?" And at his grunt of annoyance, she asked, "Do you want something to drink?"

Callahan allowed her to lift him into a half-sitting position, finding himself amazingly weak. He took the canteen from her hands. "What happened? Was I sick?" he asked in between long swallows of water.

Mattie nodded, forgetting he couldn't see her in the dark.

"Well, was I?"

"You were, but you're better now."

"Why the hell do I hurt like this?"

"Your cuts were bad. I had to open them and clean them out."

"That must have given you a great deal of pleasure."

"Callahan." She breathed his name, suddenly so angry she had to force aside the urge to commit violence. How dare he so callously remark that she would enjoy his suffering? How dare he be anything but grateful after all she'd done? "You've got to be the most ungrateful bastard."

Callahan grasped at her hand when he felt her move away, but managed only to take her shirt tail in his hand. "Don't go."

"Why, so you can insult me some more?" She tugged at the shirt.

He tightened his hold and grinned in the dark. "This is the last wagon train for you, lady. You curse as fine as any man I know."

"You don't like it?"

"No."

"Good," she snapped as she yanked her shirt from

his grasp.

"Mattie, wait," he said, as forgetting his injuries, he came to a half-sitting position. Suddenly he groaned as the darkness swam dizzily around him.

"What?" she answered, instantly alert to the sound of his discomfort.

She was on her hands and knees crawling back when her head butted against something. She heard another groan and a simultaneous "Ow" came from both their lips. Callahan fell back, his hand over his face.

Mattie rubbed her head. "What are you doing?"

His voice was muffled beneath his hand. "Bleeding."

"What?"

"You gave me a bloody nose."

Mattie breathed a long, weary sigh. "Callahan, you have to be the most ridiculous man."

"Why? Because I bleed when I'm hit?"

"Because you move around in the dark."

"You were moving too. I suggest that makes you equally ridiculous."

Mattie laughed as she handed him one of the rags that she had used for his fever. "I guess it does. Only I'm not the one who's bleeding."

"Come back here."

"What do you want?"

Callahan laughed. "Except for a long bath, some hot food, a clean soft bed, and you, I can't think of a thing."

Mattie grunted. "I noticed I came in last on your list."

"If I put you first, will you come back?"

"Are you lying down?"

"Mattie," he warned. "Don't make me come and get you."

Mattie laughed as she came back to his side, this

348

time with considerably more care. "Weak as you are, I wouldn't put it past you, Callahan." Mattie settled herself against him and sighed, "You really are the most stubborn man."

"While you, on the other hand, haven't a stubborn bone in your body."

Mattie giggled at his obvious sarcasm. She didn't blame him for being so out of sorts. No doubt she'd be far worse if she'd suffered as he. "The truth at last. Now doesn't that make you feel better?"

"Shut up and go to sleep."

"Will you tell this man how sick he was? How sick he still is?" Mattie said while pointing to the one in question. "Will you tell him he cannot drive this wagon?" Mattie glared at a grinning Jake and Nora. "Will you!?"

"Why don't you listen to the lady?" Jake offered.

"Why don't you mind your own business?"

Mattie threw her hands up in the air and made a sound of pure exasperation. Suddenly she spun on her heel and stomped up to Callahan, who was leaning weakly against the wagon. She grabbed him by his shirtfront. At his wince, she almost let him go. But Mattie knew she couldn't let him win on this score. She never wanted to see him sick again. She glared as she pulled, forcing him to bend to her height. "If you don't listen to me, I'm going to give you more than a bloody nose."

Callahan knew she was right. At this moment he doubted he had the strength to fight a feather. Certainly he didn't have enough energy to go up against this tiny firebrand. "You win," he said with a long sigh of exhaustion. "I guess I should wait another day."

Mattie released his shirt and snorted as she walked

349

away.

"What was that about a bloody nose?" Nora asked, not bothering to hide her merriment.

"None of your business."

Mattie's voice rang out along with Perry and Jake's as she urged the slow-moving oxen on. A sharp whistle pierced the air and she grinned. It had taken enough practice, but she was getting pretty good at that.

"How am I supposed to sleep, with you making so much noise?"

Mattie gave him a look of annoyance as she watched him crawl over the wagon seat and settle himself beside her. "If you can't sleep, at least rest."

"I can't do that either."

"Why not?"

"Because I've been watching you for most of the morning and imagining the things I could do to you, except that you're too far away."

"Callahan," she warned, knowing by the softening of his voice, if not the words themselves, his exact intentions.

A smile curved her lips as his hands moved unerringly to her breast. She shoved him away, only to find his hand instantly returned. "How am I supposed to fight you off while I'm driving this team?"

"That's just the point. You're not supposed to fight me off."

"Callahan, stop it." She giggled when his mouth nuzzled the curve of her neck. She squirmed on the wooden seat. Her hat fell forward. She set it right again, thereby affording him easier access to her most obvious charms. "Someone will see."

"No they won't. They're too busy."

"Callahan," she insisted, hoping her glare would get him out of this playful mood.

"All right," he breathed on a sigh. "I'll stop. But you don't know what you're missing."

Mattie only smiled, not daring to say a word lest she find herself pulled into the back of the wagon and loving every minute of it.

"Is it all right for me to put my arm around you?"

"No it's not."

"Suppose I need you for support?"

"If you're that weak, go back and lie down."

"Do you realize you're taking all the fun out of my convalescence?"

Mattie grinned, her heart almost melting as she caught sight of his tender smile. "Do you realize I . . ." She stopped in mid-sentence, a soft gasp escaping her throat. She turned beet-red. She had almost told him she loved him! The words had very nearly slipped out without a thought.

"What?" Callahan coaxed. "What were you going to say?"

"Only that I'm tired and haven't the time for this nonsense."

"No."

"No, what?"

"That wasn't what you were going to say."

Mattie shrugged. She knew she looked guilty, but it didn't matter if he believed her or not. There was no way she was going to admit her feelings for this man. She couldn't just tell him she loved him. Not when he had no intentions of marrying. Hadn't he told her that? Hadn't he made it clear he wanted her only for a time?

"Can I talk to you?" Mattie asked as she intercepted

Nora coming back from a short trip outside the wagons.

Nora smiled and nodded her head as the two women moved toward the back of her wagon.

"I want to apologize for my childish behavior. I had no right to judge any of you." She was silent for a long moment. "For some reason I wanted to believe the worst. Can you forgive me?"

Nora smiled. "Why did you want to believe the worst?"

"I don't know. I think I was protecting myself against . . ." She hesitated and then shrugged.

"Against falling in love with Callahan?" Nora finished for her. And when Mattie made no effort to deny her words, Nora smiled again. "And now you know you love him, no matter what he might be."

It was Mattie's turn to nod, her cheeks pinkening at her silent admission. "And because you love him, he can't be doing anything all that bad, and we, being his friends, can't either."

Mattie laughed. "You make me sound ridiculous."

"Not ridiculous, just a bit starry-eyed. It's natural to trust the man you love."

"Are you telling me I shouldn't?"

"Not at all. In fact, I believe I once told you you'll never find another more worthy."

"It's not easy, you know, this blind belief."

"I can imagine it to be most difficult. I wish I could have told you the truth of the matter."

"I wish you could have too. It might have saved me many sleepless nights."

Nora smiled. "We're almost to California." She nodded over her shoulder at the men sitting around the campfire. "He'll be able to tell you soon."

Mattie smiled and wondered why it suddenly seemed so much less important to know.

"And yes, I forgive you." She took Mattie's hand in hers as they moved toward the welcoming light of the fire. "Actually I might have done much the same were our positions reversed."

Chapter Twenty-three

Mattie couldn't control the urge to laugh, and without thinking, her arms flung themselves around Callahan's neck, when late on the fifth day of traveling they mounted a small rise to find, at last, the circle of wagons and welcome of cheery campfires.

Wide smiles greeted them as they finally brought the three wagons to a halt. Exhausted oxen were led away for a much-needed rest as the wagons were added to the circle.

"Oh my dear," Mrs. Stables remarked as she gave Mattie an almost smothering hug, "we were so worried. Were you treated very badly?"

"Mattie became lost during the battle, Mrs. Stables. She wasn't captured by the Indians."

Mattie glanced up as Callahan came to stand at her side. His arm slid possessively around her waist, his eyes hard, silently daring any man to call him a liar. Mattie felt a moment of intense relief, for already the leering looks in some of the men's eyes were fading. Thank God he had thought to set their minds at rest. Wisely he realized the prejudice most held for their red brothers and the opinion they'd surely form about her, if it were known that she had spent even one day as their captive.

"That's a relief," Mrs. Stables sighed. "Jim and some of the others went out every night, after we made camp, to look for you. Everything is all right, isn't it?" she asked as her gaze scanned the weary travelers and their wagons.

Mattie said a silent prayer of thanks that they had not stumbled upon the train the first night. All would then know of her capture, for she could never have explained away her costume.

Callahan couldn't help but notice Jim Stables's gaze return again and again to Mattie. For a moment he was filled with rage, but when he felt her answering hug, he forced down his jealousy. Suddenly he realized, even after all she'd been through, she was beautiful beyond belief. How could any man be found at fault for staring?

Still, Callahan was not happy to realize again her many admirers. And although she seemed not to notice the stir she caused, he vowed to keep a watchful eye, for he trusted no man when it came to her.

Jim, as did many of the others, offered his hand before leaving the young couple to the privacy of their supper, supplied by his wife. "Glad to see you made it back."

Despite his usual perceptiveness, Callahan never heard the depth of feeling in the words as his attention turned to another and his congratulations on a safe return.

More so than most did Mattie long to leave behind this raging river and the mountain range that loomed up ahead. Nothing, no matter the extra guards posted, nor Callahan's ever-ready rifle could stem the terrifying memories of these plains. For a time Mattie had put up a good front, but in the end it was obvious her experience with the Indians had not left her unscathed. It had taken nearly two weeks, but reaction had finally set in. Now she found herself constantly on edge, always waiting to hear again the eerie, high-pitched, savage screech of coming death.

355

It had been weeks since she had rested easy. It seemed the more time that passed since her escape, the more did her fears grow, until they controlled her every action, taking from her life the simplest joy.

The telltale strain on her nerves was easy enough to read. Her eyes darted nervously about. She couldn't concentrate on even the simplest conversations. Her appetite increased and yet she lost weight. Many were the nights she lay sleepless upon her pallet, knowing the morning would find her exhausted and yet finding it beyond her power to conquer this fear.

If she could only be allowed to forget, Mattie knew her tensions would ease. But that was not to be, for each day brought renewed evidence of the red man's outrage. The Indian depredations committed thus far went almost beyond her ability to bear. She shivered with revulsion, knowing she should have been numb to a savagery that was by now all too common; only the horror of it never seemed to lessen.

The time was long gone that she gave a second glance to the many beautifully carved, sometimes truly exquisite pieces of furniture left to wither unto dust beneath the unrelenting savagery of the sun. Furniture and personal belongings meant nothing when countless were the human bones, the skeletal remains of oxen, the broken wagons, discarded children's toys, feathers, and bloody, ripped clothing. It got so Mattie began to wonder if ever the time would come when she could walk more than a rod and find the road uncluttered with this clear evidence of death.

Mattie gazed now with sorrow at the abandoned wagons that lay forlornly along the edge of the road and wondered how the poor souls, once the proud owners of these pitiful remains, had fared when continuing on with little more than the clothes on their backs. Silently she cursed those who had traveled this road before them. How dare they allow these unsuspecting souls to begin such a journey, without telling the truth of it?

Certainly what she had read on the subject had not readied her for what lay ahead. It gave not a clue to what she would have to withstand. It pointed out no lack of water, nor absence of grazing for the animals. It mentioned not the rain, the mud, the insects. It warned not of death, nor the haunted eyes of childless mothers. Had she known, had she an inkling of the hardships that seemed to eagerly await her, she would have gladly suffered the incapacitation rendered by a swaying ship.

Word had it that grass was close to nonexistent from here to the western slope of the Sierra Nevada. The idea was enough to make a body laugh. Certainly the lack of grazing couldn't be any worse than the stark, inhospitable desert over which they had already tread. For the endless, breathless heat, lack of water, and grass had left cattle by the hundreds, perhaps thousands dead. Their carcasses rotting under a glaring sun caused an ungodly stench that brought flies by the millions to fill the air with one continuous black wave of motion.

Mattie, as had the others, wore a kerchief over her face for days on end, for the swarming insects knew not the difference between the living and the dead and crawled happily over every surface, moving and still.

Mattie remembered the tears she'd shed when the cow and two of their oxen had died. Only she couldn't be certain, even as yet, if the tears were of pity or fear for herself. In truth, Mattie and Callahan fared better than some, for many a traveler was forced to stand helplessly by and watch the last of his team crumble to the ground, leaving his wagon without the means to go on.

Mattie felt the first stirrings of relief when at last they camped at the Humboldt River. Here they would rest, oxen and human alike. Wagons would be carefully examined and readied to begin the last and perhaps the hardest part of the journey.

Tonight the emigrants would celebrate the happy fact that the end of their journey was so near at hand.

It was after dinner. Mattie could hear the revelry farther on down the line of wagons, when Callahan asked, "Would you like to join them?"

Mattie shook her head. "I'm too tired. I couldn't dance tonight if my life depended on it."

Callahan smiled and lifted her to sit before him on the wagon's tailgate. Their faces were almost even as he played with a curling strand of midnight hair that had escaped her bonnet. His eyes glowed with tenderness. "Would you prefer a smaller, quieter celebration of our own?"

Mattie knew well enough what he had in mind. God, did the man never tire? It didn't matter how many miles they traveled, or what work was accomplished. He always seemed to have enough energy to take her to bed, once night had fallen.

Mattie couldn't imagine what had come over her tonight. True, she was often tired at the end of a day, more so than usual of late. But now, instead of feeling excitement and elation that this journey was all but over and the threat of Indians behind them, all she could think of was sleep. Everything, even Callahan and the enticing memories of how he could set her body on fire, paled beside the inviting softness of her quilts. Mattie smiled. "I wish I knew your remedy."

"For?"

"For replenishing energy. You never seem to tire, even after the hardest days."

Callahan chuckled. "Oh, I tire, all right, but seeing you at the end of each day reminds me there are other, more interesting pastimes than sleep."

"Really?" she asked while covering a yawn with her hand. "Right now, I can't think of one."

"Can't you?" He smiled gently, his hands cupping the sides of her face. "Would you rather rest tonight?"

"Would you mind terribly?"

Callahan grinned as he leaned closer and deposited a light kiss to the tip of her nose. The tenderness in his eyes was unmistakable. "Terribly." He made to move away. "I'll sleep outside tonight."

"No!" Mattie returned with more vehemence than she had intended. Her cheeks pinkened at the unconscious pleading she heard in her voice and she lowered her gaze to the ground.

Callahan's eyes twinkled with laughter. "Have you changed your mind, then?"

Mattie shook her head, and unwilling to look at him, she investigated the floorboards of the wagon. "I just . . ." she shrugged. "Never mind."

"You just what?" And when she only shook her head, he insisted. "Come on, Mattie, out with it."

She wanted him at her side. She wanted to sleep in his arms. Why did she have to give up that pleasure simply because she was tired and wanted nothing more? "There's no need for you to be uncomfortable, is there? You can sleep inside."

Callahan grinned. "And not touch you?"

Mattie bit the inside of her lip, never knowing her gaze took on an almost pleading quality, one Callahan could never resist.

He never bothered to try. "You don't ask much of a man, do you, lady?" He grinned at her look of surprise. "Come on," he said as he jumped into the wagon, "let's go to sleep."

Callahan snuggled close to her tiny form and breathed the sweet essence of her deep into his being. "Mattie, take this off. If I'm going to sleep next to you, it's not cotton I want to feel."

"I thought we agreed . . ."

"We agreed," he interrupted. "I'm not going to do anything. Just take it off."

Mattie did as he asked, and once in his arms again, remarked drowsily, "I think you're asking for trouble."

"Probably," he concurred and breathed a low groan of pure sensual enjoyment as their naked flesh entwined. Callahan held her tightly to him and smiled with some surprise when only seconds later he heard the shallow, even sound of her breathing. "Poor darling," he soothed in a low murmur as he cupped her head to his neck. She was totally exhausted. When they reached California, he vowed she would stay in bed for a week. And he didn't care if he had to hog-tie her to keep her there.

A smile teased his lips at the thought of what delights a soft, large bed could afford them. How they might roll and twist and . . . He grimaced, feeling the instant results of his wayward thoughts. If he didn't get ahold of his rutting nature she wouldn't find much rest there either.

Callahan slid his hands down her side in a purely soothing gesture. She hadn't been herself lately. She was often tired and obviously nervous. And as if that weren't enough, she seemed to have picked up something. Although she appeared well enough during the day, she was sick every morning. So sick, in fact, that she was helpless but to allow Callahan's administerings.

The strain of this trip was beginning to show in the soft purple smudges beneath her eyes and the delicate frailness of her body. She ate almost as much as he. Many were the times when he teased her about her appetite and yet she was growing thinner each day.

His hands moved reassuringly over her body only to suddenly still as an incredible thought came to mind. His body stiffened. His heartbeat accelerated with burgeoning excitement.

Gently, so as not to awaken her, he eased her to her back. His breathing grew irregular, his heart pounded, so badly did he want his suspicions proven

360

true. Slowly he ran his hands over her stomach. He uttered a low moan and for a moment forgot to breathe so crushing was the disappointment he felt. And then he almost laughed at the absurdity of his conclusions. Of course it was still flat. If she was in a family way, it would be too soon for any change in her body. Except for . . . His fingers moved to her breasts and he sighed as the mindboggling proof lay heavy in his hand. Her waist might be as tiny as ever, but her breasts had filled out in a most enticing fashion.

Callahan groaned with delight as he pulled her into his embrace again. His mind raced back over the last few months, remembering correctly that she hadn't had her monthly time since they had come together. He knew that for a fact since he rarely missed a night making love to her. That would make her two months along. He grinned into the darkness and forced aside the desire to laugh as pure joy threatened to burst through his chest.

It was usual for the woman to tell the man of his impending fatherhood. In this case Callahan wondered if the opposite wasn't more appropriate?

He was certain she had no idea she was carrying his child. "God," he groaned into the dark. Carrying his child. What a delight to be able to say those words. Callahan sighed, almost overwhelmed with the love he felt for this woman. He nuzzled his face into the warmth of her neck and breathed in the sweet, intoxicating scent of her body, all the while wondering what her reaction would be when she realized the fact.

Mattie snarled with disgust. "Would you mind telling me what is so funny?" Mr. McMillen had ordered them to lay over an extra day so the travelers might see to the care of their wagons. Callahan was just crawling out from under theirs after applying a final coat of tar to the bottom, lest the heavy load it carried

361

cause the wagon to sink while crossing the river.

"Funny? What do you mean?" he asked while shooting her another of his mirth-filled glances. Damn, but he couldn't help himself. All he wanted to do was laugh with the pure joy of what he'd come to know. It was near impossible to hold back.

"Callahan," Mattie sighed with no little disgust, "you've been shooting me the oddest looks all day, watching everything I do and grinning like you've pulled off some miraculous feat."

"Don't move that!" he nearly bellowed.

"What?" she asked in sudden fear as she flung herself away from the box she had been about to move and crashed up against another, nearly falling in the process. "What is it?" she gasped, trembling with fear. "A snake?"

"No. Just don't move the box," he said more gently. "I'll do it."

Mattie took a deep, calming breath. Her brow arched dangerously and her mouth thinned into a white line, due to the sudden and she believed quite unnecessary fright he had caused her. She breathed a long sigh trying to get control of her rising temper and pushed herself off the crate. "Was that necessary? Did you have to scare me near to death?"

Callahan grinned. He could see she was getting riled. She looked so damn adorable standing there, her dark eyes flashing fury, her cheeks pink with anger, while tendrils of black curls, having escaped their pins, lay against her damp neck. God, but he wanted to pull her into his arms and kiss her until the both of them were breathless. Suddenly he couldn't think of one good reason why he shouldn't do just that.

Mattie watched him wipe his hands on a rag and walk determinedly toward her. It was easy enough to see he had something on his mind. What Mattie didn't know was what.

"Callahan, what are you doing?"

362

Callahan grinned. "Lady, first you fault me for my happiness. Now will you say I may not kiss you as well?"

She glanced around the camp and took a step back. "Callahan! Stop it this minute. What in the world has come over you?" She continued to back away, a smile flirting with the frown she was desperately trying to maintain. "Everyone will see."

Callahan shrugged, obviously unconcerned. "I think their eyes can withstand the shock of watching a husband kiss his wife."

Mattie giggled as she took another step. "You are acting so . . ." His lips stopped her words. "Oddly," she breathed when he finally allowed their lips to part.

"For your information, I'm acting as rational as any man in love."

Mattie gasped and stumbled back a step. "What?!" Her eyes were huge. "What did you say?"

"You heard me." He was grinning.

Mattie couldn't help but wonder if he was teasing. Certainly one didn't remark upon such a serious matter with so flippant an attitude. She leaned against the crate, trying to force her world to steady itself. Her eyes were searching his for the truth. Suddenly she smiled at what she found there. "If that don't beat all," she whispered softly almost to herself, and then laughed at the leering look he was giving her. "I give up."

"Can I have it?" he asked as his hips suggestively pressed her to the crate.

"Have what?" she asked, not following his train of thought.

"Whatever it is you're giving up."

Mattie giggled at the nonsensical conversation. "Is this how a man tells a woman he loves her?"

"I don't know. Did I do it wrong?"

Mattie shrugged, a smile teasing her lips. "I would have thought a bit of romance appropriate."

363

"I'll give you romance later," he said, while nodding his head toward their wagon.

Mattie shook her head, unable to keep her laughter at bay. Why did she want to laugh? This was supposed to be a serious moment, wasn't it?

"Don't you believe me?"

"No." She shook her head. "Yes." She nodded. Her eyes grew wider than ever. "It's just." She hesitated and then gave a long sigh. "Should I?"

Callahan laughed at her confusion. "That's one of the things I love most about you. You're so positive."

Mattie's lips twisted in a wry grin. "You can't expect me to accept your words as calmly as you said them," she explained. "Why, you might have been discussing the weather for all the emotion involved."

"Is it emotion you're looking for?" he grinned, his eyes darkening with meaning.

"It couldn't hurt."

Callahan took a deep breath as he lifted her into his arms and turned toward the wagon. "I hope you're ready, lady," he warned, his voice softening to a deep growling whisper, " 'cause you're about to get all the emotion a body can handle."

The river wasn't as wide as it was fast. Mattie felt no little apprehension as she stared at the murky brown water rushing by. The thought of crossing brought shivers down her back, especially since two wagons had already been washed downstream, their occupants even now sitting forlornly upon the opposite shore.

There had been a mad scramble to save the floundering emigrants as the wagons turned quite suddenly and the river washed all over the sides. Mattie had breathed a sigh of relief. She could only imagine their joy. Even though everything they had owned was lost, at least they were safe. From the opposite shore, Mattie had watched as sobbing mothers took their sodden children from the men who had quickly ridden after them, and held them close to their breasts.

Mattie sat beside Callahan on the wagon's seat. Her teeth bit down on her bottom lip as she tried to control her fear, lest she make a total fool of herself and beg those in charge to find another way.

Callahan's arms strained as he pulled at the reins and swung a heavy whip over their heads. Mattie cringed at the curses he screamed. She would have told him to control his foul mouth had it not forced her mind from her fears. Two riders rode on each side of the lead oxen. Their intent was to guide them in as straight a path as possible as well as to urge the obviously reluctant animals to the opposite shore.

They were crossing one wagon at a time. The cattle and oxen were terrified, and it took the strength of both riders, plus the driver, to get each wagon across.

Perhaps he was too anxious to await his turn, or maybe the animals had panicked listening to the bellowing fear that filled the air. Whatever the cause, the Blacks' wagon dashed into the water and came suddenly up alongside. Mr. McMillen, who had moved back and forth between shores, yelled for Mr. Black to hold up, but it was too late, the man had lost control of the beasts.

Mattie could see the oxen's eyes, wild with fear as they strained against their yokes. In their terror they screamed high-pitched sounds that eerily resembled human cries. Black pulled hard at the reins. Mattie could see the muscles in his arms tighten, his teeth clenched with the strain, but to no avail. The team turned to the left, unconcerned that they were certain to collide with Callahan's wagon. Their terror clearly lay beyond their driver's control.

Mattie saw the movement. Her soft gasp of dread was lost in the sound of rushing water and did not bring Callahan's attention from his task. Suddenly she was on her feet, in a useless effort to dodge the on-coming oxen. The curses that always filled the air grew more potent and explicit as riders struggled against the current to reach the Blacks' wagon in time. A moment later the first of the oxen smashed into the side of Mattie's wagon. The shock of the blow nearly tumbled her into the rushing water. She held on for dear life.

But those upon Black's wagon didn't fare half as well. The shock of impact sent Mrs. Black sprawling into the rear of the wagon, her skinny legs swaying helplessly high above her head, while Mr. Black reached out a desperate hand to prevent his fall. The only problem was his bony fingers closed over the first solid thing they touched, which was Clay. Mattie screamed as she watched the two of them tumble into the raging river.

An instant later she realized her mistake. Without thought she had jumped in, her intent to pull the boy out. Mattie was a strong swimmer, having spent many a lazy afternoon rollicking with Melanie in the river that snaked through their land, but she'd never before encountered water with the force of this.

Mattie never heard her name called over her own horrified screams. The water flung her about as if she were no more than a feather in a windstorm. She tried to get her head up, and succeeded for a moment, only to be pulled almost instantly under again.

Mattie knew the task she had taken upon herself was hopeless. She'd never save Clay. Vaguely she wondered if she mightn't die in her feeble attempt.

She was being dragged down. Her hands and knees scraped along the rocky bottom. Mattie pushed against the rocks and forced herself up. Her head broke water and she gasped for a lungful of air before the churning, speeding rapids pulled her down again.

Mattie grunted as something hit her. By the feel of it it was a man. His hand reached out, desperate to

366

grasp anything. His fingers twisted in her floating skirt. But the pull of the water was too much and the skirt ripped away. Mattie saw through the bubbling foam the terrified look in his eyes as his head went under for the last time. Instinctively she tried to grab at him, but Mr. Black was already gone.

The water pushed her along, smacking her carelessly into sharp, unyielding rocks. She tried to hold on, but everything she reached for was wrenched from her grasp as the water pushed her on. She felt dazed from the shock of each blow encountered. How many more would she withstand before the final jolt brought oblivion?

Through the mass of bubbles that foamed around her face, Mattie saw the tree. Its thick trunk leaned crookedly over the water. Three of its many heavy branches dipped beneath the surface. If she could only . . . The thought came almost too late, for she had nearly passed it by the time she was able to raise one lethargic arm and catch its heavy limb. The rush of water jolted her entire body as she hooked her arm over the limb and clung with nothing less than desperation.

Holding on for dear life, she leaned her body over the branch. Choking and gasping for breath, she lifted her shoulders from the water.

Mattie was trembling with shock. She couldn't think, but to take her next breath. Dazed, for a moment she couldn't remember what had brought her to this dilemma.

A heavy piece of wood, probably a plank from a wagon, almost caused her to lose her hold as it slammed into her. Mattie moaned from the blow her legs had taken, but tightened her hold about the limb. After a few minutes she managed to squirm higher upon the branch.

She looked around, her gaze searching for a sign of Clay. Had the water tumbled the boy to the bottom?

Had she passed him unnoticed in her desperate need to save her own life?

Mattie cried out as she saw him at last. Was he dead? Was this all for nothing? "Clay," she screamed, watching with horrified eyes as he swept past, just beyond her reach.

The water carried him effortlessly along. And just when she thought he hadn't a chance, it pushed him up against a rock. Mattie watched, a low, unconscious prayer forming, as small arms grasped desperately at the rock. He tugged at the sharp edges only inches above the water line and, to Mattie's breathless relief, finally managed to lift himself just enough to free his face of the river's foaming surface.

Suddenly there were men on horseback racing along both shores of the river. Mattie couldn't hear their calls above the sound of water. She knew they were telling her to let go and grab at the rope that had landed upon the same branch she held to, only she couldn't.

For an endless second, Callahan simply sat upon the wagon. To say he was dumbfounded was to put it mildly. But his astonishment lasted only until he saw her head go under. At that moment it was instantly replaced with panic, later would come the rage.

All eyes turned to him as Callahan screamed a mighty roar that sounded clear even above the rushing water. He almost knocked McMillen off his horse. Actually, he pulled him off, nearly throwing him upon the seat he had just vacated while screaming curse words like a raving lunatic.

It took a minute before anyone could decipher his hysteria into clear English. Once the other riders finally understood him, they separated into two groups and raced as fast as possible down both sides of the river.

He almost didn't see her, at first. Her brown shirt matched exactly the color of the branch. Muddy water had dulled her shining black hair and darkened her skin, so that she almost blended into the landscape.

He was off the horse before it came to a stop, his body propelled forward at a dangerous pace with his careless dismount. The rope in his hands was flung out to her, even before he gained his balance. It landed exactly where he wanted it to, but she merely looked at it.

"Take the rope, Mattie," he called. And when she continued to merely stare at it, he screamed, "Take the goddamned rope!"

Still nothing.

Callahan cursed again, threw the rope to the ground, and rushed into the water, which wasn't as deep as he had imagined. Here, near the shore, it came only to his waist, but was moving so fast and with such force that it knocked him down twice before he could reach her.

He wrapped his arms around her and pried her stiff fingers from the branch. The water knocked him down again. He came up sputtering, still holding her close to his chest, her arms around his neck nearly closing off his breathing.

Callahan stumbled onto dry land. He was surrounded by men offering any aid they could. Each of them was covered with blankets.

Mattie leaned weakly against him as she watched another group of men pull Clay from the other side of the river. A low sob escaped her throat when she realized the boy was all right.

Callahan said a few words to the hovering men, and a moment later they were alone. Mattie neither realized the fact that they had been there nor that they had gone. She was safe. She couldn't for a moment fathom the truth of it. For a time they simply stood in each other's arms, each, in their own silence, thanking God for this most special of gifts.

369

Callahan moaned into her wet neck as he held her tightly against him, his arms crushing her, stealing what little breath she had. "Are you all right?" He didn't seem to expect an answer. He didn't wait for one, in any case. "Mattie, my God, I was so scared," he choked. His throat seemed to close up and he had to force the words. "When I saw you go under, I thought I was going to die."

He was rubbing his hands up and down her back beneath the blanket when he suddenly stiffened and held her away from him. "Why did you do it?" he demanded, his voice cold, filled with an icy rage that blocked out every tender emotion. Callahan took her surprise at his tone of voice for deliberate silence. He was building himself up into a fine rage, believing her silence a refusal to answer him. "Damn you," he groaned as he gave her a hard shake. Callahan's lips tightened. He would get an answer. He demanded to know why she would jeopardize everything he held dear. Only he hadn't given her much of a chance. Barely two seconds passed and he began to shake her in earnest. Her teeth rattled, her neck threatened to snap. "My God, why did you jump? You could have killed yourself, not to mention the baby."

Mattie, still stunned from her close brush with death, never realized his desperation. She was about to answer him when he started shaking her. She wrenched herself from his hold. Her legs wobbled and she was forced to allow him to hold her again, lest she fall to the ground. "Stop shaking me, you maniac! I saw Clay fall in. I didn't think." She was gasping for air, trying desperately to quell her trembling reaction from the ordeal she'd just suffered and the tears of anger his lack of consideration brought about. Her voice broke. "I can always count on you to bring comfort and solace, can't . . . What baby?" she asked, stepping out of his embrace. The silence that followed was deafening.

A puzzled look turned into shock as her eyes rose to meet his cold, stony expression. She watched him for a long moment before the truth dawned. Mattie gave a soft gasp. She felt like a fool. How could it be that he knew before her? Her monthly time hadn't come since . . . Oh God, why hadn't she noticed? Why hadn't she realized the reason behind her morning sickness? Now she knew why she was always so tired, why her breasts ached ever so slightly and felt so much heavier.

A smile of pure joy began to tease the corners of her mouth when her eyes suddenly widened as a terrifying thought occurred. Her body stiffened with dread. Is that why he told her he loved her? Could it be he felt none of the tenderness he proclaimed last night? Could it have all been a lie?

Mattie gave a low, horrified moan. She could tell by the look in his eyes her thoughts were correct, for she found not the slightest tenderness in their blue depths. She neither realized the softly whispered, "No," nor its implication as her world came crashing to a million jagged, shards of pain and regret. Her eyes begged him to tell her he had meant what he said, that he didn't say what he had because of the baby. *Please tell me it wasn't a lie,* she silently prayed.

But Callahan mistook the reason behind her pleading look. A cold icy rage wound tightly around his heart and squeezed until he thought he might die of the pain. His mouth turned grim and he cursed himself for ever believing she was different from the others, for ever allowing this weakness for her. From the beginning he had known it could only lead to pain. Why hadn't he heeded his own warnings? Why hadn't he run from the witch while he had the chance?

It was there, the horror showed clearly in her eyes. She was almost sick with the thought of having his baby. "I can see the idea brings you no pleasure." He shrugged. His only defense against the torment he

371

was suddenly plunged into was to feign indifference.

Make her believe . . . Make her believe anything but the truth. Don't give her that weapon. "Don't worry, your condition won't last forever. After it's over you can leave."

Mattie couldn't believe her ears. "What?" she said, not really expecting an answer. What was he saying? Good God, it couldn't be true. She couldn't have been that ridiculously naïve.

"When it's over you can go," he repeated, believing her stunned response a real question.

Mattie blinked, unsure of her own sanity. She couldn't have heard him right. "What are you talking about?"

Callahan gave a long sigh. "After you have the baby, you can go about your business. I'll take the child, of course, but I won't try to keep you with me."

Mattie only stared at him in disbelief.

Callahan felt a niggling of doubt. Had he been mistaken? Had he misunderstood her reaction to the news? "You want to go, don't you?"

"Where?" she asked stupidly. Mattie gave a silent curse. She was acting like some dimwit. She had to get control of herself, control of this conversation.

"How the hell should I know?" He was almost sneering now, his hurt so deep and intense he wanted to tear something, anything apart. "You don't want my baby, do you?"

Mattie considered his last remark the most cruel yet. At this moment she hated him more than any living creature. But to give up his child? The thought was ludicrous. Her teeth clamped together as she sneered, "Do you think I'd give up my child to the likes of you?" She hurt so bad every breath became an effort. All she could think of was what a gullible fool she'd been. All she wanted was to hide somewhere and lick her raw wounds. But first she was going to show this beast up for the liar he was. "Last night, you told me . . ."

372

"I know what I told you." Callahan interrupted. He shrugged and forced a stiff smile to his lips. "It seemed like the right thing to say at the time," he lied, his flippant attitude belying the pain that knotted his insides. "Besides, you said as much. I'd say we're even."

Mattie was too caught up in her own misery to notice his smile was one of the unhappiest she was ever likely to see. It couldn't be any clearer, in her mind. She'd heard it with her own ears, and the words confirmed her darkest suspicions. The bastard! God, but curse words weren't near enough to describe this lowlife. Her body stiffened, her voice grated, and she smiled with menace, "Not quite, Mr. Callahan."

Mattie held up her hand as if to halt his words, when he would have countered her remark. "A few words, if I might? First of all, you're wrong. The idea of having a baby brings me much pleasure. Had I paid attention to the signs, I would have realized the fact sooner, therefore the more time to savor this joy."

But her eyes held not a flicker of the joy she proclaimed. Instead the pain shown was so stark, so raw, he couldn't begin to fathom the depth of it. "You seem to have gotten the impression I wouldn't have wanted this baby." She tipped her head slightly and inquired, "No doubt the reason behind last night's performance?" She shook her head. "Not to worry, Callahan. Your act, although very well played out, was unnecessary. I want this baby."

Mattie took a deep, calming breath and forced aside the need to cry. There would be time aplenty for tears, she knew. Now she needed to say these words or burst with the effort of holding them back. "I'm tempted to say I want it to spite you." She shook her head. "But that wouldn't be true. No, I want it despite you.

"You're a liar, Callahan. That makes you less in my

eyes than one of those oxen." She nodded over her shoulder in the direction of the train. Her gaze held to his with contempt and she smiled sadly. "You have poison in your soul and win nothing with your deception. My pride doesn't suffer to admit to having believed you loved me, or to have loved you in return. No, I'm not the fool here.

"And lastly, I most certainly will take you up on your offer to leave, but not after. I'll be long gone before this baby is born." Mattie took a deep, calming breath and smiled with a sorrow that tore at his heart. *"Now,* we're even, Mr. Callahan."

Callahan stared dumbly at her retreating back, closer to tears than any time in his life. Pain coiled like a snake around his innards, knowing he was the biggest fool alive. He didn't know how he had managed it, but he had just lost his only reason to live.

Three days had gone by. Three days of torture. Three days when nothing passed between them but silence. Callahan's every effort to talk to her met with a cold look and stony silence. When he persisted, as he often did, she merely walked away.

He had hoped, at first, to see her anger pass. But once it had, pure terror filled his being, for each day she became colder, calmer, and more deathly silent. If ever there was a time to panic it was now, for he couldn't have imagined anything more frightening.

Callahan sighed with disgust. He had to do something. He had to shake her out of this icy control. He gave a silent groan at the thought. No doubt he would only make matters worse, and yet he had to try. In truth, nothing could be quite as bad as the thick silence that lay between them.

Callahan's heart fluttered with despair as he realized every day brought them closer to the end of this journey, and perhaps closer to the end of them as well.

He had to force her to listen to him. The thought was impossible. He couldn't let her go. It was too late. He couldn't make it without her.

Callahan watched from a distance as she walked along the top of the grassy knoll. A gentle breeze tugged at her skirts. Mattie held her shawl around her shoulders and faced into it, her thick black hair glistening clean in the sunshine and falling in loose waves down her back.

Mattie never acknowledged his presence as he suddenly appeared beside her, except to turn slightly away. Callahan lost every softly spoken word he had practiced with that one movement. Damn her, he silently raged, all the while cursing his own inability to control the moment. "All right, lady," he finally blurted out. "I'm going to say this once and only once. You're not going anywhere, except with me. Do you understand?"

The words had barely begun before Callahan knew he had made a mistake and yet he seemed helpless but to finish his tirade. But Callahan didn't know the meaning of helpless until he watched her shoot him a blank look, turn, and walk down the slight incline.

Callahan gave a groan of frustration. Damn, but he was every kind of fool. A wry smile twisted his lips. *No one can say you don't know how to sweet-talk a lady, Callahan.*

But Mattie was mistaken if she thought she'd heard the last of him. He wasn't about to give up. He was going to talk to her. He was going to tell her exactly how he felt and, if necessary, force her to listen.

Mattie was sitting upon a fallen log when next he found her. Callahan might have been invisible for all the attention she gave him. He began to pace. Back and forth he moved in front of her, his fingers running nervously through his hair.

Finally he stopped directly before her and declared,

"I love you."

No reaction.

"Did you hear me?"

Mattie raised expressionless eyes in silence.

"Let's stop this nonsense and go back to the way things were."

Mattie stood, but instead of taking a step toward him, as he hoped, began to move off again.

Callahan was helpless but to follow her. "Where are you going? Damn it, Mattie, will you talk to me?!"

"Why?"

"Why?! Because I just told you I love you, that's why."

Mattie stopped in her tracks. The smile she gave him brought an icy chill of fear down his spine. "If memory serves, Mr. Callahan, you said that before. You spoke lies then. I can only assume the same holds true."

"Oh Jesus, Mattie. I didn't lie. I did love you. I do love you." She was walking again, and for some reason Callahan was having a time keeping up with her. He took her arm and brought her to a stop. His expression showed clearly his desperation. "What more do you want from me?!"

Mattie's eyes widened with surprise. "I? Mr. Callahan, there is nothing I want from you, save to be left alone."

She was walking again with Callahan once more stumbling close at her heels. "Mattie, be reasonable. People don't chuck it all just because they've had a fight. You can't walk away from what we have."

Mattie came to a sudden stop, spun on her heels, and laughed. "What we have? You will forgive me, won't you? I seem to have forgotten. Exactly what is it we have besides a few illicit moments spent in bed?"

Callahan's mouth hardened. "It was more than that and you goddamned well know it!"

"Was it? One wonders why you are so anxious to

see me leave if that's the case?"

Callahan breathed a long sigh of remorse. "Mattie, please. Can't you understand I thought you didn't want the baby? I spoke in anger."

Mattie shook her head. She had had many hours to think since their blowup, and she knew it was more than anger that caused his hateful words. "You weren't angry, Callahan." Suddenly her eyes widened as a thought occurred. "You were scared."

"Scared?" He laughed in ridicule, but by his expression it was obvious she had hit her mark. "Of what?" His heart was suddenly pounding with trepidation.

Mattie sighed with disgust at his instant denial. She didn't have it in her to press her point. If the man refused to admit to his feelings, she couldn't force him. "Oh God. Just go away."

She was about to begin walking again when his hand came to her arm and gently restrained her. "All right. All right. I was afraid." He hesitated a long moment before he found the courage to go on. Callahan had faced murderers who didn't make him tremble with fear like this one tiny woman. He closed his eyes, forcing the words from his tight throat. "I was afraid of your rejection, so I rejected you first." His voice lowered and grew husky with emotion. "I was afraid you didn't want my baby." Callahan seemed suddenly to realize what he was admitting to. He pushed his fingers through his hair again and groaned almost angrily. "Jesus, can't you allow a man his pride?"

Mattie ignored his plea. Both of them knew pride had no place here. "And now?" she insisted.

"Mattie," he gave her a determined glare, "I could always force you to stay."

Her chocolate eyes filled with ice as she silently dared him to try.

"All right," he groaned, knowing the uselessness of threats. "Maybe I can't force you." To do so would no doubt only ensure her hatred, thereby bringing untold torture upon himself.

Mattie watched him, waiting for him to go on.

Callahan dug his hands into his pockets and sighed with resignation. It was difficult enough to say what he had to; he couldn't seem to find the courage to look at her while he did it. "It's hard, Mattie. It's hard to admit to something that means so much."

Her gaze softened.

"I swore, a long time ago, I'd never again allow the hurt of losing someone." Almost embarrassed, his voice lowered. "After my wife, I swore I'd never love anyone again."

Mattie watched him in silence, waiting for him to go on.

His gaze clung to the toe of his boot. "I was assigned to New Orleans, during the war. I met her there." He breathed a deep sigh. "She played me for a fool. Married me to gain information for the southern cause. I killed her lover when I found them in bed together." He shook his head, weariness showing in the slope of his shoulders. "She died not long after that. I think the South losing the war and her lover's death were just too much for her."

"Did you love her terribly?"

Callahan uttered a sound not unlike a moan of pain. "I thought I did. Now I realize it was my pride that suffered most of all, for I felt nothing compared to what I feel now."

"What is it you feel?"

Callahan's eyes locked with hers for a long moment before he answered. "For the first time in my life, I find myself in love. Honest to God crazy in love, and it scares the shit out of me."

Mattie lowered her head to hide the smile his coarse language brought about. If she wanted softly spoken words of love, she'd have to look elsewhere, for it wouldn't be Callahan to whisper sweet nothings. Idly she wondered how many women could imagine the thrill of listening to so startling a declaration. For an instant she felt genuine pity for those who would never know this ecstasy.

"Why?" she asked softly, her heart pounding with his admission.

"Why? Why what?"

"Why does it scare you?"

"Because I feel helpless, that's why. And I don't like feeling helpless. I don't like knowing you can tear me apart with a few well-chosen words."

"What words could do that, Callahan?"

Callahan took a long, deep breath. He was laying everything on the line. A vein throbbed in his throat, his stomach tightened into a knot as he pulled his courage from the depth of his being. "If you told me you didn't love me. If you told me you never wanted to see me again."

"I'd never say that," she whispered hoarsely, astounded and thrilled beyond anything she'd every known at how this proud man had bared his soul.

"Why?"

"It wouldn't be true."

"Does that mean you still love me?"

Mattie sighed as she took a step toward him. "Silly man. Love isn't an emotion that can be turned on and off. I'll probably always love you."

Callahan's arms circled her back. His eyes closed with relief, his head lowered so that his forehead rested upon hers. "Do you have to say that with such despair?"

Mattie laughed. Her finger stroked his beard. "Is that how it sounded? On the contrary, loving you brings me much happiness. Except when you tell me you want me to leave."

Callahan groaned as he hugged her close, his face buried in the warm curve of her throat. "I never said that. I said you could go if you wanted to." Suddenly he pulled his face from her neck and gave a sheepish grin. "I lied. There was no way I was going to let you leave me."

Mattie laughed again and moved her body seductively against his. "Never?"

"You're going to marry me."

"How sweet of you to ask," she remarked, her words clearly pointing out that he had not asked at all. Mattie's smile was pure deviltry and Callahan groaned and closed his eyes again with the painful knowledge that this woman had the power to make or break his world. "You do have a way with words, darling. Have you ever thought of writing poetry?"

Callahan's only admission that he had heard her was a light slap to her bottom. Mattie giggled at his glare and sighed with delight as his arms tightened with determined possession. "And then I'm going to keep you locked up, so no one will steal the prize I've gained."

Mattie eyed him suspiciously. "If I thought you were serious . . ." She let the sentence go unfinished.

Callahan grinned, growing more confident and at ease with every passing minute. "And if I were? What would you do?"

Mattie breathed a long sigh. "Marry you anyway." She shrugged, trying hard to hide her grin. "I'm afraid loving you does not make a great statement for common sense."

For that she received another blow to her bottom, only this time he forgot to take his hand away.

Chapter Twenty-four

Mattie sighed with delight as she eased her weary body into the first hot bath she'd taken in almost eight months. She leaned back, resting her head against the tub's wooden rim and closed her eyes silently swearing there was little in life to compare to this pleasure.

Mattie's lips curved into a delicious smile. Well, perhaps that was overstating things a bit. There might be one or two things equally enjoyable, she silently amended as a picture of Callahan flashed suddenly in her mind's eye. Her breasts swelled and a gnawing ache began deep inside. It took no effort at all to remember the things he could do and had done to her. Mattie sighed her disappointment. Except for these last few weeks.

Although she loved him all the more for his consideration, she'd had enough of being treated as if she were a porcelain doll. She was a woman, a woman with needs, and it was his fault she felt these needs. She was only having a baby, for goodness' sakes. That very natural fact didn't make her an invalid. Mattie smiled, listening for his step, never more anxious to show him just how healthy a pregnant lady could be.

The lavender soap lathered into a rich creamy foam and Mattie sighed at the pure luxury of running the sweetly scented cloth over her arms and shoulders. Then again, she mused, despite her intentions to see to the delights that awaited her in Callahan's arms, there was a strong possibility that she might never leave this tub. Mattie giggled as she imagined the ridiculous picture of Callahan trying in vain to pull her out.

It wasn't until she moved her hands over her gently rounded stomach that a thought suddenly occurred. It had been months since she had thought about her plan to revenge Melanie's murder. Somehow she had quite forgotten her original intent.

Mattie gave a soft, helpless sigh. She had waited and planned for so long. It was disquieting to suddenly realize she felt no hatred for the man. Mattie shook her head, not at all happy at the turn of events. Her sister's murderer would continue on enjoying his freedom, for she no longer had it in her to seek revenge.

A rueful smile curved her lips. In truth, the child she carried wasn't responsible alone for the change in direction her life had taken. Although she'd never chance its life, Mattie knew it was Callahan above all, and the love they shared that so filled her life, she was hard put to find the space needed to nurse her hatred.

Mattie grinned at her newfound knowledge, suddenly happier and more at peace than she could ever have imagined. Her smile was clearly in evidence when she turned as the door to her room opened.

Callahan, covered still with the dust of the trail, entered. "What are you thinking about to cause so sweet a smile?" he asked, so madly in love he found himself jealous of every thought unshared.

Mattie's smile grew into low, seductive laughter as she turned back to her bathing. "Nothing earth-shattering."

Callahan almost groaned aloud at the sound. He felt an unwanted stirring in his body and gave a silent curse. *Damn rutting bastard. Can't you think of anything but your own selfish needs?*

A frown creased his forehead and caused his brows to nearly meet above burning eyes as he flung his hat

382

to a chair and walked farther into the room. He never knew the sound of his gasp as it filled the silent air. His mouth went dry and the vein that throbbed in his throat threatened to cut off his breathing.

He was facing her now and there wasn't a power on earth that could bring him to tear his eyes from the sweet sight encountered. He had intended only to glance her way, never expecting the water did not cover her completely. He groaned as his gaze took in the luster of glistening flesh, almost glowing in the afternoon sunlight. Sweat broke out over his lip and forehead. Never had he seen a more beautifully haunting sight. Entranced, he watched her breasts above the foam-dotted water's surface and licked at his lips as clear droplets fell from the rosy tips.

It had been weeks since last he'd made love to her, touched her, lost himself in her scent.

Realizing her exhaustion, he had left her each night to much-needed sleep. Not trusting himself, he had purposely kept his distance, knowing things would be better once they reached Sacramento and she had sufficient time to rest. He had convinced himself that perhaps in a day or so, they might . . . Callahan couldn't finish the thought. He cursed again. He should have taken two rooms. Why hadn't he realized the temptation?

"What then?" he asked, his voice husky, his breathing shallow and gasping as he tried to bring his gaze from her.

Mattie clearly read the longing in his eyes and felt not a moment's shyness. Her arms at her sides, she allowed his hungry look, knowing it was matched only by her own. "I was thinking how much I love you."

Callahan raised his eyes to hers. "And you don't think that earth-shattering?" Callahan shook his head, never releasing her gaze. "Lady, every time I hear you say it, the ground literally rocks under my feet."

Mattie watched his eyes widen as she arched her back. She knew full well the effect she was having on him and gloried in the fact. "Perhaps I should only say it then when you are seated," she whispered breathlessly.

Callahan was stripping off his shirt. He couldn't help himself. He had to hold her, touch her, breathe her. If she was tired, he'd ask no more than the exquisite torture of having her near. "Perhaps you should say it more often. I could get used to it then."

"Oh never that!" Mattie countered, a smile touching the corners of her mouth and exposing her crooked tooth, and all Callahan could think was to run his tongue over its adorable surface. "I wouldn't want you to take it for granted."

Callahan was pulling off his boots and socks. "I wouldn't, you know."

"Take it for granted?"

He nodded, his gaze so solemn Mattie found herself fighting the urge to cry. At last his trousers fell upon the growing pile of discarded clothes. He walked toward her, totally at ease in his nakedness, while Mattie swallowed convulsively. She had not, as one would suppose, often had the pleasure of seeing him thus, and found herself helpless but to scan his entire body with a look that threatened to sear his skin with its burning heat.

He was climbing into the tub before she came to her senses and realized his intent. "I don't remember inviting you to join me, Mr. Callahan."

Callahan laughed. He couldn't remember a time when the word mister had sounded so erotic. Gone, he hoped forever, was the cutting tone usually associated with the title. "Oh, you invited me, lady. That look you just gave me was as good as an engraved invitation."

Mattie's cheeks darkened. "I didn't."

He laughed and slid in behind her. His breath was warm as it brushed against her neck and shoulder. "I love those long sultry looks you think I don't see and then the blushes when you realize you've been caught in the act." His mouth came to nuzzle the sweet curve of her neck. "Are you tired?"

Mattie sighed, giving up all hope of denying his words. Her head tilted to allow him greater access as she breathed a shaky "No."

"Sure?"

"Sure."

"The preacher is ready anytime we are," he murmured against her skin as his hands reached for her breasts and gently worried the tips between his fingers.

"Is he waiting downstairs?" she asked, her breath catching in her throat as delicious sensations raced up her spine.

"Mmmm," he breathed, not at all sure he was answering her question or simply enjoying the feel of her against him.

His hands slid beneath the water, around her waist, and down her belly to the juncture of her thighs. "Oh God," she choked as his fingers found his objective, already aching with need, "I hope he's a patient man."

"It's a miracle we didn't drown that time," Callahan gasped as he struggled to steady his breathing and wondered if the thundering in his chest would cause any permanent damage.

Mattie giggled, still sitting astride his hips in the tub. "I don't think I was ever in any danger."

"You weren't the one on the bottom."

Laughter lurked in the depths of her dark eyes. "And whose fault was that? We could have used the bed, but for your lack of restraint. Why, one might believe it years since last we . . ."

Callahan grinned, realizing the trouble she had referring to their lovemaking. "It felt like years."

"Did it?" Mattie smiled. "Why did you wait?"

"I didn't want to tax your strength."

She laughed. "And my lack of strength no longer

poses a problem?"

"I promised myself I'd wait until we reached Sacramento. You'll have time to rest here."

"Mmmm rest. The idea is deserving of some merit, but first . . ." Mattie moved her hips. Her eyes widened and she gave a little moan of surprise as renewed sensation shot through her.

Callahan grinned, feeling himself growing hard again. "I probably should have warned you not to play with things you're not all that familiar with."

Mattie laughed. "You know, after some careful consideration, I believe I like this position."

Callahan gave her a grin so wicked Mattie felt a shiver of excitement run up her spine. "And exactly how much time have you given over to considering this problem?"

Mattie shrugged a shoulder, watching as the movement drew his gaze to her swaying breasts. She couldn't seem to control the slight trembling in her voice. "Oh, a very, very long time."

Callahan's finger traced the soft curve swaying deliciously before him. His gaze lifted to hers as he asked, "Are you trying to tell me that a lady like you harbors thoughts so wicked?"

Mattie's eyes narrowed as she poked his chest with a not too gentle finger. "Don't tell me I'm the only one here to have such thoughts, Callahan. I can only imagine what goes on in that mind of yours."

Callahan laughed, his heart soaring with the knowledge that she fantasized about him. "No, you couldn't."

"Really?" she asked, her eyes widening with surprise. "Is it that bad?"

Callahan slowly shook his head. "It's that good."

"I confess you've managed to perk my curiosity." And when he offered no answers to her unspoken questions, she finally asked, "Well? Are you going to tell me or not?"

"Or not."

"Really?"

Callahan shrugged. "Some things are best when shown."

"Oh, well, I couldn't object to that now, could I?"

"Lady, I'm going to see to it that you're much too busy to object to anything," he said as he stood, taking her slight weight easily up with him and moved toward the bed.

"Callahan," she gasped, stiffening as she realized his intent. "We'll soak everything!"

Callahan placed her on the bed and followed her down with his own body. He smiled as he nestled himself comfortably against her. "But the heat we generate will soon see all dry again."

Mattie giggled, her brow raised in disbelief. "That confident, are you?"

The glitter in his eyes belied his slightly bored tone. "I suppose I must prove it."

Amazingly Mattie felt a tremble of excitement. "How else can I be certain you speak the truth?"

He rolled to his side, his eyes moving hungrily over her smooth form. "You wouldn't simply take my word for it, I take it?"

Mattie's breathing grew shallow and uneven. He hadn't touched her and yet she could swear she felt the heat of his caress. Her eyes fluttered helplessly closed and she murmured, "On something of this importance?"

Callahan smiled, knowing full well her response to him. "There's no help for it then. I'd best be about this chore."

"If I'm going to marry you . . ."

"What do you mean if?" he interrupted, as he finished with the last of the tiny buttons that ran the length of her slim back. Callahan pulled her against him, his arms wrapping tightly around her waist. His mouth deposited playful little bites along the side of

387

her throat.

Mattie ignored his question as she watched his lips move over her skin through the mirror they faced. "If I'm going to marry you, don't you think it's time I knew your first name?"

Callahan groaned and tightened his hold.

Mattie smiled. "I promise never to use it unless I'm very very angry."

Callahan's gaze caught hers through the mirror. The twinkle of laughter in her eyes could not be denied. "Is that a warning to keep you happy?"

"You might take it that way, I suppose," she said with feigned innocence, while examining a fingernail and losing badly the struggle to keep a smile from her face.

"All right, you'll know before the night is out, in any case. I wouldn't want to hear you burst out laughing in the middle of the ceremony. Galahad."

There was a long moment of total silence. Ever so slowly Mattie's eyes began to grow wide, wider, until they threatened to absorb her entire face. And then, "Galahad?" A strangled voice. "Galahad Callahan?" A soft giggle. "A tongue twister?"

Mattie turned into the circle of his arms. Desperately trying to fight her laughter, she buried her face in his chest.

She was almost choking when she finally managed, "I'm afraid to ask this, but do you have a middle name?"

Callahan grinned. There was no help for it. It was a ridiculous name, more so when combined with his last. "Michael."

Mattie managed to quell the worst of her laughter. She cleared her throat and compressed her quivering lips. "Perhaps we might use that name this evening."

"I'm not sure it will be legal."

"You wouldn't want Jake and Nora to hear it, would you?"

Callahan groaned in despair, realizing the two of

them as witnesses to his and Mattie's vows would hear all. "Oh God, I forgot about them." He gave it a moment's thought. "Perhaps if I use only the initial and my second name?"

Mattie nodded, her eyes bright with unshed tears of laughter. "I'm positive it would be all right."

A second later, after wiping her eyes with the backs of her hands, she collapsed weakly against him and burst out laughing again. "I can't help it. Didn't your mother like you?"

Callahan's smile held a touch of sadness as he cuddled her against him. "Not enough, I guess. She left at the first opportunity."

Mattie's laughter was instantly stilled. Her eyes widened with the horror of her careless words. "Oh God, I'm sorry."

"Me too. Imagine giving a poor kid a name like that. I can't count the fights . . ."

Mattie took his face between her hands. The action stilled his words. "I'm sorry she was such a fool. How could anyone leave you?"

Callahan shrugged. "I didn't find out till years later that she fell in love with one of my father's business partners. She didn't have much of a choice. My father kicked her out." He shrugged again. "She died not long after that."

After a few moments of silence, Mattie said, "It doesn't matter, you know."

Callahan searched her face, on guard for any signs of pity. What he found lurking in the depths of eyes blacker than midnight brought him dangerously close to disgracing himself with tears. His heart swelled with the exquisite truth. In her, he had finally found his home. "I love you enough, Callahan. I love you more than enough."

"Let's go."

Mattie shot him an exasperated glance. "Callahan,

it's only half over."

"It's boring," he whispered, his mouth close to her ear, his warm breath sending chills down her back.

Mattie blessed the darkened theater and the privacy their box afforded as his arm circled her shoulder and his wayward fingers came to lightly brush against the tip of her breast. "It's lovely," she countered, her voice suddenly husky despite her best intentions to ignore his deliberate teasing of her senses.

"You're lovely," he stated, his eyes bright with laughter as he listened to her uneven breathing and watched the warning look in her eyes. "Need I remind you, madam, we're on our honeymoon?"

A soft smile curved her lips. "Callahan, you are a rogue. Can you not control these base instincts for an hour or so?"

He never bothered to deny her words. "It seems I cannot, although I thought I was doing exceedingly well till now." He gave a low growl as his mouth nuzzled against her cheek.

"Are you in pain?" she asked. Her eyes straight ahead, she forced herself to watch those on the stage, never realizing the delicious smile that curved her mouth.

Callahan took her hand and placed it in his lap, in order to show her the exact scope of his suffering. "You might say that."

Mattie shot him a look of surprise as she realized what her fingers had encountered. Her teasing smile almost brought a groan to his lips. "Are you secreting something in your trousers? I'm sure I felt something."

"Shall I show you what I've got? I've been saving it for you."

"A present?" Mattie giggled and the couple in the box beside them turned their way, shooting them looks of disapproval.

"I think you laughed at a most serious part of this play."

"Oh dear," Mattie sighed, her whisper low and thoroughly intoxicating to his mind. "I'm afraid you've quite ruined this outing for me."

"I'll gladly take you to every play you can stand. Only take pity on my present condition."

"And what condition is that?"

"Mattie," he warned. "If we don't leave now, the best part of this play will be here in this box."

"Are you sure you'll be able to walk?"

Callahan ignored her teasing and nearly dragged her out of the box. Once in the darkened hallway, he pushed her up against the wall. Mattie's gasp of surprise was the perfect opportunity for Callahan's hungry mouth to enjoy what it would.

Mattie's low moan of pleasure did little toward easing Callahan's need. He was gasping for breath by the time his mouth finally tore itself from hers. "Ah, lady," he whispered, "I feel like I've been waiting hours for that."

Someone cleared his throat behind them. "Excuse me" came a low voice filled with laughter as a man brushed past them.

It wasn't so dark in the hallway that what they were doing couldn't be clearly seen. Mattie felt her cheeks burn, only now realizing Callahan had caught her up to him and was even yet holding her to his hips with hands positioned familiarly on her bottom.

"Callahan," she glared at his grinning face, "I'm going to . . ."

"I know exactly what you're going to do. And I deserve a medal if I make it back to the hotel before we do it."

Mattie couldn't help her smile. She'd probably never understand this new side of her. He had caused her untold embarrassment and yet she felt like laughing.

They were out on the street before he eased his hurried pace. Mattie was breathing hard, in an effort not to be dragged along. "Callahan!" she snapped, digging her heels in and forcing him to slow down. "You are the most, the most . . ."

Callahan grinned, stopping to look down at her. His arm automatically circled her waist and brought her hips scandalously close to his. "The most?" he prompted.

Mattie forced a frown she did not feel. "The most annoying . . ."

"But desirable?"

"Arrogant . . ."

"And handsome?"

"High-handed . . ."

"Completely besotted?"

"Irritating . . ."

"Madly in love?"

"Beast."

Callahan laughed. "Which one?"

"All of them," she countered after a moment's thought. The slightest trace of a smile touched her lips. "And especially wonderful and funny and oh so appealing." Unconsciously she insinuated her hips against his.

"Stop right there!" he warned. "I won't be held accountable for my actions if you say another word."

"I'd best stop then." She grinned. Even in the dark, he could see a slight flush rise to her cheeks. "I want to hold you accountable. Actually I want to hold you any way I can."

"Oh my God," Callahan groaned, his voice shaking as he momentarily allowed her provocative words to form rapturous pictures in his mind. It took some effort, but he finally managed to release her and shake himself of her seductive spell.

They were back at the hotel in record time, and if they encountered startled looks as they hurried along the way, neither seemed to notice, so caught up were they in the pleasure they knew to await them.

"You're going to pay for that, lady," Callahan warned as he opened the door and almost shoved her into the darkened room.

392

Mattie giggled. "It's no more than you deserved, Mr. Callahan. Imagine taking such liberties at the theater. Why I've never heard of such goings-on. Suppose . . ."

A discreet clearing of a throat brought to an instant stop her next words. Mattie spun around and gasped with surprise.

"Sorry" came a voice from out of the dark as a match flared to life.

Mattie felt her head bang against the wall as Callahan shoved her behind him. "Jesus! Why the hell are you sitting here in the dark? I could have shot you."

Perry grinned as he lit a lamp. "I don't think so." He eyed the small revolver that seemed to have instantly appeared in Callahan's hand. "As far as I could tell, you had other things on your mind." Perry shook his head, a smile fighting his serious expression. "Getting careless, Callahan?"

Perry walked toward Callahan holding a small piece of paper out to him. "The time and place are set. Sorry," he shot a look at Mattie's startled expression, "we leave at first light."

Perry closed the door to a stream of Callahan's curses.

"What does he mean, you leave at first light? Where are you going?"

Callahan looked down at his wife, replaced the gun in the pocket of his coat, and gave a long, obviously unhappy sigh. "Mattie, you know I can't tell you."

"What difference does it make? Do you imagine I can do something to stop you?"

"Orders."

"Whose orders?"

"The people I work for."

Mattie nodded. "Very informative, Callahan," she remarked with no little sarcasm and then joined him in another sigh, hers tinged with disgust. "You're delivering the guns. Am I right?"

He didn't answer her, but pulled his saddlebag from

393

the closet and haphazardly threw a few pieces of clothing inside.

"And since I can no longer believe you're doing anything wrong, I can only assume whatever you're doing is right. Right?"

Callahan grinned at her simplistic logic, watching her pace the small room as she spoke.

"So, let's see. What have we got? You and your friends are transporting guns. Now who would be in the business of transporting guns inside the law and outside of the government?" Mattie stopped, her eyes widening with newly discovered knowledge. She faced him with a triumphant smile. "Why didn't I think of it before? It doesn't have to be outside the government, does it, Callahan? It could be for the government."

Mattie gave a small laugh at his closed look. "I think I'm on to something here."

"I could definitely put you on to something if you stop pacing and meet me over there." He nodded toward the bed.

Mattie giggled. "I'm sure you could. If you came right out and told me what you're up to, we could get right to it."

"Mattie," he sighed.

"I know, I know. You can't." She gave a short dismissive wave of her hand and began to pace again. "All right, so you're bringing guns west, under government orders. Who is it you're giving them, or selling them, to?

"It could be the Army, I suppose," she mused half to herself. "But if so, why all the secrecy?" She shook her head. "No, probably not the Army. Army personnel would have accompanied the shipment, I think." She shot him a look. "And definitely not the Indians, or you would have had bargaining power when I was captured.

"So who does that leave? Who is it that is in need of three wagonsful of guns out here? And why would the United States ship them?"

Mattie stopped her pacing, her mouth dropping open with surprise. "Of course. It's simple." She gave a soft laugh filled with relief, realizing the close proximity of their southern neighbor and the civil war that was even now being waged. "Mexico, right?"

"Mattie," he warned.

Mattie laughed with delight. "Do you know the pain you could have saved me, if you had just told me?"

"I couldn't."

"Why?"

"You might have been one of them."

"One of whom? The Mexicans?"

Callahan shook his head.

Mattie's eyes widened. "There are others who want the guns?"

Callahan simply stared at her.

"And you thought I was one of them?" She began to laugh. "Me?" And at his pained silence, she only laughed harder. Finally she managed, "How do you know I'm not?"

"I know. Now if you're finished playing detective, I suggest we use what little time we have before I leave."

"You're leaving without me, I take it?"

"Most definitely," Callahan remarked.

We'll just see about that. "How do you know I won't follow you?"

Callahan gave her a long hard look before he seemed to suddenly relax. "You won't."

Mattie didn't like the gleam in his eyes. She realized she might have made a serious tactical error here, but knew too this wasn't the time to push home her point. "Is it dangerous?"

Callahan shrugged. "I doubt it."

"But you're not sure."

"I'm sure enough. Take off your dress."

Mattie gave a secret smile as she began to unbutton her bodice. There was no way she was going to allow this man, this wonderful, hardheaded man, to take himself into any situation more dangerous than cross-

395

ing a road. Not without her, that is. "I love you, Callahan."

Callahan smiled as he watched her slip the gown from her shoulders, thankful that the thin chemise beneath it left nothing to his imagination. "I take it that means you will allow me the peace of mind to know you'll be waiting here safe and sound?"

Mattie gave a tender smile for an answer while stripping off her chemise. She faced him wearing only her petticoats, stockings, and shoes.

Callahan swallowed. What the hell was he saying? Damn, but this woman was dangerous. One look at her was enough for him to lose all thought. Dangerous. That was it! He couldn't allow her to involve herself with danger. "Mattie," he growled.

Mattie glanced his way. Her smile was sweet, too sweet, but he never noticed. She was just stepping out of her drawers, when his voice, thick with emotion, caused her to look up.

"Don't," he gasped. "Leave them on."

"My stockings?" she asked, her hands at her garters.

Callahan swallowed and nodded. "Come over here."

Mattie did as he asked and smiled as she heard his ragged, "Undress me."

"Ah, now I see why you married me." She grinned.

"Why?"

"It's ever so convenient, don't you think?"

"Is it?" he asked, not paying all too much attention to her words, since his greedy gaze, nearly devouring her breasts, left little space for thought.

She nodded. "Free labor."

Callahan smiled. "Free? Is that what you call it, after all the money I've spent on clothes these last few days?"

Mattie giggled. "Is that why I'm forced to perform these menial tasks? To pay you back?"

"There are better ways to pay me back," he suggested.

Mattie opened his shirt and swallowed at the darkly

396

tanned skin left to her view. She didn't think but to give in to the temptation it offered, and pressed her opened mouth to his warmth.

Callahan closed his eyes against the rapture that filled his being. "Oh, Mattie," he groaned. "My God."

"Don't touch me," she whispered as his hand closed over her breast. "I don't want to lose my train of thought."

Callahan's low chuckle filled her mind, mingled erotically with his scent and taste, until Mattie felt the world sway dizzily about her. She pulled slightly away. "You won't think me too bold, Mr. Callahan, if I have my way with you?"

Callahan struggled to form the words, but nothing came to his effort save a garbled groan.

Mattie's busy fingers released the buttons of his trousers. Callahan joined her in a low sigh of delight at what she found awaiting her pleasure.

Chapter Twenty-five

Mattie forced her breathing to remain even and shallow. She felt the bed give under Callahan's weight as he leaned down and bestowed a light kiss upon her forehead. A moment or so later she heard the door close with a gentle click behind him.

In a flash she was off the bed and facing the armoire. Without thought she pulled out the first thing her hand came in contact with and began to dress. Her fingers hurried over the buttons of her blouse and secured her split skirt at her waist. All the while her mind imagined Callahan downstairs, finishing off a quick breakfast and readying himself for the dangerous journey that lay ahead.

She was securing her hair into a neat twist at the nape of her neck when the door opened silently behind her. "Just as I thought."

Mattie whirled around, arms swinging wildly. As she searched for balance, she fell back on the bed. Her mouth opened in a silent cry of alarm to find Callahan leaning comfortably against the door. "You have a ways to go before you perfect that sleeping act of yours."

"You scared me!" she accused.

Callahan shrugged, apparently unconcerned that her heart was pounding with fright. "So I see."

Feeling at a great disadvantage in her present position, Mattie scrambled back to her feet just as Callahan moved toward her. "Where do you think you were going?"

Mattie shrugged, a pulse throbbing at her throat, her cheeks flushing with guilt. "I thought a bit of shopping."

Callahan shook his head. "You'd never make a decent

agent, Mattie. First lesson, one must never lie so obviously."

Mattie shot him a hard look, refusing to take back her words, no matter his obvious disbelief.

"The shops won't be open for hours," he pointed out all too reasonably.

Mattie bit her lip, realizing her mistake. She nodded her head, determined to cover her error. "I know that. I was looking forward to a long leisurely breakfast while I waited."

Callahan pulled his watch from his pocket. "Do you often breakfast for three hours?"

Mattie shrugged. "Now and then," she lied outrageously.

Callahan grinned without a trace of humor as he closed the trap. "I thought you never take breakfast? You wouldn't touch a bite of food until the noonday meal while on the trail."

Thinking fast, Mattie found her only possible out. "I'm having a baby, Callahan. Eating habits change when a lady is . . ."

"Exactly," he thundered, his cool composure vanishing in an instant as he grabbed her by the shoulders and almost threw her back on the bed. Callahan loomed menacingly above her. On his hands and knees over her prone body, he glared his rage. "You're having a baby. Are you so simple-minded as to believe the child will survive if his mother is dead?"

"You said there was no danger," she reminded him, completely abandoning any further attempts to deny what they both knew as truth.

"I said, I doubt there would be danger. I doubt it, do you hear me? That means I'm not sure."

"I hear you. I'm not deaf. Stop yelling, before everyone in this hotel awakens."

"I don't give a shit about anyone in this hotel. All I care about is you!"

"You have an odd way of showing it then. Do all men scream at their wives when they are not instantly obeyed?"

A flicker of regret shone in Callahan's eyes, but he soon forced aside the emotion. His words and the harsh tone of his voice clearly showed anger. "Not instantly obeyed? Is that what you call this?" Callahan's lips thinned further in an effort to keep his hands from her throat, for never in his life had he felt so close to throttling a woman. "No doubt another husband would beat his wife soundly. Had I any sense, I'd do as much."

Mattie never realized the extent of his anger, but took heart from the tenderness he had tried so hard to hide. "Callahan," she sighed, "how can you expect me to sit here and wait? I'll go mad worrying about you, and I'm sure that kind of tension is not good for the baby."

Callahan ground his teeth. It took superhuman control not to give in to this woman's gentle plea, for there was nothing he wouldn't grant her, except the chance to endanger herself. "You'll just have to manage."

"But that's unfair."

"Perhaps, but that's the way it will be."

"All right, all right," she snapped, not unlike a sulky child. "I can see there's no use arguing with you. I'll do as you say."

Callahan watched her for a long moment. He almost smiled as he realized just how easy it would be to fall under her spell. Loosened from its pins her hair lay disheveled, a black cloud of curls haloing her beautiful face. Her eyes were huge and dark with pleading her cause, her lips moist and entirely too kissable. Callahan grunted and moved off the bed, breathing easier once temptation was more than an arm's length away. "Get up."

"Why?"

"Madam, you insult my intelligence if you think me such a fool as to believe this new act."

"What new act? I said I'll wait."

"So you did. The problem is, I don't believe you."

"I promise, Callahan."

He shook his head. "Too little, too late. Let's go."

Mattie followed him to the door. "Does this mean you've changed your mind? Are you going to let me go with you?" she asked hopefully.

Callahan said nothing. In silence he escorted her out to an almost deserted street. The sun was just beginning to show the promise of its warming rays over the mountaintops and Mattie breathed in the sweet scent of clean, moist morning air. She smiled with confidence, knowing she had won out against Callahan's arguments as he took her arm and guided along the wooden sidewalk, toward the livery where the wagons were being kept.

"I'll be very good. I'll obey any order."

Callahan shot her a quick sideward glance. A smile touched his mouth and he nodded in agreement. "I believe you will."

Mattie's heart sang with delight, and a huge smile lit up her face. Whatever the danger that lay ahead, they'd face it together. She hadn't realized till now the power she exerted over this man. Never would she have believed he'd be so easy to convince.

She was never more wrong.

"I just have to make one quick stop," he announced as he entered a small wooden building, one of a dozen that ran along each side of Sacramento's main street.

With his hand on her arm, Mattie had no choice but to accompany him inside. Mattie hadn't ever before visited a jail. Her eyes widened as she took in the two tiny cells, each hardly large enough to hold a narrow bed and both completely surrounded by iron bars.

For a second she wondered why Callahan found it necessary to confer with the local authorities but soon brushed off her momentary surprise, realizing this meeting would obviously have something to do with the business at hand.

A man was seated at a desk just inside the doorway. He glanced up as the two of them entered, his gaze growing warm with pleasure as he returned Mattie's lovely smile. "Morning, folks," he said. "Can I help you?"

401

Callahan nodded as he returned the greeting. "Sure can, Sheriff."

The man shook his head. "Deputy Wilson. Sheriff Parker won't be in till later."

Callahan shrugged. "You'll do just fine, Deputy. I want to leave my prisoner here for a few days. Maybe as long as a week." Callahan pulled a small black wallet from the inside pocket of his coat and flashed identification at the man as he spoke.

Mattie squashed a tiny sense of alarm as her heart began to beat somewhat erratically. What was he talking about? What prisoner?

"Sure. No problem. Where is he?"

"He is a she and she's right here."

Mattie gasped as Callahan's fingers took her arm in a clamplike hold, understanding all too well, and obviously too late, his meaning.

She should have known! Why had she been so foolish to believe he'd listen to her plea?

"No! Callahan, please," she whispered, realizing herself for a fool to beg, and yet unable to simply abide by his actions. "Don't do this to me."

Callahan hardened his heart and refused to be swayed by her soft words of pleading. "You won't find any more wily, Wilson. My advice is to ignore anything she says. It'll all be lies."

Deputy Wilson was having a hard time fathoming the possibility that this woman was a wanted criminal. She didn't fit the type at all, not that he'd seen many females in her line of work. It took a moment but he finally managed to close his gaping mouth and ask, "What's she done?"

"Have you heard of 'The Widow'?"

The deputy shook his head. "Can't say as I have."

Callahan shrugged as if the man's knowledge was of no importance. "She marries a man and then . . ." Callahan gave a swipe at his throat with the tip of his finger while emitting a sqeaking sound. "She's been doin' right well for herself. As far as we know, there's been six husbands so far. And each time her pockets grow thicker."

"I'd say I took one husband too many," Mattie mumbled as she glared her anger.

"How come I ain't seen no wanted posters?"

Callahan shrugged again. "She don't leave many witnesses."

Obviously the man was unwilling to believe this dastardly tale about so appealing a young woman. "And the Justice Department is now hunting down murderers?"

"Actually, no. It just so happens I came across her while on another assignment."

Deputy Wilson nodded, knowing, despite his reluctance to do so, he had no choice but to believe this government man. He took a ring of keys from his desk drawer and sighed as he came to his feet.

"You don't have to do this, Callahan," Mattie whispered as she was being dragged toward one of the cells. "I promised you . . ."

"I know what you promised me, lady," he interrupted, loud enough for the deputy's benefit "I can't say I wasn't tempted, but you ain't goin' to make me husband number seven. I like my throat just the way it is."

"I'm going to kill you," she grunted as Callahan shoved her inside the cage.

"I know, I know," he returned. "You and every other prisoner I've ever helped send away."

The idea flashed that she might run by the two men and make good her escape, but Callahan's large form stepped directly before her and blocked the doorway. Belatedly she realized the notion must have clearly shown in her eyes. Callahan grunted as he shoved her to the bed. He was instantly beyond the opening in the bars before she could come to her feet. The iron bars clanged horribly as the door shut.

"I'll never forgive you for this," she warned, so calmly that Callahan felt a shiver of fear race down his spine along with an unreasonable urge to beg her forgiveness. Still, his resolve to ensure her safety did not waver in the least. This woman was going to remain behind. It didn't matter her anger. He would gladly face her rage, even her hatred, to keep her safe.

Silent tears of frustration ran down her cheeks as she faced him through the bars.

Callahan's heart ached. He longed to take her in his arms and kiss away every tear, but dared not give in to the impulse lest he lose his resolve. Finally he sighed and gave a weary shake of his head. "I love you," he mouthed in silence. A moment later he turned, and without another glance walked out of the building.

Mattie sat in self-pitying silence, her mind systematically running over every curse word she had heard while on the trail, and attributing each one, with great relish, to her husband's character. It didn't take her long to come to the conclusion that, in general, all men were a sorry lot indeed. In her opinion, the fool behind the desk ranked almost as high as that rat she'd married.

It accomplished nothing to proclaim her innocence. He ignored her every word. To no avail, she explained who she was. She begged him to wire the marshal, any marshal, for proof of her innocence. Wouldn't he then realize the charge against her ridiculous? But what did he do? He sat there reading a paper, pretending she hadn't even spoken.

Suddenly the door to the jail opened and Clay walked in. "You all be wantin' your breakfast, Deputy?"

Mattie stared in surprise. She knew Clay's mother was working at the café down the street, but she hadn't realized Clay had taken to running errands before school. She supposed he was helping his mother out financially.

Clay hadn't seen her yet. And it wasn't until the deputy spoke that he glanced her way. "Two breakfasts this morning, son."

Clay's mouth rounded with astonishment, and Mattie gave a quick shake of her head, lest he speak aloud his surprise. It wouldn't matter if he proclaimed her inno-

404

cence. It wouldn't matter if the whole train did. This man wasn't going to listen to anyone but Callahan. She gave a snide twist of her lips. He was after all a government agent. Why should anyone doubt his story. No, she didn't need a word spoken in her defense. What she needed was to get out of here.

Clay walked over to the cell. "Somethin' special you want, ma'am?"

Mattie looked toward the deputy and thanked God his nose was still in his paper. She nodded toward the desk and mouthed the word, "Keys."

As so often happens to those of tender years, Clay was unhappily experiencing his first bout of unrequited love. Actually, it bordered on hero worship, rather than love. He believed Mattie to be the epitome of everything good and sweet in womankind.

She had kissed him once. Although he wouldn't have admitted it to another living soul, he wouldn't have minded if she did it again. He didn't understand his reasonings here, for the mere thought of kissing brought instant disgust when associated with anyone else. Clay gave the slightest of shrugs. It only went to prove she was different. She was brave and strong. Hadn't she defended his mother and himself from his stepfather? Hadn't she and Mr. Callahan protected him from first a tornado and then a buffalo stampede? He knew he owed her his life. And besides that obvious fact, she was the prettiest lady he'd ever seen. There was absolutely nothing he wouldn't do for her.

Clay didn't give a thought to the trouble he would no doubt find himself in. He knew he would do as she asked, and do it without the slightest hesitation.

Clay walked over to the rifle that stood propped up against the wall behind the deputy. A moment later he had the gun pressed against the man's neck. "Put your gun on the desk, Deputy, and git into that empty cell."

"Clay," the man warned in a voice calmer than any would have expected, "you don't want to do this."

"Move!" He increased the pressure against the man's

neck and the deputy came to his feet. "Put your gun on the desk."

Deputy Wilson hadn't a doubt that he could draw his gun and shoot the boy dead before the lad was able to squeeze off a shot. But the idea of killing this boy did not sit at all well. On even this short acquaintance, he knew Clay and his mother, especially his mother, for kind, decent folks. And if he had anything to say about it, he was going to know the boy's mother on more than just a friendly basis. Killing her son would, of course, put an instant end to any notion he had concerning the wooing of the shy, sweetly fragile Mrs. Ada Black.

With a sigh of resignation, Deputy Wilson took his gun, laid it on the desk, and walked into the cell. The door swung shut behind him. His mouth hardened at the sound of the lock clicking in place.

Wilson watched in silence as Mattie bestowed a quick kiss to the boy's forehead and fairly flew out of the building's back door the moment Clay managed the tricky lock and opened her cell. "Your ma ain't going to be happy about this. You know that, don't you."

Clay shrugged, his expression one of misery, and yet he was obviously prepared to accept the consequences of his actions. "I couldn't let you lock up Miz Callahan. She's my friend." Clay turned bright red at his admittance and Deputy Wilson realized it was more than just friendship the boy suffered. Wisely he kept that knowledge to himself.

"Callahan!" Deputy Wilson exclaimed a moment later. "Is that her name?"

Clay nodded glumly, imagining the years he would now spend locked behind bars. What was his mother going to do without him? She'd be alone now. Who was going to take care of her?

Wilson groaned with disgust as the name registered. So she was telling the truth, after all. She was his wife! Why would Callahan make up a story like that? Wilson's thoughts were a jumble of confusion, unable to fathom the man's reasoning. Why would any man have his wife locked up? Finally he gave up trying to find an answer to this bizarre circumstance. He knew he'd come across the truth soon enough.

Wilson smiled at the worried look on the boy's face. "You can let me out now, son. I won't bother your friend. I won't even tell your ma."

Clay nodded, feeling a rush of relief, and immediately unlocked the cell. He didn't know why, but he wasn't going to get in trouble this time. He gave a sheepish smile. "You still want breakfast?"

Wilson grinned. "Hot cakes, this high," he motioned with his hands. The sound of a heavy wagon plodding on by the office brought his gaze to the office's window. Wilson looked out over the street. Callahan was driving the team of oxen. He watched as the wagon moved on and then nearly laughed out loud as he saw Mattie's dark eyes, huge in a face gone totally white, peer cautiously out of the back. An instant later she ducked under the white flapping canvas.

Mattie's eyes opened with alarm at the sound of a low moan. Guiltily she looked around, praying no one heard the unwitting sound of her discomfort.

It was unbearably hot. Why hadn't she thought in advance of her need for water? Mattie leaned back, huddled in a corner, protected from sight by the crates of guns, and gave a soft sigh. A dozen questions filled her mind. How far had they gone? How much farther till they reached their destination? How much longer could she stand this cramped discomfort and stifling heat?

Mattie rained silent curses upon the one who had forced her into this position. What she couldn't figure out was why she loved him so much. Surely he was the most obstinate, ungrateful wretch she'd ever known. Instead of being thankful that she was willing to help, he raged at her, calling her every type of fool.

Mattie sighed. If it weren't for Callahan's thick head, she could be sitting at his side right now, enjoying what there was of fresh air. But no, because of him, she was forced to secrete herself in the back of this wagon.

Mattie never once considered the fact that had she listened to her husband in the first place, she wouldn't now be suffering any discomfort.

A wide grin flashed sparkling teeth as she imagined his expression when she stepped out of the wagon tonight. It would be too late to bring her back. He'd have no choice but to allow her to continue on.

The first thing she realized was the weight pressing heavily against the length of her and the slight restriction in her breathing. Mattie knew she had been asleep. She knew too that she must have been dreaming, but she couldn't seem to shake away the effects of the dream. She tried to move, but found it impossible. Why?

Mattie's eyes opened wide to encounter his angry glare. He heard her gasp and felt her stiffen beneath him. His teeth flashed white in a menacing grin. "Did I scare you again? What a shame," he gritted out, his sarcasm never more apparent.

His hand was over her mouth, his body pressed the length of hers. "You know," he whispered, "if I strangled you and dumped your body out here, it might take years before anyone found it. If they ever found it."

Mattie bit his hand and grunted with some satisfaction at the low curse he emitted.

He was sucking at the injury when Mattie sneered, "You don't scare me, Callahan." She tried to buck his weight from her. "Get off!"

Callahan groaned. "I gave you more credit than was due, Mrs. Callahan. Do you realize the danger you're in?"

"No. Why don't you tell me?"

Callahan ran his fingers through his hair in frustration as he leaned back, keeping her hips pinned between his thighs. "Jesus, Mattie. I've got a job to do. How am I supposed to concentrate on my work when I'm worrying about you?"

"Well, how could I stay behind worrying about you?" she countered.

Callahan shook his head. How had he ever involved himself with this female? Why hadn't he realized she was nothing but trouble? What was he going to do now? He had no answers. There was no way he could guarantee her safety. He sighed. "Oh God, you're driving me crazy."

Mattie giggled at his admission. "Am I?"

"This isn't funny, damn it!"

"Callahan, stop raging at me. I couldn't let you leave without me. Suppose you get in trouble and need my help?"

Callahan shot her a look of disgust. "I'm afraid you don't realize how serious, how deadly serious," he emphasized, "this mission is."

Her eyes rounded with surprise and a shiver of fear raced down her spine. "What do you mean?"

Suddenly a thought occurred. "How the hell did you get out of jail?"

Mattie shrugged. "What does it matter? I did, that's all."

"Is no one immune to your charms, lady?"

Suddenly the silent night was alive with sound. Guns fired. A man screamed in agony. A moment later the heavy sounds of racing hooves came charging into their camp. Mattie gasped, her eyes wide with panic. For an instant she thought it was Indians again. She tried to sit up, her first instinct to run, but Callahan, amid a stream of curses, pressed her firmly to the floor of the wagon. "No matter what happens, don't move," he ordered just before he scrambled out the back of the wagon, his gun drawn and ready to fire.

Callahan crouched behind the wagon, trying to make out what was happening, when the cold butt of a revolver was pressed to his back. "Easy. Just put the gun down."

Callahan cursed, instantly recognizing his friend's

409

voice. "Jake! Jesus, not you! Why?"

There was no way Jake was going to allow Callahan to get off a shot. The man was too damn good to miss, and Jake had to keep everyone alive, for the time being. At least until he knew who was behind it and where they were keeping her. "Sorry, Callahan. Some decisions aren't ours to make. Let's go."

Mattie lay inside the wagon, her mouth open with horror. Jake! What was he doing? What in the world was going on?

More gun shots. Mattie's hand flew to her mouth to stifle her fearful cries. Please, God. Please, she begged in silence. Let him be all right.

Callahan blinked in astonishment as Mitchell trotted his horse into their camp and dismounted. Jesus, what the hell was he doing here?

"Surprised, Callahan?" Mitchell grinned.

Callahan gave a silent groan. Was there no one left he could trust? First Jake, now Mitchell? Was Nora in on it too? "Not much surprises me anymore." He shrugged. "We were waitin' on someone. Just didn't know who or when we'd be hit."

Mitchell's mouth twisted in contempt. "That fool, Manning. If I'd have known what he was going to blurt out," he gave a shrug. "Won't be butting his nose in where it don't belong again," he said, leaving no one in doubt as to his young assistant's penalty for enthusiasm.

Jake was obviously as astonished as Callahan to find Mitchell the culprit behind this mission, but made no remark as the two men carried on their stilted conversation.

Callahan grimaced with disgust. "Guess it was you and the missus all along," he said as Jim Stables walked into the circle of light of the campfire.

Jim Stables's grin was all confidence.

The sound of Mitchell's voice brought Callahan's gaze back to his former boss. "Ain't no need for you to get all fired up, Callahan. I ain't taken nothing from you personally."

410

" 'Cept my reputation."

"Nobody's perfect." He shrugged. "It's unreasonable to expect you to succeed in every mission."

"But you took something from me, Mitchell," Jake interrupted. "Where is she?"

"Perfectly safe. I assure you."

"You don't mind if I make sure of that?"

"You didn't expect me to bring her here?"

Jake moved out from behind Callahan and pointed his gun directly at Mitchell. "The deal was the guns for my daughter, Mitchell. I left word where we'd be tonight." Jake hardened his heart against the ache he felt at Nora's soft gasp. He wouldn't look her way. He couldn't stand the disappointment he'd surely find in her eyes. "If you don't bring her, I figure she's already dead, so the deal's off." Jake cocked his gun and aimed it at Mitchell's belly. One look at Jake's grim expression and there wasn't a doubt in anyone's mind that the man was a second from being a memory.

Mitchell held up his hands, palms forward, as if to ward off the coming shot and almost yelled, "Take it easy. Take it easy. I'll get her."

Callahan took in the situation. There were two men lying dead just outside the circle of firelight. Perry's shoulder was bleeding. Robinson stood almost exactly at his side. Both men had their hands raised in the air, while Nora stared with disbelief at the unfolding situation.

Mitchell nodded toward Stables. "Kill them."

Jake's gun never wavered in his intent. "I wouldn't," he suggested easily.

"I told you I'd get her here."

Jake shook his head. "It ain't that I doubt your word, Mitchell, but nobody is going to die till I get Sarah back."

Mitchell shook his head. "Whatever happened to honor among thieves, as the saying goes?"

Jake's smile was a horror to behold. Mitchell felt a chill of fear race down his spine. "No problem. It'll take a few hours, but I'll get her here." He spoke to Stables again. "Tie them up." And then back to Jake. "Is that all right with you?"

Jake shrugged, uncocked his gun, but wisely kept it aimed at the man he hated most in this world. He pressed his back up against one of the wagons and asked, "Where are the rest of them?"

"The rest?" Mitchell asked with apparent surprise.

Jake shook his head. "Three wagons? Four men? I figure you wouldn't take those kind of odds. Call them in."

And when Mitchell hesitated, Jake cocked his gun again. "Call them in."

"Come on in, boys," Mitchell called.

Almost immediately two men stepped into the light of the fire.

Callahan, Perry, Robinson, and Nora were bound, ankles together and hands behind their backs. Sitting in a stiff row, they leaned uncomfortably against one of the wagons. Mitchell, Stables, and a man answering to the name Ed were sitting at the campfire drinking coffee. Jake nervously prowled the campsite.

At least an hour had gone by since one of the two men had been dispatched. His mission, to bring Sarah back as quickly as possible. All knew it would take most of the night, since Sarah was reportedly established at the hotel in Sacramento, in Mrs. Stables's care.

Mattie was stiff from lying still for so long. She had heard the men talking, but had kept her silence even when that one man had ordered Callahan and the others killed. Now she thanked God for her control. Somehow, no matter Callahan's orders, she was getting out of this wagon and setting them free.

Wouldn't Callahan be happy she hadn't listened to him. Mattie smiled. She could just imagine the wonderful ways he might show his gratitude. Why, if it wasn't for her, none of them would have had a chance.

Mattie peeked out of the back of the wagon. All was as she supposed. Three men sat at the fire. The other four, including Callahan, were leaning up against the wagon across from the fire. She didn't see Jake anywhere.

Mattie slid silently out of the wagon, taking care this time to bring a knife along. If Callahan hadn't had the weapon the last time, she never would have been able to make good their escape.

Knife in hand, she moved into the darkness. Far from the light of the campfire, she began to circle the camp. Suddenly a hand clamped over her mouth, the knife dropped to her feet, and she was dragged back against a solid male form. "What the hell are you doing here?" came a rough whisper near her ear.

When Mattie mumbled something against his hand, Jake sighed and released his stranglehold. "Never mind. Real soon, there's going to be a lot of trouble. I want you to get over beyond those rocks and stay there until one of us comes for you."

Mattie looked in the direction he pointed out. In the shadowy distance, she could see darker shades of black. She imagined those to be the rocks.

"Are you going to just stand there and let them die?"

Jake sighed with disgust. "No, I'm not going to let them die. Now do as I said."

"Well, cut them loose then."

"Mattie, will you butt out of this?"

"No! I'm not going to let anything happen to him."

Jake cursed in angry frustration. "I can take care of it."

"Suppose you can't? What then?"

Jake groaned, not at all sure he didn't need her help. "All right. What do you want to do?"

"I'm going to crawl under the wagon from the other side and cut their hands free."

"And then?"

"What do you mean and then?"

"Their feet are tied together as well. You can't cut that or risk being seen." Jake took a few steps in each direction. Suddenly he stopped pacing. "Stay right here," he ordered as he moved off to one of the wagons.

A moment later he was back holding two heavy revolvers. "I don't have more than these two." He nodded toward the men at the fire. "They took the others." He pushed the guns into her hands. "Give one to Callahan, the other to Robinson." He stopped her when she would have moved away. "After you cut their hands free, leave the knife with Nora and then get the hell out of there."

At first Callahan thought it was a rat nibbling at his fingers. And then he felt the pull of the ropes against his wrists. Suddenly his hands were free. Callahan groaned as he heard Mattie's whisper. Would this woman never listen to him? "Jake said to leave this with you." A gun was laid across his opened palm.

Next Mattie divested Nora's hands of the ropes. Then Perry, then Robinson. She left the second gun with him as she was told and slid the knife handle into Nora's palm.

"There's going to be a lot of shooting in a minute or so. Get as far away as you can," Nora whispered.

Mattie realized she hadn't any other choice. She didn't have a weapon, which, considering her marksmanship, was probably a good idea. This time she was going to do exactly as she was told.

Or so she thought.

She was just edging into the shadows beyond the small circle of wagons when a thick arm grabbed at her waist, clutching her to the man behind her.

Mattie listened to the low laughter sound near her ear. For a second she thought it might have been Jake again but instantly realized the error of her thoughts. She was being dragged out into the open, toward the fire, her strength no detriment against this man.

"Look what I found," Jim Stables said as the other two men jumped to their feet with surprise.

Callahan closed his eyes against a silent groan as he watched her useless struggles. He was going to strangle this woman the minute he got his hands on her.

"Where did you come from?"

Mattie lowered her eyes, too scared to face this vicious-looking man, too scared even to reply.

"I asked you a question, girlie."

Stables pulled Mattie closer and Callahan uttered a low curse of frustration. Her body completely blocked any opportunity he might have had to kill the bastard.

"I was in the wagon."

Mitchell swore. "Why the hell didn't you check them?" he asked of the two men standing on either side of him.

Both of them gave a sort of shrug, having no answer.

"Check them now," Mitchell ordered.

Mitchell kept his gun pointed at Mattie's middle until the two men returned.

"Who is she?" Mitchell called to Jake, who was again leaning against one of the wagons.

"Mattie Callahan."

Mitchell shot Callahan a look of surprise. And then gave an almost apologetic shrug. He raised his gun as if to shoot, when Stables swung her up close to him again. "Wait just a minute, Mitchell. What do you want to waste a bullet on this pretty thing for? I've been watching her for a long time. Let me have some fun first. You can kill her later."

"I ain't got time for this."

"Come on, Mitchell. What's it going to hurt? We got hours before the girl comes."

"All right, but keep her quiet. I don't want to hear her scream."

Jake moved closer to the three men. "I know you're dirt, Mitchell. Anyone who'd take a kid . . ." He left the sentence unfinished. "But how the hell did you hook up with slime like this?"

Mitchell shrugged. Jake was right. Stables was slime, but it didn't matter none. He didn't care what Stables did, as long as it didn't interfere with his plans. For twenty years he'd broken his back for the Department. For what? The Department was his wife, his family, his life. He'd given everything, everything he had! And now they were going to retire him after this mission was completed. Retire him with their heartfelt thanks and maybe a gold watch for all the years of faithful service. He shook his head. A gold watch and a pittance for retirement. He deserved more than that.

He didn't care who won the war in Mexico. What the hell difference did it make to him? All he cared about was the money the French would be willing to pay to see that these guns never reached Juarez. Mitchell finally faced a silently raging Jake. "It don't matter none. She's going to die anyway."

Mattie shivered with disgust as Stables ran his hand over her breast.

Blood thundered in Callahan's brain. He was going to kill this bastard. The man was going to die for daring to touch her. His fingers tightened around the gun in his hand. Callahan growled out his rage as he watched Stables's hand move familiarly over his wife's shuddering body. *Patience, man, patience,* he warned, knowing the impossibility of getting a clean shot from this angle. *God,* he prayed, *let him move.*

Stables muttered, "I've waited a long time for this. If you're nice to me, I might be able to get you out of here."

Despite her trembling and almost paralyzing fear, Mattie struggled against his crushing hold. She wanted to scream out her disgust, for no matter how she fought, she couldn't stop his hands from touching her. She shivered with horror. Low, whimpering sounds mingled with harsh grunts as she continued her struggles. "You make me sick."

Stables's harsh laugh sounded demented to her ears. His breath rushed heavily against the side of her face. "Remember what I did the last time you said that?"

"What?" Mattie asked, some rational part of her mind realizing the longer she kept him talking, the better her chances of finding a means of escape. "What did you do?"

Stables cursed and then shrugged. He hadn't meant to say that, for just a second he been confused, but it didn't matter now. She wasn't going to be telling anyone anything he might say. "Susie. She tried to fight me, just like you."

"You! You killed her."

Stables grinned, relishing the memory. "She was a bitch. She would wriggle herself all around me, teasing and taunting, letting me watch when she went to the river to wash. She thought it was funny, me being so hot for her, but when I touched her, she threatened to tell." Stables grunted as Mattie kicked out behind her. He shifted and ran his hand down her thigh, holding her more firmly against him. "I couldn't let Cassidy put us off the train, could I? I had to stop her."

As Stables spoke he began to drag Mattie into the darkness that surrounded the fire. Callahan held back a scream, wondering if he'd survive the effort. In a minute it would be too late. He couldn't shoot blindly into the dark. Jesus, he couldn't stand it. He was going out of his mind. Why didn't she do something? Why did she simply stand there with her mouth hanging open in shock?

Move, Mattie, he silently screamed. *Get out of the way!*

So caught up was she in the horror of what he was admitting to, Mattie realized almost too late that he was inching her away from the light. She couldn't fight him, her strength was as nothing compared to his. Suddenly she slumped in dead weight, her knees going out from beneath her.

It wasn't much, but it was just enough to knock him slightly off balance. Stables staggered. His arm tightened around her. He started to grin as he realized her feeble attempt at escape. She should have known he'd. . .

He never finished the thought.

Mattie screamed as the night exploded with the horror of death. Three guns fired, all with perfect accuracy. Three bullets tore into flesh and left his face unrecognizable. The force of the shots flung him back a good four paces. With his arms locked around her still, she was carried helplessly along with him until his body seemed to realize it was dead and crumbled to the ground.

417

She wouldn't look at him. She shivered in disgust as the last of his breath brought gurgling sounds as blood filled his air passages. His arms, no longer secure around her, lay limply at his sides.

Mattie rolled away. Shaking uncontrollably, she scrambled to her knees and crawled as far from him as she could before her arms and legs collapsed weakly beneath her. She huddled in a small heap as the sounds of gunfire continued.

When the shooting stopped, Ed, with gun drawn, was lying facedown, never knowing the lower half of his body lay across the campfire. Mitchell, crouched low to the ground, cursed. He should have known better than to let any of them live. He should have killed them the minute he had the chance. Where the hell had they gotten the guns?

Mitchell knew he hadn't a hope against three guns pointed directly at him. He smiled with resignation, dropped his weapon to the ground, stood, and raised his hands in surrender. "It was nothing against you, Jake," he remarked, facing the deadliest foe he'd ever known in all the years with the Department. From the back of his mind a tiny glimmer of hope held that, because of Jake's decency, he might find a way out of this yet.

Mitchell, never having had a child of his own, was ignorant of the rage and despair a father would know when his child is taken. He was dead wrong.

"Afraid I can't say the same," Jake countered as he squeezed the trigger without the slightest flicker of conscience. All watched with more than a little satisfaction as their former boss fell dead over his comrade in crime.

At the sound of the last gunshot, Mattie seemed to come suddenly to her senses. Completely forgetting the fact that Callahan's feet were still tied together, she saw only that he was lying on the ground. She screamed as she lunged at his prone body, believing him injured. "Are you all right? Are you? Oh God, are you?" she asked as she hugged his head tightly to her breast and rocked him as if he were a baby.

Callahan's groan was a mingling of anger and relief against her breast. "I've had it" came the muffled sound of his voice. "I absolutely, positively quit." He pulled away, shaking his head with disgust. "I hope you'll like the life of a trapper's wife, 'cause you got it, lady."

It took a moment before Mattie realized he wasn't hurt. And still a few seconds more before she understood his words. Finally she blinked in amazement. "Why?"

"Why? Because I haven't a doubt that I'll be allowed to go on another assignment without you trailing along!" His face came level to hers as he glared. "You never listen to a goddamn word I say. And there's no way I'm going to take a chance with your life."

Mattie shook her head, a soft smile of admiration touching her lips. "I don't think you can give this up," she remarked, knowing him just a bit too well for his liking.

"I already gave it up," he insisted. "It's finished, do you hear?"

"Don't you think we make a good team?"

"Sonofabitch!"

Chapter Twenty-six

Mattie walked along the sidewalk heading for the cafe and a longed-for cup of tea. She was meeting Nora and Sarah and then the two women were going to take the girl on a shopping spree.

Mattie grinned, knowing no limit to her happiness. Life was sweet, sweeter than she ever could have imagined. Callahan had done as he promised. He had quit the Department and they'd soon be on their way back East.

The guns had been delivered as planned to Juarez. The mess with Mitchell left no lasting effects. No charges were brought against Jake, since everyone realized the reason behind his actions.

Sarah, a pretty little girl of eight, was about to get a new mother. Nora and Jake planned to be married by the end of the week.

All in all, Mattie imagined things couldn't have worked out better.

Mattie fumbled with the packages that filled her arms, wondering if it might not be a good idea to deposit her purchases at the hotel before joining Nora. Her fingers held to a small package, and a dreamy smile lit up her face as she imagined Callahan's reaction when he saw her tonight in the filmy black gown she had just purchased.

Her mind was still on the possibilities of the night to

come when a familiar and yet not familiar face broke into her imaginings. Her eyes narrowed as she tried to remember where she had seen him before.

Suddenly Mattie closed her eyes and groaned. She'd never seen him in person, but she couldn't be mistaken. He looked older than the fuzzy photograph she had managed to confiscate from his files through the help of one of the cleaning women she had befriended. But she hadn't a doubt that he was the one.

Mattie felt the blood drain from her face. Her purse and packages slipped from lifeless fingers as she watched him move toward her. How odd. After all these years of hate, she felt only a sense of misery as she watched his approach. This man was responsible for her sister's mistreatment and subsequent death, and yet her hatred had disappeared. At this moment she felt nothing, not even fear.

It was the shock of seeing him, she reasoned, but even as she thought it she knew that wasn't entirely true. Mattie felt a stab of guilt. Melanie's murder would go unavenged, for she had forgotten how to hate.

Her eyes widened with surprise as he stopped before her. She had forgotten the packages she had dropped and stared in amazement as he gathered them up.

"Haven't we met?" he asked, obviously puzzled that she should look so familiar.

Mattie managed a stiff smile. "I'm afraid not."

Ellis grinned, knowing her answer for a lie. He knew this woman. Never would he have forgotten a face like hers. Suddenly he remembered that rainy night just outside of Richmond. "It's Melanie, isn't it? Melanie Trumont?"

Mattie stared in amazement at his audacity. He acted as if he had once been a suitor, rather than the vicious beast who had repeatedly raped her sister. Did he believe all honor was abandoned in times of war? Did he believe all was forgotten and forgiven, now that the war was over? Mattie felt the stirring of a hate returned, so great as to leave her nearly breathless.

She thought she had forgotten. And she nearly had. But how could she forget when this man dared to leer, obviously remembering his enjoyment but none of her sister's horror?

Mattie didn't trust herself. Her fingers shook with rage and she knew, without a shadow of a doubt, had she a gun she would have killed him here on the spot, regardless of the punishment she'd be sure to suffer.

The only thing to do was to get away. She had to find Callahan. She had to remember what they meant to each other. She had to forget again this animal and the hate he could so easily instill.

"I'm afraid you're mistaken, sir," Mattie returned as she tried to brush by him.

Ellis's grin was decidedly suggestive as he caught her arm, nearly causing her packages to fall again, and restrained her from moving on. "I don't think so. I think you're Melanie, all right. I couldn't have forgotten a face so lovely."

Mattie shivered. What kind of a monster was this? Did he expect Melanie to acquiesce to his wants? Did he not remember the screams that would haunt Mattie for the rest of her life?

"I expect you have a good reason for touching my wife."

Ellis dropped his hold on Mattie's arm as he turned to face a stony-eyed Callahan. "The lady looked as if she were about to faint. I hope she is well."

Callahan's murderous glare settled on his wife. "Are you all right?"

Mattie nodded, her cheeks flaming with guilt. In that instant, she made up her mind. Callahan was never going to know who this man was. She shivered

422

with fear. There was no telling what he might do. And she wasn't going to see Callahan hanging at the end of a rope. Not if she could help it.

Ellis bid them a good day and moved off, his arrogant smile not diminishing in the least.

It was obvious to Callahan that something had happened. There was something between Mattie and the stranger. Mattie couldn't lie to save her soul. He waited for her to tell him, and when she didn't he felt a stab of anger.

"Who was he?"

Mattie blinked, hoping her look was blank. It wasn't. "Who?"

"Let's go," Callahan snapped as he took her arm and nearly dragged her to their hotel.

Once inside the room, he gave her a small shove. "Who was he?"

"If you mean the man on the street, I haven't the vaguest notion."

"You're lying, Mattie, why?"

"Callahan," she laughed tightly. "Why would I lie? I never saw the man before."

"Is that so? Then why did you look so terrified?"

"Me? Why should I be afraid of someone I don't know?"

"A good question." Callahan gave it a moment's thought. "Perhaps it wasn't him you were afraid of. Perhaps it was me."

Mattie looked at him with some amazement. How did he ever come up with that? "Callahan, you're being ridiculous."

"Goddamnit! Mattie, I know when you're afraid."

"I wasn't. Stop badgering me!"

Callahan's hands closed into fists. His lips tightened into a sneer. His eyes hardened to blue chips of ice. "Fine. No problem. I'll see you later." He slammed out of the door.

Mattie ran after him. "Where are you going?" she asked, grabbing on to his coat at the top of the stairs.

Callahan turned, and the smile he gave her sent a shiver of fear up her spine. "You might not tell me, but he will."

"Callahan," she pleaded. "There's nothing to tell. Come back inside."

"Callahan," she called softly as he tore himself from her hold and descended the stairs.

Mattie paced the room, wild with fear, imagining Ellis lying dead and her husband in custody for the crime. Oh God, why didn't she just tell him? After some clear thought, she realized he wouldn't have felt this need to find justice for her sister. Why didn't she just trust in his control? After all, it was Melanie who had been raped, not her. Oh God, she'd made such a mess of things.

There was a knock at the door. Mattie hurried to answer it and blinked with amazement to find Ellis standing there.

"I saw him leave. Figured maybe you'd like some company."

Mattie tried to close the door, but he was already pushing past her. Ellis slammed the door behind him and locked it.

"What do you want?" A silly question, Mattie. What do you think he wants?

Ellis grinned. "Thought maybe you and I could take up where we left off."

Mattie heard the low groan and felt the room sway dizzily around her, but forced aside her weakness. She couldn't allow herself to faint. No telling what this beast would do in that case. Mattie moved a few steps away and held to the bedpost for support. She looked at the floor as she spoke. "Mr. Ellis, I'm afraid you've mistaken me for my twin sister. Melanie is dead. She was murdered by a pack of animals during the war."

Ellis chuckled. "I don't know. You look pretty good to me."

Mattie lifted her eyes from the floor and gasped to find the man calmly undressing. His jacket was off, his shirt already unbuttoned. "I'm telling you, I'm not Melanie." Her voice began to rise in panic. "I'm Matilda Trumont. Mattie, her sister. Her twin sister."

"Have it your way. It don't matter none to me who you say you are. I remember what you looked like underneath." He nodded at her dress. "I've a hankerin' to see it again."

"Oh God," she groaned. She knew there was no talking to him. It didn't matter in any case. She looked enough like Melanie to satisfy. Mattie gave the locked door a look of longing.

Ellis shook his head and smiled. "You'll never make it."

Mattie felt a scream bubbling up inside her. He was taking off his pants. She didn't care if she made it or not. She wasn't going to stand here and let this animal abuse her, not without a fight.

Mattie lunged for the door, but he caught her easily. Ellis struggled hardly at all. Mattie screamed as she was flung through the air and landed on the bed. A heartbeat later, his body was sprawled over hers.

He was tearing at her clothes. She screamed again. His hand came to muffle the sound.

Mattie never heard the pounding at the door, so frantic were her efforts at escape, so loudly did her heart pound in her ears. Suddenly Ellis jumped from the bed. At that exact moment the door crashed in and fell upon the floor.

Callahan took one look at his wife and the near naked man who was climbing out of her bed. His hand reached for the gun at his hip. Callahan never heard the man's yell. He never realized the gun was in his hand. He never knew he pulled the trigger. The choking smell of gunpowder filled the room.

Now that it was over, Mattie began to shake so, she could hardly pull herself into a sitting position. An instant later her eyes widened with surprise as Callahan silently turned the gun on her. Their eyes met and Mattie gasped with shock. She had never known hate like the hate in his eyes. A muscle twitched under his eye and a pulse throbbed in his neck. Mattie watched his love die before her eyes.

If it were possible for a heart to break then Mattie's did as she realized his accusatory stare. For a wild second she wondered how they could have fallen in love, when each of them seemed always ready to believe the worst of the other.

Callahan watched as Mattie's gaze held his own. God, but she was a brazen bitch. He almost grinned at the perfection of her performance. When had she mastered the art of consummate actress? She was so good, he could almost believe her an innocent, even though he had seen her lover leave his bed with his own eyes.

He never realized the torn state of her dress. All he could see were her bare breasts, exposed to his gaze like some tempting jezebel. Callahan cursed his body's weakness. How could it be that the sight of her, fresh from another's arms, could so entice? He wanted her despite what she was. Surely this was madness. For a moment Callahan couldn't think which one of them he despised more. His mouth twisted with disgust. "History repeats itself."

She should have told him then, but she couldn't get a word passed the ache in her throat. Mattie licked her lips and waited, silently wondering if a denial would only push him over the edge of his control.

Finally Callahan closed his eyes with a sigh and

holstered his gun. "Fix your dress. Someone is coming."

Mattie moved through a haze of torment. Her whole world was crumbling down around her and she didn't know how to go about putting it back together. Callahan never spent a daytime moment in her company anymore, only at night was he there. And you really couldn't count that, not when he crept into the stateroom and collapsed in a drunken stupor, smelling of whiskey and perfume. She didn't want to think about what that meant.

It had been two weeks since he'd killed Ellis. Two weeks of total and complete silence. No, that wasn't entirely true. She had talked to him. On numerous occasions she had begun to tell him the truth of the matter, but Callahan, without fail, had walked out of the room, every time she attempted to explain.

Right from the first night, after all the business with the law had been settled, she had tried, but Callahan had warned her if she continued on with her story, he wouldn't be responsible for his actions. He had scared her then. Really scared her. For the first time, she knew he was barely holding on to sanity. Even when he held the gun pointed at her, she hadn't felt this violence, or the fear instilled by his icy cool contempt.

What was she going to do? After the first time she had insisted he know the truth, he had simply walked out. How was she going to make him listen?

The problem wasn't hers alone. Callahan wouldn't talk to anyone. Jake caught a black eye when he tried to bring up the subject and the two of them had barely spoken since.

Mattie sighed as she gazed out into the fog-filled night. She smiled as Nora came to her side. "How are things going?"

Mattie nodded, having not the strength to tell her the depth of her pain.

From behind them came the shrill sound of a woman's laughter. Mattie and Nora turned to find the woman looking adoringly up at a smiling Callahan as she held to his arm.

Mattie bit her lips and turned back to the ship's railing. "He's killing me. Too bad he didn't get it over with that night." She gave a long sigh. "It would have been easier."

"He's not doing anything, you know. Perry tells me he's in the saloon playing cards every night."

Mattie nodded. "I know. He told me as well." She shrugged. "It almost doesn't matter."

"What are you going to do?"

"I don't know. He won't listen. He won't let me explain." Mattie sighed again. "Did you know he killed a man in his first wife's bed?"

Nora gasped. "So he thinks . . ."

"Yes, he thinks," she nodded wearily. She turned suddenly to her friend. Her desperation couldn't have been more in evidence. "Nora, help me. Give me an idea. I can't think what to do."

"I suppose he's too drunk when he comes in at night."

Mattie's smile was almost heartbreakingly sad. "If you mean too drunk to be taken advantage of, you're right."

Nora bit at her lip for a long moment, her mind racing on as she sought a remedy to this problem. Suddenly a huge smile flashed and her eyes twinkled with relish. She had just the thing. Too bad she'd never witness the brute atone for his sins.

Mattie's heart pounded as she sat across from him and prayed she had the courage to see this thing through. At the time, Nora had made it sound rational enough. But now, faced with the actual act, Mattie wondered if she weren't out of her mind to even consider this.

Once he awoke, he was going to be like a madman. Mattie trembled knowing the curses that would fall upon her head when he realized he was tied to the bed. She released a shuddering sigh and only hoped the ropes would hold.

The hour grew late and Callahan slept on. Mattie was tempted to awaken him and get this over with but put aside the notion. He was going to be mad enough, she reasoned. It was best he get all the sleep possible.

Mattie jumped when she heard his low moan. Her heart pounded in her throat when she saw his head move. Her mouth went dry as she listened to the groan that grew into a grunt of discomfort. He was trying to shift positions. "Oh God," she whispered desperately, "give me strength."

Callahan opened one jaundiced eye to a dimly lit cabin. Thank God the curtain was pulled over the porthole. He could only imagine how much greater his pain if he'd been subjected to sunshine.

Callahan grunted and tried to turn to his side. He blinked with surprise and stared silently at the ceiling. He couldn't seem to move. Why? Had he had an accident? He tried to remember but nothing came out of the haze that was last night. Jesus, had he finally drunk himself into paralysis?

Oh, that's great, Callahan. Now you've done it. Now you've really done it.

But something was wrong, or maybe right. He wasn't paralyzed. He was moving his hands. He could shift his hips. So why couldn't he turn over?

Callahan moved a throbbing head and squinted through bloodshot eyes, trying to understand what he saw. He almost laughed. And perhaps he would have if the pain in his head hadn't been quite so bad. It looked like he was tied up. Ridiculous. He must be dreaming. Maybe he was still drunk. Drunk and hung over at the same time. That must be some kind of a record. He didn't care. Not as long as he didn't have to think, to remember. Callahan sighed. What he needed was a few more hours of sleep.

Mattie came suddenly into his line of vision. He watched her face as she moved closer. What the hell was the matter with her? She looked like she was scared to death.

"Are you awake?"

"No, I always sleep with my eyes open."

"Do you want something to drink?"

Callahan's dry tongue ran over dry lips. "Yeah, I could use another drink and about ten more hours of sleep."

"I meant water, Callahan," Mattie said, unable to hide the disapproval in her voice. She held a glass to his mouth and he downed it almost in one gulp. "Have pity on the other passengers. You're leaving them not a drop to drink."

"What the hell is going on?" he asked as he looked again at his hands and realized what he had thought impossible was true. His hands were tied. He hadn't been dreaming. Slowly he raised his head and then groaned with the effort it took. He tried it again, his eyes widening as he realized his feet were tied as well.

His gaze moved to Mattie's worried expression. "Answer me, damn it!"

"We have to talk, Callahan."

"Sonofabitch! Untie me!"

"Not until you hear me out."

"I'm going to kill you when I get out of this. Untie me now!"

Mattie's smile of courage wavered just a bit. "Your threats are a convincing argument to keep you in place. Maybe I'll never untie you."

Callahan told her just what he thought of her intentions with a few explicit curse words. "You're wasting your time. I won't listen."

Mattie sighed. This was working out exactly as she thought it would. Nora couldn't have been more mistaken. She *was* wasting her time.

"I'll send Jake in to untie you. I'm leaving you."

Callahan gave an ugly laugh. "You have nowhere to go. I killed your lover."

"He wasn't my lover, you fool!" Mattie's lips tightened and her eyes flashed with anger. "I've been trying to tell you that for days."

Callahan laughed humorlessly. "Tell me I didn't see it." He glared, daring her to deny the scene he'd come upon.

"You didn't see it," she said so calmly, so gently, so deliberately that Callahan wanted to smash her beautiful lying face.

Callahan nodded, his throat constricting with the very pain he'd been trying for two weeks to keep smothered in an alcoholic haze. "You're getting better, I'll give you that. At least you're learning how to lie."

"No doubt the company I keep," she snarled as she moved to the porthole, pushed aside the draperies, and peered out.

Callahan closed his eyes against the blinding light but said nothing.

Mattie let the curtain fall back into place and turned toward the bed. Damn him if he wasn't the most beautiful man. Snarling lips, bloodshot eyes, sickly yellow complexion, and still she knew not another to compare. She couldn't help it, she had to try, no matter how he would likely rebuff her attempt. She loved him too much to simply give up and walk out of his life. "Callahan, I just . . ."

"Shut up. I don't want to hear it."

431

Mattie sighed. Oh, Nora, you were wrong, so very very wrong. It isn't working. What should I do? How can I make him listen? What would you do? Suddenly an idea dawned. Mattie pushed the outrageous thought aside, knowing it would surely make things worse. But the thought refused to abate. Maybe, just maybe, it would make things better.

Mattie watched him for a long moment, knowing she'd need every ounce of courage she ever possessed were she to put this plan into action. He'd rant, he'd curse, he'd fling insults. Was she up to it? Could she withstand anger like that and not cower in the face of it? Mattie smiled, knowing she could. For this man she could do anything.

Mattie moved to the corner where their bags were stacked. With fumbling fingers she began her search.

"What are you doing?"

"Looking for something."

"What?"

"A knife."

Callahan's eyes widened. What the hell was she planning? Was she going to kill him? Or worse, herself?

"Why?" he asked, holding his breath as he awaited her answer.

"Because I need it," she returned, bringing him not a smidgen closer to understanding her actions.

Mattie gave up her search with a soft sigh and moved instead to the small table that held his shaving supplies. "Ah, ah" came her low, triumphant exclamation as she picked up a straight-edged razor.

Callahan felt every muscle in his body tighten as he watched her move back toward the bed. He held his breath as the razor came closer, filling his vision. "Not afraid, are you, Callahan," she asked, noticing for the first time the look in his eyes.

"Should I be?"

Mattie gave a smug smile. "I think you are. Don't worry, it'll be over in a minute." She grinned, unable to resist adding, "You'll hardly feel a thing."

Hardly? What the hell did that mean? His heart was pounding now with real fear. He knew she wasn't cutting him loose. He could tell by the look in her eyes. So what did that leave? What was she going to cut? He had completely forgotten the pain in his head. "What the hell are you going to do?"

Mattie didn't answer. She stood over his helplessly prone body and pulled at his shirt. Calmly she then proceeded to slice into his clothes, slitting his garments into shreds up his body and arms, down his legs, until he lay naked to her gaze, the useless remains of his clothes still under him. Mattie nodded with approval. "A very cool character, Callahan. You didn't even take a deep breath." She smiled, a devilish gleam in her eyes. "Not even when I ventured dangerously close to vital parts."

Mattie returned the razor to the table.

Callahan couldn't keep his eyes from her as she began to undress. There wasn't a doubt in his mind as to what she was going to do. "It doesn't matter what you do." He shook his head. "It's not going to work," he swore, but he knew his words for the lie they were as he watched her pull her dress over her head.

There was a possibility that Callahan might have persuaded her to believe his desperate words. But when she pulled her chemise down and stood half naked before him, he couldn't stop the groan that slipped by his lips.

She was smiling triumphantly when he said. "This will come to nothing, Mattie. I don't love you."

Mattie's fingers shook at the ties to her petticoat and tears of hurt misted her eyes. Was it true? Was it too late? No, please God, no. It couldn't be. She wouldn't let it be. This man wasn't going to send her away in

433

tears, at least not until she tried everything there was in her power to do.

Mattie forced aside the pain that filled her heart. You knew he would say hateful, hurtful things. Ignore his words. Concentrate on his eyes. His eyes are telling you the truth.

Callahan groaned and closed his eyes in agony as her petticoats and drawers were pushed over her hips. He wasn't going to be able to stand this. She was a witch, trying to drive him out of his mind. It wasn't enough she had taken his love and almost killed him with her betrayal. She wouldn't be satisfied until she possessed his soul, his mind, his very being.

"Afraid to look at me, Callahan?" she taunted.

Callahan opened his eyes and stared at her, forcing aside his need, praying she'd only see disgust. "I can't begin to tell you the hate I feel for you. There are no words to measure its depth." Callahan allowed his gaze to move over her nakedness with cool, insulting scorn. "You are a whore." He saw her stiffen, watched the pain in her eyes, and prayed it could only match his own. He laughed hollowly. "A whore without a shred of pride. Doesn't it bother you to know all the women I've had since this ship left port?"

At first Mattie could only gasp with shock. She had imagined him to be vicious, but she hadn't expected even him capable of such cruelty. She hadn't thought he would go this far.

She watched him for a long moment before remembering his words. Her shoulders began to relax by inches until she finally sighed with relief. He'd almost done it. He'd almost sent her away from him forever, but, thank God, he'd gone on too long. If he hadn't mentioned the other women, Mattie would have believed everything he said. But she knew he hadn't taken another to bed. Hadn't he, in a drunken stupor, told Perry as much? Hadn't he cursed the fact that he couldn't bring himself to bed another, for none compared to his wife? A wife he professed to hate? Damn him and his stubbornness.

Mattie gritted her teeth, mustering all her strength against his ravings. "No doubt you tried, Callahan, or at the very least the thought occurred. And for that I'm going to find a particularly nasty form of punishment. But you didn't bed another."

"What the hell do you know about it?"

"Shut up, Callahan, or I promise I'll gag you next. It doesn't matter your nasty words. You're not going to stop this."

"I don't want you! Doesn't that count for something?"

Mattie's gaze moved deliberately to his hardened sex. Her voice was a low, husky taunt. "Yes, I can see you don't want me."

Callahan gave a silent, helpless curse, knowing his body belied his words. He wanted her all right. God help him, at this minute he wanted her more than salvation.

Mattie moved toward the bed. Her hand reached out. Gentle fingers ran over his chest.

Callahan felt his body jerk at her touch. If ever there was agony, it couldn't compare to the torment he was about to suffer.

"My head is killing me," he said. *That along with every inch of my body,* he added silently.

"I know you love me."

"I don't love you."

Mattie smiled as she crawled over his stiff form and settled herself comfortably upon his stomach. "Give it up, Callahan. Give up the lie."

"Is it your intent to rape me?" he asked with disbelief, his voice dripping sarcasm.

Mattie laughed. "I'm not at all sure of the possibility." Callahan closed his eyes to her lying, tender gaze.

"No, Callahan, it's my intent to love you. I do love you, you know."

Callahan laughed without a shred of humor. "Your kind of love is sick."

"Is it?" She leaned down and ran her mouth over his chest. "You might be right," she murmured against his skin. "It holds me like a madness I cannot control. No matter how mean you are, no matter how cruel, no matter what you believe of me, I only seem to love you more. No doubt that makes me quite a fool. But I can't help it."

Mattie teased the corners of his mouth with light feathery kisses. Deliberately, she avoided his lips, using every bit of the knowledge he had so eagerly imparted. He cursed his own idiocy as her mouth and tongue taunted the flesh of his jaw and throat.

Callahan took a shaky breath. He tried to think about anything rather than her deliberate seduction. He wouldn't let her win. Not this time. He didn't want her, would not revel in her sweet caresses, would not delight in the heat of her moist kisses.

Her warm breath whispered near his ear and chills ran up his spine. Determinedly he pushed the sensation away. But he might not have bothered, for she had learned her lesson well and the gentle tugging of her teeth at his lobe almost brought a groan from his throat. He caught it just in time.

When her mouth came to brush feathery kisses against his lips, his remained firmly together. He swore she could do as she would. There would be no effect on his senses. But even as he swore it, his mouth turned slightly, against his will, against all good judgment, to meet the fleeting touch of her. Her mouth was gone almost before it touched his.

Callahan could feel the groan coming from deep within his chest as her mouth flirted with his eyes, his cheeks, his jaw. She laved the flesh of his face with her

436

tongue, biting at his throat and then easing the tiny injury with the soothingly, oh so sweet caresses of her tongue.

Again her mouth came to tease his lips and Callahan forgot his determination not to give in to this need. His mouth opened beneath hers, his lips softened and silently urged her to complete the kiss.

And when she did, he knew he'd die were she to ever let him go. The low groan that rumbled in his chest went unheard. All he could think was her mouth, all he could want was more.

Mattie's hands smoothed down over the rough hairs of his chest and belly, retracing their movement to his shoulders and up under his arms. Never had he known such delightful torture, such aching need.

Her hands came to cup his face, her lips refusing to part from his even to breathe, while her tongue took all it was possible to give.

Her breasts grazed his chest, searing his flesh as she slid lower. Her mouth brushed lightly over his chest, his belly. Continuing the torturous delight lower, lower until his hips raised with undeniable aching need.

She stopped and pulled back. His breath caught in his throat. His eyes opened to find hers, gazing black fiery want.

Her fingertip traced lightly upon his sex. Her smile was seductive and so damn erotic it was almost enough to send him over the edge of madness. For she seemed to take particular delight in swirling the tiny droplet of moisture found there over the tip. Callahan closed his eyes, for the pain of wanting was not to be borne.

He waited with silent, aching agony, waiting, waiting. He prayed she wouldn't, for if she touched as he most wanted, he'd be lost forever. And yet he knew if she didn't he'd surely die. His body trembled, his breathing grew nonexistent.

His body gave a startled lurch and a hissing indrawn breath filtered through his teeth and filled the silent room when the heat of her mouth encompassed him. Yes, she had touched her mouth upon him before, but the light shy kisses she had bestowed were as nothing compared to this. Never had he imagined her capable of such mastery, such avid, lusty enjoyment. Callahan knew not an ecstasy on earth to compare. It was hopeless, he knew, for there'd never be another woman for him. Her sensuality was all and more than any man could want. He longed to run his fingers through her hair, to hold her head in place, perhaps for eternity. But the notion was forgotten as her tongue began its mind-boggling magic.

"Mattie," he choked. "Ahhhh, lady." He shivered as wave after wave of unspeakable pleasure overtook his body. "Oh, Mattie, Mattie, love," he chanted, never knowing he had spoken.

Working on sheer instinct, Mattie couldn't have been a more practiced lover. Her hands slid down his legs. Her nails slid back and up, grazing his inner thighs to meet with hungry pleasure at her mouth. Callahan was writhing beneath her, the insistent movement of his hips letting her know his limit of endurance was about to be reached.

Callahan's dazed mind hadn't time to register the absence of her mouth when her body raised above his and sheathed the pulsing, thickened evidence of his desire into the roaring heat of her flesh.

Callahan moaned, delirious with pleasure as her lusciously tight body engulfed his and took him deeper, deeper, until he began to doubt his own senses, for nothing could be this good.

She leaned forward. Her mouth held to his and grew impatient. Her body tensed. Her tongue imitated their frantic movement. Callahan strained with a sudden frenzied need, lost to reason, knowing only

438

this woman, this moment. He felt her stiffen, her strangled murmuring of his name adding momentum as the fever grew in strength.

His brow creased. He couldn't decipher pain from pleasure. There was no difference. There was only her and the hunger he knew for her, until at last he cried out, knowing nothing but the sweet, blissfully aching sweet ecstasy of release.

Mattie lay slumped upon him, her breathing shallow and gasping as she strove for a calming breath.

Callahan too was gasping for breath, but his soul knew a darkness of despair so powerful and horrifying that tears slid from his eyes. "Mattie, what did this prove? That my body can still respond to a beautiful woman?" Callahan knew his words for the lie they were, for he'd never know a greater rapture than in her arms, and her beauty had nothing to do with it. He loved this woman beyond all sense and reason. No doubt he always would.

"I'm going to tell you something." Mattie leaned back, supporting herself with her arms across his chest. She wiped at his tears. Neither mentioned their existence. "And you're going to listen."

"Don't bother. I won't believe you."

Mattie ignored his words. "The man you killed was Ellis."

Callahan laughed. "Now that is a startling piece of information. I already know his name."

"I mean, he's the one I was coming west to kill."

Callahan stared at her for a long moment. Despite the pain that throbbed like a drum in his head, he gave a great roar of laughter. "That's good. That's really good. And I'm supposed to be just stupid enough to believe it?" Ah, Jesus. Why didn't she just shut up. The more she talked the worse he felt, for the pain in his head was as nothing compared to the agony in his soul.

439

Mattie's mouth hardened with aggravation. "Callahan, the fact that you are stupid is something neither of us can deny. Still, it doesn't change the truth of the matter. He was the one I was going to kill."

A hard smile lingered at his mouth. "And you just wanted a few minutes with him before you finished him off, is that it?" he asked with cold sarcasm. "What was it, some perverse curiosity to sample what your sister suffered?"

Callahan shrugged as best he could with his arms spread out above his head. "Shame on you, Mattie. Surely, after two weeks of thinking on it, you could have come up with a better story than that?"

Mattie nodded her agreement. "No doubt I could have had I been thinking of a good story. But it just so happens that this is the truth."

Callahan shook his head. "It doesn't make sense. If you're telling me the truth, why did you invite him to our room? Why didn't you tell me who he was from the first?"

"I didn't invite him to our room, he barged in. And I didn't tell you who he was because I was afraid you'd kill him."

His smile was dry, barely a smile at all. "And deny you the pleasure? Hardly."

Mattie sighed. "Callahan, I haven't thought about killing him since I fell in love with you. When I saw him on the street, I knew I hated him still, but I only wanted to run away. I knew I couldn't jeopardize what we have."

"Had," he corrected.

"Have," she insisted.

Callahan closed his eyes. "I don't want to hear any more lies."

Despite his obvious unwillingness to listen, Mattie proceeded to tell him the whole story. Callahan lay silently beneath her as she spoke, trying to block out her words, swearing them to be lies and yet greedily absorbing every syllable, praying them to be truth. With all his soul he wanted to believe her. Should he? Could he take the chance? Would he survive the pain if he believed her, only to find she'd lied?

Callahan sighed with despair. It didn't matter. Nothing mattered but that he loved her. God help him, he loved her no matter what she'd done.

"If it's true, why didn't you tell me he was trying to rape you from the first?"

"I saw the hate in your eyes after you killed him. I knew you wouldn't listen."

"Later then?"

"You wouldn't speak to me. You wouldn't let me explain."

Callahan studied her face for a long moment, trying to dispute her claim of innocence. But he had to admit what she'd said made sense. If she was going to take a lover, wouldn't it be a wise move on her part to use the man's room? When he had found them together, she was still completely dressed. Only the fact that her bodice was ripped gave any evidence to what she was about. But if she were willing, would Ellis have found a need to rip at her clothes? Was it possible that he had brought this suffering upon himself, and all for naught? Hesitantly he asked, "Did he finish the act?"

Mattie shook her head. "You knocked the door in before he had a chance."

Callahan took a long, calming breath and forced aside the surge of happiness that filled his being, too afraid of the consequences should he be proven wrong in his belief. "Untie me."

Mattie swallowed, her heart pounding with dread as she listened to his almost bored tone. She bit her lower lip as tears came dangerously close to the surface. He didn't believe her. After all this, he still believed only the worst.

441

Enough! She'd had enough. The man was the cruelest beast, thick-headed, to boot, and an arrogant monster on top of that. She was better off without him. Probably a hundred times better off. What was she knocking herself out for? The man would believe what he wanted in any case.

Mattie flung herself away from him. "You know, Callahan," she remarked angrily as she took the razor and began slicing viciously at the ropes, "I'm beginning to see that this is probably for the best. I can't imagine why I insisted you listen to me. Even in the best of times I can hardly stand you."

"Is that so?" he asked, unable to hide his grin, watching her breasts bob back and forth just above his face as she sawed away at the ropes. It was her anger that finally did it. Suddenly there wasn't a doubt in his mind that she had told him the truth.

But Mattie never noticed his smile as her fury mounted. "Yes, it's so," she snapped in return.

"And in the worst of times?"

"In the worst of times, I hate your guts."

Callahan laughed with delight. He couldn't love her more than when she was mouthing off to him, for she was never more intriguing, more delightful, more enticing in his eyes. "Not as much as I hate yours, surely."

"Probably not." She was finished with the ropes and threw the now useless razor somewhere in the vicinity of the table as she grabbed at her drawers. "But then again I haven't your capacity for hate."

"Maybe," he remarked as he came stiffly into a sitting position. He was flexing his aching shoulders. "But you seem to be learning fast enough."

Mattie pulled her chemise over her head and smoothed the material against her lips. "You're right about that. And that's the reason I'm getting out. I don't want to end up a miserable bastard like you."

442

"Mattie, you know I don't like it when you curse."

Mattie's laugh was hard and filled with scorn. "Isn't that a shame?" she asked sarcastically. "And just how do you propose to stop me?"

"Suppose I kiss you every time you do it."

Mattie snorted her disbelief, only half realizing what his words meant. "Not an easy accomplishment, Mr. Callahan, since you're going to have to find me first."

"Come over here, Mattie."

"Drop dead, Mr. Callahan!" She started for the door, finishing the last of her buttons as she moved. "I'll send for my bags." She disappeared before he had a chance to say another word.

Callahan growled. If she thought that was the end of it, she could think again. In a flash, despite his aches and pains and the stiffness in his legs, he was out the door, running along the passageway, oblivious to his naked state and the startled shrieks of two of the female passengers.

Mattie spun on her heels at the unholy screams sounding behind her. Her mouth dropped open with astonishment — no — astonishment, amazement, surprise, none of them fit. There were no words to describe the emotion she felt at seeing him running toward her without a stitch of clothes on.

In an instant she was scooped into his arms and he was running back from whence he had come. The door to their cabin slammed behind them and Mattie was tumbled upon the bed. Callahan stood menacingly above her. "I hope you're satisfied? No telling what that did to my reputation, or yours."

Mattie's silent, wide-eyed stupefaction turned suddenly into giggles, and Callahan actually blushed. She turned her face into a pillow, almost sobbing her hilarity, unable to catch her breath. She couldn't believe what he'd just done. God, what was she going to do

443

with this impossible, wonderful, totally obnoxious, beautiful, stubborn man? When her laughter calmed to an occasional giggle, she turned to face him, a smile lingering. "Why did you do that?"

"Because I love you, damn it! Why the hell do you think I did it? I forgot I didn't have any clothes on."

Her smile became bubbling laughter as her soul filled with joy. She came to a sitting position. "I take it you believe me then?"

"Of course I believe you. What do you take me for, an utter fool?" There was a moment's hesitation before he quickly added, "Don't answer that."

Mattie grinned, wisely keeping her opinion to herself.

"If I had any sense . . . if I didn't love you quite so much, I probably would have realized from the first that you weren't a willing participant. As it was, when I saw you, I . . . I . . ." His throat closed with emotion. Raw agony filled his eyes and he couldn't seem to go on.

"You thought about your first wife?" she prompted.

"No. Not at first. At first I thought, 'I wish to God I was dead,' for death would have been preferable to the pain."

Mattie came to her knees. She pressed her face into his chest and slid her arms around his waist. "Oh, darling, never wish that." She rubbed her face into the crisp hairs. "What would I do without you? Who would aggravate me?"

Mattie smiled at Callahan's rumbling laughter. His large hand came to cup her head. Her arms at his waist tightened. "I'm happy to hear you find me good for something."

"Mmmmm," she murmured. "Now that I think on it, I do believe there are a *few* things you're good for," she remarked in an exaggerated southern drawl.

"You wouldn't mind showing me, would you?"

Her hands slid down his back and cupped his firm buttocks. "I guess I could, if you're really interested."

"Oh, I'm interested, lady."

Mattie spread a line of kisses over his chest. She was lowering her mouth to his waist when Callahan's hands cupped her cheeks and held her from him. "Mattie," he groaned desperately, unable to believe how good it felt to have her arms around him again. He pushed her to her back upon the bed and lay down beside her. "I love you so goddamn much," he murmured against her throat, his voice breaking with emotion, and tears came again to mist his eyes.

Mattie giggled as she looked up into his tender gaze. "You don't just love me? You love me so *goddamn* much?"

Callahan laughed at her mimicry. "I warned you, lady, about this habit you have of cursing. I can't imagine where you're picking up these words."

Mattie grinned wickedly. "What do you propose to do about it?"

"I told you before what I'd do."

Callahan felt his stomach tighten with aching hunger for this woman as Mattie's eyes half closed with a taunting promise. "Watch out. You might get more than you expect."

"Ah, lady, I'm counting on it," he groaned as he buried his hands in a cloud of midnight curls and his tongue in the sweetness of her mouth.

ROMANTIC GEMS
BY F. ROSANNE BITTNER

HEART'S SURRENDER   (2253, $3.95)
Beautiful Andrea Sanders was frightened to be living so close to
the Cherokee—and terrified by turbulent passions the handsome
Indian warrior, Adam, aroused within her!

PRAIRIE EMBRACE   (2035, $3.95)
Katie Russell kept reminding herself that her savage Indian captor
was beneath her contempt—but deep inside she longed to yield to
his passionate caress!

SAVAGE DESTINY
A REMARKABLE SAGA OF BREATHLESS, BOLD
LOVE IN A WILD AND SAVAGE LAND!

SAVAGE DESTINY #1:
SWEET PRAIRIE PASSION   (2635, $3.95)
A spirited White woman and a handsome Cheyenne brave—a forbidden love blossoms into a courageous vision. Together they set
out to forge a destiny of their own on the brutal, untamed frontier!

SAVAGE DESTINY #2:
RIDE THE FREE WIND   (2636, $3.95)
Abigail Trent and Lone Eagle had chosen passionate love over loy-
ality to their own people. Now they could never return to their separate lives—even if it meant warfare and death!

SAVAGE DESTINY #3:
RIVER OF LOVE   (1373, $3.50)
Though encroaching civilization is setting White man against Red,
Abigail's and Lone Eagle's passion remain undiminshed. Together
they fight the onrush of fate to build their own empire of love in the
wilderness!

SAVAGE DESTINY #6:
MEET THE NEW DAWN   (1811, $3.95)
Frontier progress threatens all Abigail and Lone Eagle have struggled for. Forced to part to hold together what they cherish most,
they wonder if their loving lips will ever meet again!

Available wherever paperbacks are sold, or order direct from the
Publisher. Send cover price plus 50¢ per copy for mailing and han-
dling to Zebra Books, Dept. 2574, 475 Park Avenue South, New
York, N.Y. 10016. Residents of New York, New Jersey and Penn-
sylvania must include sales tax. DO NOT SEND CASH.

EXPERIENCE THE SENSUOUS MAGIC
OF JANELLE TAYLOR!

**TURN TO CATHERINE CREEL — THE
REAL THING — FOR THE FINEST
IN HEART-SOARING ROMANCE!**

CAPTIVE FLAME   (2401, $3.95)
Meghan Kearney was grateful to American Devlin Monta-
gue for rescuing her from the gang of Bahamian cutthroats.
But soon the handsome yet arrogant island planter insisted
she serve his baser needs — and Meghan wondered if she'd
merely traded one kind of imprisonment for another!

TEXAS SPITFIRE   (2225, $3.95)
If fiery Dallas Brown failed to marry overbearing Ross Kincaid, she would lose her family inheritance. But though Dallas saw Kincaid as a low-down, shifty opportunist, the
strong-willed beauty could not deny that he made her pulse
race with an inexplicable flaming desire!

SCOUNDREL'S BRIDE   (2062, $3.95)
Though filled with disgust for the seamen overrunning her
island home, innocent Hillary Reynolds was overwhelmed
by the tanned, masculine physique of dashing Ryan Gal-
lagher. Until, in a moment of wild abandon, she offered
herself like a purring tiger to his passionate, insistent caress!

*Available wherever paperbacks are sold, or order direct from the
Publisher. Send cover price plus 50¢ per copy for mailing and handling to Zebra Books, Dept. 2574, 475 Park Avenue South, New
York, N.Y. 10016. Residents of New York, New Jersey and Penn-
sylvania must include sales tax. DO NOT SEND CASH.*

THE LADY PROTESTS TOO MUCH

Mattie's spine stiffened as Callahan tried to tell her when she could and couldn't go out. "Since when do I have to answer to you?" she spat out.

"Since you hired me to get you to California," he sneered. "You're my responsibility, lady. It's my job to see that nothing happens to you."

Callahan was beginning to calm down. The only problem was his body was also beginning to take notice just how much she had on, which was nothing. His eyes moved to the long length of naked leg and hip. Her gown was crushed in her fists, lying over the length of her, covering only the bare essentials.

"Get out of here, Callahan," Mattie breathed softly, only her words sounded like a plea for him to stay.

Callahan smiled as his fingers moved to the buttons of his shirt. "You say the right words, lady, but . . ."

"I mean it," she said more firmly.

"Do you?" he dared, his brow lifting with mocking humor. "I wonder what you'd do if I joined you on the floor."

His low laugh was awful in what it did to her. He shouldn't be allowed to laugh like that. Mattie felt her will slipping away, and contrary to what she protested, every inch of her skin begged for his touch, his kiss, his most intimate discovery of her . . .